RUTHLESS REIGN

STEEL ROSES MOTORCYCLE CLUB
BOOK 5

JENA DOYLE

DIRTY WORDS PUBLISHING LLC

Line Editor: Misha Robinson at Verity Ink Editorial

Proof Reader: Kimberly Hunt at Revision Division

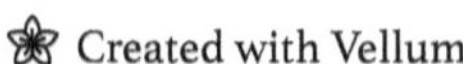 Created with Vellum

For you, my dirty little smut slut.
Turn the page.

Good girl.

1

JULIA

I stared at the paperwork on the table in front of me, the words blurring as I scrambled to catch up to what my lawyer, Angelo, said.

"If the marriage were to be dissolved, my client would walk with all of the assets she had coming into the arrangement." He scribbled something into the margins of the contract before glancing up at the other people across the room.

"That won't be necessary," my brother, Leo, said. He tapped his forefinger to his lips and looked at me before shifting his focus to my betrothed. "Caputis do not believe in divorce."

"Nevertheless," Angelo continued, "this is to protect your investment...and Julia."

I squirmed as he added my name at the last second, like I was an afterthought in this charade, like I didn't matter more than what my name would do for us in this situation.

Leo pursed his lips and nodded. Angelo went on, reading the rest of the legal jargon that would dictate the entirety of my life from here. My attention drifted to the heavily tattooed man next to the other lawyer.

Roman "Bear" Montgomery. My affianced.

At first glance, he was beautiful. He had dark hair, deep, soulful brown eyes, and a jaw cut from marble. But I knew the truth. He was a monster, a villain from a children's fairy tale. He'd been named the acting president of the Steel Roses Motorcycle Club and, as such, my family's sworn enemy.

That was until my brother allied with him two months ago. Leo had been captured by the bastards last year, and now that he'd sobered up and gotten to know them better, he thought he could end the bloodshed between our families with a blessed union.

This was how we found ourselves in this drab conference room, decked out with lawyers, going through the technicalities of a relationship that had been forged in hatred and decades of shared animosity.

Roman caught me staring, and I quickly averted my gaze, but not before I saw him scowling and narrowing his eyes.

What did he see when he looked at me? Was I only the Caputi princess to him? Or did he know how I seethed with my own vengeance? Did he know how badly I wanted to take down my aunt for what she'd done to me? That the only reason I'd agreed to this farce was because I hated her more than I could ever hate anyone else, except for maybe my father. Did he know about the secret plans I'd made since Gabriella attacked the Roses two months ago?

Of course, those schemes were superseded by my want for peace. No one else needed to die for this useless blood feud. It was time for it to be over, and I'd do whatever I could to help that along. If I happened to get revenge in the process, well, what a happy coincidence that would be.

"Section four, subsection three, paragraph six," Angelo said. "Cohabitation."

I took a deep breath as I prepared myself for this battle. Roman and Leo both wanted me to reside in Madison County. They believed it was safer for me, especially after Gabriella found out I'd been spying for the Roses and she set her men to beat me. The bruises on my face had only just gone away, but I didn't see how I could continue to be of any use from such a distance.

The information I'd given to the Roses had gotten them this far. How would they stage a coup without someone on the inside? Of course, how effective could I be now that my cover had been blown?

I still had family members that were against Gabriella. I had cousins and uncles willing to push her out in favor of someone else. But my brother had insisted we would figure it out, and if I needed to contact them, I should do so with a burner phone from the comfort of Roses territory. It would be harder for her to get to me there.

"We will live at my house," Roman said. "In Madison."

Leo scoffed and picked at imaginary lint on his suit. "I've seen your house. How do you propose to make a Caputi princess happy in such a hovel?"

Roman shifted and set a penetrating gaze on my sibling. "As opposed to some drug den easily infiltrated by anyone with half a brain? Or perhaps you mean the Rose house currently given to you as charity?"

The Roses had snatched my brother out of his mansion on the Eastern Shore one night when he'd been having a drug party. He'd been so high, he didn't know what had happened to him until two weeks later when most of that nasty stuff was out of his system. Since then, he'd been living in one of the Rose houses, trying to set up his takeover from there to avoid our aunt. Eventually, he'd have to go home. He'd have to make an appearance on Caputi territory to show the bosses he was a strong leader, that he could undermine Gabriella and steal back his throne. He'd have to get the rest of the family on board first, and I wasn't sure he had the votes.

No, they wanted someone else, someone made of sterner stuff, someone with a guaranteed sober mind.

"Do you have the money to purchase something more suitable?" Roman asked, raising an eyebrow. But the question was rhetorical. Since Gabriella had found out about my betrayal, she'd seized control of my family's estate. I only had what I'd managed to siphon off in the years leading up to it. It wasn't a small sum, but it also wasn't enough to fund the life Leo and I had grown accustomed to.

"A house is a house, Leo," I said to him in Italian.

"Not for my only sister," he replied. "You deserve the best."

"If that were the case, you wouldn't be selling me off to this godless mongrel."

"Hey, I believe in God," Roman cut in with perfect pronunciation of my native tongue.

"I've already agreed to go along with this." I rolled my eyes, muttering obscenities to myself. "I'll live in whatever shack my new *husband* deems appropriate for his bride."

"My house is perfect for two people," he said. "It's on a mountain, and it overlooks the city. You'll be safe there."

Out of one monster's land, into another.

"It's settled," said Roman's lawyer, Berkshire. "Ms. Caputi will reside at Mr. Montgomery's residence until further accommodations can be agreed upon."

Angelo checked that item off before flipping the page. "Section five, subsection two, paragraph three—last name."

"Caputi," I said at the same time Leo and Roman said, "Montgomery."

Shocked but desperate to hide it, I looked at my brother with murder in my eyes.

"This is an alliance," Leo said. "You must play the part if anyone is to believe it."

I took a deep breath to calm the rising fury in my gut, knowing it would get me nowhere. My life had always been rooted in doing whatever the men around me deemed appropriate. My uncle, Benito, had been the Caputi boss before he died, and my father, Giuseppe, had been his brother and most trusted adviser. I'd had to act a certain way, dress a certain way, conduct myself a certain way to appease their conservative mentality, no matter what it cost me. This would be no different.

"Perhaps you'd be open to a compromise?" Roman said, looking directly at me. "Caputi-Montgomery?"

Ugh, what a mouthful.

I already had four middle names, but perhaps this was Roman extending a tiny olive branch over the vast divide between us.

"Thank you," I said. "Montgomery is fine."

Roman cleared his throat, shifted in his seat, and gave Berkshire a glance of approval.

"Okay," Angelo said. "That brings us to the next section. Procreation."

I sighed, knowing this was coming.

"What?" Roman said, leaning forward, blinking incredulously. "What about it?"

"You will produce a child within a year," Leo said, his tone calm and dignified despite how manipulative this whole thing was.

Roman laughed and shook his head. "You must be joking."

"I am not," Leo continued. "The only way this works is if Rose and Caputi blood are mixed. We need to be family. A child will go a long way to smooth over any...opposition...on both sides."

"There is already a child of both Caputi and Rose blood," Roman said. "And surprise, surprise, she doesn't want anything to do with you."

"Alba did not grow up in the Caputi family. Except for a few individuals, no one else knows she exists." Leo raised an eyebrow. "Besides, everyone loves babies."

Roman blew out a breath and shook his head with a sarcastic laugh. "Fucking hell."

"Language," Leo said. "Especially in front of my sister."

"Your sister has said worse to me personally." Roman looked at me with a sly smirk, and I bit back a grin at the thought of the first time I'd ever met him. He'd been keeping Leo prisoner for months, and my brother looked like hell. I'd read Roman the riot act for not taking better care of him.

"Nevertheless," Leo said. "Show some respect."

"You're okay with this?" Roman asked, brown gaze trained on me. "Be honest. If you're not, we'll shut it down."

"Julia will do—" Leo started.

"I'm not talking to you," Roman interrupted. "You're not the one I have to fuck, are you?"

I bit my lip as Leo adjusted his hips and let out a low growl of frustration.

None of this was how I'd ever imagined my life would go. Once upon a time, I'd been in love with a beautiful boy from my high school, Vittori. But he was a Morelli, and therefore, not fit for a Caputi. When my father learned we were together, he quickly disposed of my beloved and shattered my heart. After that had been Hugo. From the moment I met him, I had stars in my eyes. I'd always thought we'd run away together and have six kids by the time I was thirty. Now, I knew better.

I was cursed to have a violent family, violent blood. Any man who dared love me would need to be bulletproof lest he end up a casualty of my wretched relatives and my family's strict moral code. It was my burden to bear for all the sins the Caputis had committed. After Vittori and Hugo, I'd promised to never love again.

Now I stared down the barrel of my thirty-first birthday. They were dead, and I hadn't even been married. Hell, I'd barely been bedded properly. I wasn't a virgin, but I'd been raised a good Catholic woman. Both of my previous lovers were incredibly conservative and entirely too scared of my brothers.

When Leo first proposed this asinine idea of wedding Roman Montgomery, he'd convinced me by suggesting Gabriella would give me to an underboss's son. If I'd been less conniving about maneuvering myself in other directions, it would have already happened.

After Alba's mother died/ran away, I became the eldest Caputi princess. A rare jewel. Worth more than a marriage of convenience to some underboss's dusty boy. So, I thought, "Fine. Why not marry for an alliance? Why not end the war?" Never mind they'd killed my eldest brother, Julian. Never mind Roman's hands were so soaked in Caputi blood, it might as well be dripping from every venom-laced move he made.

Could I push this aside for the sake of my family? Could I lie back and think of Italy anytime I had to couple with him?

He wasn't the ugliest guy I'd ever met, nor was he the most violent. Sex with him might even be enjoyable...if I got over the fact he was a Rose and a Montgomery and my family's worst enemy. I'd never love him, but maybe that was the point. After all, how upset would I be when he died if I never cared about him to begin with?

"A child within a year," I said with a nod.

Roman made a low noise of disbelief and leaned back in his seat, running the length of me with an assessing gaze. "Is there nothing you won't do for your brother?"

Not just my brother, but the principle. I wanted peace. I wanted the curse to end. I wanted this madness to stop.

"You have three siblings of your own, do you not?" I said. "Isn't that why you're sitting at this table?"

He considered this before asking, "And if we can't produce a child? Lots of couples have problems with infertility."

"If that is the case," Leo said, "Julia has enough sense to seek a doctor. You must make an effort, understand? There can be no pretending in this marriage. Commitment is essential. There must be a true alliance."

"Fine," I said, raising an eyebrow at Roman.

"Fine," he repeated.

"Wonderful," Angelo said, moving his pen down to the next paragraph. "This coincides nicely with section seven, subsection two, paragraph two—infidelity."

I steeled myself against Roman's reaction or lack thereof. Based on how my previous relationships had worked out, he could rest assured I wouldn't be interested in anyone else. But I knew how these biker men were—only enough sense to operate their brains or their dicks at one time but not both.

"That won't be a problem," Roman said, shaking his head. "I barely have time for this relationship, much less anyone else."

"Regardless," Leo said, "should it be found out that you've been unfaithful, Julia will be within her rights to seek restitution in the form of seventy percent of assets gained, not to mention alimony and a trust for any children."

Roman snorted and glanced at me. "And is the reverse true as well? Will I have to chase off any Caputi men who come sniffing around my property?"

"Don't flatter yourself." I tilted my chin up and stared at him with every ounce of defiance I could muster, tempering my reaction to being associated with his...*property*. "I likewise do not have the time, patience, or desire for multiple lovers."

Roman ran his perfect pink tongue over his lips. "Fine."

"Fine," I agreed.

"Great," Angelo concluded, flipping the pages of our contract closed. "We have no further arguments."

"We agree," Berkshire said before reaching for another stack of papers and grabbing the one on top. He handed it to Roman and pointed at a spot on the bottom. My betrothed picked up a pen, signed it, and pushed it across the table to me.

The marriage certificate.

We'd agreed to the contract, and now came the final step. After this, there was no going back. I picked up my pen and glanced at Roman one last time, steeling myself against the ever-simmering rage in my belly for him and everything he stood for.

Then, for the first time, a hint of kindness echoed out of his gaze, like he sympathized with me, like I could see deep down to his soul and it was good and sweet and generous. Perhaps this marriage wouldn't be as horrible as I feared. Perhaps there could be a solid foundation to our relationship, however screwed up and ridiculous as it began.

I signed my life away right next to Roman's.

"By the power vested in me by the Commonwealth of Virginia," Angelo said, "I now pronounce you husband and wife. Congratulations."

GROWING up in a family constantly feuding with another, I'd often wondered what I would do to end it. What price would I be willing to pay to stop the bloodshed? Where was the line between doing enough and doing too much?

I loved my family. I was proud to be a Caputi. But when I learned my father had been responsible for Vittori's death, I started plotting a way out. Hugo and I nearly made it. I'd almost gotten free. But Gabriella caught up to us, and after that...well...I'd been willing to make a deal with the devil to topple her from the throne. For years I had pondered these things, and as I drove to my new husband's house with whatever I could salvage from my old life, I still didn't know the solution. I prayed I'd made the right call.

I had lived in mansions for most of my thirty-one years. Between expansive townhomes in the heart of DC and the enormous sprawling houses in Potomac, my family had spared no expense raising my brothers and me in the lap of luxury. My wardrobe alone could have funded a small nation's economy for a decade.

But now Gabriella controlled my estate, and I'd been cut off from everything. My closest cousins, Della and Chesco, had managed to smuggle a few sentimental items—my arsenal of guns and some family photos—but that was it. Anything I brought with me had been recently purchased with my own secret funds, something not even Leo knew about.

This new arrangement came with the harsh smack of reality when my driver pulled up in front of Roman's two-story cabin almost a month after we signed the contract. There had been legal issues to sort out and trusts to be formed, etc. Now that it was all finalized, I took a deep breath and steeled myself against my new life.

Roman hadn't lied. The residence was in the mountains, surrounded by enough woods to ensure our privacy, complete with a massive wraparound porch on both levels and a bench swing next to the front door.

Compared to the opulence I'd grown up with, this reeked of rustic poverty. I silently regretted agreeing to live here in the contract and wished I had fought harder to make him purchase something more opulent. Of course, if I didn't have the money for that, why did I believe he would?

"Are you sure this is the right address?" my driver, Williams, asked.

Roman walked out the front door wearing jeans and a white T-shirt, one hand in his pocket and a cup of coffee in the other. I sighed.

"This is the one." I swallowed against a dry throat as Williams put the car into park and opened the driver's door. But Roman was already walking toward the vehicle, and when they met at the back door, Roman clapped Williams on the shoulder and opened the door for me. He held his hand out, as if he meant to help me.

I ignored it and climbed out on unsteady heels, gripping my purse to my person like he might snatch it away from me.

"Your movers already came and left," Roman said. "Your room is mostly unpacked."

Mostly. They wouldn't have touched my personal effects or my weapons. No, those were specifically for me to unload alone...once my *husband* had gone to bed.

"Thank you, Williams," I said to my driver, giving him a pleasant nod and a smile. "That will be all for now."

"Take care, miss," he said before circling the vehicle again to the driver's seat, leaving me alone with my husband. I followed Roman up the wooden stairs and across the porch into the house, where I froze and glanced around. The foyer gave way to a great room with a kitchen in one corner, the dining area next to that, and the living area on the opposite side next to a wood-burning fireplace. The walls had been painted a neutral shade of beige, but there were no paintings or artwork. The drab furniture indicated a bachelor living on his own—hand-me-down accoutrement with no style whatsoever.

Just as I expected.

Leo told me Roman had never had a serious relationship and had lived alone for most of his adult life. Being a mechanic and leading a gang of murderous bikers must have taken up so much time as to keep him from properly decorating the space. It felt cold and unwelcoming, and I clenched my fingers around my bag as he led me farther inside.

"Kitchen, dining room, living room, the bathroom's through there." He pointed around the corner, and I bit the inside of my cheek to keep from grimacing. I could only imagine what that looked like. "Your room is upstairs."

I followed Roman to the right, grabbing the railing to keep myself steady on shaking knees as I climbed the steps to the second floor. There was another bathroom at the end of the hall with two doors on either side in front of it.

"This one is me," he said, gesturing to the one immediately at the top of the staircase. "And this"—he opened the door opposite his room and clicked on the light—"is you."

I stepped inside and assessed the damage. My luggage sat in a far corner, already emptied by the movers I'd hired. My bed had been made in the center of the room and two dressers stood on the opposite wall. My closet at home was two times the size of this space, but alas. My life had become a miserable train wreck, and now I paid the piper.

Staring at these meek surroundings, I told myself this was the sacrifice I'd made for the good of my family. I wanted this war to end. I didn't want to lose any more of my loved ones, and if I had to live in this hovel to prove it, I would. I bit my bottom lip and moved to the French doors opposite the main door, holding back a gasp at the view.

Because the house was so high up, we looked down into the valley of Madison County below. Beyond that, the mountainous skyline of western Virginia rose out of the horizon. The deck wrapped around this side of the house, and I envisioned myself taking coffee out here every morning for a better view. Sure, we had outdoor patios at the Caputi estate, but this...well, this almost made it all worth it.

"I know it's probably not what you're used to," Roman said from his spot in the entrance, running his hands back through his hair. "But I promise you, it's safe. No one will harm you here."

I'd heard that before from every member of my family, including my aunt. In the end, I decided the only one who could keep me safe was me. Which was why there was an army's worth of guns and ammo in one of those suitcases and my favorite knife in my garter belt under my dress. I even slept with it under my pillow.

"Thank you," I said, forcing a smile before turning to the patio windows. "I'm sure this is...sufficient."

Roman pushed upright and cleared his throat. "I have to go to the clubhouse in about an hour. There's a session tonight and I need to be there."

"Right." Because he was the president. The president of my enemy. The proverbial king. He'd have to lead the great fight, and now that he had his prize in the form of a Caputi princess, my brother would likely be there as well.

"Right," he said. "You should come, too."

I'd rather swim through hot garbage.

I swallowed against a dry throat, remembering the *real* reason I was here, and licked my lips, willing myself to agree.

When I said nothing, he narrowed his brown eyes and tried a different tactic. "It would look much better if we put on a united front."

I scoffed before I could stop myself. "United."

"Yes," he said. "The Caputis are not the only ones who might have a problem with our marriage...our alliance. There are those within the Roses that want you all dead."

I tsked through my teeth and rolled my eyes, murmuring in Italian. "Despicable, rotten villains. Who will they kill next? Every Caputi child?"

"Yes," Roman answered in the same language. "If they have their way."

I'd forgotten he could speak my mother tongue, and a small pulse in my heart nearly had me softening toward him. *Nearly.*

"Where did you learn to speak Italian?" I asked, raising an eyebrow. His accent could use some work, but I wouldn't hold that against him.

"I have an ear for languages," he said with a shrug. "I know

German, French, Spanish, and Portuguese as well. My high school teacher called me a savant, said I should go work for the CIA."

"Why didn't you?"

"It's a long story." He sighed and glanced around, crossing his arms. "Look, I promised to protect you, and the sooner the club sees us together, the sooner they'll get used to it."

I nodded, remembering all of the other conditions of our marriage. Living together and changing my name had only been two points of contention. The other... I shivered, wondering when we would have to fulfill that request. Would he expect it tonight? Would he hold me down and force himself on me while I closed my eyes and pretended to be somewhere else?

No, he didn't seem the type. But then again, how well did anyone know anyone? I'd never thought my father would break my heart, that Gabriella would set her goons on me. I never thought men I'd known my entire life would blindly follow her order to beat me within an inch of my life.

"Will we have to take the deathtrap there?" I raised my chin, implying that I would sooner walk in my six-inch heels than get on the back of his motorcycle.

"You mean the bike?" He laughed. "Well, yeah. I'm the president of a motorcycle club."

I sucked in air through my teeth. "You'd have to knock me out and throw me over your shoulder before I'll ride on one of those despicable machines."

"That can be arranged." His cheeks flushed, and I could tell I was getting to him. My heart raced at the thought, my fingers itching to curl into fists.

"And where would your precious alliance be then?" I sighed. "Barely married and already planning my demise. How... predictable."

"Trust me, wife," he said, taking a few steps inside the room, closing the distance between us so I had to stare up at his considerable height. Despite my heels, he still towered over me. "If I wanted to get rid of you, you'd already be dead."

"Trust me, husband," I replied, mocking his tone. "The sentiment is mutual."

"A stalemate it is then."

"So it seems." I took a deep breath, ignoring the enticing appeal of his cologne and deodorant and whatever else made his scent so masculine. The first time I'd met him, we had fought over his negligent treatment of my brother. I remembered how passionate he was as he argued with me in Italian, how he'd stood firm against me while I banged on his chest and shoved at his shoulders. He took it all with a gleam in his eye, like he enjoyed getting a rise out of me as much as I did to him. It made my blood run hot for reasons I didn't care to examine. Nor would I ever.

This wasn't about attraction. This was about an alliance, a compromise. But I'd always thought it was easier to attract flies with honey.

"Fine, I will accompany you to your club meeting," I said, "as long as you drive me in your truck. If not, I can call Williams—"

"We'll take the truck." He pulled one side of his mouth into an annoyingly beautiful smirk, his eyes twinkling with victory. "We leave in an hour."

"Is that all, husband?" I asked, trying to put as much animosity into that one question as I could. If I wasn't going to have an easy marriage to my worst enemy, neither would he.

He snorted and shook his head while he turned toward the hallway. "That's all, wife."

The word came out like he was trying to wipe excrement off his shoe.

Roman grabbed the door, shut it, and left me alone in my miserable little room.

2

BEAR

My new wife spent the majority of the ride to the clubhouse looking at her phone, which was fine with me because I wanted to talk to her about as much as she wanted to talk to me. This wasn't a love match, and I wouldn't pretend I had anything in my heart for the Caputis other than suspicion and animosity.

But if I wanted to end this war between our families, I would do what I had to do...including putting up with the mafia princess and ignoring the way her indignant gaze made me want to claw her eyes out. Sure, my house wasn't as big as any blood-money mansion she'd lived in, but it wasn't a fucking shack.

Whatever. I didn't give a shit what she thought about our living arrangements. Her opinion changed nothing. We were stuck together regardless.

When I pulled into the clubhouse driveway, she glanced at the building with a sneer, her dark gaze sweeping over the gravel pavement and ancient vinyl exterior with incredulity.

"It truly is a wonder the Roses have managed to hold my family off for so long," she said. "Everything you own reeks of dereliction and decay."

I put the gear shifter into park before turning to face her. "Well, feast your eyes, princess. Everything I own is fifty percent yours now."

She gave me a side-eye before opening the passenger door to hop out. I sighed, running a hand back through my hair. Julia could hold her own, but I feared what would happen when we walked through these doors. I'd never had reason to be afraid of my brothers before, but only half of them had wanted this alliance. The other half had threatened to walk because of it. I was barely holding the fractured pieces together.

Three months ago, the FBI had raided the Steel Roses headquarters and arrested my father, the former president. In his absence, the rest of them had elected me the interim leader, but I didn't think I was ready for the responsibility. I wasn't sure I'd ever be ready. I could count on one hand the number of people I trusted, and my wife wasn't one of them.

Get it together, Montgomery, I scolded myself before climbing out of my truck to lead Julia inside.

At this time of night, most of the members were already here. The old ladies, MC princesses, and hang-arounds mingled about, gossiping and talking and getting rowdy. Normally, I would have found one (or two) to flirt with, but those days were long gone. Recently, I'd been too focused on ending this war to fuck around, and now that I was a married man (with an infidelity clause in my contract), I didn't see the point.

The room went quiet when we walked in, all eyes turning in our direction. Julia froze, stiffening her spine and steeling her jaw against the pervasive onslaught. Some were curious, my sister among them. Verona sat in her boyfriend's lap with his arms around her while my acting vice president, KC, looked up from his spot next to his wife, Alba. For the first time in probably all of SRMC history, none of these motley motherfuckers had anything to say.

A tiger had entered lion territory, and all waited to see who would attack first.

"Well?" I said, jumping to my new wife's defense. "What the fuck are you all staring at?"

Some cleared their throats and went back to their activities. V and Hollywood, a.k.a. my best friend who had started dating my little sister, stood and walked closer.

"Congratulations?" V said, opening her arms to hug me before turning to Julia. "You must be my new sister-in-law."

"Indeed," Julia said, holding out a hand for V to shake.

"What's it feel like to be a married man, huh?" Hollywood clapped me on the shoulder and threw an arm around my neck. Of everyone in the club, he was the comedian, the one most likely to crack a joke to break the tension.

"About the same as it felt being single," I said, which caused Julia to snap her attention to me and raise an eyebrow.

"It's nice to see you again, Julia." Hollywood flashed her his trademark grin and a wink.

"Likewise," she said, but her tone suggested it was *not,* in fact, nice to see any of us.

I nodded toward the back of the clubhouse where the MC usually held church. "Is Leo here yet?"

Julia straightened at the mention of her brother.

"No," Hollywood said. "He texted he's running five minutes late. He should be here soon."

I nodded and headed in that direction, but KC and Alba cut me off. My buddy looked suspicious of the Caputi princess. Alba only pushed her glasses higher on her nose and smiled.

"Julia, this is Alba," I said, introducing the two relatives.

"Right," Julia said, raising an eyebrow. "Alessandra's daughter."

"Penny's daughter," Alba corrected. "It's wonderful to meet you."

"Well," Julia said, "any Caputi blood in the Rose thorn bush is sure to make me feel right at home."

I winced because despite being *technically* related to the Caputis, Alba had never considered herself one of them. Her mother had run away from that life and faked her death after getting pregnant with her. She'd lived on Rose territory ever since. Alba didn't know this about herself until two years ago, but now that they were standing side by side, it was easy to see the family resemblance.

They had the same nose, the same mouth, the same cheekbone structure.

"C'mon," Alba said, nodding toward the bar. "You look like you could use a drink."

Bless Alba and her friendly disposition.

Julia gave me a hesitant glance before following KC's old lady to the bar with the other MC princesses.

Just as I was heading toward the back room, one of the hang-arounds I used to fuck, Amber, saddled up next to me.

"Hiya, prez," she said, smiling with her sexiest grin. "How have you been?"

"Oh, just fine," I said. I hadn't meant it to be an invitation to flirt, but ever the opportunist, she took it as one.

"Ya know." She pressed her hands to my chest before sliding them to my neck. "If your bed is still cold after marrying the frigid Caputi bitch, I can warm it just as good as I used to."

I bit back the insult to my wife and grabbed her wrists, forcing them down. "I'll keep that in mind."

She deepened her smirk. "Good. Maybe I'll see you later."

I didn't respond because I wasn't interested, even if I hadn't signed a marital contract with a firm infidelity clause. I pushed past her and into the meeting space.

"How's it going?" KC asked, seemingly holding back a grin at Amber's blatant invitation. "With Julia, I mean?"

"I'll be surprised if she doesn't murder me in my sleep." I rounded the SRMC table and sat in the president's chair at the head, gazing over the logo burned into the wood: a rose with a blade going down the center. My father had occupied this seat for over twenty years, and I prayed I could fill his jumbo-size shoes.

"I'm not so sure about that," Hollywood said, barking out a laugh as he took the road captain's seat on the left. KC lowered himself into the VP seat on the right, lighting a cigarette as Hollywood continued. "I saw the way she looked at you when Leo announced your 'arrangement.'"

"What's that supposed to mean?" I asked. "She hates me, then and now. This isn't a love match."

These two fuckers were my best friends in the entire world, and I trusted them with my life. If I could confide in anyone, it would be them first...even if Hollywood had been known to be a gossip worthy of a flock of clucking hens.

"I don't know, man." Hollywood huffed a teasing breath. "The way she got up in your face? I've never seen a girl with balls that big. She's the only one who would dare talk to you like that."

KC raised his eyebrows and blew out a lungful of cigarette smoke. "You know Bear likes 'em rowdy."

"Shut up," I said, rubbing my fingers over my eyes at the memory. The first time I'd met Julia, she'd given me a raft of shit for the way her brother had been held captive for months. She'd banged on my chest and shoved at my shoulders, and I was man enough to admit, I *did* like a woman with passion. Even if she was a Caputi.

"How'd the wedding ceremony go?" KC asked. "Sign your life away?"

"Leo wants a child within a year." I leaned back in the seat and glanced between them.

Both Hollywood and KC went silent. I had evidently gasted their flabbers.

"A child?" Hollywood said with disbelief.

"He demands too much," KC said. "I told you he'd try to steamroll you."

"She agreed," I said.

Hollywood slammed his hand down on the table and leaned his head back to howl with amusement, causing me to glare at him. If looks could kill...

"Within a year?" He guffawed. "I bet you're pregnant before winter."

"I'll take that action," KC said, holding a hand out across the table.

"Can you two knock it the fuck off?" I growled.

"Two shifts at the garage," Hollywood said, taking KC's palm, ignoring me. "AND a security shift at the Beacon."

I sighed at the mention of the club-owned BDSM club where my sister liked to take her flogger to my best friend's ass and tried to push the mental image away.

"You're on," KC agreed, giving Hollywood's hand a firm shake before a few of the other officers filed into the room.

Thor, the MC's sergeant at arms and KC's brother-in-law, sat down next to him and cracked his neck. At six-three and built like a Viking, he'd earned his nickname because he liked to beat mother-fucking heads in with a sledgehammer. There was a reason he was the sarge. He gave off a "don't-fuck-with-me" vibe that sent most idiots screaming for the hills. He'd recently married KC's sister, Selene, and if two people were the definition of opposite sides of the same coin, it was them.

After that, Doc came in alongside Saint, whispering to each other. Doc had been the MC's enforcer for the last ten years and had earned his reputation as the proverbial Doctor Jekyll. He'd been trained as a surgeon but had suffered some personal tragedy that created in him a Mister Hyde who liked to carve up disloyal fuckers and throw their bits in the fire. I'd seen him do things that nearly made me retch. Saint, on the other hand, had been raised in a Catholic orphanage. He had a complicated relationship with his God that sometimes came out in the form of beating Caputis to a pulp. It was his mercy that had saved Leo from death and his friendship with Julia that had led to the position we were in today.

Doc sat next to Hollywood while Wheels, the MC's treasurer, sat down next to Thor. I waited until the rest of the Roses filled in around us, all grizzly, haggard motherfuckers that had seen better days.

Three months ago, Gabriella Caputi had ambushed our ranks and killed more Roses in one day than the Caputi fucks had in years. Since then, they had interrupted our trade routes and taken more of our men from us. Things were escalating quicker than I could put a lid on them.

I couldn't blame my crew for being skeptical of this new match with Julia or the alliance with Leo. I only hoped it didn't come back to bite me in the ass.

Finally, Leo came into the room. At six-five and wearing a suit that probably cost more than my truck, he dominated the space as he walked. I'd stabbed him in the kneecap the night we captured him so he still used a cane to walk. But other than that, he seemed much healthier than he had in nearly a year. This time, he was flanked by two burly men with guns in holsters under their arms—his security detail. I couldn't blame him for that either, especially considering Gabriella had put a price on his head worthy of a Powerball lottery. He came to stand next to me, giving me a wink and a shit-eating grin that I ignored.

Once everyone was assembled, someone shut the door to the front and KC stood to bang his rings on the table.

"All right, you fucking pricks, listen up. Church is in session." He stabbed out his cigarette and nodded at me to go on.

Taking a deep breath, I stood and glanced at the assembled crowd, wishing not for the first time my father was here to guide me. I'd been trying to reach him at the pen, but until his trial, the DA wouldn't allow any contact with SRMC members, even if they were related to him. All correspondence had to go through my sister, and that chafed most of all.

"Brothers," I said, taking a deep breath, "we are closing in on the end of the war with the Caputis. Very soon, Gabriella will be dead."

Whoops came from the crowd, echoing a boisterous applause. Leo shifted next to me and cracked his neck, but didn't say anything, so I continued.

"I've contacted the Steel Roses in New England, Ohio, North Carolina, and Georgia. They're all riding in for the convention. How are we on arms?" I glanced at Thor.

"We're stocked," he said. "After Gabriella stole our last shipment, the IRA was willing to step in. This time, we're ready for her."

"Good," I said, looking to Doc. "What about supplies?"

They knew what I meant. If this went the way we wanted, we'd kill Gabriella and usher in a time of peace. But until then, we'd have to pick off her cronies for information. Doc had a secret stash of poisons he liked to use when he...*interviewed*...such people.

He smiled. "I'm ready."

"Fantastic." I was happy Doc had gotten on board with this plan. A few months ago, he'd been skeptical, taking every opportunity to let his opinion be known. He didn't trust Leo Caputi, didn't think we should partner with him, and didn't agree my match with Julia would be good for anyone involved. Thor had threatened to beat some sense into him, and he'd come around. But when I glanced back to the sixty or so other club members, I saw a mix of emotions on their faces. Some were agreeable, others more distrusting.

"What's the plan, then?" asked Stallion, a grizzly old-timer who had been in the club nearly as long as my father. His much younger brother, Skulls, had been murdered by Gabriella the night she attacked us, something that had aged the man nearly two decades in a matter of weeks. "Are we gonna sit back and hope that Caputi fucker can get his family to accept this deal?"

Leo tensed and stepped forward, probably preparing to rip into Stallion, but I held up a hand to stop him.

"We're working on that," I said. "Leo and my wife have close ties with Caputis who are unhappy with how Gabriella has been running things."

"And?" Stallion asked, crossing his arms. "What are they saying? When is this supposed to go down?"

"We're still putting the final pieces into place," Leo said. "My uncle Sulli and my uncle Frankie are—"

"Uncles?" Stallion scoffed. "You mean Benito's brothers? There's no fucking way they side with us." He shifted his hard gaze to me. "Bear, you gotta realize this is stupid. If your old man—"

"My old man is locked up because of Gabriella." I slammed my hands on the table to get his attention, and he straightened, inhaling at my outburst. I met the gazes of my younger brothers, Castor and Pollux, across the room. Earlier this year, Pollux was in the hospital after Gabriella had the Beacon blown up, and three months ago, Castor had a gun to his head. He barely escaped with his life.

"Picasso, Slip, Coins, and Skulls are dead because of her. I almost lost my brothers and sister because of her. They've been fucking up our business all year."

"And how many more did we almost lose because of *him*?" Stallion sneered at Leo. "I speak for a lot of us here when I say this plan is fucked-up. You're leading us in the wrong direction."

"My father wanted this before the Feds grabbed him," I said, narrowing my gaze at the dissenter. "Are you suggesting I don't know what I'm doing? That Crow didn't know what he was doing?"

Stallion pursed his lips and shifted his stance as if he meant to tell me just that.

Lore cleared his throat and stepped forward before he could. "Look, I understand why everyone's tense about this. If anyone gets it, I do." Last year, Leo had taken him hostage and carved out his eye before dumping him back on Rose territory to die in a puddle of his own blood. "It takes all of my willpower to stand five feet from that maniac and not tear his heart out."

"Reformed maniac," Leo said, "and I apologize for what was done previously...when we were under *different* circumstances."

Lore scowled and glared at the Caputi boss. "But we can't fall apart now. If this truce gets us peace...*lasting* peace...isn't it worth it? We can't spend our time bickering among ourselves, and if I can come to that conclusion, so can you."

"They took my brother," Stallion said. "They took half our leadership, and the other half is in the pen. We're sitting on our asses, letting that happen."

"Pretty soon, we'll have all the pieces in place to put that bitch in the ground," KC added. "Until then, everyone needs to trust we have it under control."

Stallion took a deep breath and let it out on a disgruntled scoff but didn't say anything else, causing Reaper, the brother next to him, to lean in and whisper something in his ear. I didn't miss the interaction, and I wondered how close those two had gotten in recent weeks.

I glanced at Thor, who watched them like a hawk. It was his responsibility to keep these fuckers in line. He was ex-military, and as far as I knew, he'd done some fucked-up missions for our government that forced him to leave and join a motorcycle club, so whatever it was must have been some heavy-hitting shit. If anyone in the club were plotting, he would find them out.

Then, I looked at Doc, who smoked a cigarette and eyed Stallion with a neutral glare. He had been the most vocal about not trusting this plan, and if there were Roses who were thinking of doing anything against my wishes, he'd be the one they'd go to for guidance. He had a seat at the table. He was the enforcer, the one who carried out the MC's sentencing.

"So?" I said, directing my attention back to Stallion. "Is there a problem?"

The crowd held its collective breath, and KC tensed, preparing to handle Stallion if he moved too quickly. Phrasing it like that meant something. If there was, Stallion had two choices—he could challenge me or tear off his patch and leave. But when someone joined the Roses, they made an oath to be loyal until death. If he decided to leave, the rest of the brothers would go after him. I wouldn't be responsible for what they'd do, but I could guess. Until I became president, I would have been a part of it.

"No problem," Stallion eventually said, shaking his head.

"Anyone else got a problem?" I glanced at Reaper and finally to Lunchbox on the other side of Stallion. They stood in the back with a few other guys grouped around them, seemingly sectioned off from the rest of the crowd.

When no one said anything, I moved on. "You were saying, Leo?"

He nodded. "Sulli and Frankie are in the same boat as us. They're tired of Gabriella's bloodbath and eager for a regime change. I've talked to a few of my cousins, who have been gathering intel from the underbosses. If we can rally support from the majority, we'll have her outnumbered and surrounded."

"Are you certain they'll go for an alliance with the Roses?" Hollywood asked.

"They don't have a choice," Leo said. "Not anymore. Julia is married to Bear. If I'm the boss, we'll be family. I can assure you, there's nothing we Caputis hold in higher esteem."

I ignored the bristle building at the back of my throat and watched as the rest of Roses swallowed that information. In my family, a marriage happened at the clubhouse with the entire membership in attendance. We toasted the health of the couple and the promise of future generations of little Roses running around. The couple announced their love in front of everyone so the rest of the club knew who would come for them if anything happened to either one. None of that happened with me and Julia. So why should they believe it?

Leo had told us everything about our union needed to appear legitimate to win Caputi loyalty. I needed to do the same for my own men, as much as the thought chafed. Julia was my wife in name and image only. To throw a big party celebrating our union seemed to spit in the face of what the Roses held sacred about it. But when we agreed to this thing all those months ago, I knew it needed to be public. It needed to be loud and proud so everyone understood—the Feds, the Caputis, the other bosses and MCs in the surrounding area. This wasn't some minor truce between two feuding nobodies. This was the end of an era, of decades worth of fighting and territory wars.

"To spill Caputi blood is a sin worse than any other," Leo said. "Gabriella has overstepped her reach. She'll pay for that."

"When there's more at play, I'll give you all an update," I said. "Now, what about the run in a few weeks?"

Hollywood stood and explained his plan for the upcoming trip to our allies out west in Montana. We'd recently made an agreement with the Royal Bastards MC in Helena, who were all too eager to help us with our supply shipments.

"Lore, I'm letting you take the lead on this," Hollywood said. "Pick your team and let me know the details."

Lore nodded and smiled before clapping a few of his buddies on the shoulder. Wheels gave the treasury update next, and the realist in me grimaced. The FBI raid and the Caputi massacre had caused us to dip into emergency funds, and now we were running low.

"I don't wanna scare anyone," Wheels said, rubbing a hand over his head. "But if this deal with the Bastards doesn't go well, we'll be up shit's creek."

"Work with the prospects and the old ladies on shoring up a few fundraisers," I said.

"Once I get access to the Caputi funds, I can help," Leo added, raising a few Rose eyebrows.

"Thank you," I said as I shook his hand. "All right, brothers. That's enough for tonight. Go have some fun, huh? Let's remember why we do this shit in the first place."

KC knocked his rings on the table to announce the end of church, and most of the brothers filed out to the front room. The sounds of music and clanking pool balls declared the start of another rowdy night.

While the club had dispersed, the officers stayed behind. Thor and KC shifted their attention to Doc, who rubbed a hand over his mouth and glanced between them.

"I know," he said, seeming to understand his obvious dissent had fueled more among the rest of the group.

"We need to be united," KC said. "Especially now. The old leadership is dead or locked up. With us so newly in charge, it doesn't look great that you've been bucking against our ideas. Fear spreads and spreads."

"I know." Doc sighed and lit another cigarette.

"Fix it," Thor growled before pushing to his feet. "Before I have to. Understand?"

"I'll handle it." Doc nodded, stood, and walked out front, hopefully to set Stallion and the others straight.

Thor glanced at me with distrust echoing in his gaze before following the enforcer out.

"Don't worry about them," I said, turning to Leo. "We'll get them in line."

Leo smirked and winked. "I'm not worried, brother. We're on the same train now. We'll get where we're going in one piece." He clapped my shoulder before limping away, his two bodyguards on either side.

"That's a problem," KC said once it was just us and Wheels. "Doc should have kept his mouth shut."

"I don't trust Stallion," Wheels said. "My brother got shot that day, too, so I understand why he feels the way he does." The only difference was Hollister had lived, despite the vicious scar on his head. "He's up to something."

"Thor will keep an eye on him," I said.

"You need to marry Julia publicly," Hollywood said. "That's the only way they see this as a true alliance."

"Yeah," I said with a sigh. I'd been thinking the same thing.

"Otherwise, they'll eat her alive," he continued. "If they don't think she's your old lady, they're never gonna respect her. One drunken night is all it's gonna take, and they'll chew her up."

"Got it," I said, nodding toward the door. "Go on. Go get laid. Let me deal with that bullshit."

Wheels, KC, and Hollywood stood to leave, and I ran my hands over my face, taking a deep inhale and again wishing I could talk to my father. I didn't know how he'd done this for so long. I'd only been in charge for three months and I nearly drowned with the pressure. The responsibility for everyone in this clubhouse rested on my shoulders. Every drop of Rose blood spilled from here on would be the result of my action or inaction. If someone died, that was my fault. If this plan didn't work, it would be my fault.

Fuck, Stallion, Reaper, and all their buddies would drag me out into the woods and rip my limbs off before shooting me between the eyes, and I would deserve it.

A hot lance of panic went through my chest, making my heart pound against my rib cage, turning my lungs to ash. I gasped for air, praying the sweet oxygen would soothe me, but it only made me more desperate for a reprieve.

Uneasy lies the head that wears the crown, and all that shit.

3

———

JULIA

I watched as the Roses filed out of the back room and resisted a sneer. Four months ago, I'd been their informant, the one who had an ear to the ground in the Caputi stronghold. Now that I was an "old lady," I wasn't even allowed in the meeting. Didn't they realize this had also been *my* war long before our alliance existed? If Gabriella was coming apart at the seams, they needed to act strategically, not with anger and vengeance.

While Alba, Verona, and the other MC princesses chatted around me, I texted my cousin, Della. She was only a few months younger than me and had been my best friend growing up.

Me: I can't wait to come home for a visit. Wait until you see my new house.

Della: Is it terrible? Where is it?

Me: In the sticks. It's dreadful. What is going on at home? What is Gabriella planning?

Della: Nothing good. Word has spread about Leo being alive and your marriage to the Roses. Uncle Frankie is in an uproar. My mother is pleading with Gabriella to step down, but she won't. What about the Roses?

Me: Don't know. They won't let me in—

"Julia?" Alba said, breaking my concentration. I glanced up at the expectant faces of my cousin, my new sister-in-law, and two others. Sue and Ailene? I hadn't been paying attention when Alba introduced them, my mind too focused on how my husband had flirted with that ugly brunette *puttana* in the corner. She eyed me with a smug grin that said she could have Roman if she wanted to, and being so new to this environment, I didn't know if she was wrong. We had agreed on the infidelity clause, but that didn't mean he wouldn't push his limits.

"Sorry," I said, holding up my phone. "My cousin."

"We were thinking about having a girls' night next Friday, just the four of us," Alba said, pushing her glasses up her nose. "Would you be interested in coming?"

"Don't be too sweet, Alba," Verona said. "Surely, the Caputi princess has better things to do than slum around with the likes of us."

I pushed my shoulders back and forced a smile, trying not to show how much I would rather stab myself in the thigh than spend time with the Rose women. Alba was married to the man that killed my eldest brother, Julian, and my uncle, Benito. Despite being blood related to her, I seethed with hatred for both of them. The rest were nearly as bad as their men—cutoff shorts, tank tops, disgusting flip-flops. The goth one had tattoos all over her body, even on her fingers. What did they know about me? What could I possibly have in common with them?

"Uh," I started.

Ailene cut me off with an indignant snort and shook her head, taking a sip of beer. "You're right, V. Check out the look on her face. It's like she stepped in flaming dog shit."

Am I that transparent?

"Well, this isn't exactly where I'm supposed to be, is it?" I raised an eyebrow. "A Caputi in Rose territory is a precarious thing, indeed."

"V, Selene, knock it off," Sue said, and I winced internally at having gotten the name wrong. This one blinked at me with eyes nearly as big and blue as Alba's. "You saved my fiancé's life. I'd like to at least do a shot or two with you if you don't have anything else going on."

Oh. This one was *Ru,* not Sue. This was Saint's girl, the one he'd been smitten with and talked about all the time. A few years ago, I had saved Saint's life, and he'd saved mine. We owed each other more than I would ever admit, which was why I'd started leaking information to the Roses in the first place.

"Right," I said. "Next Friday?" I tried to think of any reason I couldn't, but being that my social calendar had all but disappeared after I'd been disowned by my family and agreed to marry Roman, I figured I might as well get it over with. Perhaps I could put in a few hours and they'd leave me alone for a while afterward. Besides, it wasn't like I had any other friends in Madison County. "Sure. Count me in."

"Great!" Alba said. "We usually binge a TV show and drink and gossip. You'll have fun, I promise."

I wasn't so sure about that, but I didn't argue with her. Instead, I eyed my brother as he came out of the back room and walked toward me.

"There she is," he said, holding his arms out for a hug, which I gladly obliged. "How are you fairing?"

I answered him in Italian. "How dare you leave me with these people, Leo."

"Come now," he said in the same language. "Of the two of us, you've always been better at making friends."

I glared at him. "You said we'd be in this together and you throw me to the wolves. Some brother you are."

Leo laughed and kissed my temple. "You'll be okay, dear sister. I've got to go."

"Where are you going?" I didn't want to be separated from the only family I had here, the only family that mattered.

"I've got a meeting with Rancone and Davila." He brushed hair behind my ear. "If I can get them on my side, I'll have the Baltimore underbosses."

I took a deep breath and ignored the nervous churning in my gut.

I didn't like the thought of Leo going to these meetings alone, even if he had two hired hitmen on either side.

"Take me with you," I said. "Together, we can—"

He tsked at me and shook his head. "I can't do that. Your husband would have my head."

"Who cares what he thinks?" I couldn't hold back the scoff that shot out of my throat. "My husband doesn't care what happens to me."

"Hmm." Leo's eyes narrowed like he didn't believe me before he gave me one last kiss on the cheek. "I'll call you later."

At that, he turned and left, and I tried not to look as useless as I felt while I watched some of the Roses walk closer to our little group. Saint threw an arm over Ru's shoulders, and Hollywood pulled Verona closer from behind.

"You hanging in there?" Saint said, eyeing my glass of water. The rest of the ladies had been slinging back beer, but I didn't trust this situation enough to lower my guard.

"Oh, you know me," I said, "I always land on my feet."

"Uh-huh," Saint continued. "And the married life?"

"She's coming to girls' night on Friday," Ru said, tucking herself tighter into his torso.

"Girls' night?" He curled his lips into a smile. "*You're* going to girls' night?"

I tilted my chin higher, trying to appear as nonchalant as possible. "What's wrong with that?"

He shrugged. "Nothing. I'm glad you're fitting in."

"Well," Alba cut in, "technically, we're family. Right?"

I still hated the way that sounded. "Right."

Ru turned to Saint and whispered something low that made him chuckle and drift his hands lower on her hips. KC grabbed Alba and led her away, while a tall guy with long dirty-blond hair stole Selene's attention. Suddenly alone with nothing else to do, I went back to texting my cousin.

Della: What do you mean? You've been giving them information for years.

Of everyone in my family, Della had been the only one who knew what I was doing. She claimed to hate Gabriella as much as the rest of us. Somehow, the information had gotten out a few months ago and my dear favorite aunt had her men abduct me from my own home and beat me nearly to death. I still wasn't sure how she'd learned of my betrayal. Perhaps I had been sloppy or perhaps she'd had my phone tapped. I'd never know for sure, but I did trust Della. Now that I couldn't be physically in the mansion, listening and learning the way I'd used to, I had to rely on her and my other sources.

Me: The situation is confounding. Find out what you can, would you? I need some leverage.

Della: I think they're planning an arms trade soon. Even though Gabriella stole that supply shipment from the Roses, she doesn't think it will be enough.

Me: When and where? Can you find out for me?

Della: I'll try. Invite me for a visit soon. I miss you.

Me: Miss you, too.

I switched gears. Della may not be in the right rooms at the right time, and being a princess, the bosses would stop any important conversations when she appeared. But the staff? Caputis barely noticed the people who worked for them, and most had NDAs preventing them from talking to anyone outside the family. But I wasn't outside the family, and I had a few close informants on the payroll who would always answer if I was the one who asked.

I contacted Titus first, and when he didn't immediately answer, I went for Hannah. They'd been servers for nearly a decade now, and if there was one thing that was true about Caputis, we lived to talk around the dining room table.

"Are you ready to head out?" came my husband's voice, and I lifted my focus to see him standing in front of me with his arms on his hips, a blank expression of indifference on his face. To my right, Alba whispered sweet nothings to her husband, something that made him bite his bottom lip and smile. To my left, Hollywood was in the process of dragging Verona toward a back room. All these old ladies with their MC men, and here I sat, choking back my annoyance while mine deigned to talk to me.

"Sure." Standing, I walked toward the front door, focusing on the sound of my heels click-clacking on the concrete instead of how his club members eyed me as I passed. Roman put a hand on my lower back, and I tried not to react to the foreign touch.

The stifling, humid air of summer in Virginia hit me in the face as soon as we walked outside, sweat immediately pooling at my hairline. Augusts in the mid-Atlantic were notoriously vile, but it was almost like the weather fates were mocking me, making my miserable circumstances all the more intolerable because I couldn't be comfortable, no matter what I did.

He helped me into the passenger seat of his truck, and I checked my phone again for updates, dismayed when no one had responded. Would they change their minds about helping me now that I'd been "married" to a Rose? Or had something happened? Had they been found out?

No. Della would have mentioned something if Titus and Hannah were removed from service. Perhaps they were busy or—

"Did my sister behave herself?" Roman asked, drawing my attention up to him.

"I've been invited to a girls' night next Friday," I told him. "I've accepted. I hope there were no other pressing matters."

Roman raised his eyebrows. "You accepted?"

"Is that so shocking?" I rolled my eyes. "Perhaps I will get along with your extended family better than you."

"I doubt that," he said with a laugh. "V hates pretty much everyone except Hollywood and her friends."

I took a deep breath, considering that perhaps Verona and I had more in common than I previously thought.

"How did your *church* go?" I said the word like it meant nothing because, in my opinion, they had nothing if I didn't give them the information they needed.

He ran his fingers over his forehead. "Fine. There's some dissent, but it'll blow over."

"Dissent?" That surprised me. "And here I thought you were all a bunch of mindless brutes set on doing whatever your little leader told you to do."

"Hmm," he said. "And why would you think that? Is that how things go in the Caputi household? All the king's soldiers blindly follow commands until someone else steps in?"

I scowled at his incendiary tone. "And just how do you propose to deal with these dissenters?"

"We need to have a wedding. Soon. In the next two months."

Laughter bubbled out of my throat before I could stop it, and when he snapped his insulted gaze to me, I realized he was serious.

"Why are you laughing?" He raised an eyebrow. "I would have thought you'd like something like that. A chance to spend a ton of money and wear an overpriced dress and be the center of attention?"

"You know nothing about me." Sure, I looked like the type of woman who had been planning her wedding since she was in grade school, but I'd only ever wanted someone to love me...and someone to love in return. I had that with Vittori. I had that with Hugo. We were going to elope with whatever remained in my trust, run away, and hide from my family so no one would ever tell me how to live my life again. Then, Gabriella had snatched that from me, and I'd been out for her blood ever since.

"Regardless," he said, "it needs to be in front of the other Roses. A piece of paper means nothing to them. Leo was right; we need to show them this is a true marriage for them to accept it."

"A true marriage?" That almost made me laugh again. "You and I will never have that."

"Not with that attitude." Roman's stoic voice made me want to slap him, and had he not been driving, I might have.

"Well, get used to it," I said. "It's the only one I've got."

"Some partner," he said, seemingly under his breath.

It set my temper ablaze. "Partner? Oh, is that what you wanted when you bought me from my brother?"

"You agreed to the marriage," he said. "Don't blame me for this."

"I do," I hissed. "I blame you and your stupid club. If it weren't for you, none of this would have happened."

"Is that what you think?" His voice grew louder, his cheeks flushing with what must be his fury rising inside him.

"That's what I know," I said. "This whole war started because your idiot president couldn't keep his hands to himself." The president before Crow had been in love with Gabriella. When she chose Benito over him, he went ballistic and took out a bunch of Caputis in one night, trying to get to her. Some men just couldn't handle rejection.

"And if Gabriella Caputi had left her legs closed long enough to get married, there never would have been a bloodbath to begin with," he snarled.

"Sure, blame the victim," I yelled, balling my hands into fists so I didn't start swinging them. "I can see what marriage with you is going to be like."

He pulled up in front of his house and shoved the gear shifter to park. I opened the door and climbed out before he could reply, stomping up the porch steps despite my heels.

"You should be grateful I agreed to this at all," Roman yelled, trailing after me. "Thirty-one and still a spoiled, frigid bitch. I can't imagine why no one wanted you."

Grateful? I'd never been more insulted in my life. He put his key in the door, twisted it open, and stepped aside so I could go first. But my anger had taken over, and I couldn't stop myself. My hand swung out and connected with his cheek before I knew what I'd done.

He whipped his head to the side from the impact and slowly looked back at me, his gaze twinkling with both fury and something else, something sinister and enthralled. My heart pounded, and I gasped for air, my palm stinging from where it had connected with his cheek. Anticipation flooded my blood as I waited to see what he would do, but my wrath did not dissipate.

"I am not *unwanted*," I said, remembering my beloved Vittori and Hugo. "Don't ever talk to me like that again."

"Or what?" He leaned in, twisting his features into a sneer. "What will you do, *wife*?"

I reached up to smack him again, but he reacted quicker this time. He grabbed my wrist and hauled me back against the doorframe, holding my arm above my head with one hand and wrapping the other around my throat—not tight enough to hurt but enough to tell me that he was in charge, that he would take control of the situation if he needed to.

The heat of his body seeped into my thin blouse, tightening my skin, making me shiver. My legs spread to accommodate his, and a distinct bulge pressed against my hip bone. That too sent trembles through my body. He smelled like deodorant and cologne and wind and leather, and the delectable concoction stoked the flames of my rebellion. I hated him more in that moment than I ever had, and yet, as he leaned in closer, pressing his forehead to mine, I had an insatiable desire for him to close the space between us and press his lips to mine.

He terrified me in the best possible way, like jumping out of an airplane and not knowing whether the parachute would open. He could kill me, but wasn't that the point? Everyone needs a thrill every once in a while.

"The last person who hit me ended up as pig feed," he murmured.

I took a deep breath to squelch the rotten images that generated in my mind.

"Getting rid of me so soon?" I scoffed. "And here I thought you were made of sterner stuff."

"Oh, *mia cara,*" he whispered, and the tendrils of hot breath shot down the front of my shirt, coasting across the tender skin of my breasts, squeezing my nipples into tight balls that ached for his perfect teeth. "For you, I'd be willing to make an exception."

I pretended the lurch in my lower stomach had nothing to do with the endearment pouring off his lips, coating my skin like a tender caress. He rubbed his thumb over my pulse as he brushed his nose across my cheek, my pulse hammering between my temples.

"You hit me again, and I'll do much worse than shove you up against the doorjamb," he said, and I couldn't tell if that was a threat or an innuendo. Probably both. He backed away, and the rush of humid nighttime air filled the void he left, making my skin break out in sweaty chills.

I took a deep breath to try to stem my racing heartbeat, and when I turned to follow him inside, I found the space empty. He might have gone to the bathroom or went ahead to his room, but I didn't care. After how disturbing my reaction to him had been, I secretly hoped I never saw him again.

On unsteady legs, I sauntered through the great room to the stairs, taking them as slowly as I could manage with a respectable gait up to my room, quietly clicking the door closed behind me.

4

———

BEAR

I wasn't supposed to find her so damned attractive. The fact she was a Caputi meant that I should hate her, that I should be repulsed by everything she represented. But she smelled like heaven and looked like a siren devil and, when she smacked me, I wanted to bend her over the nearest surface, turn her ass pink, and bury myself deep inside her.

Did I deserve it? Most definitely. I'd been angry and my tongue reacted before my brain could stop it.

Did I like it? Fucking fuck. Her beauty was matched only by her zeal, and when she set all of that on me, I wanted to consume it like the raging, spiraling void of a black hole. When I had my hand around her throat, her pulse beat like butterfly wings under her skin, and I wanted to see how much faster I could get it.

Shaking that off, I retreated for the bathroom to cool down, and when I came back out, she was already in her room. Which I figured was for the best because I needed a drink and some time alone.

After I had my tumbler of whiskey, I went to my bedroom and pulled out the research we'd managed to compile on the current Caputi players. Based on what Julia and Leo told us, there were a few of Benito's siblings who would be willing to hear us out, but looking at their family tree, I wondered if it would be enough.

These bastards bred like bunnies, and there were a dozen cousins we'd have to get on board as well, not to mention the underbosses Leo had promised to visit.

As if summoned by my thoughts of him, my phone buzzed with a text from the Caputi prince himself.

Leo: Rancone is on board. Davila may take some work.

Me: What's he want?

I sat back and rubbed a hand over my mouth, waiting for the reply.

Leo: A bigger piece of the pie.

Fucking figures. These crime bosses, all they ever wanted was more—more money, more power, more status.

Me: How big?

Leo: Another territory. Higher percentage.

Me: And?

Leo: I'll consider it. I'm reaching out to Frankie and Sulli tomorrow morning.

I left it at that, and I massaged my burning eyes. I had my own shit to deal with. Stallion, Reaper, and Lunchbox would be a problem, one I wasn't sure Doc could fix. He'd planted the idea there could be dissent when he'd been vocal about this alliance not working, and now we reaped that harvest. Other people in the club thought it was okay to rebel, to make their opposition known loud and clear. Instead of coming to me man to man, Stallion had openly expressed his dissatisfaction and fear that the Caputis would betray us.

That wasn't to say I didn't harbor that same fear myself. Julia and Leo could be playing us, but I didn't see how that worked out to their advantage. The Caputi princess and I were legally bound to each other. She could kill me in my sleep, perhaps. But what remained of the club would come for her. She was on Rose territory, knee-deep in the thorns. Leo wouldn't risk his only remaining sibling like that if he planned to turn coat at the last second.

I would have to do something about Stallion, Reaper, Lunchbox, and whoever else joined in with their scheming. An incoming text came from my sister, telling me our father had reached out. While she was Rose adjacent, she wasn't a patched member. Therefore, she could talk freely with Crow, and as much as that chafed, I was glad one of us could communicate with him.

Detective Jordan was up his ass and the DA had plans to rake him through the coals. He would fall on the sword for us, the way the president was supposed to, but that didn't mean I liked it. Sick desperation brewed in my heart, and I wished for the millionth time that I could talk to him myself, that I could get some of his old-fashioned guidance.

On top of all this, the Hell's Knights MC were seen riding through North Carolina, much farther north than their territory would predicate. When Gabriella enacted her murderous plan four months ago, she had made a deal with the Hell's Knights to get information about us through my sister. In exchange, Gabriella had sold Verona to the president as retribution for his brother's death, something my father had done before any of us were born. We now had more enemies than we could count, and the walls were quickly closing in on every side.

I took another drink of whiskey and sighed. A soft murmur echoed through the house, and I grabbed my gun, clicking off the safety before remembering I had a new roommate.

The sound came again, this time louder, a moan or perhaps...a stifled plea. I stood and walked toward the hallway, holding the nine millimeter in one hand while I turned the door handle. The moaning grew more intense when I opened the entry, but as I got closer to Julia's room, it turned into words.

"Please, don't," she said. "Please. Please, stop. He didn't do anything. I didn't do anything." She groaned again, the pained sound turning into a muffled scream. I opened her door and held my gun up, prepared to shoot any intruders, but the room was empty. Moonlight trickled in through the French patio doors, bathing the space in a soft glow. I stepped closer, tilting my head to the side as her cries grew more despairing.

"Zia, stop it. Please. He had nothing to do..." She trailed off into a mumble, something unintelligible and pained. I squatted in front of the mattress, bringing myself to eye level with her. She gripped the sheets in a tight fist, her knuckles white, and wisps of her hair stuck to her forehead from the sweat of her nightmare.

"Julia," I said softly, trying not to startle her. She didn't wake.

"Please, don't. Please. Please. Let him live." She thrashed, her body shaking as she cried, small tears tracking down over her cheeks.

"Julia," I said louder this time, gently brushing hair out of her face to grab her cheek.

She woke on a gasp, snapping her eyes open and jutting a hand out toward me. The cold kiss of metal met my throat, and I stiffened, recognizing the blade in her tiny fist.

"Relax," I said, holding up my palms, showing her the gun pointed toward the ceiling. "It's just me."

She took a long, deep breath, her golden eyes glancing around her room. "What are you doing in here?"

"You were having a bad dream," I managed to say despite the prick of her blade's edge digging into my skin. "I was just trying to help."

"Help?" She still didn't lower her guard or her weapon. "Do you think scaring me awake in the middle of the night is helping me?"

"Well, it's certainly better than whatever was happening inside your head," I said. She pressed the knife harder against my windpipe, and I sat up straighter, trying not to back down but also not wanting to get my throat sliced open. I ignored the lace nightie she had on and the delicate dance of fabric over her perfect perky tits. If there was ever a good time to ogle my new bride, it wasn't after she'd had a nightmare.

"What were you going to do with that, huh?" She nodded toward my pistol, still in my left hand. "Shoot me in the head to protect me from myself?"

"I thought someone snuck in," I explained. "I thought someone was hurting you."

She paused, seeming to consider that for a moment before sneering. "I don't need your help, Roman."

"Fine," I said, and when she didn't lower the knife, I dropped my hand to her wrist and tenderly...oh so gently...slid it down to her elbow, hoping the contact would ground her, would make her realize she'd nearly murdered her own husband because of whatever she'd been dreaming about.

"What time is it?" Perhaps trying to get me to stop touching her, she moved her weapon away from my neck and looked at her phone, resting on the table next to her bed.

"Two in the morning," I said, running my fingers back up her forearm, ignoring how soft and delicate her skin was as I took the knife from her grip and placed it next to her phone.

"Were you still awake?"

"Yeah," I said. "Couldn't sleep."

"Why?" She furrowed her brows and pouted her lips, and in that moment, I didn't care about family titles or where she'd come from or what she and her brother might have planned for us. She looked so delicate, so precious, that I wanted to climb into bed next to her, wrap my arms around her, and protect her from every evil thing haunting her.

The thought confused me, so I stood and put distance between us. She'd bled for this war, sacrificed as much as any Rose. I should find a way to trust her, especially if I wanted to have a real marriage with her. But she was still a Caputi, my enemy, and everything I'd been raised to hate. Trust had never come easy to me, and it definitely wouldn't in this relationship. She wasn't even trying to meet me halfway.

"Get some sleep, Julia," I said instead of answering her question. "We've got a long road ahead."

I walked toward her door, but she called out to stop me.

"Roman," she said, making me turn back to her. "Thank you for being prepared to protect me." She nodded toward my gun.

"I said you were safe here," I murmured. "I mean to keep my word."

"Even if it's from you?" She raised an eyebrow, her lips twisting into a cute grin. "What if I have to smack you again?"

"Well, now," I teased, "let's not get carried away."

I closed the door behind me to her soft giggle and took a deep breath to slow my racing pulse. Something tickled the side of my neck and when I reached to swipe it away, my fingers came back crimson. I walked to the primary bathroom in my room and clicked on the light, grimacing at the cut on my throat. It was barely a flesh wound, nothing more than what I might have done shaving, but the thrill of her having caused it sparked something in my gut, echoing down to my balls.

My cock had been half hard when she smacked me earlier in the night, and now that she'd pulled a knife on me, I ached with the need to release. I wanted to hold her down by her little wrists and make her come on my face before burying myself deep inside her.

Yes, I was married to her, but this compulsion was a problem for so many reasons, not the least of which was how deeply her hatred for me ran. Despite agreeing to the patronizing and revolting "procreation" clause in our marital contract, I wouldn't sleep with a woman who didn't want me. I wouldn't force myself on her unless she begged me for it, and I wouldn't sully the image of our alliance by fucking around with other women, infidelity clause aside.

Which meant only one thing.

Letting out a deep exhale full of regret and self-deprecation, I shucked off my clothes and climbed into the shower. When I fucked my fist thinking about the beautiful half naked woman in the other room, I told myself it was because of physical attraction. Nothing more. And certainly not because of how her ire matched my own in the most delectably deplorable ways.

WHEN I WOKE up the next morning, I made breakfast for both of us and checked in with my sister. She'd talked to our father that morning and he told her to tell me to keep going with the Caputi truce, despite the Roses that disagreed.

"Shit will even itself out," he'd said. "But keep an eye on your six."

I had a shift at the garage, so by the time Julia came downstairs in her fluffy pink robe and matching slippers, the prospects I assigned to guard her had already shown up and posted outside.

"Sleep well?" I asked, ignoring the cute rumpled look on her face.

She dropped her gaze to the nick on my neck before returning to my eyes. "Fine. You?"

I shrugged and lied. "Perfect."

Julia nodded and headed to the carafe of coffee, opening the cabinet above to grab a mug.

"I have to go to work," I said. "There are three prospects outside to stand guard."

"Stand guard?" Julia dropped one spoonful of sugar into her cup before pouring the hot beverage and adding a little bit of cream. I took a mental note just in case that information became useful sometime in our eternity together. "Afraid I'll tear the place apart?"

I smirked. "Do your worst, *wife*. We both have to live here. It's in our contract."

She scowled, and I scooted the plate of tepid food toward her on the counter. "Here's breakfast."

She glanced down at it and raised an eyebrow, perhaps assessing whether I'd dosed it with something lethal. Just to be a menace, I picked up a strawberry and stuck it in my mouth. "It's not poisoned."

Julia rolled her eyes and took a drink of coffee. "You don't seem like the type to kill me in secret."

"Oh?" Since I had a few more minutes before I'd be late, I entertained her. "And how do you think I'd kill you?"

Julia hummed and ran her gaze over the length of me. "You'd stab me in the heart. You'd make sure the last face I ever saw was yours."

The thought made me laugh, and perhaps once upon a time, I'd almost done that very thing to her dear brother.

I turned toward the door, throwing a quick, "Don't burn the place down," over my shoulder before I pulled it closed behind me. Mick, the prospect just outside, looked at me as I exited. "No one goes in or out without my permission. If she wants to go somewhere, take her, but I need the details."

"Ten-four, boss," he said.

I clapped him on the shoulder and headed down to my bike, bringing it to life and taking off toward Rose Garage. It was only eight in the morning, but the humidity was enough to have me sweating by the time I got there, despite only wearing a white T-shirt, my cut, and jeans. I pulled into the parking lot and parked next to Hollywood's bike, putting out the kick stand before swinging my massive leg over the back and taking off my helmet.

Then I caught sight of a black Crown Vic on the other side of the parking lot and alarm shot down my spine.

What the fuck are the pigs doing here?

I walked inside the office, trying to temper my rage when I found Detective Jordan and her partner, Detective Green, talking to Selene. She stood behind the counter with her hands on the top, chewing a piece of gum. Thor and Hollywood stood behind her, the former with a sledgehammer in his hands, the latter with a huge, charming grin.

"Well, well, well," I said, tilting my head as I made my way next to my brothers and cousin. "To what do we owe this very great pleasure?" Disdain dripped from my words, and I crossed my arms to show how much I found their presence irritating.

"Roman Montgomery," Jordan said. "We've come to ask about searching the premises."

I snorted. "And what in God's good name makes you think we'd agree to that?"

"This land belongs to Aris Washington, correct?"

I raised an eyebrow but didn't answer.

"They were already snooping when I got here," Thor said.

Green shot his gaze to the brother in question. "The sign says you open at eight. We were here at eight."

Thor cleared his throat and shifted his stance.

"Do you have a warrant?" I asked.

"No," Thor and Selene said at the same time.

"Then, there's the door." I pointed to the entry. "Kindly fuck off."

"Your smart mouth is gonna land you in a cell right next to your daddy, son." Green smirked.

"I'm not your son." I sneered. "And thank fucking fuck for that. You look like you—"

"Hey," Selene cut in, stopping me from letting my attitude get the best of the situation. "If you don't have a warrant and you're not taking us in, there's nothing else to talk about."

"Roman," Jordan said, bringing my attention back to her. "Could I have a word?"

I grimaced.

"In private," she added, causing a glare from her partner. Evidently, she hadn't cleared this with him beforehand.

I pursed my lips and considered her request. This could lead nowhere good. Nothing she wanted to ask me would work out well for the club, and I'd had enough of her pig shit to last me a lifetime. She'd personally arrested my father, and even though I wasn't there when it happened, I imagined she gleefully slapped the cuffs on his wrists. She'd had it out for him for years, and if I weren't so interested in what she had to say, I would have told her to go pound sand.

Instead, I ran my tongue over my teeth and nodded toward the mechanic's bay. Jordan took the lead, her bright eyes missing nothing as she pushed open the door so I could follow her in.

"So?" I asked when she turned to face me. "What do you want?"

"How are you holding up?" Her features softened, and she brushed her brown hair behind an ear.

"You wanted to talk to me in private to ask how I'm doing?" I balked. "Well, let's see. My dad's in lockup and the Caputis are still out there killing my family. How would you feel, detective?"

She took a deep breath and let it out slowly through her nose. "I heard you got married."

"Oh yeah?" I raised my eyebrows, surprised it had gotten around that quickly. We hadn't put an announcement in the newspapers yet, and unless she was watching the county registrars like a fucking hawk, she couldn't have known. "Where'd you hear that?"

"Around." She shrugged. "Now, it does surprise me *you* of all people would marry Julia Caputi. Your families have been at odds for years." She put her hands on her hips. "All of a sudden, you're bedfellows."

I chuckled at her mafia reference. "I suppose the heart wants what the heart wants."

"Uh-huh," she said. "And how did you and a Caputi princess even come across one another? Would this have anything to do with the rumors I've been hearing about Leo?"

Now, I was curious. "What might those be?"

"That he's still alive and living on Rose territory, cutting deals with the people who held him captive for over six months."

I trained my features into my best poker face, zeroing my focus to her and her tells. Objectively, she was a beautiful woman. In her early thirties, she had deep ebony skin, defined cheekbones that gave her a model-esque brilliance, and eyes so hazel, they were almost the color of the sun. But her lips quirked when she wasn't sure about something. If we were playing poker, I'd say she was bluffing. So she might have heard about Leo, but she wasn't sure, and now she was fishing.

"I don't know where Leo is," I said. Which was objectively true. He could be at the house we'd given him or back on Caputi territory, making deals with underbosses. Who the hell could say?

"Hmm. Convenient." She raised an eyebrow, returning my skepticism.

"You know what's convenient, *detective,*" I started. "An FBI raid on my clubhouse at the same time as a Caputi attack twenty miles from here."

"What are you insinuating?" That seemed to get her attention.

"I don't know where you're getting your information, but if I were you, I'd start looking a little closer to home."

Jordan didn't say anything. She trained her features into a stoic expression, one she must have learned in all her years of investigating us lowly criminal scum.

"How did you know our clubhouse would be mostly empty that day?" I continued. "How did the Caputis know you'd be tied up there so they could savage our brothers?"

"Roman," she said, glancing to the ground, "I'm sorry for your loss, but if you've got something to say, out with it."

"I think someone on the inside is slipping info to the Caputis. I think someone cut a deal, and judging by the look of indifference on your face, you either don't know or you're covering it up."

Her lips twitched again.

She doesn't know.

"Trust me," I said, "when I find out who it is, I intend to plug that leak."

She stiffened. "Is that a threat?"

I laughed cruelly and tried not to sound too much like a cliché. "It's a promise."

She pursed her lips, her eyes searching mine for sincerity.

"Now, if you'll excuse me." I turned back to the office, where it seemed Thor and Detective Green were in a good old-fashioned stare down.

"Roman," she called, making me pause to look back at her. "What if I could help your father?"

I didn't have a comeback to that, cliché or otherwise. "What do you mean?"

"Since we've taken both Montgomery and Washington into custody, they've said nothing. They've been uncooperative at the best of times and downright belligerent the rest of it."

I huffed to myself. That sounded like them. Both the president and the vice president, Aris, had been arrested that day concerning an attack on the Holabird docks some two years before. It had taken all that time for Jordan to get the evidence she needed to arrest them, and now that she had it, I didn't see why she'd be willing to help either of them.

"My father's not a snitch," I said. "And neither is Aris."

She stepped forward and put her hands on her hips, lifting her chin to look me in the eye. "What if I could get you visitation rights? What if...what if you tried to talk some sense into him?"

My heart nearly leaped out of my chest. I wanted to see my father so badly it itched. But even if I made such a deal, he wouldn't listen to me. Just like I wouldn't listen to him if the roles were reversed. He was in the pen with other Roses, other MC members, other outlaws. None of them would suffer a former president with loose lips, no matter how hard his son may plead with him.

"That's a pretty offer, but it's no good. Crow won't do that. You'd be better off trying to paint the sky purple than to get him to talk. But I do wish you luck in both efforts."

"I want to help him," she said. "I want the people who hurt your family to find justice, but I can't ignore all the terrible things he's done, too."

Fair enough.

"Find out where your leak is, detective. Then maybe you have a case."

5

JULIA

No one had ever made me breakfast before. I had serving staff that prepared my meals every day, but I paid them to do that. Not even Hugo had lowered himself to cooking. And yet, I couldn't bring myself to eat it. I stared at it for entirely too long before eventually chucking the whole plate in favor of drinking coffee instead.

The gesture was too kind, too personal, and after the way he'd stared at me when he woke me up from my nightmare, I felt too vulnerable to accept such a gift.

What did it mean? Why would he do it?

Did he simply make himself too much food and decide to give me the leftovers? Or was it a show of peace, a white flag over the vast divide between us? Was he trying to tell me he expected the same of me, and I was too well-bred to know the difference?

Should I start making him food? Was that what a wife of his... *standing* would expect? I hardly knew how to operate a vacuum, let alone an oven and stovetop.

Frustrated with myself, him, and the whole ridiculous thing, I showered and dressed before reviewing my texts from the previous evening. Titus replied with his typical precision. He knew the details of the upcoming arms deal and Gabriella's conversations with various underbosses.

Titus: She's still trying to ascertain whether Leo is alive. Davila may be a problem. He seems to know Leo's location, but he wants more money.

He rattled off more information about my aunt's itinerary and where she planned to be in the upcoming days. I decided to wager that against what I wanted from Roman. With this type of information, we could track her down. We might even be able to get her alone if we were lucky.

Hannah, on the other hand, hadn't answered. I tried again, hoping to hear from her soon. Both of them knew the dangerous game they played, so I prayed nothing nefarious had happened to her. I prayed she hadn't been found out.

My phone buzzed, flashing Della's name, so I answered.

"It's good to hear your voice," she said. "How are you? Where are you?"

"I can't say," I replied. "But it's good to hear from you, too. How are you?"

We caught up for a few minutes, and tears nearly burned my eyes at the thought of having to do this all without her. But she was being carefully watched on Caputi territory, and I had three "bodyguards" outside who wouldn't let me have visitors without my husband's permission, as if I needed that. What was supposed to be a healthy alliance had quickly turned into a cage.

"I'm planning a wedding," I told her. "Something big and flashy."

She scoffed. "And how are you going to do that without your family there?"

I didn't answer her because I didn't know. The Roses would attend, surely. But the Caputis? A proposition started to form in the back of my mind, something devious and maniacal. But it could work...if the chips fell in the right spots, if the Roses were on board, if *Roman* was on board.

"Sneak out and come home, Jules," Della said. "I miss you. We all miss you. Chesco is going berserk without you."

Chesco was my Uncle Frankie's son, one of my closest cousins. He'd been born with a screw loose, more likely to shoot first and ask questions later than have a civil conversation. It had taken an act of God to convince him to let me go, that this was my idea and there was nothing he could do to stop me. Besides, after Gabriella's raid, I'd been disowned. She couldn't allow me back on Caputi territory even if Chesco convinced her to.

"He has a funny way of showing it," I said. "He hasn't answered any of my texts."

"He's mad at you," she replied. "They all are. We didn't want this."

"Well, Gabriella forced my hand. You know that."

Della sighed. "I know."

"Tell him to call me," I said. "Tell them all I still love them. I love you, too, Della."

"I love you more, Jules." We said our goodbyes and promised to find a way to get together soon before hanging up. And then I let the tears fall, allowing myself a few minutes of grief for my old life. It would never be the same again. I would never be able to walk into my home and have dinner with my family and drink with my cousins until I passed out. I'd never be able to go shopping with Della, or play cards with Chesco and tease him about the women he brought home. There were only two options at the end of this road: either they sided with Leo and the Roses, or they sided with Gabriella. There was no middle ground. There was no third option. And if they didn't end up with me, I had no doubt my brother and my husband would kill them. The Potomac River would run red with Caputi blood by the time this was over, and that pained me most of all. We were family. I had a history with every single one of them, and to know at least half of them wouldn't make it out alive cut me open.

A deep rumble came from outside, and I perked up, wiping the tears from my eyes. In all the moping, planning, and research I'd done throughout the day, I'd lost track of time. It was now close to five o'clock, and that noise could only mean one thing. I started to get up so I could hustle back to my room, but the sounds of boots on the porch outside made me pause.

"All right, man," Roman said. "You can head out."

The sentry just outside left as my husband opened the door and walked inside.

I had to swallow the reaction I had to him like this. Covered in grease stains and oil marks, he certainly looked the part of the filthy mechanic. His white shirt had been soiled with various finger swipes and his jeans were likewise just as grimy. His dark hair was windswept and tousled, likely from the helmet in his hands, and his face had a shiny gloss from sweat and sun. The veins in his arms protruded, hinting at the powerful muscles under his tanned skin, and his fingers were rough and callused and covered in black soot.

It shouldn't have been attractive. I could nearly smell his long, hard day from across the room. But the heat of a sudden need to clean him off hit me in between the legs, making me want to see how badly he could mark me up with those worker's hands. I clenched my thighs together, ignored that reaction, and raised an eyebrow.

"Nice of you to finally show up. I've only been sitting here all day like a trapped zoo animal."

"You're not a prisoner." He sighed and set his helmet on the table next to the door before reaching into his pockets for his keys and wallet. "I thought you had a wedding to plan."

"And how do you expect me to do that from your living room?" I tsked through my teeth. "I can hardly go dress shopping from here."

"If you want to go out, go out." He gestured to the door. "You've got three escorts anywhere in Madison County."

"And they'll report back to you anywhere I go."

"Bullshit," he said, taking a step closer. "They need to ask my permission before taking you anywhere."

I scoffed. "And is that how our marriage is going to go? I'll need your *permission* to do what I like?"

"Only while it's not safe for you to leave," he said. "Only while I'm not sure I can trust you."

"Trust me?" How insulting. Hadn't I done everything he asked? Hadn't I married him, agreed to sleep with him, and spared him from cutting his throat open when he startled me last night? "Trust is only earned by trusting."

"And do you trust me, *wife?*" He came closer still, his massive body backing me up to the kitchen island.

"Ugh, never." The words came out, but I didn't feel them as keenly as I had yesterday.

"Hmm." He looked down at me, tracing his gaze over my expensive A-line dress, which was more costly than anything else in this house. His eyes twinkled like he had nothing but thoughts of putting his greasy paws all over it to see how badly he could mess it up. My heart skipped as I wondered if I would stop him. I took a deep breath and held his stare, trying not to shiver, trying not to be intimidated. I'd been right, of course. He smelled like oil and man and wind, nearly as overpowering as it was when he'd had me backed up against that doorjamb. For one mind-numbing moment, I thought he might kiss me. I thought he might actually put his dirty fingers under my skirt and rip my panties to the side and finally make good on our contractual obligations.

Instead, he curled his lips into a sexy grin, almost like he knew I'd been thinking about it, and stepped back.

"I need a shower." He turned and walked upstairs, leaving me breathless, hot, and bothered in the kitchen. I rubbed my hands over my face, trying to get my mind back in the game.

Get a grip, girl.

I had things to tell him, deals to make. I wanted to give him the information I'd learned, but only if he came to a compromise with my place in his life. I wouldn't be the princess in the tower ever again. When Hugo died, I swore to do whatever I needed to bring Gabriella down. Roman would have to give me a spot at his table. He didn't have another choice. Leo didn't have the sources I did, and until Roman conceded that fact, I had to remain resolute.

I couldn't let my silly sexual frustration get the best of me.

Yes, that's all this is.

It had been so long since I'd been intimate with anyone in any real way, and now that I was in a confined space with a man who drove me to my wit's end, my hormones were taking over.

Enough, I told them. *We need to be smart about this.*

I walked up the stairs to head to my bedroom, but as I passed Roman's room, I noticed the door was cracked. The sound of running water muffled his voice, but I could have sworn I heard a soft, *"Mia cara,"* come from inside.

Curious, I stopped and peered in. From this vantage point, I had a direct line of sight to the primary bathroom on the other side of the room, where that door had been left completely open. Through the mirror above the sink, I saw Roman in the shower. He'd thrown his head back, his long, muscular throat on tantalizing display as water dripped down his defined chest and over his corded abs that ended in a V, as if pointing to the best part of him. One hand braced his upper body against the tile wall, the other disappeared down his body, out of view.

But judging by the quick jerking motion, it was obvious what he was doing.

Heat flooded my body, my cheeks burned, and I clenched my fingers into fists as I stood there and watched with rapt attention. I couldn't look away. I should have gone to my room. I should have let him have his privacy. But he was so glorious in all his naked splendor that the very feminine parts of me responded.

My lower stomach tightened, my thighs automatically pinching together to ease the ache. Without thinking about it, I tucked my right hand between them, rubbing my fingers over my most sensitive part.

I couldn't help the moan that tripped out of my mouth, and at the sound, he opened his eyes, his gaze connecting with mine through the mirror. Humiliated that I'd been caught spying on him, I expected him to stop...to confront me...to degrade me for having the audacity to enjoy watching my enemy masturbate.

But instead, he kept going. He held my stare, his lips twisting into a smirk as he jerked himself faster. I gasped and held my breath, pressing my clit harder as he licked his lips. The connection overwhelmed me, bringing me back to reality—one where I hated him and everything he stood for. It didn't matter if he was beautiful. Even if, logically, I knew I would eventually have to get over this animosity and indulge myself, that day had yet to come.

This is wrong. This is so wrong.

But that didn't stop me. No, if anything, it spurned me on. If he thought he could mess with me, I wanted to show him I could give as good as I got. I worked my fingers faster, harder, holding his stare, and just as he groaned with his release, mine crashed over me. I moaned and shivered with the weight of my ecstasy, and when I was done, I brought my fingers to my lips to lick them clean, raising an eyebrow to dare him to do anything about it. He smiled as I backed away and headed toward my room. Once I was alone, I took a deep breath and ran my hands through my hair, wondering if I'd completely lost my ever-loving mind.

6

―――――

JULIA

Roman didn't mention my little voyeuristic breach of privacy, and when I asked him the next morning if he enjoyed the show, he only smirked and winked in response. Then, I spent the next two hours analyzing the whole situation. Did he want me to see him? Did he want me to hear him call out for me?

I decided I didn't want to know.

Days passed. Every morning, I woke up to breakfast and coffee. Roman updated me on his day before leaving to go to work. I passed the time plotting against my aunt and compiling as much information as I could about her. I wanted to ensure I had a compelling case before I went to Roman with my plan.

When that was done, I gathered ideas for the wedding. Roman said it needed to be at the clubhouse, but if we did what I wanted, it would have to be somewhere more private, somewhere no one would stumble upon us unexpectedly. When I lost interest in that, I demanded my bodyguards take me out shopping for decorations for the proverbial bachelor pad, small accent pieces to make it feel more like a home. If Roman noticed, he didn't say anything, not even when

I replaced a cheap broken lamp with a frilly vintage one Leo would certainly label as garish.

In the afternoons, before Roman came home, I experimented in the kitchen, telling myself it had nothing to do with *him,* only that I wanted to learn for myself. I tried to make steak, but they ended up tasting like concrete (literally), so I threw it away before he got home and retreated to my room. He must have sensed I was trying, especially as the things he'd wanted to cook for himself disappeared. But like the decorations, he didn't say anything about it.

He only showered, made himself dinner, and retreated to his room. I didn't want to impose, and selfishly, I didn't want to owe him more than I already did, so I existed off whatever I could find ready-made.

If there was church at the SRMC, he dragged me along, insisting we put on the good show. I watched from my perch with the MC princesses while hang-arounds flirted with him, that filthy brunette ceaselessly flaunting her *assets* in his face. He never indulged her though, despite the smirk on his lips. And he never invited me into the sessions with the club. Nor did he ask my opinion about whatever they discussed.

I made nice faces with the other women and did my best to get along with them, knowing they only tolerated me so much as I did them. None of us asked for this, but after awhile, I'd gotten lonely. I was woman enough to admit I needed friends, and they *were* trying. At the end of every night, Roman politely collected me, drove me home, and disappeared into his room. I did the same.

We lived around each other like magnets with matching polarities. He went right, I went left. He stepped forward, I stepped back.

One day, he didn't have anyone to guard me, so he demanded I accompany him to the shop.

"Why can't I stay here?" I asked, crossing my arms as I raised an eyebrow. The idea of spending an entire eight hours at that filthy, disgusting rathole made my stomach churn.

"Because I promised your safety, and I need my prospects elsewhere." He nodded toward the door. "Let's go."

I glanced down at my Prada dress, my Jimmy Choo heels, and my diamond necklace, deciding I would ultimately sit in a corner anyway, so what did it matter? I reluctantly followed him out.

Thor, KC, Hollywood, and Roman worked in the garage while Selene ran the front desk. She snorted and rolled her eyes when I sat next to the coffee machine and pulled out my phone. Just because I wasn't at home didn't mean I couldn't be productive, and I had wedding dresses to select. She blew a piece of gum into a bubble, popped it, and reeled it back into her mouth, eyeing me with disdain.

"What?" I finally asked when I couldn't take it anymore.

"You going to sit there the whole time or…" She raised her eyebrows.

"That's the plan." I saved a beautiful Versace gown I could get at the boutique in DC.

"There's a stack of receipts that need sorting in the back office," she said. "If you're going to be here all day, you might as well be useful."

I took a deep breath and let it out. *Useful.* She didn't know planning this wedding and researching my despicable aunt was my way of being the most help I could to this new life, but hey…I'd been trying to get on her good side. Maybe this was a way to soften her resolve. Girls' night was in two days. It might be less awkward if I helped, right?

Swallowing down every rotten retort I had, I stood and walked into the back room. Besides, how long could the sorting possibly take?

Hours, it turned out. They needed to be filed by month and then alphabetized by the last name of the customer, and they were printed out on an old machine that used some kind of ink transfer. My hands, fingers, nails, and dress were covered in the stuff by the end of the day.

That was how my husband found me at five o'clock—purple, filthy, and frustrated.

"How could you let it get like this?" I blew hair out of my face and shoved another receipt into the filing cabinet. "It's like you haven't organized a thing in years."

He laughed, crossed his arms, and leaned against the doorjamb. He was also dirty from head to toe. Dark oil patches smudged his massive arms, and his fingers were nearly black with grease. I ignored the rush of heat that gathered between my legs and went back to my filing.

"You almost look like you're enjoying yourself." He raised an eyebrow and smiled. "Maybe I'll bring you here more often."

I scoffed. "Like I don't have better things to do with my time than sort your orders. Some of these are so old, I'm surprised they haven't disintegrated into ash."

"Well, I think you've earned your keep for the day. Let's go home, huh?" He nodded toward the front, and I shut the drawer I'd been working on to follow him out. When Selene saw me, she giggled hysterically and threw me a towel.

"Rubbing alcohol and vinegar," she said with a wink. "Nice work today. See you at the clubhouse tonight?"

I smiled, surprised by how much her compliment warmed my midsection. Maybe I could get along with the princesses after all. Maybe all I had to do was figure out how to exist in this new world. It wouldn't be easy, but I'd done harder things.

"We could use you at the garage, ya know," Roman said from the driver's seat. "If you ever wanted something else to do besides sitting around the house all day."

Part of me wanted to agree. Despite the mindlessness of the task I'd been given, the time had flown by, and I found organizing had actually been...well...fun? Normal? It was certainly better than entertaining thoughts of how to destroy the matriarch of my family. But then the mafia princess in me spoke up, demanding I be reasonable. Caputi heiresses *did not* file paperwork.

Of course, once I got home and saw myself in the mirror of my bathroom, I understood why Selene had been laughing at me. I had ink patches on my face from where I'd brushed hair out of my eyes or scratched at my cheeks.

Hilarious.

It took me an hour and an entire container of 90 percent proof rubbing alcohol to get it all off.

When I got to the clubhouse that night, Selene threw her arm over my shoulders and announced to Ru, V, and Alba that I was the employee of the month at the garage. If I kept it up, she'd have to find devious new ways to get Thor to hire me full-time.

"Well, let's not get ahead of ourselves," I said, holding up my hands. "I look like I've got frostbite. My manicurist is going to murder me."

"I know a good one," Ru cut in. "We'll get you fixed in no time."

V, Ru, and Alba laughed and clinked their beers against my glass of water, and some of the weight that had been on my chest vanished. After that, the princesses seemed to soften toward me, as if I'd been put through some demented hazing and come out the other side still standing. Maybe they just wanted to see me get my hands dirty... literally.

Now if I could only figure out how to cook.

By girls' night, I'd started to look forward to hanging out with them, so I woke up on Friday morning regrettably grateful Alba had invited me out. Roman couldn't tell me no, especially not when his sister and cousins would be around to babysit me.

"KC's gonna be here the whole time?" Roman said when he dropped me off at the house Alba shared with her husband. I stood to the side and glanced around at the tiny space, my focus catching on the soft feminine details that must have been Alba's influence—a vase of flowers on the dining room table, matching towels hanging from the oven, bright decorative lamps in every corner.

"Yes, oh my God!" Verona rolled her eyes and huffed. "You're so overbearing."

"Where is he?" Roman said, raising an eyebrow. "I want to talk to him."

"I'm here, too, dickwad," Selene said from the living room. "Your precious Caputi princess will be fine."

Roman snorted, glancing at me with a mild hint of concern. "Are you okay?"

"Aw, be still my heart," I teased, clutching my chest. "It's almost like you care."

My husband glowered before glancing around one more time. "Text me when you're ready to come home."

"Nonsense," Alba cut in. "She's spending the night, right?"

"Uh." I tried to smile, feeling like an idiot for not assuming such a thing. "I didn't prepare for that." I hadn't brought an overnight bag or a toothbrush.

"It's fine," Alba said. "You can borrow some of my clothes and—"

"Let the girl breathe. Jesus." Verona shook her head and nodded toward the kitchen. "Come on. We've got pizza and beer." She set her incinerating stare on Roman again. "Goodbye, brother."

He hummed a deep grumble before turning to leave, shutting the door behind him to leave me alone in enemy territory. I swallowed my nervousness and followed my new sister-in-law, the smell of greasy takeout making my stomach rumble. I didn't normally eat junk food, but seeing as I didn't know how to cook for myself, I'd been dependent on cereal and whatever leftovers I could scrounge from his fridge (which, admittedly, wasn't a lot). I'd been trying to remedy that. Despite how much I hated him, maybe it wasn't fair he worked all day and came home to an empty table with a clueless wife who expected to be pampered.

"Look at you," Ru said, walking into the room with her dark curly hair up on top of her head. "You act like you've never seen pizza before. What's Bear feeding you over there, huh?"

I forced a tight grin. "Breakfast."

"Okay." She laughed and nodded to the paper plates. "Help yourself. Beer's in the fridge."

"Oh, I, uh—" I shouldn't drink around them. I still didn't trust them or myself enough to be inebriated.

"What, you don't drink?" Selene said, raising a dark eyebrow.

"Which is fine if you don't," Alba added, elbowing the taller woman in the ribs. "Not everyone likes the taste."

I didn't want to be rude and decline, especially when I'd been trying to find common ground. They were technically family now, right? Would they lure me into intoxication only to rip the rug out from under me? Would they humiliate me or sell me out to my aunt the moment I'd lost control? Judging by the camaraderie and warmth between them, I doubted it.

Besides, Alba and V were *technically* my family. Selene and Roman were cousins, which made her my cousin, too. Ru and Alba had the same father. The four of them were as close as sisters, and even if I cherished my real cousins deeply, I'd never had a sister before.

"Sure," I finally said. "I'll take a beer."

"Cool." Ru smiled and opened the fridge to hand me a bottle, and I glanced at the label. I'd never had an IPA, but after I twisted off the top and took a drink, I decided it wasn't too bad. I was usually a dry wine sort of girl, but I supposed I could get used to this.

Selene opened the pizza box so I could grab a slice of cheese for myself and sit in the empty spot at the table.

"So," Alba said, taking the seat next to me. "How is everything going?"

"Yeah," Verona said, glancing up from across the table. "Is my brother being a fucking twat?"

I snorted at her vulgarity and took a small bite of pizza. "He's fine. It's all...fine."

"Fine?" Ru raised an eyebrow. "I'd feel like a fish out of water if I were you."

"Yeah, that's a good way to put it." I pursed my lips and sipped my beer, visions of the time Gabriella had abducted us flashing through my mind. The four of them had been bound and gagged on that dusty wooden floor, staring down at me while I moaned and curled in on myself. Men I had known my whole life had beaten me nearly to death, and I hadn't been able to see out of one eye, but I knew they were there. All of us had almost died that day. "But the war needs to end. I don't want any more bloodshed. If this is what I have to do, then I'll do it."

"Well, I admire your spirit," Alba said, clinking her beer bottle against mine.

"Bear's a pigheaded alpha asshole sometimes," Ru said. "They all are. But he's a good man deep down. He'll never hurt you."

"And if he does," Verona added, "you tell me, and I'll handle it, you understand?"

I thought of when he'd woken me up from my nightmare and I held a knife to his throat. The gleam in his eye hadn't been fear or fury, but something much more dangerous...bordering on lust. I couldn't help but laugh.

The conversation drifted to other things. I learned Alba ran a website where she and her husband had sex on camera for money. Ru and Verona worked at the MC-owned BDSM dungeon called the Beacon. In a few weeks, they were having a massive end-of-summer party, and everyone who was anyone in the area would be there.

"You should come. Bring Bear along...or not," she said with a wink.

"I'm not sure that's my scene," I said, trying not to sound snotty and prudish.

"Have you ever been to a dungeon before?" Ru asked.

"Well, no. But I also don't like the thought of anyone else watching me while I...*do that*," I explained.

"You don't have to do anything," Alba explained. "And if you decide you do, there are private rooms where you can sneak away."

I tried to imagine Roman and me going to her club and what we might see. Undoubtedly, we would encounter things I'd never considered, which might lead to other things I needed to confront but hadn't yet dared to face. The memory of him masturbating in the shower came back to me: how beautiful he'd looked, how hard I'd come watching him watching me, how much I wanted to do it again. I'd gone out of my way to avoid bringing it up since, but that wasn't to say I'd forgotten about it. My cheeks burned a scalding flame that echoed into my ears and down my chest.

"I'll talk to my husband about it," I said, taking another drink of beer to quench how suddenly dry my throat had become.

We ate the rest of our dinner in amicable conversation, and I realized I liked these women. They were strong and smart and exactly like Roman had said—not at all damsels. They tried to make me feel included, though that was hard considering our vastly different backgrounds. They were salt of the earth, and I had been raised with a silver spoon. Still, I'd entered this arrangement of my own free will, so I might as well make the best of it.

After the pizza, we went to Alba's living room to watch an old movie, something about a vampire who fell in love with an average high school girl for a completely unrealistic reason. I'd heard of the cult classic, of course, but never had the opportunity to watch it with any seriousness. Neither, it seemed, did these women. They laughed and joked and made fun of the characters the entire time.

A few hours later, after I drank another two beers, I went outside with Verona while she had a cigarette. I didn't smoke, but she'd invited me and I could use the fresh air.

She sat on the porch swing and patted the spot next to her, which I took with a grateful smile.

"Thank you for insisting I come," I said. "I'm enjoying myself."

"Shocking, right?" Verona laughed, reassuring me she'd meant it sincerely and not as ridicule. "When I first came home from college, I thought I'd rather be anywhere else than stuck with these three all night. But they're not so bad."

I appreciated her candor.

"But seriously," she said. "How's it going with Bear?"

Sighing, I ran a hand over my forehead and debated what to say. I didn't want to tell her the truth, seeing as it was her brother, but I also didn't have anyone else to confide in. Three IPAs into the night had lowered my inhibitions and raised my ability to trust her, at least enough to spill my guts.

"It's tolerable," I said.

"Tolerable?" She whistled incredulously. "Well, that's what good marriages are made of."

"We barely talk, and when we do, it almost always leads to a fight. We've been living together for two weeks, and I feel like the divide between us now is greater than when we signed that contract."

"Hmm," Verona said with a nod, taking a long drag on the cigarette.

"We're supposed to be partners, to have an alliance in every sense of the word, but I..." I trailed off because I wasn't sure how much I should tell her, how much she'd want to hear.

"Go on," she said.

"I'm not supposed to want him," I admitted. "I'm not supposed to like any of you. Yet here I am, drinking with the enemy."

Verona gave me a small smile and nudged me with her shoulder. "I admire you, ya know."

That got my attention, and I sipped beer to hide my embarrassment at her admission.

"I'm not sure I'd be able to do it...if roles were reversed. If Bear had asked me to marry Leo?" She blew out a breath. "That's a tough spot to be in. On one hand, I want the war to end. On the other, I've wanted to claw Leo's eyes out for a long time."

I grinned. "He has that effect on people."

"So does my brother." Verona let out a deep sigh. "My mother died when I was nine. She was in a car with Selene's parents. It was your father that blew them up."

I held my breath, unsure of what to say in response. I knew about this, of course, but it had happened so long ago I barely remembered it. Giuseppe Caputi, my father, had later died in his sleep from an apoplexy, or so we thought.

"After that, my father never really recovered. He loved her and her death..." Verona shook her head and wiped at a cheek, perhaps brushing away a tear before I could see it. "Bear took over in a lot of ways. He got me and my brothers up for school and made sure we did our homework. He cooked dinner for us every night and packed our lunches. The boy was fourteen going on forty, and he never once complained about any of it." Verona met my gaze then, hers sympathetic and seemingly gentle despite sitting next to the daughter of her mother's killer. "And when Dad fell on hard times, Bear started working at the garage to pay our water bill and put food on the table. He had his own shit going on and he put it all aside so we didn't go without."

"Verona, I…" I choked back my tears. She'd lost family to his war, so had I. Where did it end? Could Leo and I really put a stop to it? "I don't know what to say."

"Bear wanted to go to college. He wanted out of this life, and he never got it," she said. "Now he's under the pressure of taking over the mess my father left him, this fractured kingdom. He's the king." She took another long drag on her cigarette before stabbing it out. "And you, darling, you're the queen, even if you don't like it, even if you don't know what to do with it."

She could have smacked me and it would have shocked me less. I had never known any of this about him, but nor had I asked. I'd been too focused on my plight to consider exactly what type of mess I'd stepped in. But she was right. Roman was holding things together by his fingernails, praying Leo would come through in the end. But my brother wasn't the one who had the information, the one who had a plan, the one who was supposed to be his partner.

Roman needed me. And begrudgingly, I needed him.

"Take it from one princess to another," Verona said. "If you can make Bear respect you, the others will, too. From what I've heard from my boyfriend, you've got enough spirit to have all of them eating out of the palm of your hand."

I tried not to blush, but couldn't help it. I could only imagine the stories Hollywood had told Verona.

"My brother loves a woman who will stand up to him," Verona said. "So keep doing that and things will get better."

"Thank you," I said. "Truly."

"Yeah, you're welcome." She gave me another friendly smile. "You know, it may be the four beers talking, but I've always wanted a sister, and if you're what fate's gonna give me, then I guess I can find a way to make my peace with it, no matter what our families did to each other."

"Yeah, me too," I told her.

Then, she stood, grabbed my hand to haul me up, and threw her arm over my shoulder, guiding me back inside.

7

———

BEAR

Watching her watch me in the shower made me come harder than I ever had, and when she stood there to finish, it took everything in me not to stalk across the house, throw her on the floor, and make her scream my name. Her smirk when she licked her fingers had me half hard just thinking about it. But two weeks passed, and she mostly ignored me. Other than the one day I'd brought her to the garage, she continued to plan our wedding, and I went about my life like nothing had changed.

By the time I got home at the end of the day, she'd already gone to her room, and when I brought her to the clubhouse, she hung out with the other old ladies until it was time to leave.

It couldn't go on like this.

Living together was one thing, but being a true marriage, one born out of partnership and trust, needed cooperation on both sides. Knowing that did not stop me from remembering her family had been responsible for the deaths of so many of mine. She was beautiful, yes, and fucking her wouldn't be a hardship, but the cognitive dissonance of our situation kept us in a stalemate.

To top it off, Leo hadn't made it very far in his mission with the underbosses or his uncles.

"Rancone is in," he explained, shifting his weight while he held his cane in front of him. "But that means nothing without Davila. He controls the southeast. If we don't have his territory, we don't have the ports."

I sighed and rubbed my tired eyes, leaning back in the president's chair at the Steel Roses' head table. We had an officer meeting this afternoon, so I'd come right from the garage without stopping to pick up Julia. Perhaps that was a mistake, but I needed some breathing room.

"What can we do to get him on our side?" I asked.

Leo took a deep breath. "I don't know what Gabriella has offered him. He won't budge."

I nodded. "What about taking him out of the equation? Is there anyone who works for him that might be loyal to you?"

He shrugged. "Hard to say. I'd need to talk to Julia and a few people on the inside."

It had occurred to me before now that my wife had been our main source of information for the last several years. She had every right to be at these conversations. But at the same time, we were fighting dissent among my own club members, and I didn't want to put her in any more danger. Leaving her with the prospects all day already set my panic to high alert. Bringing her here, letting the guys have frequent access to her, it opened doors to things I didn't want to contemplate. That chapped my ass more than anything else. This was supposed to be our safe space where I didn't have to worry about shit like that. But Stallion, Reaper, and their buddies had been talking together in hushed corners, even after Doc and Thor made it clear the shit wouldn't be tolerated. My suspicion had run so high I'd put my brother, Castor, on investigating them. He could do things with computers that boggled my mind. After this conversation with Leo, I'd check in to see what he found.

"Let me know what you need," I said. "I'll make it happen."

Leo nodded, twisting his lips into a grin. "How are things at home?"

I purposely held myself still to keep from shifting uncomfortably. "What about it?"

He eyed me with a look that said I knew what he meant. Of course, I did. He wanted me to knock his sister up already. The sooner we had a child, the sooner both families would see us as a combined unit.

"Is Julia treating you okay?" He raised a brow.

"Now that she's my wife, you don't need to worry about that anymore," I said, hoping to make my point clear. We'd signed his damned contract. That was where his involvement ended.

"She was my sister long before she was your wife," he said.

"Perhaps you should have thought about that before you offered her to me as a show of alliance." I left little to the imagination with the harshness of my tone.

He held his hands up in solidarity. "I meant no disrespect. I only wanted to make sure our agreement was on track."

"That's none of your fucking business," I snapped.

He pursed his lips and let out a small, amused chuckle. "All right, Montgomery. I appreciate your possessiveness."

"One day, you might have your own wife," I said. "And perhaps you'll understand."

"Fair enough." He nodded and turned toward the door, pausing to turn back one last time. "Don't leave it too long. Julia gets agitated when she's bored."

Yeah, no shit. But I remained resolute on not touching her until she wanted me to, and based on our family's long history of bloodshed, that day may never come.

"Have a nice night, Leo," I said, and he walked away. After he left, I went to the back of the clubhouse where our IT gurus, Switch and Castor, had set up their operation. They affectionately called the area "the trench," but it was really an old storage closet turned into our server shed. Castor sat perched in front of four monitors, typing on his keyboard with his headphones over his ears. Switch was on the other side with the same number of screens in front of him. At my approach, Switch turned to face me and smiled.

"Descended from on high to mingle with the plebs, huh?" He shoved my brother in the shoulder to make him pay attention.

"Hey, shithead," Castor said, moving his headphones to hang around his neck. "What brings you to the trench?"

"Just checking in." I glanced at whatever he had been doing, grimacing when I saw security footage of the Hell's Knights MC in Southern Virginia. They'd officially trespassed onto our territory, and we'd have to be prepared to fend them off sooner or later. "They're getting close."

"Too close," he said, typing on his keyboard to pull up another screen. "I intercepted a text from Stallion to Coffin, their acting president."

"And?" That got my heart racing. If this was the smoking gun, I would put those traitors in the ground before they knew what hit them.

"Nothing good," Switch said. "Stallion is asking for an ETA, wanting to know when he might have backup."

"Do we know for what?" I asked the question, but I already knew the answer. Stallion was teaming up with the Hell's Knights to overthrow me, probably kill my wife and new brother-in-law while he was at it.

"I can guess," Castor said. "But I don't have any evidence yet. He's keeping all comms squeaky clean."

I sighed and blinked against the headache starting to form between my temples. "All right. Keep your eyes peeled. Let me know what you find."

"Ten-four, prez," Switch said.

"Hey, you eat dinner?" I rubbed at my little brother's head the way I'd done since he was a kid. "You're looking scrawny." He'd always been tall and thin, but his hours behind the computer screen hadn't helped, especially if he wasn't eating.

"Get off me," Castor said, shoving me away. "Now that Pollux is seeing that hot nurse, I can't cook at my place." Around November of last year, Castor's twin had been severely hurt in a bombing at the Beacon. He'd been on a ventilator for months, and for a long time, we thought he'd never recover. But the little shit pulled through, and after he'd been released, he started dating Phoebe, the nurse that had cared for him until he was healthy again. They spent a lot of time together, apparently too much in Castor's opinion.

"And I can't go to V's," Castor whined. "She and Hollywood fuck pretty much all over the place."

I pretended to plug my ears and groan. "I don't need to hear about that shit."

"I wish I didn't know," Castor said. "I only needed to walk in on Hollywood tied to the kitchen table once for me to never eat off it again."

Fucking hell. Maybe at the start, I'd had an issue with my best friend dating my sister, but now that I saw how happy they made each other, I didn't have a problem with it. That didn't mean I wanted to know about it.

"If you need a place to crash, come to my house," I said. "I've got those extra rooms in the basement."

"And ruin your honeymoon?" Castor scoffed. "Pfft. No, thank you."

There wasn't much honeymoon to speak of, but I didn't tell my brother that. I rubbed his hair again and turned to leave, calling, "Get some food," over my shoulder as I went.

I EXPECTED to arrive home to the same thing I normally did—dark downstairs, Julia in her room, the entire evening to myself. But when I said good night to the prospects and dismissed them to go inside, I froze at the sight.

The dinner table had been covered with a peach tablecloth and two proper place settings in front of the chairs. Long-stemmed candles lit the center with a plate of steaming vegetables in between them. My mouth watered at the sight of Julia placing chicken next to that, complementing the risotto on the other side. At my entrance, she paused and glanced up at me, crossing her hands in front of her polka-dotted apron.

It smelled delicious, and when my stomach grumbled, I realized Castor wasn't the only one neglecting his nutritional needs.

"What's this?" I asked, setting my bike helmet on the table next to the door.

"Dinner," she said. "Isn't it obvious?"

"No. I mean..." I cleared my throat and ran my hands through my hair, stepping toward her. "Why did you make it?"

She licked her lips, and I dropped my focus to the tiny movement, entertaining the idea of what that perfect pink tongue might feel like on my own skin.

"I thought...perhaps we could talk?" She phrased it like a question, like I could turn her down if I wanted.

I didn't know what to say. I was disgusting, having spent the entire day in the sweltering garage before going to the clubhouse to mingle in politics all evening. I reeked of leather and oil and sweat, and I was in no condition to sit down and have a meal with her. Besides, what would we talk about? How much we hated each other? How much I wanted to fuck her and choke her with equal intensity?

"It's okay if you don't want to," she said, murmuring in Italian as she bent over to blow out one of the candles. "Stupid girl. This was so stupid."

"No, wait," I said and held up a hand to stop her. "This is great, Julia. Really. It's just...uh...I need a shower. Can you wait another two minutes? Let me go—"

"Oh," she said, blinking and smiling an adorable grin. "Of course. Please."

"Okay." I raced up the stairs and stripped faster than I ever had. I jumped under the water and scrubbed like the world would end before I could get out. And after I dried off and dressed, I took a deep breath before I went back downstairs to find Julia sitting at the table, spinning a glass of wine between her fingers. My stomach rumbling louder, I walked to the other side and sat, meeting her curious gaze as I did.

She'd already plated our food and waited for me to arrive before eating.

"This looks amazing, thank you," I said, grabbing the napkin to put in my lap.

She did the same before taking a sip of her drink. I brought my own glass to my nose and inhaled. A pinot grigio, and I put that in my mental notes for next time. My wife enjoyed dry wine. *Good to know.*

"Thank you for breakfast these past few days. I wanted to return the favor." She picked up her fork and knife to slice off a piece of chicken for herself.

"I didn't know you cooked." I, likewise, stabbed into a piece of chicken, nearly wincing when I stuck it in my mouth. It tasted like sandpaper and salt dunes had a baby, and that baby looked and talked like a chicken, but had never actually been alive at all.

"Oh, damn," she said, nearly knocking over her glass of water when she reached for it.

I coughed and choked the meat back, swallowing it down before going for my drink.

"Evidently, I can't," she said with a deprecating chuckle. "Here I thought I'd followed the recipe."

"It's okay," I said, smiling as I took another bite. Just because it didn't taste like the best meal I'd ever had didn't mean it was inedible. "Chicken is hard. Maybe try spaghetti next time."

"Why? Because I'm Italian?" She raised an eyebrow and twisted her lips into a cute grin.

"No, because it's easy. Noodles. Pasta sauce. Done."

"Hmm. You've been severely sheltered if that's all you think of spaghetti." She narrowed her eyes and took another sip of wine. "You don't have to eat it. We can order in or—"

"Nonsense. I've eaten worse." I winked at the innuendo, taking another bite and swallowing it before my tongue could really taste it. Suddenly, the last few weeks became clear—the missing food, the smell of burned meat in the house. She'd been practicing, and I laughed internally at what *those* might have looked like if she thought this turned out okay. "What did you want to talk about?"

She cleared her throat and shifted in her seat. "I thought perhaps we could start over."

Start over?

"Okay," I said tentatively.

"These past two weeks haven't worked for me," she continued. "I won't live this way. Moving around one another. Pretending the other doesn't exist."

She hadn't acted like I didn't exist when she was spying on me in the shower, but I didn't bring that up. Instead, I took a bite of the mushy overcooked vegetables and shoveled that down with some wine.

"I can't go to the clubhouse and sit outside with the other women," she continued. "If you're the king of this ruthless reign, then I'm its queen. We should at least act like it."

I put down my fork at her metaphor and sat back in my seat, contemplating her meaning. Her serious gaze burned holes into me like she was trying to get through the facade I showed the world—the one that put everyone else first, the one that resisted buckling under the weight of a burdensome crown.

"I thought you didn't like me," I continued. "I thought you said we'd never have a true marriage."

"I don't, and we won't," she explained, holding her head higher. "How are things coming along with Leo, hmm? Making any progress?"

We weren't, but I was curious how she knew that.

"It's almost like he's not the Caputi you should have in your meetings."

"Are you suggesting you would be a better option?"

"I fed the Roses information for years. What makes you think I am not still in contact with the people close enough to know things no one else does? Did it never occur to you that *I* should be the one at your side?"

It did, actually. "I want to keep you safe."

She scoffed. "I'm in more danger by being kept in the dark than by helping you plot and scheme."

I was man enough to admit my wife made a good point.

"All right, I'll bite." I didn't see another way around this other than to simply suffer each other until we died. "What do you suggest?"

"We pretend," she said, brushing her long brown hair over her shoulders. "When we're at the clubhouse, I go where you go. We make decisions as a team. We bring Gabriella down together." She reached under her seat and put a folder on top of the table, resting her hand over it.

I eyed it but stayed silent, waiting for her to continue.

"In return, I will give you the information you need to take her down." She drummed her bright red fingernails on the folder. "I have a plan."

I considered her request, looking for any obvious flaw. She was right, of course. She had fed Saint information before Gabriella found out about it, and if she truly had a network of spies, I couldn't do this without her. Leo had been ousted from the family for almost a year now, and she'd been holding it all together in his absence. From the club's perspective, making a grand gesture like that would show I was serious about this alliance, about her.

"Okay," I said. "But I have a few conditions."

Julia sipped her wine. "Such as?"

"When we pretend, we *really* pretend. We act like a couple, like we enjoy each other, like we *love* each other."

"To what end?" She narrowed her eyes.

"There is no end," I said. "Not until one of us is dead. You signed the paperwork, the same as me."

She paused, seeming to consider that.

"If we want the world to believe our partnership," I continued, "it needs to look real."

"You plan to kiss me in front of them?" A perfectly plucked eyebrow rose up her forehead as her cheeks turned a rosy shade of blush, and I wondered what succulent memories flicked through her mind.

"Among other things." Kiss her, hug her, sit her in my lap, rub my hands all over those magnificent curves, prove to my brothers she was mine and I was hers, and if anyone dared touch her, I would cut their fucking fingers off. Maybe it made me fucked-up to want this, but what could I say? She was a beautiful woman and all mine.

"What about limits?" She grabbed the bottle of wine to pour herself another glass, reaching over to refresh mine as well. "What if I feel uncomfortable?"

"We'll have a safeword," I said, taking a cue from my sister's BDSM 101 rule book. "If you don't like something, say it and we'll talk about it."

"Fine," she said. "Since we're star-crossed and forcing our way through it, our safeword is Mercutio."

"Fine. Agreed." Laughing, I finished my chicken before scarfing down the rest of the vegetables and rice. "Now, what's this plan of yours?"

Julia scooted the folder across the table toward me, and I flipped it open, looking over a list of places Gabriella went to and common hideouts. According to Julia's sources, Davila had been offered a shit-load of money and a promotion in the family business if he backed Gabriella. I had her schedule of events for the next month as well as contacts who would be next in line for her to try to secure.

"I would go after the right column first," she said. "They'd be more willing to turn on her for the right price."

"Damn." I blinked as I flipped through the rest of the pages. "You compiled all of this in two weeks?"

"I did all of this in three days," she said. "I've been sitting on it as I waited to see what you would do. I had hoped you would come to some kind of arrangement on your own, but you know what they say about Roses." At that, she paused to smirk. "All brawn, no brains."

"Is that what they say?" I asked in Italian, causing her cheeks to flush as she pursed her lips.

Ignoring my flirtation, she continued. "When you and the Roses showed up at that abandoned cabin four months ago, you messed up her plans. She won't make a mistake like that again. She won't allow herself to be that vulnerable."

"Okay." I flipped to the last page, containing an apparent list of wedding invitees.

"You need to draw her out," she said.

It all clicked together like one brilliant puzzle piece. "The wedding."

"Precisely." Julia nodded and sipped her wine. "She wants Leo. She'll do whatever she can to eliminate what she perceives as her biggest threat." She leaned forward on the table, intertwining her fingers under her chin. "She doesn't realize Leo is only a pawn. *I* am her biggest threat."

I acted like that didn't turn me on in a million different ways.

"You think this will work?" I raised my eyebrows, trying to imagine a world where we did it, where we got rid of Gabriella and made peace with what remained of the Caputis.

"You could ambush her the way she did to you," Julia continued. "You could intercept her trade routes and steal her supplies, and that might be a good way to intimidate her. But a lion in wait rests while the wolf exhausts itself chasing its prey."

"Who told you that?" I'd never heard that proverb before.

She cleared her throat and looked down to her half-eaten plate. "My father."

I resisted the urge to shift uncomfortably at the reminder of our parents. Her father had killed my mother, my uncle, and my aunt. Selene would never admit it, but I suspected she had then retaliated by killing Julia's father in return. KC had killed Julia's brother, and her other brother had nearly killed Lore. On and on the bloody rampage went.

She hated me for it, and I returned the sentiment. But lately, it seemed like I had room in my heart to put aside that loathing and open it up to new possibilities...like accepting this marriage and leaning into it.

Pretending would be a start. I could pretend to like her. I could pretend to want her. Fake it until you make it and all that bullshit.

"This is amazing, Julia," I said. "Thank you."

She nodded. "Don't thank me yet. We don't know if your club will go for it."

"It's something to work with." I closed the folder, filled with a new sense of warmth and adoration for the woman sitting in front of me. The candles lit her features in a beautiful, hazy glow, making her seem like a succubus here to tempt me into damnation. Her mind matched her beauty, and it made me want things that I shouldn't want, that I knew she wouldn't want. "When it comes to pretending, do you think we should practice?"

She ran her tongue over her lips, forcing my gaze to the motion again. Such a tender pink tongue, I bet it could make my knees shake.

"Practice? What did you have in mind?"

I shrugged. "How real will things look if the first time we kiss is in front of my club? It might be obvious we don't do it in private."

Julia paused, seeming to consider that. "Are you asking to kiss me, *husband?*"

The use of that word in her condescending tone sent shivers down my spine, ending with a lurch in my balls. It started as a taunt, true, but now it sounded more like a promise.

"Is that what you need to admit you want it?" I asked. "Do you need to hear me ask for it?"

"Who says I want it?"

"*Wife,*" I teased. "I saw you watching me when I was in the shower. I saw your hands between your legs and the desire in your eyes. I watched you come, and I know you liked it."

She blinked and dropped her gaze to the table, clearly avoiding me. "That was a mistake."

"Was it?" I hummed. "As you say, I *am* your husband. If there's one person who can give you those things, who *should* give you those things, it's me."

Julia took a deep breath but didn't respond.

I waved two fingers at her, gesturing her over to me. "Come here."

8

JULIA

I should have been offended that he summoned me like a dog, but when I stood and walked on unsteady legs over to him, it seemed to come from a part of me I couldn't control. I dragged my fingers across the table, hoping the cool tablecloth would ground me. When I got to Roman, he scooted the chair out from the table and spread his legs, leaning against the back as he looked up at me with big brown eyes.

"Well?" I asked, ignoring the steady pounding of my heart.

"Sit," he said, gesturing to his thigh.

I normally didn't like being ordered around, but his commanding voice made me feel strangely cared for, like all I had to do was what he told me and the world would be right. Which was ridiculous, of course. Only I could take care of me.

But still, I found myself stepping in between his legs and lowering onto the one farthest from the table. The smell of his soap and deodorant and natural male scent assaulted me, and I steeled myself against the trembling that echoed down my spine.

He wrapped an arm around my waist and pulled me closer to his body so we connected from my shoulder down to my hips, the entire length of my arm touching his firm chest. I'd been raised around powerful men who simply took what they wanted from the women in their lives. Being the president of the SRMC meant Roman would hardly be different. I'd bet he walked into rooms and women fawned over him. I'd seen how the hang-arounds threw themselves at him when he entered the clubhouse.

"Why are you shaking?" he murmured, gripping my hips, digging his fingers into the tight fabric of my dress.

"Being close to you annoys me," I lied, knowing it was really my nerves. I hadn't been kissed by anyone since Hugo died, hadn't even wanted it. And not that I would ever admit it to him, but the thought of pressing my lips to his sent heat to places that made my thighs clench.

He grinned and ran his tongue over his canine, drawing my focus. "I thought we were pretending."

"I'm trying." Even my voice shook.

"Try harder."

I scoffed and rolled my eyes, glancing away, but he grabbed my chin and forced my face back to him. He pressed his forehead to mine, ghosting his fingertips down my neck, over my pulse point, to the bare skin on my chest. I took a deep breath, preparing myself to kiss the enemy, the one who had spilled so much Caputi blood, he might as well bathe in it.

I shouldn't want this.

Those strong, callused fingers brushed over the mounds of my breasts at the top of my neckline, tracing along the ridge of the fabric like he meant to duck them under. Heart pounding, I arched into the touch despite myself, praying he would just do it and save me the embarrassment of wanting it any longer.

Roman tilted his head forward and tentatively brushed his mouth over mine, delicate and sweet at first, shooting ripples of sensation through my blood. I melted against him, twisting my fingers in my lap to keep from tangling them in his hair. His lips were soft and warm and, when he opened them to lick over mine, I sighed into the contact. The noise turned into a moan when I reciprocated with my tongue, wrestling against his in a pathetic attempt for dominance. But I wanted to submit to him. I wanted him to win, to make me his, to show me how strong he was, how capable he was of protecting me and keeping me safe.

One hand snaked up my back to my neck, twisting in my hair to hold me in place. The fingers on my chest danced lower, rubbing over my dress to my nipples, which had pebbled from the kiss and the anticipation of what was to come.

A low masculine noise echoed from the back of his throat, and I sighed, my overheated skin suddenly too small to contain this rush of feeling inside my veins. I brought my hands to his jaw, cupping his face before moving to the back of his head, gripping, clawing, wanting more, desperate for all of him. His index finger twisted in the front of my dress and dragged it down, the rush of cool night air tightening the most sensitive parts of my breasts.

I wanted more. I wanted all of him. I wanted him to crack us both open to see if our insides matched.

Gasping into the kiss, I arched toward his touch when he grabbed one nipple between his fingers and pinched, tugging it in just the right way to send shocks of pure pleasure down my spine. In retaliation or perhaps in competition, I bit his bottom lip and pulled, and he groaned, leaning into it.

My pulse hammered against my ribs; he must have felt it, and my body whispered things I had no desire to investigate. I should have stopped this while I still had my wits, but he lifted me up and shifted me around so my knees were on either side of his hips, my feet dangling to the rungs of the chair. He grabbed my ass and yanked me closer, nudging my soft center up against the bulge in his sweatpants.

"There's a good girl," he murmured, dragging his hands up over my hips to continue tugging at my breasts.

I couldn't stop myself, almost like I was compelled by some force greater than the two of us in this room. I rocked against him, lust combining with years of pent-up tension as I sank into this depravity. He was the enemy, and I was supposed to hate him.

I did hate him. But oh, it felt too good to stop it. The smell of him, pine and citrus and *him,* amped up my arousal, and when his cock flicked against my clit, a moan barreled out of my chest unwillingly. I coasted my hands up over his arms, so hard and strong under his shirt, and balanced them on his shoulders while he worked me. Panting, he broke away from my lips to pepper kisses over my jaw and down my throat. I leaned my head to the side, granting him more access, and when he licked over a tender spot near my pulse, I trembled. Chills skated down my spine and the back of my legs, pooling in the most ravenous part of my anatomy. My belly fluttered, clenching deep inside of me.

"You smell like heaven," he murmured. "Perhaps this Rose isn't completely brainless, huh?" He punctuated his taunt with a bite near my shoulder, and I quaked again.

"You're a monster," I said, rocking harder against him. The contrast of his sweats with my lace panties was simultaneously too rough and just the right amount of agony, and I knew the wet spot on his lap would only grow larger the more I let this go on, but my mind had long since lost control of my body. I was acting on instinct now, and my nerves were too ignited to stop. "It's pretend. It's only pretend."

I didn't know if I was mumbling that for his sake or mine... perhaps both.

"Uh-huh," he said. "Such a good little wife, pretending for me."

The praise knocked over a tumbler in my restraint, the rest of my reasons for resisting finally falling away. I bit my lip and ground down on him, swiveling my hips to make that pleasure echo through my entire body.

"There ya go," he said. "Are you going to make yourself come? Huh? Are you such a good pretender that you can convince me you like this?"

I don't. I don't like it.

But it felt so tantalizing, and no one had ever handled me like this. The volcano building in my body inched closer to erupting with every heartbeat.

"Nothing to say?" He let out a sick, twisted laugh and bit my earlobe, the heat from his breath cascading over my bare skin and down to my breasts, which were tender from his ministrations. "Wow, who knew all I had to do to get you to shut up was ruck up your skirt?"

Frustrated, I snaked a hand into his hair and yanked, glaring down at him while I rode him, searching for my climax, desperate for release. He winced at first, his lips curling into a smirk as he let out a dark, sinful chuckle.

"Oh, so we do like it rough?" He dug his fingers into my hips to guide me, rocking me harder and faster. "Get yourself off, little *wife,* and then I'm going to bend you over this table, smash your face into that appalling excuse for dinner, and fuck you so hard you can't stand tomorrow."

That image sent me over the edge. It shouldn't. I didn't want him to fuck me. I didn't want his body to do the things it was doing to me, but when my orgasm broke through my hesitation, I moaned and threw my head back and every muscle in my body tensed with the rush. My toes curled, my nails dug into his scalp, and I bit down on my bottom lip so hard I tasted blood.

For that one heart-shattering moment, the world ceased to exist. It was just me and him and the smell of wine on our breath. My over-heated skin cooled, and when I looked at him, his cheeks were flushed with excitement, his eyes shimmering with desire and wanton possession.

But in the aftermath, reality set in. This was supposed to be pretend. This was supposed to be practice for us to convince his club the next time we were paraded in front of them. I had taken it too far. He'd *let* me take it too far. And I didn't know if blaming him made me feel better or worse.

Suddenly coming to my senses, I jumped off him, backing away so fast I nearly tripped over my feet and had to steady myself with one hand on the table.

He sat there and stared at me, adjusting his hips as he grabbed his cock to seemingly relieve his own tension. The V of his legs enticed me, making me want to kneel in between them and finish him off with my mouth. But no.

No!

This was wrong...so terribly wrong. He was a Rose. He was evil and vile and wretched, and everything about him repulsed me.

"What's wrong, wife?" he asked, raising an eyebrow and tilting his head to the side. "Too ashamed to admit you liked how hard you got off on my lap?"

I swallowed against a dry throat and took another step back, trying to reason with myself about the wickedness of my situation. *He'd forced me into it. He goaded me. Lied to me. He told me it was pretend, but it wasn't...and I liked it. I liked it so much.*

"You disgust me." I wanted to run away. I wanted to hide and act like this whole thing had never happened.

Roman shoved to his feet and stormed toward me, towering over me, making me seem small and insignificant in comparison. "Do I? I think you like that, too."

I shoved at his shoulders, but he grabbed my wrists and twisted me around, ramming my hip bones into the table as he slammed me against it. He overpowered me, forcing me to bend over it, rattling the wineglasses and plates, spilling pinot on the tablecloth. The candle flames flickered, and my stomach twisted, churning with anticipation and longing and...something darker. Part of me was scared of him. He'd done so many awful things, only some of which I knew about. He was a powerful man, and he could so easily force me to do whatever he wanted. But the other part...the wretched little slut I kept deep down inside, she liked everything about it, and she wanted more.

The heat of his legs brushed against the back of my thighs, the thick ridge in his pants pushing against the curve of my ass as he leaned over me, holding my wrists at the base of my spine. His lips brushed against my ear when he whispered, "Tell me to stop, *wife*. Tell me to stop and go away and I will."

I said nothing, just gasped for air to fill my lungs.

I wanted it to stop...didn't I? This was pretend, only pretend, and I should have ended it before it even began. But wasn't this what I set out to do by making him this meal? Wasn't this what we were supposed to practice? This was how a husband and wife lived, and we *were* married. If I allowed anyone to treat me like this, if I allowed anyone inside my body, it should be him.

Just then, I *ached* to be filled...especially by him.

I opened my mouth, prepared to tell him to get off me, but that wasn't what came out. Instead, I hissed, "Is this how the Roses treat their women? You depraved fiend. Some *husband*."

I arched into the feel of his cock on my backside, despite the harsh words pouring over my lips.

At that, he laughed again and wrapped one giant hand around my wrists, using the other to wrench up my dress. His heavy palm slid up the side of my leg to the holster where I kept my knife, and he yanked it free, leaning over me to stab it into the table next to my face. I jumped at the loud *thunk* but didn't move to grab it. Then he shoved my panties down to my ankles, nearly ripping them off my legs as I lifted one foot, then the other, to step out of them.

Quivering against the cool air on my wet vulva, I took a deep breath to prepare myself for what was coming, but that did not stop me from sinking into the table when the tip of his cock brushed through my soaked skin.

"Last chance," he whispered. "Say the word, and this ends."

"Oh, c'mon, you Rose bastard," I snarled. "Surely, you're not this much of a coward."

Why...oh, why...did I goad him? Perhaps I was tired of being the barely touched princess. Perhaps I longed to be fucked so hard I couldn't remember my own name. Or perhaps I just wanted to rip off the weight of expectation between us. He'd had the most issue with this part of the marriage contract, and because of that, our sex would always mean more than it would to any other newlyweds.

He shoved into me so hard I surged up on my toes and sucked in air, my back curving into the contact. Once fully seated inside, he froze, shifting his weight behind me, using his feet to spread mine farther apart.

"Fucking hell, you're tight," he said. "So fucking hot and warm and..." He trailed off, murmuring soft perversions I couldn't hear.

No, all I could focus on was how big he was, how much he stretched me in the most delightful ways. His fingers dug into my wrists, nearly painful in how hard he held me, and he grabbed my neck with the other hand, a sort of collar that both held me in place and labeled me as his possession. It should have been revolting, but the sensation of being claimed...*by him*...amped up my excitement.

His thrusts came slow at first. He eased out only to carefully push back in, and while that felt amazing, it frustrated me. He promised to smash my face into the table and fuck me so hard I couldn't stand. How would he accomplish that with such a tedious pace?

After an eternity of fretful teasing, I growled and met his ruts with punishing ones of my own. His grip on me tightened.

"Is that all you've got?" I hissed, glancing over my shoulder at his clenched features. His eyes were wide and sparkling, his lips parted in exasperation, and his brows had pulled together to make an adorable scowl between them.

At my taunting, he held on to me harder and changed his angle, surging into me so rough and deep, I could swear I felt him in my bones. He hit my cervix, and it sent stinging anguish up my body and down my legs. I whined, shifting my hips to accommodate his length. But he wouldn't let me.

"Oh, no," he growled, moving his hand to my hair and gripping it to hold me in place. "You wanted this, you fucking take it."

I struggled against him, trying to push myself up to no avail. He outweighed me by at least a hundred pounds of muscle, something that should have terrified me but only made me more aroused. Finally defeated, I relaxed into the pure debilitating bliss, the pressure of my carefully calculated control slipping from my chest. With him, I didn't need to worry about it. He would take me how he wanted, and I liked it more than I should and there was nothing I could do about it.

In that submission, I found the purest form of ecstasy. My body tensed around him, my cunt turning to a vise grip the longer his savage pounding continued, every nerve lighting on fire. My toes curled at the sound of the table legs scraping across the floor. My fingers clamped into fists. Some deep-seated emotion in me snapped as my climax finally yanked me under. Moans poured out of my mouth, turning to sobs and eventually to screams when the sensations became too much.

Roman grunted and sank his nails into me, but I couldn't feel any of it through the haze of my own explosion. The heavens parted to welcome me into their righteous kingdom. Had I died right there on that table? Was my heart still beating? I hung suspended between earth and purgatory for an eternity, and when I crashed back into my body, he had stopped moving.

His cock twitched inside me, indicating he had reached his release, and his hand rested in front of my face, bearing the weight of his body as he panted on top of me.

"Fuck, Julia," he whispered. The scent of his cologne and sweat brought me back to my right mind, and I took a deep breath before wiping at an itch on my cheek. When my fingers came away wet, I realized I'd been crying, and tears stained the tablecloth under my face. "Are you all right?"

I shook with the fury of my suddenly released emotions, all the anger and frustration and sadness so callously wrenched from me by my new husband. He took a step back, sliding out of me, leaving the evidence of our combined orgasms to run down the insides of my legs.

"Fuck, come here." He touched my shoulder, perhaps trying to help me stand, but I pushed away from him, holding myself up on the dining room table as I finally met his gaze. He genuinely seemed concerned, which contrasted with the wonderfully monstrous way he'd handled me only moments ago.

"I'm fine," I said, my tone curt and cold. "Do you think that's the first time I've been bent over a table and fucked like a wild beast?" It was. *It definitely was.* But my pride forced me to scoff, determined to make sure he couldn't see my vulnerability or how he'd turned my insides to mush. "I think we've sufficiently practiced enough for one night."

I grabbed my knife from the table, turned, and forced myself to walk toward the stairs, steeling myself against my wobbly knees as I gripped the railing for dear life. When I made it to my room, I let out a deep breath and headed to the bathroom to clean myself up.

9

JULIA

I tossed and turned most of the night, struggling with how much I liked what had happened between us. He was a Rose, a deplorable man with a villainous history and I should *not* enjoy fucking him—especially not like that. But every time I moved, I ached between the legs, and it reminded me of how adequately he'd split me open.

I still felt his hands in my hair, and when I rolled out of bed the next morning, there were bruises on my shoulders and neck from where he'd gripped me hard to rail into me deeper. They should have repulsed me, but a sick smile pulled at my lips and a demented sense of accomplishment rattled down my chest.

You should be ashamed of yourself, whispered my mother from beyond the grave. I couldn't imagine what my father would have thought. His only daughter, his princess, married to a Rose. Not just *any* Rose, but the prince. The heir apparent. The new president.

If you're the king of this ruthless reign, then I'm your queen.

We'd made that official last night, and even if it was only pretend...*practice*...my stomach fluttered with the thought of doing it again. I didn't even care if it started as a fight. In fact, I preferred to get him all wound up and flustered. I liked it rough with him. I liked when he took control, when he forced me into submission and held me there in his capable hands.

For the first time in a long time, I almost felt...*safe*. He had the power to hurt me, to kill me, but he wouldn't. Not only that, but he wouldn't let anyone else do it, either. I'd slapped him and held a knife to his throat, but all he did in return was smile and lean in. It was maniacal, certainly, but also strangely comforting. I existed in a world of madness, and my marriage to the Rose president had become a tentative safety net.

Still, I didn't trust him completely, and now I knew I couldn't trust myself around him. Even if I wanted to like him, even if I wanted to lose myself in the ridiculous emotions bubbling in my chest, I couldn't. I was cursed. Anyone I loved had been eventually killed by my family, and of them all, Roman walked precariously closer to the edge. Gabriella would get a great thrill in dispatching him in front of me, torturing him until my heart gave out.

No, I needed to keep that stupid, tedious organ protected. There could be no fluttering romantic notions between us. Roman and I had an understanding, nothing more.

I dressed and did my makeup (leaving his marks exposed) and ensured I smelled amazing before heading downstairs for breakfast. As usual, he'd already cooked and now stood on the other side of the island in jeans and a white T-shirt. I'd grown up around men who wore suits unless they were sleeping, so the sight of him in such casual clothing should not have sent such an ache down my spine. Yet, there I stood, raking my gaze down to his boots and back up again, shivering with the memories of last night.

"Good morning," he said, sipping his coffee. He ran the length of me with a heated stare, pausing for a moment on my neck before reaching my eyes. "How'd you sleep?"

"Fine," I lied, walking toward the coffeepot. "You?"

"Hmm," he hummed, straightening so he could turn to face me as I squeezed between him and the counter. "Let me see."

Roman grabbed my shoulder to twist me around, ghosting his

fingers over my throat to my jaw, holding my head in place while he assessed the bruise. "I got you good here, huh?"

I wanted to whip out of his hold, to shove him away, and smack him for having the audacity to touch me without asking first. But when I glanced up at him, sincerity echoed out of his dark brown eyes, a heady mix of playfulness and care that turned my insides to jelly.

"Don't worry about it," I said. "Leo will see it and know what it is. He'll leave us alone for a while."

"I don't give a fuck what Leo thinks," Roman said, taking a step closer to me, bombarding me with his ambrosial smell and the hard plane of his chest. "Are *you* okay with it?" He cleared his throat. "With what happened last night?"

"I told you I was fine," I said, glancing down to the ground, avoiding his stern gaze. But he put his finger under my chin to tilt my face back to his.

"And then you isolated yourself for the rest of the night," he said. "I'm sorry I went so rough on you. I shouldn't have done that. I should have—"

"I liked it," I admitted, the words tumbling out of my clumsy mouth before I could hush them. "I just...I shouldn't have."

"Why?" He raised an eyebrow. "Because I'm a disgusting Rose coward?"

I licked my lips and smiled. "Yes. Exactly that."

"Hmm." He nodded again and ran his thumb over my bottom lip, sending shocks down to my toes and back up again. I almost wilted, and I focused on his mouth, remembering the way he'd consumed mine so skillfully. "Are you ready for today?"

Right.

We'd have to enact my plan, the entire reason we'd ended up in that situation to begin with. We'd have to pretend to like each other in front of his club, to play the part of the happy couple to convince everyone that this alliance was real, that we wouldn't end up killing each other in the end.

Jury's still out on that.

I nodded. "Yes."

"There's a good girl." He leaned in to kiss my forehead before grabbing his coffee and moving around me to the microwave. I ignored the way his praise made my heart beat faster, telling myself it had nothing to do with him and was more representative of the trauma in my life that had developed into a despicable praise kink. He grabbed a plate of food and sat it down in front of me, nodding to it while he took a long sip of caffeine. "Eat. You'll need your strength."

I sat and picked up a fork to follow his command. That, too, I ignored. It felt good to listen to him. I was relieved to not have to think about it, to just sit and eat and know he'd provide for me. How long had it been since I'd been so cared for?

Christ, girl. It's just eggs. Stop fawning.

"Before I bring you into that room, there are some things you should know about the club." He put his hands out to either side of the island and leaned on it, his shirt pulling around his muscles, making him seem big and domineering and strong.

So amazingly strong.

"Okay," I said before biting into a strawberry.

"Most of the leadership is on my side. KC, Hollywood, Thor, and Wheels, they're all good men. They're in favor of ending this war by any means necessary, and they approved of our marriage."

I nodded, memorizing the information while I ate.

"But there are others...Stallion, Reaper, Lunchbox, and maybe Doc, who are against it. I don't know what they'll do to prove they're right. Stallion has been sending messages to the president of a rival MC—The Hell's Knights."

That sent a shock of anxiety through my belly, and I stopped chewing to take a sip of coffee, glancing up at him. Gabriella had worked with them last year. They'd wanted revenge on Crow and had arranged to abduct V as payment for information. Gabriella had been all too eager to accept. "Do you believe they're mutinous?"

He crossed his arms and my focus dropped to the veins accenting his muscles. How had God made someone so beautiful and so completely horrid?

"Perhaps," he said. "Doc says he's changed his mind, but that he questioned it at all gave the others leeway to dissent. I don't have any evidence against Stallion and Reaper yet, but I will."

"How does the MC usually handle people like that?" I took another bite of eggs, but the taste turned sour when he didn't immediately answer.

He ran his tongue over his lips and drank his coffee, and I understood what he didn't say. In this, the Caputis and the Roses were similar. Should a coup be unsuccessful, any members of such a resistance would magically disappear. I looked at Roman's hands again, wondering how much Rose blood they had spilled in addition to Caputi.

He is a bad, bad man.

"But," Roman continued, "I think your idea is a good one. And when I tell the others that it *is* your idea, that should earn some respect."

"Aren't you upset that our expensive decadent wedding will be used as a trap?" It wasn't like I'd been particularly looking forward to it, but it *was* my wedding. And the only one I'd ever get unless something happened to Roman.

He sighed and let out a sad laugh. "I just want the war to end. I'm tired of losing people."

That, at least, we could agree on.

We talked while I ate, and he told me about his family. I'd already met his siblings, of course, but he had a special glimmer in his eye when he mentioned his father. I knew Gabriella had worked with the FBI to get Crow locked up, but seeing the effect it had on Roman made my heart strangely heavy. He clearly missed him, and that he wouldn't be at our nuptials, even if they were a ruse, made him melancholic.

"I'm sure he'd be proud of you," I said. Roman glanced up at me with his eyebrows raised, surprise in his expression. "As far as cowardly Roses can be proud of each other, that is."

He glowered before shaking his head and laughing. I helped him clean up, and after that, we headed to the clubhouse. I still refused to get on the back of a motorcycle, so he drove us in his truck. Much to my immense astonishment, we continued our conversation the entire way there. He showed me places he'd grown up: his middle school, his high school, the place he'd taken his first girlfriend—though all they did was make out.

"She let me touch her boobs though," he said with a grin.

Heat flushed my cheeks, and I laughed at a younger version of him finally feeling up a girl for the first time. Then, my memories went to last night and how those strong, capable hands had held me, had played with my breasts, had touched me with such deliberate competence. Perhaps I owed that girl my thanks.

When we got to the clubhouse, he put the truck in park and looked at me. "Are you ready?"

I understood what he meant, and it wasn't just sitting in the corner the way I had the last few weeks. We would have to pretend. We would put on the act and show the others that we were completely in this marriage, and they'd have to deal with it.

"Absolutely," I said, opening the truck door to climb out. When we got to the door, he held his hand to me with that adorable grin on his lips, and I pushed down my girlish response to that, placing my palm in his. He led me into the clubhouse, and I took a deep breath at the eyes that immediately flicked to us.

For being so early in the day, the place was packed. My focus immediately went to V, Selene, and Alba by the bar, and normally, I would have taken an empty seat by them. But Roman squeezed my palm and rubbed a circle over my skin with his thumb before bringing it to his face so he could kiss my knuckles.

"Come with me, little wife," he said, nodding toward the back room. I followed his lead, never letting go of him, and five sets of eyes looked at us when we walked through the entry. KC, Hollywood, Thor, Doc, and Wheels sat around the table, each with a different expression. Thor and Wheels seemed impassive, Hollywood smirked, and KC grinned in that jovial way of his. But Doc eyed me with suspicion, inhaling a cigarette before stabbing it out in the ashtray.

"Morning, prez," Hollywood said before glancing at me. "Lady prez."

"Morning," Roman said, walking over to his spot at the head of the table. He sat and opened his legs, gesturing me into his lap, the same as he'd done last night. Gulping and trying not to seem nervous, I sat before pushing my hair behind my shoulders. One of his hands settled on my lower back, the other splayed out on the table in front of him.

KC looked at me before shifting his gaze back to Roman. "This is new."

"She's in this with us," Roman said. "She's the one who knows Gabriella the best, the one who has the best source of inside information. We can't do it without her."

"And Leo?" Thor asked.

"Leo will be here any second," Roman said, raising an eyebrow in expectation, like he'd been waiting for anyone to disagree.

"So we're just bringing old ladies into church now?" Doc blew out a disbelieving breath.

"She's not *just* an old lady. She's my wife, so watch your fucking mouth," Roman argued. "She's been feeding us information for years. We need her to bring down the enemy."

"*Her* aunt." Doc shook his head. "You wanted me to get Stallion and the others on our side. This is not the way to do it."

"I don't give a fuck what *you* or Stallion think. If you don't like it, challenge me." Roman's features remained stoic. "How about it? Do you need a reminder why my road name is Bear?"

Doc took a deep breath and let it out through his nose. "I'm not that stupid, but Stallion and Reaper are fucking idiots, especially if they got Lunchbox involved. They're having a hard time with all this."

"That's why she's here," Roman continued, giving me a little hug. "The more they see her, the more they understand her brilliant mind, the more they'll come around."

Doc shifted in his seat but didn't argue. The door to the back room slid open and my brother walked through, flanked on either side by his bodyguards. He wore an impeccable suit and loafers with his hair brushed back, the same uniform I'd seen him in my entire life.

"Well, well, well," he said when he set eyes on me. "What do we have here?"

"Brother," I said when he leaned down to plant a kiss on my temple. "It's good to see you."

"You too." Leo looked at Roman. "To what do we owe this great honor?"

Roman reiterated that I was the one who knew Gabriella the best, and I tried not to balk under Leo's scrutiny. His focus zeroed in on the bite mark on my neck and he grinned, apparently giving it no more thought than that.

"Very well," he said, taking up a spot to Roman's left. And when no one else said anything, Roman shifted me closer to his body and nodded at Hollywood. "Where are we?"

"Lore and the others reached Helena last night," he said. "The Royal Bastards send their love."

"Fantastic," Roman said. "What else?"

"Switch and Castor have reported that the Hell's Knights are getting closer," Thor explained. "I'm keeping an eye on the comms going in and out, but everyone's being careful."

Roman nodded and listened as Wheels gave a financial update and KC filled him in on the rest of the MC. "We need a plan, something to tell them, something to keep them engaged."

"Well, it's a good thing I married who I did." Roman smiled up at me. "My wife has a good idea. I want to run it past you before I take it to the group. If we decide it's worthwhile, we'll start working on it as soon as possible." Roman looked at me and brushed a piece of hair behind my ear. "Go on, beautiful. Tell them."

I took a deep breath and faced these violent men with their steel gazes, reiterating to them the same thing I'd said to Roman last night. Gabriella wouldn't be easy to trap, especially not since her plans went sour four months ago. We needed to lure her out, give her a reason to come out of hiding. Our wedding would be the perfect opportunity.

"It'll be crawling with Roses," Thor said. "We have four different chapters coming in to stand guard."

"She won't be able to resist," I explained. "If Leo is the one who walks me down the aisle, if we spread rumors that he'll be there, she'll come to the bait."

"I have to say, dear sister," Leo started, letting out a short laugh, "this is quite daring."

"It will work," I said.

"Oh, I have no doubt of that," he continued. "If we can hold her off that long."

"Do you think we can't?" I raised my eyebrows at him, anticipating what his argument might be. Based on what Della had told me, Gabriella was losing her grip on her allies. She could have spiraled even more since the Roses spoiled her plans, and if she'd lost control of the family, she'd have nothing left to lose. That would make her a wild card.

"No, I think it is a brilliant idea," Leo continued. "She'll come with the whole family, and if we do our job right, they'll turn on her when it matters most."

Roman shifted in his seat with a pleased smile before turning to his officers. "Well? What do you all think?"

KC ran a hand over the back of his head, his brilliant blue eyes wide as the wheels churned behind them. "A Rose wedding is meant to be more than a trap for our enemies. It's your opportunity to show the club that you're tied, that you're one."

"They're already married," Hollywood argued. "Neither one of them *wanted* this, and if it'll put an end to the madness and put Leo back on the throne, why wouldn't we do whatever we can?"

KC shook his head. "Inviting them onto our turf, giving Gabriella any chance at our family, I don't like it."

"Seconded," Doc cut in.

Roman looked at the man on his left. "Thor?"

The big blond Viking shook his head and ran a hand over his face. "I don't know. I'm inclined to agree with KC, but I can't think of another way to draw her out."

"I have Rocco, Enzo, and Matteo in cahoots," Leo said, mentioning the underbosses he'd gotten on our side. "Stefano and Frankie are coming around. Rancone and Davila are right behind them."

"Davila is playing both sides," I said, explaining the information Titus had given to me. "He wants more money."

Leo blew out a breath and shook his head. "No problem. If he won't come around, I'll replace him."

"You won't be able to win the underbosses by killing the ones that don't agree with you," I said. "We're trying to stop the bloodshed, not create more."

"What do you suggest, *mia sorella?*"

"What about Sulli?" He was our father's cousin on his mother's side, and the patriarch of that arm of the family. If we were trying to make the biggest show of force, we'd have no choice but to get his buy-in. "If you get Sulli, you get Davila. They've always played hand in hand."

"You know Sulli's always been ambitious," Leo said. "If Gabriella is out of the way, he'll want the seat for himself."

"Can you convince him you're the better option?" Roman asked.

Leo pursed his lips and nodded. "I'll work on it."

Roman returned his attention to his officers. "Wheels, what do you think about this plan?"

"I say do it," he said, crossing his arms. "Take it to the club, get their approval. I don't want to ever stare up at that bitch from my knees again."

"I agree," KC cut in. "But Bear, this is— If it goes sideways, if she comes heavily armed, if she makes another deal with the Kings of Carnage or the Hell's Knights, we're putting our entire family at risk."

"Do you have a better idea?" Roman asked. "Short of storming her castle and executing anyone in our way—"

"Not an option," I said. "There are good people there. Not everyone in my family is as bloodthirsty as she is."

"So you're asking me to choose between your family and mine?" KC raised his eyebrows. "That's not a difficult decision."

"Hey," Roman said. "We're all family now. That was the whole point of this, wasn't it?" He gestured between me and him.

KC sighed and lit a cigarette. "All right, brother. I trust you." Then he looked at me before glancing at Leo. "But if it comes down to my wife or your family, don't expect me to put Alba's life—"

"No one is expecting that," Roman said. "This is going to work."

"Yeah?" KC exhaled a deep cloud of smoke. "How can you be so sure?"

"Because it has to," Roman replied. "We don't have another choice."

10

BEAR

Convincing the rest of the club took more work. Stallion, Reaper, and their buddies stood in the far corner, staring Julia down the entire time. When it came to a vote, they were the quickest to shove their hands up in defiance. They were outvoted though, and by the end of church, we had decided to move ahead with Julia's plan. Between the Caputi siblings, they would start rumors of the wedding among the staff, which would eventually creep into the ears of the family proper.

I held her on my lap the entire time, the sharp, heavenly scent of her perfume mixed with her natural smell to intoxicate me, reminding me of last night. Yeah, catching her watching me in the shower was one kind of deviant pleasure, but rocking her against my cock, making her fall apart, it made me feel like a new man.

I hadn't meant to be so rough, but once she goaded me, there was no stopping my reaction. I loved it when she fought with me. I loved her tempting, horrible mouth. I loved the way she moaned and tried to act like she didn't want it.

Then she told me this morning she'd *liked* how rough I'd been, and it took everything in me not to bend her over every available surface in the house.

I couldn't say that, of course. This was pretend, a farce, a charade we practiced so the club would take our alliance seriously. She didn't actually *want* any of this, and neither did I. *I really didn't.*

After the session was over, we went out to the front room where I bullshitted with the guys while she socialized among the princesses.

"Things seem cozy," Hollywood said, throwing an arm over my shoulders. "Much better than yesterday."

I didn't answer him, just sipped my beer and raised an eyebrow.

"Y'all finally working on that baby clause?" Hollywood flashed his shit-eating grin, and I shoved him away.

"Fuck off," I said. "Don't you have something better to do?"

"Whew." He blew out a breath. "You know what, you're right. I wonder if V's ready to put on the strap and peg—"

"Ahh!" I palmed his face and pushed him again. "I don't need to hear that shit."

Hollywood laughed and sauntered over to my sister, wrapping his arms around her from behind before leaning down to kiss her shoulder. I would rather stab myself in the eyes than have the mental image of my baby sister doing anything to my best friend, regardless of what he liked to have shoved in his ass. Alba led KC over to the front door with a mischievous grin on her face, and Ru grabbed Saint by the belt loops to pull him toward the back rooms.

I tried to dampen the rising tide of heat in my blood, the flush in my cheeks that hinted at envy. I would never have what they had. I'd never have someone who had looked around their life and chosen me out of everyone else. I'd never have that end-all-be-all love that my brothers did for their old ladies, and what a fucking shame that was.

Sure, Julia matched my temper and my wits. She even had a beautiful brain behind those mesmerizing eyes, but pretend was all this would ever be. She'd never love me, never choose me, and once we popped out a kid, I didn't know if she'd ever warm my cock again.

Do I want her to?

In the deepest, darkest part of my heart, maybe I did. Maybe I lamented that our marriage had started the way it did. Maybe I loathed the thought of our union only being a duty, a means to an end. I watched her as she stood at the bar with V, Hollywood, Wheels, and Hollister. She was obviously telling them a funny story, gesturing with her hands in a way that made all four audience members laugh. I wondered what it was. I wondered what she said. Why didn't she try to make me laugh like that?

I imagined her belly round with my child. Something stirred in my chest, something wicked and depraved. Yeah, I'd fought the procreation part of our contract only because I didn't want either of us forced into something neither wanted. But I'd always thought I'd be a father one day, that I'd have a family of my own. And envisioning my wife pregnant shifted a kink gear I didn't know I had.

"Hiya, Bear," came a soft voice from my right. When I pulled myself from my brooding, I focused on Amber. She stared up at me with those big blue fuck-me eyes, her shirt cut incredibly low and her shorts cut incredibly high. She was gorgeous, and once upon a time, I'd already be in the back with my cock down her throat. But I was a married man now, and even if I didn't have the same connection with my wife that KC had with his, I would never fuck around on her.

"Hey ya, Amber," I said. "Whatcha doing?"

She shrugged and ran a finger down my forearm, trailing it over my hand and fingers before ghosting it back up again. "Just wondering how you've been."

"Fine," I said, pulling away as I refocused on Julia, now talking with Wheels and sporting a huge grin.

"How's married life?" Amber asked with a tiny pout. "Do you miss me already?"

I'd been paying so much attention to my wife that I almost missed her question.

"Married life is great," I said. "Fucking wonderful."

"You don't sound very convincing." Amber pushed up on her toes, pressing her breasts to my stomach while she leaned into my ear. "You could take me in the back room so I could kiss it better?"

She'd been pawing at me for weeks now, and if it had been before my marriage, I would have heartily agreed. But I was a faithful man. I wouldn't let anyone put a finger on Julia, so I likewise wouldn't let anyone put a finger on me. Just like all the times before, I grabbed Amber's shoulders and pushed her away, taking a step back from her.

"No, thanks," I said.

"C'mon, that Caputi bitch can't keep y—"

"Shut your fucking mouth," I snapped, my blood heating her casual insult of Julia. "That's my wife, the president's old lady. You'll respect her, or you can find a new place to slut around. Understand?"

Amber's eyes widened, like she hadn't expected that response from me.

"Husband," came Julia's voice from the other side of the hang-around. Distracted by putting Amber in her place, I hadn't seen her approach. "Are you ready to go home?"

"Of course," I said, setting down my beer so I could hold my hand out to her. "Have a nice night, Amber."

"Yeah, you too," she said, sneering at Julia while we passed. I held my wife's hand all the way out the door to the truck, where I helped her into the passenger's seat before circling to the driver's and starting the truck.

"Well," I started once we were on our way, "that went better than I expected."

"Hmm." She smiled, but it didn't reach her eyes.

"What?" I said.

"Nothing," she said. "I'm happy most of your club seems to be on board."

I nodded. "Yeah, it was a good plan. Truly, Julia."

She took a deep breath and let it out slowly, keeping her focus on the window. "I'll text Hannah and Titus tomorrow. We should consider making it a big event."

I mulled this over while I drove, turning onto my street that wound up into the mountains.

"Take out an ad in the paper," she said. "Announce it on all the social media platforms. It will be most impactful if we rub her nose in it."

"Do you think that might be going overboard?" I asked. "Roses don't generally make our weddings public affairs."

"This isn't just any Rose wedding," she argued. "This is the president of the club. The leader. The king and his new queen."

"Right," I said, ignoring the giddiness that shot down my torso and into my balls. I liked it when she referred to me as a king. I liked thinking about her as my queen. I wondered if I could get her on her knees, staring up at me with those big doe eyes, calling me her king with her soft, delicate lips before wrapping them around my cock.

We finally got to my house, and I pulled the truck into the driveway to park. She climbed out before I could help her, and by the time I circled around, she'd already climbed up the stairs to the porch and stood expectantly at the front door. I used my key to unlock it and went to turn off the security system.

"There will be more sessions later this week," I said. "I saw you talking to Wheels and Hollister. It's good if you get on better terms with the brothers."

She pursed her lips and set her purse on the table by the door. "Hmm."

There was that sound again, that noise that raised the hair on the back of my neck and set off alarm bells in my mind.

"What?" I turned to face her as she slipped out of her heels and bent over to pick them up.

"Nothing," she said. "I'm tired. I'm going to bed."

She walked toward the stairs and climbed them to the second floor. I waited only a moment before following quickly behind her.

"You might as well be out with it," I continued. "You've never had a problem telling me exactly what you think. No reason to start now."

"I will do as you suggest," she said, glancing at me before heading down the hallway toward her room. "Get on...*better terms*...with the brothers."

"Why do you say it like that?" I asked. Her suggestive tone did nothing to alleviate my anxiety. "What? Do you think they didn't buy it? Do we need to do something different?"

"No, I'm sure our pretense was perfectly acceptable." She stopped and turned to face me, crossing her arms and pushing her amazing tits higher over the top of her dress. I couldn't help my stare, remembering the way they'd puckered and how she moaned when I pinched them.

Pretense.

Right. We were still pretending. None of that was real, and now that we were alone again, we could drop the act.

Unless...

"Do you think we need more practice?" The words were out of my mouth before I could stop them.

She laughed, but not in a happy way. It came out in deep, mocking guffaws that both confused and enraged me. That was certainly not the reaction I'd wanted or expected.

"Perhaps you should go practice with Amber." She sneered before moving away from me again.

Amber? What?

I grabbed her upper arm to stop her, spinning her around. "What the hell does that mean?"

"I saw the way you looked at her," she hissed. "The way she pressed up against you. Very familiar. I'm sure she'd *love* to be bent over your table."

It was my turn to laugh. "Now, now, little wife. Don't tell me you're jealous of a hang-around."

She scoffed and yanked her arm away, taking a step back. "I would have to like you to be envious of any woman you put your hands on."

"Are you saying you don't like me?" I pretended to be offended and clutched at my heart, closing in on her, forcing her up against the wall outside my bedroom. "That's not the impression I got while you were moaning on my cock last night."

She jutted her chin out, her cinnamon eyes burning into mine as she straightened against the plaster. She took long, slow breaths, the tips of her breasts colliding with my lower chest as I closed the space between us. She smelled amazing, like woman and perfume, and the blush in her cheeks made me want to see if I could turn her ass that same rosy pink.

"You misunderstood," she said. "But of course you would. The Roses have always thought with their dicks first and their brains second. Not enough sense to operate both at the same time."

"Is that so?" The fire in her taunts turned me on and lit the fuse in my temper. I tilted my head to the side and raised my hand to run it over the soft, fleshy mounds of her tits, teasing the skin until it goosed. She shivered, and I chuckled, knowing I had her. "And if I were to—" I ran my other hand along the inside of her legs, dancing my fingertips over one thigh and up under her skirt, pausing when I got to the garter where she hid her knife.

I paused. Our eyes met. She reacted first.

She grabbed the handle of the weapon before I could stop her and held it to my throat, causing me to straighten as the kiss of cold metal hit my windpipe.

"Last night was an anomaly," she said. "You move that hand any higher and I'll bleed you out on your hallway floor."

The threat sent tingles through my body, twisting around my poor, pathetic heart. No woman had ever talked to me like this, and it made me so fucking hard, I could barely stand it.

"Yeah?" I leaned into the blade, bringing my forehead to touch hers, our lips inches apart. "Go ahead."

She panted and her hand shook. Was it nervousness or arousal that had her quivering? Maybe she was afraid of me. Maybe that turned her on. To test this theory, I brought the palm between her legs higher, inching up her dress until I touched lace.

And fucking hell, she was soaking wet.

"Well, well, well," I said with a smirk. "Such a liar, aren't you?" I dove in between those thighs and rubbed at her drenched panties, pushing in between her sensitive skin until I found her clit. It was hard and swollen and nearly throbbing with her heartbeat, but oh, how that urged me on. "But that's just like a Caputi, isn't it? You were born with lies on your tongue."

She moaned, and I pushed the delicate fabric to the side, spearing toward her entrance. I teased it, circled around it, rubbed anywhere but where she wanted.

"Better a liar than a monster," she snarled, rocking her pelvis on my fingers, pressing down on me as if to persuade me to stuff my way inside her. "Not even married two months and you're already seeking out other women."

"Oh, my sweet little wife," I said, dragging my free hand up to her throat so I could circle it like a collar...claiming her...marking her as mine. "I signed a contract saying the only cunt I'll fuck is yours. And I'm a man of my word."

I rubbed my thumb over the love bite from last night, and when she leaned her head to the side to give me more room, I had to take a deep breath to keep myself from dropping my pants and fucking her into this wall like a savage.

She whimpered and rubbed herself harder against me, and I obliged her frenzy, pushing one finger inside her, searching for that sweet spot that would drive her wild. When she threw her head back and lessened her grip on the knife, I massaged that area, pushing another finger inside to give me more leverage. I gripped her neck tighter, holding her in place so I could do my worst, and when she made another mewling sound, I knew she was getting close.

"That's it," I whispered, leaning in to bite her earlobe. "You love having my filthy Rose fingers inside you, don't you? You like coming on my hand like a good girl. Tell me how much." I nudged her face with my nose, urging her on. "Go on. Tell me."

She resisted at first, sighing and groaning as she fucked my fingers with fury, one palm still wrapped around the blade, the other gripping my shirt like she might fall if she let go. Silly girl. I'd never let that happen. But I wanted to hear her consent. I wanted to know she liked this, and I wasn't forcing it on her...even if she was the one who was armed and could stop me anytime she wanted.

Just when she was about to reach her climax, I stopped and pulled my fingers out of her, leaning back so I could see her face. She whined and grabbed my wrist, urging it back between her legs.

"Uh, uh, uh," I said, shaking my head. "Use your words, wife. Tell me you like it. Tell me you want it. Only good girls who ask for what they want get it."

"You're evil," she whispered.

"Hmm." I brought my fingers up to her mouth and shoved them in between her lips, and despite her name-calling, she moaned and sucked on them. "You taste that?" I laughed. "That's how much you like me when I'm evil."

"Please," she mumbled around my fingers.

I pulled them back with a soft *pop* and raised my eyebrows. "What was that?"

She growled and huffed, and even her exasperation made my cock jerk behind my jeans. "Please."

"Please...what?"

"Please...make me come," she murmured. "Please finish what you started."

"That's more like it." I grabbed the knife from her feeble grasp and kneeled in front of her, slipping the blade under the elastic of her panties to slice them clean off her body. She gasped and jumped, but the desire in her eyes told me she'd liked it.

"Those were more expensive than your death machine motorcycle."

I snorted. "Bill me."

She opened her mouth to say something else that would piss me off, but I pushed her feet farther apart and slid in between her legs so I could taste her for myself. That shut her up.

I licked at her before latching my mouth around her delicate skin, sucking and flicking my tongue against that pulsing ache. She moaned and clenched her fingers into my hair, and that made me feel like a God, so I kept going. My wife rode my face like no one had ever done this to her before, and I lapped her up, pleased to serve her any way she needed.

I shoved my fingers inside her and fucked her like my soul was on fire, and when she came, I laughed and laughed and laughed as I gobbled her up.

Fuck, but it felt good to know I could make her shake. If the rest of my life would be like this...maybe it wouldn't be so bad after all.

11

JULIA

I told myself I wouldn't do this again, not after last night. I didn't care what was in our marriage contract. Even if I found Roman ~~incredibly~~ moderately attractive, I shouldn't find such pleasure in this masochistic thing between us. It should have been repulsive, but lord forgive me, I wanted more.

He had gotten the right of it. Seeing that hang-around put her hands on *my* husband had sent something rotten through my molecules, boiling my blood until I had to interrupt them and force him to take me home.

I told myself it was because he'd fucked me last night and now had the audacity to flirt with another woman, but if I were honest with myself (and only myself because I would never tell him this) I had started to feel possessive of him.

He was *my* husband, *my* protector, *my* king. And I would cut the hands off anyone who dared try to take him from me. I secretly liked this evil game we played. I secretly wanted to play more of it.

After he made me come on his face, he kissed my vulva and inner thighs until I stopped trembling and released my death grip on his hair. When he appeared from under my skirt, his lips and chin glistened with the evidence of how much I'd ached for him, but his cocky smirk made me want to grab my knife and stab him.

"Look at how flushed you are, little wife," he said, pushing to his feet, towering over me yet again. I tried to act like the sight of such a powerful man on his knees *for me* had no effect on my ego, but truthfully, I nearly wilted at the sight. "I think you liked that."

"You should be so lucky," I said, my voice cracking despite how desperately I wanted to sound serious.

"Still lying?" He tutted me like a disapproving authority figure before wrapping his strong hands around my throat again, tilting my face up to his, forcing me to meet his gaze. "Such beautiful lips, and you use them to say such terrible things."

"I hate you," I said. It was a weak defense, but he'd rattled me. The way he held me spoke of adoration, and the ease with which he'd licked me to a mind-blowing orgasm had me pulsing in disbelief.

"Hmm, of course, you do." He yanked me forward to collide his lips with mine, and the fierceness of his kiss sent sparks down my spine and the backs of my legs. He licked at me, forcing me to open my mouth so he could shove inside, invading all parts of me, tasting like me and him and the beer he'd been drinking before we left the clubhouse. We wrestled with each other, but he ultimately dominated me like I knew he would, like I wanted him to. When he pulled back, he stared down at me with that haunting mix of ruthlessness and villainy in his eyes. "I think that mouth is better suited for something else."

I swallowed, my throat gone dry for what I anticipated would be next. My heart pounded and butterflies lined my stomach.

"I think you should get on your knees and fuck my cock with your throat." He ran his thumb over my bottom lip, and I opened to let him dip inside.

Any number of insults passed through my mind, and the urge to let them all out tested my restraint. I'd been raised a mafia princess in the richest family in DC. Men got on their knees *for me*. The thought of lowering myself for him bucked against everything I'd been brought up to think about myself. But heaven help me, Roman was unlike any other man I'd ever been with. Wealth, station, last names, none of that mattered anymore. All I had in the world was his. I was his.

He'd turned my legs to jelly with his tongue, and I wondered if I could do the same. Could I have the same control, the same power, over him because of what I could do with my mouth?

I raised an eyebrow and slowly kneeled in front of him.

Surprise flickered through his expression for only a moment before he shut it down and returned to his stoic dominance. He widened his stance when I coasted my palms up his thighs to his belt, carefully undoing the metal clasp and sliding the leather through it. He removed it entirely while I worked on the button and the zipper. Then, I pulled the waist of his boxers down so I could free his cock. I hadn't gotten a look at it last night, though I felt through his sweatpants that it was big. Up close like this, I almost backed out. I almost pushed to my feet and told him there was no way I could deep-throat him, but doing so would mean he'd win. I'd never been one to balk at a challenge, especially not with him. I wouldn't start now.

"Well, get to it," he said, causing me to meet his gaze as I grabbed the base and licked the entire underside of him. His velvet skin tasted clean and salty, and there was something distinctly him that made my cunt throb as another surge of arousal hit me. He groaned and leaned his head back, but that urged me on. I took the tip in my mouth, sucking and lapping over the slit, swallowing down a drop of precum that amped me up even more. I liked how he tasted, and when one of his hands dropped to my head, I liked the way his fingers curled in my hair.

He encouraged me down on him, and I complied, thankful he'd given me the cue. I wanted to learn how to do it right...for him...and any guidance worked in my favor to make him melt. When he looked down at me and guided me, I hummed in appreciation. He grinned, evidently liking that sensation, and I relaxed my throat to take him all the way.

It burned, and I gagged, choking around the thick girth of him, but when his hand clenched on the back of my head, I figured he liked that, too. I hadn't done this in a long time, so long that I embarrassed myself by heaving on the third or fourth thrust. But I didn't let that disrupt my goal. I wanted to win this battle of wills.

My eyes watered and slobber dripped from my chin, but that, too, turned me on. I wanted to get sloppy for him, knowing he'd made me that way. I was a princess the rest of the time, prim and put together and expensive. But here, on my knees, *for my husband,* I would ruin myself.

I'd let him ruin me. For surely, there was no one else I could do this for, no one else I wanted to do this for.

He held me by the crown with one fist and wrapped the other around my jaw, his fingers massaging my throat while I took him as deeply as I could. A few more ruts, and he paused there, letting my esophagus convulse around him while he moaned and pushed his hips forward even more.

I couldn't breathe. I couldn't think. The edges of my vision started to soften, and just when I thought I'd have to stop, he relented and pulled out, staring down at me with that confusing affection while he stuffed himself back in his jeans.

"What a good little cocksucker you are," he said, wiping the spit off my chin before running his knuckles along the tears on my cheeks. "Do you like being my wife? My little Caputi whore?"

The degradation should have insulted me, but instead, I took a deep breath and dropped my gaze to the ground. Shame rolled in my chest at how much I *did* enjoy it. No one else saw me like this, and I'd signed a contract that said no one else ever would.

"Oh, I think you do," he said, raising an eyebrow. "Now be a good girl and stand up."

I complied, far more easily than I would have liked, rising to my feet with tears on my cheeks. I was certain my mascara had run down my face and my lipstick had smeared, but perhaps he liked that because he grinned and nodded to the door for his bedroom.

"Undress and get on my bed." His commanding tone left little room for debate, and I swallowed against my sore throat, knowing where this would lead. He would take me hard, perhaps even harder than he had last night, and I would like it. My feelings for him would only get more complex. That wasn't what this was supposed to be about, but how exactly did I plan to have children with him if I didn't have sex with him?

Perhaps I hadn't expected to like it as much as I did. Perhaps I had only thought it would remain clinical, that we wouldn't be as compatible as we were.

"Well?" he asked, raising an eyebrow. "If you want to stop, tell me to stop. You can always—"

"No," I cut in, afraid he would end this before it even began. I didn't know how to tell him I enjoyed it when he was rougher, when he made the decisions so I didn't have to. "I'm just surprised you can operate a brain and that giant cock at the same time."

At first, he smirked like he had decided to take that as a compliment. But then he grabbed my upper arm and hauled me into his room forcibly, kicking the door closed behind him. His grip pinched, but that added to the experience, and when he tossed me on the bed, I bit my lip to keep from smiling. That would only make it worse. I landed on my hands and rolled over to look at him. He stared down at me like some kind of menacing villain, and I shivered thinking about what he might do to me.

"Take off your clothes," he said. "I won't say it again."

Maintaining eye contact with him, I climbed off the bed to unzip my dress, shoving it down to my ankles so I could step out of it. The bra went next, and when I stood naked in front of him, he grabbed his cock through his jeans and eyed me up and down with a pleased tilt to his mouth.

"Lie back and spread your legs. Show me that beautiful wet cunt." He walked around to the end of the bed so he could have the best vantage point, and I did as he asked.

My body seemed to comply before my mind could fully catch up, and I simply...let go. I enjoyed giving him control over the situation. It made the constant chatter in my brain die down, and I knew that if he wanted this, he'd take care of me. I had no reason to think he wouldn't.

The duvet was soft under my shaking body and I laid my head on the pillows, bending my knees as I opened them for him. I'd certainly shown myself to lovers before, and Roman himself had even gotten up close and personal, but to be so blatantly on display sent a self-conscious heat through my veins. Cool air rushed in between my thighs, and I gasped, my pussy suddenly so needy and throbbing for him. I reached down to cover myself, but he was suddenly there, swatting me away.

"Don't you dare hide," he said. "Not from me."

I swallowed and nodded, clenching my hands into fists at my sides, refusing to back down from him. He yanked his shirt off and shoved his jeans to the floor before doing the same to his boxers. Now, we were both exposed to each other and for the first time since I'd seen him in the mirror, I got a glimpse at his gorgeous body. His broad chest gave way to abs that spoke of his physically demanding job, his arms just as veiny and defined. His adonis belt framed a thin line of dusty brown hair trailing down to his magnificent cock, jutting out straight, pink, and hard, ready for more attention. He had big thighs and thick calves, so much power in one body that I wondered if anything in this world could stop him from taking whatever he wanted.

"God, you're beautiful," he said, kneeling on the mattress. He moved between my legs and rested his hands on my knees, maybe to keep me there or maybe to ground himself in our shared reality.

The compliment was so sudden and unprovoked I nearly gasped, my heart fluttering as my belly dropped.

"So are you," I murmured.

He hummed and smiled softly, scooting closer so that his cock touched my cunt. I rocked into the connect, especially when he grabbed it to spear the head between my skin, taunting my clit before sliding downward. He teased my entrance, making me arch toward him in anticipation before he moved back up again...toying with me like I was his plaything.

By the third pass, I couldn't stand the way my body yearned for his. I huffed and tilted my hips so that he went farther in than he meant to, and he hissed in a startled breath.

"Uh, uh, uh," he tutted, shaking his head as he raised an eyebrow. "That was very naughty."

He pulled away and slapped my cunt, rattling my clit so hard I cried out and tried to twist away. But he held me there with his massive body, my knees tucked under his shoulders, keeping me in one spot.

"Only good wives get my cock," he said, leaning over me to bring his face above mine. "Are you going to be good?"

I squared my jaw and glared up at him, debating whether I would oblige this game or tell him to fuck off. But I *did* want him. I was so worked up and ready that I thought I might physically combust if he didn't do it. I could get myself off in my room, but I wanted him to do it.

For the first time in weeks, I could admit that to myself.

I *wanted* my husband, and I wanted him to want me.

"Yes," I said, my voice hoarse with desire. "Yes, I'll be good."

"We'll see about that." He grabbed my arms and moved them above my head, crossing them at the wrists. "You stay just like this. Can you do that?"

I nodded.

"Use your words, little wife," he said, nudging my nose with his.

"Yes," I replied. "I'll stay like this."

His grin lit up his entire face, and I realized how expressive his chestnut eyes actually were. In them, I could see how much he also wanted this, and he rose again to sit back on his feet, dropping his gaze to the space between my legs. He ran his fingers over my sensitive wet flesh, spreading my labia so he could explore. The touch frustrated me only because I wanted him to fuck me already, but lord, it was so erotic. I'd never had anyone take their time getting to know my body like this, like he was trying to map the entirety of me and memorize every piece. When he pinched my clit and pulled, I made a noise somewhere between a yowl and a moan, and I curled off the bed, trying again to close my legs around him.

"Such a pretty cunt," he said, holding me open for him. "And it's all mine, isn't it?"

"Yes, yes," I said, tensing my arms to keep them above my head. I didn't want him to stop, not now. I wanted to be good for him, only him, so good.

"Tell me it's mine," he commanded, that mischievous sparkle in his eyes.

"It's yours," I complied, far too eager for my liking. "It's all yours."

"That's right." He leaned over me again, lining himself up at my entrance before surging home all in one thrust, all the way to the hilt.

Air rushed into my lungs and I held it, the sensation of being filled at war with the tender ache of being stretched so completely.

"And this?" He nodded down toward his cock, retreating only an inch before rutting in again. "This is all yours. Do you understand?" Another short ease out before a harsh shove in.

"Yes." I sighed, the word sounding more like a breath than a syllable.

He held himself up with one arm and grabbed my chin with the other, forcing me to face him. "I mean it, Julia. No hang-around gets to touch. No one else."

The use of my real name snapped something deep inside, and being connected to him like this created an emotional backlash I wasn't prepared for. It was like there had been a rubber band between us, stretched nearly to its breaking point by how we'd ignored and treated each other for weeks. And now it had been let go, snapping its recoil on tender flesh, and my eyes burned like I wanted to cry.

"And if anyone so much as looks at you the wrong way," he continued, fucking me slow and deep, rubbing at the delicious spot inside me. "I'll kill them. Understand?"

My nerves fired on all cylinders as I wrapped my legs around his lower back, hooking my ankles together so I could urge him in harder and faster, consuming all of him and all of me.

"You're mine," he mumbled, leaning down to kiss me, making me tremble again.

"Please," I said in between his frenzied taking. "Please, can I touch you?"

"Touch me, little wife," he said. "Make me yours."

I wrapped my arms around his neck and held him closer while I devoured his mouth again. I speared my fingers into his soft hair, yanking and scratching however I wanted, and when my pleasure started to climb, I clawed down his chest, using his stomach muscles as leverage to thrust my hips into his. When I was just about to hit the pinnacle, I reached between us and rubbed my clit, setting off my climax.

It burst through my veins like flames and tightened all of my muscles. I sank my nails into his skin as he continued to fuck me through it, his groans accenting my screams. I'd never come so hard in my life, and I couldn't remember a time when I'd been so comfortable with someone else. Not Vittori. Not Hugo. Never. Perhaps it was him. Perhaps he put me at ease with this power dynamic between us.

But he wasn't done. When I came back to my own body, he'd only just started to chase his orgasm.

"Mine, mine, mine," he mumbled, ducking his head into the space between my neck and my shoulder. He kissed and licked at my skin, uttering other things I couldn't quite make out. And when he reached his peak, he tensed, his cock jerking violently inside me, filling me with his seed. He hovered there while I held him, my legs still wrapped around his waist, my arms around his neck, my cunt clenching around his cock.

He lifted his head and gazed down at me with a destructive passion in his eyes, almost as if he *liked* me, as if our union had ended far too soon. Roman leaned down to press his lips to mine in a tender kiss that stole my heart, and perhaps I had to admit I liked him, too. Or at least, I liked this awful thing between us.

"You're so beautiful like this," he whispered, trailing sweet kisses over my face. "Flushed and spent and relaxed."

"Don't say things you don't mean," I said.

He chuckled and pushed up, sliding out of me as he sat back on his feet. I tried not to cover myself up as he ran his hot gaze over the length of my body, from my burning cheeks to my racing heart and down to my slippery, wet cunt. I wanted to put my hand there to shield the mess of our joining from his sight, but something about his demeanor told me he wouldn't let me even if I tried.

Then he did something none of my other lovers had ever done. He reached between my thighs and ran his fingers over me, scooping up his cum and shoving it back into my vagina. I gasped and arched into the touch, still too sensitive for this abuse. But he didn't seem to care. His searing gaze held me in place while he did what he wanted.

"You know," he said in a low husky voice, "I always wanted kids. I want a big family." He continued playing with me, with our combined cum, while he talked, gathering whatever leaked out and pushing it back inside. "I can't stop thinking about what it might be like, what you might look like, all swollen with my child."

I didn't know what to say. This was the first time he'd ever been vulnerable with me, and maybe it was the after-sex hormones that made me soften to him, but at that moment, I wanted nothing more than to wrap him in my arms and never let him go again.

"Would you want a boy or a girl?" I asked, meeting his gaze when his eyes shifted to me.

"I don't care," he said. "Doesn't matter to me. What about you?"

I shrugged. "I suppose I don't either."

"Did you want kids? Ya know...before this?"

Letting out a small laugh, I shook my head. "I grew up Catholic, and even if my family aren't *good* Catholics, I always knew it would be expected of me."

"That's not what I asked." When he was finished playing with my cunt, he put his hands on his thighs and sat there, expecting an answer from me.

"Yes," I said. Though I had always expected to have them with Hugo, not the president of my family's enemy.

He nodded and glanced to the bed, perhaps reading the solemnness in my eyes, before climbing off the mattress. "Stay there. I'll get something to clean you up."

"Don't bother," I said, rolling to my side so I could stand. "I'll take a shower—"

"Julia," he cut in. "Please. Let me."

His begging stopped me, and I froze to look at him. He had his hands on his hips and a soft expression on his face, as if it was his honor to do it. So I let him. I lay down and spread my legs, and he returned with a warm washcloth to wipe away anything he hadn't played with. When it was done, he nodded toward the primary bathroom and grinned.

"C'mon," he said. "Let's play pretend some more and shower together like a real couple."

I should have told him no. I should have insisted I go back to my room and clean up by myself. But I couldn't resist him, not when he looked so damned adorable. So I took his hand and let him lead me to the amazing walk-in shower with four showerheads.

"Wow," I said, glancing around.

"Ru's father helped me renovate this part of the house. We were working on the rest before he got arrested." Roman turned on the water and held out a hand to gesture me inside. "But I'll finish it one day."

I smiled and ran my gaze over the assortment of shampoos and conditioners, mostly male oriented, but when I got to the end, I paused. Right next to his sat my favorite brand, new bottles of the exact versions I used. Picking one up, I scowled and turned to face him.

"What's this?" I asked.

He ran a bar of soap over his muscles and grinned. "I wanted you to be comfortable."

"In your shower?" I sneered and opened the lid, but he took it from me and poured some into his hand. "Quite presumptuous."

"Well"—he moved behind me so he could run the shampoo through my thick hair, massaging and rubbing at all the right spots to nearly have me moaning—"you're here, aren't you?"

"Mr. Montgomery," I said, pretending to be offended. "Don't tell me this was a ploy all along just to get me wet and naked."

He chuckled low in his chest and leaned down so his mouth was right next to my ear. "Mrs. Montgomery, there's not much I *wouldn't* do to get you wet and naked."

I couldn't help myself. I laughed and leaned into his touch while he cleaned me.

"Is this your first time experimenting with kink?" he asked.

I tensed, unsure what he meant. Was that what we were doing? I'd always liked it a little rougher in bed, but I'd never been so quick to heed a lover's demands.

"Yes," I finally said.

"How do you feel?" he asked, massaging the shampoo deeper into my scalp.

"I like when you tell me what to do," I said. "It's like...it's like I don't have to think anymore."

"I like taking control," he said, his fingers working down my neck into my shoulders. "I like when you give in to me. It makes me feel powerful."

"Is this unusual, what we have?" I turned to face him, squirting some of his shampoo on my hand so I could do the same to him.

"No, not at all." He let me wash his hair, even leaning his head back and humming when I hit a particularly sensitive spot. "But if you do like it, there's a lot more we could do. We could explore the dominant/submissive thing...only if you want to."

"I've never done anything like this." I'd been raised a good Catholic girl, and even though I'd had sex with Vittori, it was extremely conservative. Hugo had been more traditional. He'd wanted to wait for marriage. We didn't do much more than heavy petting. It had never been anything like this. Roman was the only man to ever fuck my throat.

"I've never been in a relationship with someone I've done kink with," he admitted, his voice low and husky like it pained him to say.

Are we in a relationship now? I supposed we were, even if we were doing it backward.

"How would that work?" I couldn't help my curiosity.

"There are lists online," he said. "I'll print two off. You fill out one, I'll fill out the other. Then we'll compare and see what we have in common."

A rush of heat coated my veins, but I wasn't sure if that was anticipation or nervousness. Still, never one to back down from him, I nodded. "Okay."

"There are limits to this thing," he said. "We don't have to... *pretend*...in public. Only in private. There's a lot more I'd want to do to you, but only if you consent to it."

Consent. I nearly melted when he said it. I'd been called beautiful my entire life. I'd started growing boobs in middle school and hips before I was in high school. Older men had touched, pinched, and grabbed at me for as long as I could remember. No one had ever asked me for what I wanted.

Standing under the scalding water with Roman, I could have dropped to my knees and begged him to marry me again. He was so sweet, so tender and caring. I didn't deserve him, not one bit. And I cut off that line of thinking with a harsh smack to reality. We had a bloody, violent history between us, and thoughts like that were dangerous. Those types of emotions made me vulnerable. Falling for him, letting this be real, it made me weak. After Hugo, I swore I'd never be like that again. I'd been cursed with my family, and there would never be an escape, not while Gabriella still lived.

"Do some research," he said. "My sister's website is a good place to start. She's got lots of videos explaining what kink is and what a healthy lifestyle looks like. Then, we can have that conversation."

"Thank you, Roman," I said, too emotional to meet his gaze. "Thank you for all of this."

He touched my chin and forced my eyes to meet his again. "Hey, we're in this together, right? We might as well make the most of it."

I nodded and pushed up on my toes to kiss him before grabbing the washcloth to suds it up and rub circles over his muscular frame. We joked and teased for the rest of the shower while we took turns soaping each other thoroughly. We talked about our families and what it was like growing up in our respective clubs, and not once did we mention our arrangement or how this was supposed to be pretend. And when he made me laugh again, I decided I liked Roman Montgomery perhaps a tad too much.

"Stay with me tonight," he said, shutting off the water when we were done.

"What?" I didn't believe he'd meant it.

"In my room. In my bed. Stay with me." Roman wrapped a towel around my shoulders and handed me another one for my hair before reaching for his own, circling it around his waist.

I paused, unsure of what to say. I'd grown used to sleeping on my own, but I could admit I didn't particularly like waking up in a cold sweat, terrified my aunt or her goons were after me again.

"If it makes you feel any better," he said. "It's purely selfish. I don't want to have to walk across the hall to wake you up when you have another nightmare, as much as I like a knife to the jugular."

I rolled my eyes and shoved at his shoulder, but he grabbed my wrist and pulled me closer to him, leaning down so our foreheads touched. "Come on. Let's pretend, just a little longer."

I took a deep breath and sighed, telling my poor, pathetic heart not to read too much into this. It was fake, just practice for our show in front of his family. But I wanted to give in. For now, I wanted to pretend.

"Okay," I said. "I'll sleep here. Just let me go get my clothes."

"No need." He grinned that beautiful boy-next-door smile and headed back toward his bedroom, opening a dresser drawer to toss me a white T-shirt. It smelled like detergent and him, and my heart fluttered when I lifted it over my head. Now completely consumed by him, inside and out, I'd never felt more claimed.

Julia Montgomery, indeed.

"I like you in my clothes," he said as he climbed into bed, shoving his long legs under the covers.

"Yeah?" I walked around to the other side and scooted in next to him.

"Yeah," he said. "It makes me feel like you're mine."

"Hmm." I smiled as he turned off the bedside light, bathing us in the faint moonlight trickling in through the curtains. "If we're still pretending, then I am yours."

"What if—" His voice came soft and slow, almost innocent in its quiet demeanor. "What if I wanted you to be mine for real? What if I didn't want to pretend anymore?"

I took a deep breath and let it go on a slow exhale as my stomach dropped. Maybe I'd been thinking the same thing. Maybe I didn't want to pretend anymore, either. But he'd killed my family. My family had killed his. We could never—*would never*—be anything more.

Shoving that down, I snuggled closer to him and rested my head on his chest, relishing the feeling of his fingers tangling in my wet hair.

"We have the rest of our lives to figure it out," I said.

He seemed to like that answer, and I fell asleep to the sound of his steady heartbeat. And when my dreams came that night, they were of dark brown eyes and soft curly hair and tattooed fingers around my throat in a dominant caress.

12

JULIA

The next few days went the same way. We woke up. We ate breakfast together before he went to work. I spent the day planning an extravagant wedding and planting seeds with the Caputi family. There was so much to do: finding a wedding dress and figuring out a venue. I wanted it to be somewhere that made sense for the Roses so that it wouldn't look too much like a trap, but a place that wouldn't draw attention in case things turned bloody. Roman had mentioned something about the MC owning a farm just outside of town. That would probably be the best spot.

Despite my plans, I still had to keep up the pretense of being Roman's loving wife. If there was a meeting at the clubhouse, he took me. Every night when he came home, we ate dinner together like a real couple before he ordered me to take off my clothes so he could fuck me within an inch of my life. We hadn't continued our discussion about a more negotiated dynamic, but I did do the research he asked me to complete.

Most of what I found on V's website and other various educational websites sent a jolt of heat through the center of my body and in between my legs. My hands clenched into fists with discussions of impact-play and orgasm denial. I wanted to be what Roman called me—his princess, his toy, his Caputi whore.

Then, I went to the list he'd given me and marked each item, investigating any terms I wasn't familiar with. Anal sex, cock warming, impact, throat fucking, knife-play, it went on and on. I wanted to try most of it. I wasn't into needles or excrement, but I had a feeling Roman wouldn't be either. For the rest of it, I marked either yes or maybe.

When I finally gave the list to him, my entire body shook like he might take one look at it, smirk, and throw a line of insults in my direction. He didn't. He ran his dark gaze over it, smiled with simmering satisfaction, and grabbed his list to show me.

"We're compatible," he said, leaning back in the dining room seat. We'd just finished a meal I'd ordered in because I still hadn't figured out how to cook. But I had a plan for that, too. "I think we might be able to pretend for a while."

He was right. Most of the stuff I wanted him to do to me was on his list of things he wanted to do. Spanking, hair pulling, biting, scratching, paddling, flogging, cuffing, ropes, chains, etc. He wanted to fuck my throat and cum deep inside of me, and I wanted to let him. He wanted to breed me, domesticate me, and pretend I was a fifties housewife, solely reliant on him for my pain and pleasure. Giving him that control alleviated the anxiety continuously churning in the back of my mind. Honestly, the only time it stopped was after an intense scene with him, like he was the only person I could give over to. I still wasn't sure how I felt about that, but I decided not to examine it too closely.

"What do you want to feel during our time together?" he asked, sipping his wine.

"Cared for," I said. "Adored. Even if you're degrading me, calling me your slut, the fact I'm yours makes it special."

He nodded. "I agree. And after? What do you hope to get out of it?"

"Calm," I said. "Peace."

"Hmm." He must have liked the sound of that. "And I have your consent to do anything in the Y column at any time?"

I nodded. "Yes."

His grin lit up his entire face. "Good. Now get on your pretty little knees and crawl over to me."

I did, and he took me in the dining room nearly as rough and as furious as he had the first night. Afterward, he ran a bath, and we soaked in the tub together for over an hour, talking and plotting.

Perhaps because of this, I wanted to show him I could be the wife he wanted, that I had more use than being a Caputi heiress. So a week later, I invited Alba over to teach me how to make dinner. I figured I could spend some quality time with my cousin in addition to trying to please my husband.

"You see," she said, pulling the chicken out of the oven. "You want to get it to an internal temperature of one sixty-five. That's when you know it's done."

I'd read that in the cookbook, but having her here to show me made it so much easier.

"I feel like an idiot," I said as I grabbed the tongs to plate our dinner. He'd be home in a few minutes, and I wanted to make sure everything was perfect for when he arrived.

"Don't," Alba said, pushing up her glasses. "Cooking is a difficult skill to learn. It took me forever to figure out the timing."

"Thank you," I said, giving her a soft smile. "For being so kind to me."

She grinned and narrowed her intuitive gaze. "You seem better."

"Oh?" I tried to hide my surprise. "How so?"

Alba shrugged. "More at ease, maybe."

I ignored my burning cheeks at how *at ease* Roman had made me last night. "I think I'm getting the hang of this whole thing."

When Alba turned just right, I saw Uncle Benito in her features. She'd probably hate it if I told her that, so I kept it to myself, but it reminded me I did have family here. The people I'd grown up with seemed so very far away, but Alba was my blood.

"There's not much to it," she said. "Especially when these alpha assholes start to get smitten."

I rolled my eyes. "Roman is hardly smitten with me." Except for when I took my clothes off and did whatever he told me. Except for when he gave me commands, and I nearly tripped over myself to follow them.

"I see how he looks at you when he thinks no one else is watching," Alba said, bumping me with her hip while she scooped carrots onto our plates. "I'm sure this isn't what you planned, but if it had to be someone in the Roses, it seems like it was a good thing it was Bear."

It took me a second to remember Roman and Bear were the same person. "Why does everyone call him Bear?"

Alba shrugged and shook her head. "You'd have to ask him that."

My phone buzzed and drew my attention from my cousin, and I turned my back on her when I realized it was Della.

Della: Hannah was terminated after you left. No one's seen her in months.

My stomach dropped and my heart raced.

No.

Could Gabriella have done something to her? Could she have learned that Hannah was still leaking information to me for the Roses? I tried texting Hannah again, but this time, the message was undeliverable.

Della: Gabriella is planning an arms pickup from the Hell's Knights in three days.

It bothered me that the Hell's Knights were so close to Rose territory. Had they already come through? Were they still here?

Me: Do you know how big?

Della: Big. When are you coming home? When can Chesco and I see you?

Me: Soon. I want you both at my wedding.

Della: What about the Roses? What are their plans for Gabriella?

"Are you coming to the party at the Beacon next month?" Alba's question brought me back to reality, so I put the phone down without answering Della.

"I think so," I said, putting it on my mental list to ask Roman when he got home. Between that and the wedding, I had a lot going on.

"It'll be fun," Alba said as she stacked dishes in the dishwasher and wiped her hands on a rag. "You and Bear will enjoy yourselves... if you go in with an open mind."

"I've never been to a...uh...club like that before," I admitted. I'd certainly seen my fill of naked women. The Caputis owned several strip clubs in various parts of DC, but none that catered to the kink community. Outside of Roman, no one had ever asked me what sort of things I might want to try.

"Are you nervous?" Alba asked. But she didn't seem judgmental; more like she wanted to help alleviate any fears I might have.

"A little," I said, deciding I might as well ask her about it. Della would be outraged if I ever brought any of this up, and Chesco would kill Roman for even considering half of it. "Are you and KC kinky?"

She laughed, and the sound made me wonder if I'd overstepped a line. "We run a camsite. So yes, we've done just about everything there is to do."

"Roman made me fill out a list," I said. "He wants to make sure I'm comfortable, that he doesn't do anything that would harm me or overstep a boundary."

Her features softened and sincerity echoed out of her ice-blue gaze. "That's a good thing, Julia."

"I'm afraid I might enjoy it too much," I said. "I mean, what does it say about me that I like when he takes control? He's a Rose. I'm a Caputi. It should be abhorrent."

She snorted and shook her head. "You're a Montgomery now. Same as me."

That got my attention, and I thought about the last few nights, when I'd slept in his bed wearing his shirts, smelling like him from head to toe. I realized I had started to refer to myself with that name now, and I wondered when that shift happened.

Julia Montgomery.

"I think it means you're human," she said. "Being scared. Liking sex. Enjoying your husband. These are all normal things."

"We've only been married two months."

"So?" She grabbed the wine from the counter and put the automatic corkscrew on top before pressing the button to activate it. "KC and I were together less than that when I realized I was in love with him. We got married just over a year into our relationship. When it's right, it's right."

I mulled over a response when the explosive sound of motorcycles rumbled down the street. My ears perked up, and I immediately thought Roman had arrived home.

"That's my cue," Alba said, winking. "If it's any consolation, I think you two are great together. He needs someone who can go toe to toe with him, and even if you like to submit in the bedroom, you have a lot of spine outside of it."

"Thanks, Alba," I said. "For all of this."

"You're welcome." She wrapped her arms around me and pulled me into a hug, which I was grateful to return. I didn't have much family on this side of Virginia, and as much as I missed my closest relatives, at least I had her.

Another wave of obnoxious engines echoed through the house, sending shivers down my spine. When I pulled back from Alba, I narrowed my gaze at her.

"Is KC coming to pick you up?" I asked.

"No," she said, glancing toward the door. "He's meeting the Roses from New England at the clubhouse."

It sounded like at least five or six bikes had stopped outside, and I belatedly remembered Roman had taken his truck this morning because his bike was in the shop. The prospects guarding the place wouldn't leave until Roman personally dismissed them, so who—

All thoughts stopped when gunshots rang out, one after the other, followed by shouts.

"Get the fuck out of here!" someone yelled.

"You don't want this," someone else said. "Just back down and I won't kill you."

"This is a big fucking mis—" He didn't get the rest of it out before another loud bang silenced him forever.

"Shit," Alba said. "We need to go."

"C'mon." I grabbed her arm and yanked her through the house, pressing Roman's number on my cell phone as we ran up the stairs. I led her into my room and shut the door, locking it despite knowing how futile that would be.

"I recognized those voices," Alba said. "I think one is Stallion."

My heart sank, my blood turning to ice in my veins. If that was Stallion, then that meant... *No.* Would they do that? Would they attempt outright treachery to prove their point? Roman's phone went to voicemail and Alba tried KC, but that, too, didn't work. While I attempted to get ahold of Leo, she dialed another number and a woman answered the phone.

"Sel," she said. "Come quick. We're at Bear's house. Bring your guns."

Selene didn't ask many questions, but it didn't matter. The sound of my brother's voice settled some of my anxiety.

"*Mia sorella.* What's going on?" He spoke in Italian, meaning he was around people he didn't want to know his business.

"Someone's here," I said. "At Roman's house. I can't get ahold of him, but I think they're here to hurt me. Alba's here, too."

I heard muffled conversation and the deep tones of my husband in the background before his voice came through the phone.

"What do you mean?"

"Alba thinks it's Stallion," I said as the door burst open downstairs.

"Oh, Julia!" someone called. "Come out, you little Caputi bitch."

I took a deep breath to calm my nerves. "Roman, they're in the house."

"Where are you?" His voice sounded gravelly and mean like he was furious.

"In my room," I whispered, backing Alba up toward the walk-in closet where I'd unloaded my stash of weapons when I moved in. I'd been raised a princess, but I wasn't sheltered, at least not when it came to defending myself. Leo and Julian made sure I knew my way around a gun by the time I was out of diapers, and I had perfect aim before I'd lost all my baby teeth. The heavy pounding of boots rattled up the stairs. "There's a lot of them."

"We're on our way," he said. "Shoot first, ask questions later. You understand?" Another loud bang went through the house, this time closer—like they were in Roman's room across the hall. It startled me enough to make me drop the phone, even as I heard Roman's voice call out on the other end.

"Do you know how to shoot?" I asked Alba, handing her a pistol from my dresser.

She checked the clip and cocked the chamber before nodding. I grabbed my two favorites and did the same.

"Don't hesitate," I said, moving to the farthest end of my closet as the crunch of splintering wood indicated they'd busted down my bedroom door. They were here...in my room...just on the other side of the closet.

"Where *are* you?" came a deep voice. Alba had been right. It was Stallion. "Come out, come out, wherever you are."

"What if she's not here?" That one was Reaper.

"She's here," came a third voice. Maybe Lunchbox. "Bear wouldn't just let his wife go wherever she wants unprotected."

"Are you sure this is the president's house?" I didn't know that voice, and judging by how unsure they were about this being the right location, I assumed they were with the Hell's Knights. Roman had said Stallion and the others were making contact with the rogue club, and they wanted vengeance for something Crow had done decades ago.

The door handles jiggled, and I held my breath, tensing my muscles and preparing to defend myself any second. My vision narrowed. The air in my chest grew tight and heavy, my lungs suddenly unable to get enough. I tried to stay present, but the anxiety in my blood boiled over.

Suddenly, I wasn't in the closet with Alba anymore. I was back in my room at my old house, getting ready for the day. Several men who had worked for my family for years burst into my space, grabbed me, shoved a pillowcase over my head, and dragged me out of my home. They put me in a car and took me somewhere, and as they hauled me into a freezing, dank room, I realized I had been found out. The beatings came, and I couldn't stop it. It was my own family, my flesh and blood, that had done this to me. Just as it had been Gabriella who took Hugo from me and my father who killed Vittori. Was it any surprise that I had started leaking information to the Roses? Could anyone blame me for wanting to escape?

Gunshots brought me back to reality, where Alba stood next to me, firing off rounds into big, hulking men as they tried to get into the closet. I blinked, swallowing down the rancid fear threatening to choke me, and aimed. I didn't care who I hit. If they were trying to get in, they were enemies, and they had to go.

"How dare you!" Alba shouted, but the bang of the guns was almost too loud for me to hear her. "You fucking traitors."

I hit a guy in the shoulder, and he went down, but then a hot slicing pain went through my leg and I winced, dropping to my knee.

"Stop!" shouted Stallion from the back of the frenzy. "Stop shooting at her! We want her alive!"

I tried to keep up with the number of guys barreling toward me, but it was only us two, and we couldn't rattle off the bullets fast enough to keep all of them away. A man I didn't recognize rushed in and I tried to shoot him, but I'd run out of ammo. I grabbed my knife on my thigh, holding it out as I dared him to come any closer.

He raised an eyebrow and laughed. "You think that pigsticker is going to hurt me?"

"Why don't you come find out?"

Alba had grabbed another gun from my dresser, holding it out like she meant to fire at them, but more men filed into my room, and we were entirely outnumbered.

"Come on," I roared.

He raged toward me, and I tried to stab him in the midsection, but he caught my wrist and twisted me around so my hand was behind my back. His massive arms scooped around my waist, picking me up like I weighed nothing. It took two guys to get Alba to stop fighting, one grabbing her arms, the other grabbing her legs. We'd managed to take down six of them, bodies lining the ground of my once pristine bedroom. Now, blood soaked the walls and the carpet while several other men held their wounds with angry scowls.

Good.

"Now, now, you little Caputi cunt. Calm down. We're not going to hurt you too much, not yet anyway," Stallion said, grinning as his men wrestled me out of my room and down the hall, Alba right behind me. Stallion, Reaper, and Lunchbox trailed after us, wearing new cuts that read *Hell's Knights*. Had they already been patched into a new club? How did that even work?

"You fucking traitors," I shouted, fighting the hold the guy had on me. If I could just get loose, if I could get outside, I could run to get help. Bear and my brother were on their way, but judging by the delay in hurting me and Alba, perhaps that was what they wanted.

"Oh, quite the hypocrite, huh?" Stallion laughed and raised his hand, bringing it down on my face so hard, I saw stars. Pain exploded through my cheek and that side of my body, and my vision blackened for a few moments. When I came to, we were in the living room. I kneeled in front of them, Alba at my side. They'd restrained our hands together behind our backs with zip ties and wrapped cloth around our mouths so we couldn't talk.

"Now, we're going to sit here and wait for your...*husband*...to rescue you," Stallion said from his spot perched on Roman's recliner, his disgusting boots on our ottoman. I seethed with hatred for him, my body trembling with adrenaline and my chest aching with nerves. "In the meantime, let's have a little fun, shall we?"

He glanced at Reaper behind me, a middle-aged man with disgusting teeth and horrible body odor. The former Rose rubbed his hands together and raised his eyebrows, looking down at us. "Oh, I can't wait for him to walk in on what I have planned for you both."

13

BEAR

The drive between the clubhouse and my house normally took ten minutes, maybe fifteen if we got stuck at a red light. After the call with Julia, I made it there in five.

We'd been welcoming the officers from the New England and Ohio chapters, who had driven in for a meet and greet and my upcoming nuptials. Even though we were about a month out from that, they'd arrived early to help us plan. But after hearing my wife's panicked voice, everyone raced to my place.

Rage boiled through my veins, my entire body scalding with fury when I parked my truck down the street from my house. KC hopped out of the passenger seat, the hatred in his gaze matching mine. This had been a coordinated attack. They knew we'd be held up with our other chapters, but they made a mistake. Roses banded together, no matter what. Even if they had the Hell's Knights with them, we were rolling three chapters deep, and we had enough guys to decimate them.

Thor, Hollywood, and Wheels walked up behind us, followed closely by Titan, the president of the New England SRMC, and Copter, the president of the Ohio chapter.

"I'm going to tear their fucking throats out," KC said, his body tense as he stalked toward my house.

"Leave some for the rest of us," Leo said from next to him, his bodyguards already armed and ready to go. He cocked his pistol, his limp barely noticeable with all the adrenaline pumping in his veins.

I understood. I wanted to rush in there and rip off all of their heads.

"Wait, wait, wait," Thor said, grabbing KC's shoulder to stop him. "They'd be idiots to not know we're coming. They haven't left the house."

"So?" KC asked, wide eyes glaring at Thor.

"This is a trap," Wheels said, rubbing his hands over his bald head.

"How are we going to do this?" I said.

"They want you scared," Doc said, standing next to us. "I tried to talk reason into them, but they're too pissed about everything. They want you to back down. They want you to step aside."

Footsteps sounded from the woods to our right, and I grabbed my gun, holding it up just in case it was one of the traitors. When Selene appeared with her rifle in one hand, I lowered my pistol and took a deep breath.

"There's ten of them, from what I can tell," she said, "and another five guarding the house. We can surround it, take them out, and get inside."

Thor nodded and kissed the side of her head.

"Alba and Julia?" I asked.

Selene took a deep breath and glanced at Thor. "We should move."

That did nothing to alleviate my wrath. Whatever was going on in there would make me murderous, even more than I already was.

"Titan, take your guys around the house. Bring down anyone wearing a Hell's Knights cut." He nodded and stalked off to bark commands. "Copter, your guys are with me. We're going in. Don't kill any Roses if you can help it. You know how we handle traitors."

A bullet to the head would be too clean, too easy. No, I would string them up by their insides and let them rot for days before I finally gave them release.

"You got it." Copter turned to head toward his guys, currently parking their bikes behind the rest of the Madison Roses.

With KC at my side and the rest of my brothers behind us, we stalked the rest of the way to the house, aiming at the three Knights standing outside. I didn't think, just reacted, firing at their heads, so they dropped to the ground. I stormed up the porch stairs and shot another Knight who tried to stop me. He managed to get off a round that clipped me in the shoulder, a fiery brand shooting down that side of my body, but I didn't stop. Fueled by vengeance and the weight of this sudden affection for my wife, I entered my house like a demon, like I had the entire world behind me.

The scene inside would haunt me forever. Alba and Julia were on their knees with Stallion standing behind them. Reaper had been unbuttoning his pants when we walked in, and now stood with his fingers on his zipper, staring at us with that disgusting grin on his face.

Chaos erupted so fast, I could barely keep up with it. KC reacted first, firing at Reaper and hitting him in the leg. He went down as Stallion aimed at Julia's head, but I was quicker. I hit him in the shoulder, knocking him back, making his gun go off straight at me instead. The bullet grazed my arm, but I didn't feel it. I didn't care. I had to get to my wife.

Her wide, terrified eyes met mine, and she sobbed, maybe in relief, maybe in terror, and I rushed forward. More Knights came around the corner, their guns raised, and I shifted to the side, nearly missing the rain of bullets that tore up my dining room and kitchen. KC ducked to the ground, hiding behind a side table as bits of drywall and furniture sprayed through the air.

Shattered glass rang out, and I winced as shards of the window hit me in the face, but the Knights tumbled over each other as Thor and Selene hit them from the outside. It cleared the way enough for KC, Leo, and me to rush into the living room and shoot the remaining Knights, huddled together in my hallway.

The rest of my brothers raided the house, Hollywood and Wheels taking off upstairs to make sure it was empty, and the sounds of "All clear" outside told me Titan had managed to get rid of anyone hiding in the woods.

Switch and Castor grabbed Stallion and hauled him upright while four of my other brothers detained Reaper and Lunchbox, but I couldn't worry about that. The only thing I wanted, the only thing I needed, was my wife.

I rushed to her side and pulled the rag from her mouth before cutting the zip tie from her wrists.

"Roman," she said on a cry, wrapping her arms around my neck. I lifted her with an arm under her knees and the other around her shoulders, holding her close to me while I sat on the couch so I could assess the damage.

"It's all right, little wife," I cooed, kissing her temple, her hair, her face, any skin I could touch. I needed to ground myself in her safety as much as she needed to know she was safe. "I've got you. Are you hurt?"

She trembled so hard, she couldn't talk, only shook her head and sobbed. KC grabbed Alba and took her to the kitchen, likely to do the same thing I was doing with my old lady. And when Leo kneeled in front of us to put a hand on his sister, it took everything in me not to growl at him to get the fuck away. But he loved her, too, and he was her family, her blood.

"*Mia sorella,*" he said. "Tell me you're okay. Tell me you're not hurt."

"Thank you for coming for me," she managed to say. "Thank you for saving me."

"I'll always come for you," I said, holding her tighter.

"This is a fucking mess," Thor said, drawing my attention when he came into the room. "I'll get the cleanup crew working on it, but Bear...you can't stay here. There's blood everywhere."

"Come to my house," Leo said, rising again. "There's extra space, and we'll need to talk about what to do next."

I nodded and tried to stand with my wife, but in the wake of the attack, my wounds had caught up to me and I groaned before plopping back down on the couch again.

"You're hurt," Julia said, finally glancing up at me with red-rimmed eyes and tear-stained cheeks. "Oh my God. Help him!"

"Shh," I said, pressing a tender kiss to her lips. "I'm okay. It's just a scratch."

It was a lot more than that. A bullet had gone through my shoulder and out the other side. Another had nearly hit me in the chest, making a huge gash that would likely need stitches. And my leg ached, meaning I'd at least been grazed in the thigh if not outright shot.

"No, it's not." Suddenly forgetting her own trauma, Julia focused on me, tracing her fingers over my bloody cut before she lifted my shirt to see the damage underneath. "You need to go to the hospital."

"No, *mia cara,*" I said. "There's no time for that. C'mon. Let's get you cleaned up, and then I've gotta head to the clubhouse to deal with this."

Her features turned panicked, and she gripped my leather cut like her life depended on it. "No! Please don't leave me. Not again. Please."

I didn't want her to go to the clubhouse with me. I knew what I had to do there. I had to execute Stallion, Reaper, and the others. I had to torture them for betraying us and take out my fury on their bodies before turning them into pig feed. I didn't want her to see me like that. Undoubtedly, she knew what I was capable of. She'd lived in this life since she was born. She'd heard the stories, and certainly, her family had done worse.

But there was a difference between hearing it secondhand and seeing it. By the time I was done with these dumb motherfuckers, I would be covered in their blood. I'd bathe in it for weeks if I could, if only to be certain they were dead and they couldn't betray me again. But I didn't want those images in Julia's head. I didn't want that to cause her nightmares or make her see me differently.

"You can come with me," I said, brushing the hair away from her face before resting my forehead on hers. "I won't leave you again. I promise."

"Thank you, Roman," she said. "*Cuero mio. Amore mio.*"

My heart. My love.

I took a deep breath and tried not to let the terms get to me. She'd been beaten, shot at, and nearly raped. Her emotions were high, and she'd likely gone into shock. It didn't mean anything, but that didn't stop me from kissing her again, deeper and longer, holding her tighter.

"Can you walk?" I asked, knowing my busted arm had finally given out on me.

She nodded and stood on shaking legs, only for her to wince and buckle under her weight. It was then I realized she'd been grazed in the thigh.

"Fuck, baby," I said, pushing to stand. "Thor! Get some prospects in here. Julia can't walk."

"No, I'm okay," she said, grimacing through it. "Just stay with me. I'm okay."

With her wrapped around me and my good arm holding her close, I led her out of the house and away from the most terrifying night of our marriage thus far.

14

BEAR

"You don't have to watch this," I said, grimacing as Selene shoved the needle in the skin on my ribs and pulled the stitching thread through. I skipped the numbing stuff because I didn't want anything to take away from what this night had cost me. The pain would fuel my anger and keep me focused, and I needed to be as clearheaded as I could when I went into the barn.

"I have to," Julia said, grabbing my hand. "I have to know they're dead, so they can't haunt me."

"You can trust me," I told her. "They are not going to survive the night."

We had killed half of the Hell's Knights that teamed up with Stallion and Reaper, their vice president included. The president and some other officers had escaped unscathed, but they wouldn't be free for long. Switch and Castor were already trying to hunt them down, and when I found out where they were, they would pray for mercy before I granted it.

"I do trust you," Julia said. "But I need this."

I glanced at Selene, who looked between us before raising her eyebrows and going back to stitching me up. With Doc in the barn, already tearing the traitors to pieces, she'd been left to patch us all up. We'd lost four prospects and three brothers today, five from my own chapter and two from the New England chapter. Titan was pissed, I was livid, and there wasn't enough Judas blood to pay for it.

"Please, husband," she said. And damned if that fucking word didn't make me melt. It used to be a taunt between us. A few weeks ago, hearing it fall from her lips would have made me smirk and think of the worst thing I could say in response. Now, I wilted. Now, I wanted to do whatever I could to hear it over and over again.

"I don't want you to see *me* like that," I whispered, pressing my forehead against hers.

"Nothing you could do would make me feel differently about you." She kissed me, and her soft lips against mine dissolved any remaining resistance. I wanted to believe she meant it in a positive way, but I remembered this was all pretend. If I looked behind the curtain, I'd realize she still hated me and nothing I could do would change that. It wasn't like she could dislike me more than she already did.

I'd been right about my shoulder, the bullet had gone straight through, and the one in my leg had only left a scratch. The worst one was on my side, which hurt every time I moved. Julia had been shot in the leg, but I'd made sure Selene fixed her first. Now patched up, my wife sat at my side, too afraid to leave me again so soon after the attack. That, too, turned me into a vicious man. Stallion, Reaper, and the others hadn't just broken their vows tonight, but they'd also taken my trust in my brothers, the same trust Julia had in me to keep her safe.

"All right," Selene said, snipping the last piece of thread before dropping her forceps on the tray next to her. She picked up a bandage and peeled off the stickers to place it over the wound. "I'm giving you some antibiotics and pain meds."

"Skip the pain meds," I said. "I'll take Tylenol if I need it."

Selene smirked. "Always the fucking hero."

"Whatever." I rolled my eyes, but Julia raised an eyebrow.

"I'll make sure he rests," she said.

Selene smiled. "Good. I'm glad you're here, Jules."

My wife gave my cousin a half-hearted grin, but it was time to go. We'd already waited too long, and I had to get in there to do my worst. I pushed to my feet and put an arm around Julia's waist, half helping her walk, half guiding her out of the clubhouse and into the humid summer night.

"Will it be gruesome?" she asked, brushing her hand over the shirt I'd given her from the spare clothes I found in my truck. She'd been covered in blood, and we'd come straight to the clubhouse to regroup and deal with the fallout. Now, the white T-shirt swallowed her, making her seem small and delicate. But fuck if I didn't love the sight of her in my clothes. It sent a possessive, territorial spark straight down my spine.

"Yes," I said. "You really don't have to come to this."

"No. I need to see it done." She took a deep breath and raised her chin in defiance. "Besides, we're a team, right? We need to convince the rest of the club we can do this together."

I wanted to scoop her up and take her home, to bury myself so deep inside her that nothing and no one would ever touch her again. I hated that I hadn't had my phone on me when she needed me. I hated that someone had gotten close enough to hurt her. If we hadn't gotten there when we did, it could have been so much worse.

The Roses' clubhouse sat on a huge piece of property that had luckily been transferred to me in the weeks before my father's arrest. A few hundred yards behind the main building sat a big barn where we did our dirty work. Once upon a time, Leo had been held captive in it for months. Now, the rest of my club had gathered to deal with the traitors who had tried to take out my wife. Would they have hurt Alba, too? I didn't know. I'd like to think not, especially since she'd been part of our family for years. But they had gone all in with the Hell's Knights, and they wanted to hurt us where it counted. If the men were the muscles of the Roses, the women were the heart and soul. Hurting them sent all of us into a rage.

I opened the wooden door and stepped aside so Julia could enter first, steeling myself against the smell. It used to reek like animals in here, but after the last few years of Doc's handiwork, it now stank of old blood and rotting flesh.

Stallion, Reaper, and Lunchbox were on their knees in front of the fireplace, gags in their mouths, their hands tied behind their backs. Four other Roses had also assisted them, but they'd been casualties of the shootout. Too easy a death for my liking, but at least these three conspirators were here to face the club's justice.

Doc stood next to a table covered in his tools, his hands bloody and his forehead sweaty. Wheels and Thor were off to one side with Leo, Saint, and Hollywood on the other. The rest of the club filled in around the perimeter. KC, bless him, must have already blown off some steam. His knuckles were bloody and his white T-shirt was covered in fresh crimson. Judging by the amount, it probably wasn't all his own.

At our entrance, everyone turned to face us, all eyes expecting my wrath.

I steeled myself against what I knew I had to do, taking a deep breath so I didn't back down. My father had always told me if a man was going to pass judgment, he had to be the one who carried out the sentence. Doc was our enforcer; he usually handled traitors. But this was personal, and I had to do it myself.

"Wait here for me, okay?" I kissed Julia on the temple, and she nodded, going to stand next to her brother. Which was good. He'd keep her strong through this. It wasn't going to be pretty.

I walked up to Doc, ignoring the twinge in my shoulder and the ache in my side. He laid down his scalpel and glanced up at my arrival.

"What'd you get out of them?" I asked.

Doc rubbed bloody fingers over his forehead and brushed his hair out of the way. "Not much. But there's not a lot to tell. It's easy to guess what happened."

"Hmm." I grunted and looked at the three traitors lined up on the ground. Stallion and Reaper stared back at me with hatred and anger in their eyes, but Lunchbox shook like a little bitch. I didn't know if it was adrenaline withdrawal or fear, but either way, he'd be the one most likely to run his mouth. I grabbed the machete off Doc's table and walked toward him.

"You know, I'm disappointed," I said, twirling the weapon around. "I would have thought you'd have the balls to come after *me.*"

Stallion snorted and Reaper rolled his eyes, but Lunchbox trembled harder. Now that I was closer, I could see that Stallion and Reaper had been beaten, likely by KC. They had patches of skin missing from their hands, and looking over their shoulders told me Doc had torn off the nails from all their fingers and toes, the psycho motherfucker.

"Going after our old ladies?" I shook my head and stopped in front of them, holding the blade up to run a finger over it and prove how sharp it was. "That's low—even for cowardly motherfuckers like you idiots."

Stallion groaned, but it was Reaper who tried to come after me, pushing up on his knees so he could attempt to head-butt me. I leaned out of the way and KC grabbed his shoulders to haul him back into place. Doc and Saint moved behind them to keep them detained, but I glanced at KC before continuing. The wrath and confidence in his gaze told me I had to keep going, that this was the right thing to do.

"Cut him loose," I said to Doc, gesturing to Reaper.

My brother furrowed his brows. "What?"

"Did I stutter?" I nodded and grabbed a cinderblock from next to Doc's table, sitting it down in front of the traitor. "Cut his hands loose."

Doc grumbled something to himself before doing as I asked, and the moment Reaper was free, he launched at me again. KC and Saint grappled for his shoulders, but his reaction was exactly what I wanted. I grabbed his wrist and draped it over the concrete, tightening my fist around his forearm.

"Hold him steady," I told my brothers. KC and Saint complied, leaning their weight on Reaper, keeping him in place despite his wiggling. "Listen to me, you piece of shit. You see that woman over there?" I pointed to Julia at the edge of the crowd, her hands clenched into fists, her face set in a stoic mask. "Mine. And if you touch what's mine, I take your fucking hand."

I raised the machete high in the air, only to bring it down in one harsh slice right on his wrist joint, separating his hand from his arm. The crunch of bone echoed through the weapon, and blood spurted all over my shirt and the floor. My shoulder twinged and something snapped in my side, likely a popped stitch. Selene would kill me, but fuck it. This had to be done.

Reaper screamed, struggling against my brothers, and when I shoved his arm back at him, he collapsed on the ground, clutching the wounded limb to his chest. Yeah, it was gruesome, but I had my father's temper. And right now, nothing in the world would put a stop to it.

Lunchbox cracked like an egg. He cried and screamed, mumbling something behind the gag.

"What's that?" I yanked the bandanna down.

"It was Stallion's idea," Lunchbox said, sputtering, hardly making sense. "H-H-He told us the Hell's Knights would help us, that they only wanted the Caputi girl, that's it. We didn't know about Alba."

"Uh-huh. I see." I glanced at KC, who sneered with disgust from behind the quivering coward. "And how long have you known about this?"

"Only a few weeks, I swear." Lunchbox sobbed and shook his head. "Only a few weeks."

Stallion growled from behind the gag, shoving his shoulder into Lunchbox to make him shut up. But he kept going, detailing how they planned to let Alba go if she agreed not to tell the rest of us about Julia. "We shouldn't be allies with them. They're gonna stab us in the back. We were protecting you, prez, I swear it. We only wanted the best for you."

I nodded and squatted down in front of him. "Why didn't you come to me with this?"

He shook so hard, his teeth chattered. "By the time I realized what they were doing, I was in too far. I thought you'd think I had something to do with planning it. I was just going along with it. I swear, I swear, I swear."

"Ohh, you were just going along with it." I turned to look at Julia, Leo, and the rest of the Roses. "He was just going along with it."

Some jeered while others heckled the terrified brother. But the look on Julia's face spurred me on. She scowled and pursed her lips, and I wasn't deterred. She needed to know who she married and what I would do if anyone came for her again.

"Cut him loose," I said to Doc, who agreed with no argument this time.

"Please," Lunchbox said, trying to back away from me, his wide, panicked eyes begging me for a reprieve. "Please, don't. I'm sorry. I'm so sorry."

"Yeah, you're gonna be," KC said, grabbing a hand to yank it out in front of him. Lunchbox fought it, blubbering as he tried to prevent it from happening. But KC was bigger and stronger and pissed, and when I moved the cinderblock in front of Lunchbox, he screamed.

"Wait! I'll tell you where the Hell's Knights are hiding! Please!"

"Best make it quick," KC said, holding a hand out to me.

"They came through here on their way to the Caputis," Lunchbox said. "They were supposed to bring Julia to her aunt. They're looking for Leo. They just want Leo. That's all."

I glanced back at Julia and Leo, who both seemed to agree that could be a plausible plan.

Nodding, I handed the machete to KC and took his place, holding Lunchbox so my cousin could have his vengeance. KC pulled down his shirt, revealing the sunshine tattoo on his chest.

"You see this? You know better than to touch a brother's old lady." KC raised the weapon high and brought it down on Lunchbox's wrist. "You should have come to us."

The traitor screamed and pissed himself before passing out, dropping to the ground like a bag of potatoes while his limb gushed.

"Wake him up," I said to Doc, who grabbed smelling salts from his table before kneeling over Lunchbox. KC handed the weapon back to me and I stalked to the head fucking Brutus himself, big bad

Stallion who stared at me with fire in his eyes. He wouldn't back down, not now, not even after I'd maimed his cohorts.

"Is all that true?" I asked. "Did you think you'd be able to ride off into the sunset with the Hell's Knights like I wouldn't come after you?"

Stallion sighed through his nose, refusing to cower an inch. Of course, it was this bravery that had led us to patch him in the first place.

"Did you think the Caputis would come save you?" I raised my eyebrows as my rage swelled up inside me. If I didn't do this, the others would see me as weak. The rest of the club would think it was okay to stab me in the back, to invade my home and harm my family. I wouldn't have it. "What made you think that coming after *my wife* would be okay? You really are a dumb motherfucker, huh?"

Reaper curled on his side, pushing up into a sitting position while still clutching his wounded arm. He yanked the gag down and, when Saint went to restrain him, I shook my head.

"Her father killed your mother," Reaper said. "Her aunt killed Skulls and countless more. Look at you. Not married two months and you're already pussy whipped."

"Do you think that's what this is about?" I grabbed his hair and yanked his head back. "This is about respect. I told you if you had a problem to challenge me for the top spot. Rather than do that, you go *behind my back.* You go to my house. You fuck with my old lady, with KC's old lady. Pussy whipped or not, I won't accept that treachery."

"C'mon," Doc cut in, grabbing his pistol. "We've let these cowards suck up too much air already. If you're not going to let me have my fun, then let's end it." He aimed the barrel at the back of Reaper's head.

"If I have to die to show what the Caputi cunt has done to your strength, then so be it." Reaper sneered.

"Hmm." I almost laughed. Here he was, thinking my marriage to Julia had made me weak. But I knew differently. I glanced back at my wife for reassurance.

Should I kill them now or make it slow?

She gave me a subtle nod—quick and short. But I understood what it meant. She wanted it to be done with. She wanted it over so they couldn't haunt her anymore.

I grabbed my gun from the holster under my arm and held it at his forehead, right in between his eyes.

"Make your peace with God," I told him.

"Fucking do it, you—" He didn't get the rest out before I pulled the trigger, bits of brain and skull exploding out the back of his head. Reaper's body fell over backward, nearly colliding with Doc's legs.

Lunchbox wept next to him, sobbing and snotting down the front of his shirt. Alas, I was but a merciful leader. I aimed my pistol at his head next and put him out of his misery.

Then, I returned to Stallion, who sat stock-still like none of this bothered him. Perhaps he thought he'd get away with it, or perhaps he knew he would always end up here.

"What to do with you?" I shook my head and tsked through my teeth, blood boiling with the thought of what could have happened to Julia had we been delayed. My rage nearly bubbled over, having not dulled with what I'd done to Lunchbox and Reaper. "Should I take your hands? Should I beat you to death?"

None of it fazed him.

"Should I throw you to the club?"

Whoops and hollers of agreement came from around me. I wouldn't be so delusional as to think they cared enough about Julia in two months to avenge her honor. No, this was about loyalty. Roses didn't fuck with another member's wife. Roses didn't side with another club over our brothers. Roses didn't disrespect our colors like that.

Stallion gulped and squared his jaw around the gag, training his features so he didn't react. But the twinge at the corner of his eye gave him away. If I tossed him to the wolves, they'd tear him apart.

"What do you all think?" I turned toward my brothers, toward the over sixty members crammed into the barn to witness my retribution. "Stallion came after my old lady because he disagreed with something I did."

"Boo!" came the chant from all around me.

"Should I take his hands?" I glanced around, connecting with Hollywood's stare. It could have been V, and his uncharacteristic scowl told me what he thought about that. "Should I take his skin?"

Some cheers filled the space mixed with arguably less boos.

"Should I let you have him?"

A chorus of applause echoed through the small space.

"What do you say, wife?" I glanced at Julia, tilting my head to the side.

She considered, looking around at this motley crew of outlaws. When she came to a decision, she met my gaze again and said, "Let them have him."

Stallion sighed and sagged, sitting back on his haunches while the rest of the Roses shouted their enthusiasm. But I agreed. The club deserved a chance to have their revenge. We allowed disagreement. None of us were slaves to the patch. But the way Stallion had gone about it spat in the face of everything we stood for.

"You heard the lady," I said. "Do your worst, but for the love of God, clean up after yourselves."

I walked back to Julia and put my arm over her shoulder to guide her from the barn, but I caught Leo's gaze just as we turned to leave. He nodded, approval and respect in his expression. If someone had asked me a year ago whether that would have meant anything to me, I would have said fuck no and never. But now, some small part of me ached with satisfaction that both he and my wife were okay with what I'd done. It took a monstrous side of me to deal with those beasts, and even if I didn't like it, they had to go.

15

JULIA

"*Shut the fuck up, traitor,*" *Lenny roared, smacking me in the face. He had worked for my father for years before Gabriella took over, and now he stood over me, fury in his eyes as he beat me. "How dare you betray your blood like this?"*

Another goon grabbed my hair and held me up so Lenny could hit me again. I fell to the side, biting back tears, refusing to let them break me, but I didn't know how much longer I could hold out. Gabriella had found out about me, about how I'd been leaking information to the Roses. I didn't know how she knew. I'd probably never find out, but it didn't matter. Now they had me, and I shivered at the thought of what they'd do before Gabriella arrived.

"I ought to bend you over the table and let my men fuck you bloody," Lenny said. "How disappointed your father would be in you. You're nothing better than a warm hole now."

I stared him down and ground my teeth.

Fine. Let it turn to rape. Let it be over with.

"Gabriella said no," the other goon cut in. "We're not supposed to touch her...like that."

Ahh, so my dear Zia hadn't lost all of her morals, only some.

"I don't give a fuck what Gabriella says," Lenny said. "This Rose whore deserves it, and my men are aching for a good fuck."

"Julia—" came a familiar distant voice, but I was too lost in my memories to react.

"Go on then," I said. "You fucking cowards. Do it."

"Julia, wake up. It's only a dream." The voice was louder this time, and when a warm arm draped over my waist to pull me closer to a hard, muscular body, I blinked my eyes open to a dark room and a strange bed I didn't recognize. But I inhaled Roman's clean pinewood scent, and that calmed the rising panic in my chest. We were in the safe house where Leo had been living, in one of the spare rooms. Roman's house had to be cleaned and repaired before we could return.

I turned in his arms to face him, leaning closer to breathe him in deeper.

"Thank you," I said, nuzzling under his chin.

"Want to talk about it?" he asked, his voice gravelly from sleep.

"No, it's better left in the past," I answered. Now that I was awake, I focused on my husband's features—the way his cheek sloped down to his jaw, his pouty lips, the stubble on his chin. I brought my fingers to his mouth, tracing it like I could memorize the exact shape of the curve. He truly was so beautiful, and after what he'd done to save me, to *side* with me, I could no longer deny these strange feelings developing in my chest. Yes, watching him be so brutal had made me painfully aware of the dark side of our life, but perhaps I'd been sheltered from it for too long. Perhaps that had been the hubris of thinking I could run away with Hugo and nothing would happen to me. This was war, and ending it, would be bloody.

I'd signed my life away to Roman, and in exchange, he'd given me his protection.

"Thank you for saving me," I murmured.

He opened his mahogany eyes and glanced down at me. "There's no thanks needed, Julia. You're my wife. I'll always keep you safe."

Mine. You touch what's mine, I take your hand.

"I'm sorry I didn't answer when you called," he said. "I should have gotten there sooner."

"Shh," I said, kissing him to silence his unwarranted apology. It wasn't his fault, none of this. Roman dragged his hand up my back to my hair, holding my face firmer to his, devouring my mouth. I touched his stomach, tracing the way his abs became his chest and eventually his neck. He was so strong, so powerful, honed from years of turning wrenches in a shop and riding a heavy motorcycle.

He lapped at me with his tongue, and when I opened for him, he wrestled against mine, making me moan. But that spurred him on, and he rolled on top of me, settling his hips between my legs. His half-erect cock rubbed at my clit when he rolled his pelvis, and I spread my legs farther, arching into him, granting him access to whatever he wanted. Most of the time, we played with dominance, but I sensed that wasn't what this was about. This was a reconnection, a reclaiming, a reinforcement that I was safe and protected and *his*.

His. His. His.

Which made him mine.

And oh, how I loved the thought of that. No one else would ever touch him the way I did. No one else would ever know what it was like to be under him like this, to know the weight of his body and how his cock curved upward when it was hard and how he groaned when he wanted more.

He reached down between us, pulling my underwear to the side so he could position himself at my entrance. He was big, so he didn't shove inside me the way he'd done before. He took it slow—rocking in and out a few times to prepare me. And when he slid in all the way, he held himself there for a moment to let me adjust to his girth.

"Fuck," he whispered, biting my earlobe. "You always feel so good. So damned good."

"So do you," I said, turning my face so I kissed him again.

"My wife," he said, rutting against me, fucking me in long, gentle strokes. "My queen."

"Yours," I said. "And you're mine. My husband. My protector. My Rose king."

He paused to lean back and meet my gaze, his grin nearly blinding. "I like when you call me yours."

I bit my bottom lip and rolled my hips, adjusting him inside me, hitting a spot that made both of us moan. I wrapped my arms around his neck and my legs around his hips, meeting him thrust for thrust, and when I came, he put his hand over my mouth to muffle the sounds of my euphoria. My muscles tensed and I clenched my eyes shut, but the thumping in my heart swelled down to the agony between my legs, making me want him again. I didn't think I'd ever get enough.

"Shh," he said, nuzzling into my neck. "Leo's in the next room."

I didn't care. If I had a dime for every time I'd heard Leo with a lover, I'd be rich on my own and I wouldn't need Caputi money. Still, I hummed my agreement and kissed my husband through his climax, his cock kicking deep inside me, spilling his seed. And maybe for the first time since we were married, I prayed he got me pregnant. I prayed we would have a child, something to call ours.

I watched him in his bliss, how his eyes scrunched, how his mouth fell open, how sweat beaded down his temple and over the side of his face. I couldn't admit it out loud, not yet. But in that moment, I loved him more than I needed to, more than I ever thought I would. I expected him to roll off me or maybe kneel between my legs and play with our combined release.

But he lay there with his elbows on either side of my head, his body on mine, his skin sticky and hot. He brushed hair off my face and kissed my nose, running his mouth over my eyes and forehead. His cock stayed buried deep inside me, twitching and softening, but he didn't move.

"I think I like you the most like this," he said. "Half awake and oh so pliant."

I tutted through my teeth and ran my fingers over his face, stopping at his lips. "You like when I fight you."

He sucked two of them into his mouth and bit my fingertips. "Only because you like it, wife."

I didn't know if it was the nickname, the finger-sucking, or the cock warming that set him off, but he soon grew hard again and took me once more before we fell back asleep. The nightmares did not return.

Later in the morning, we woke and showered together, joking and touching and teasing. When the water turned cold and our fingers had pruned, we dressed and joined my brother downstairs. He sat at the tiny dining room table with a mug of coffee in one hand and a newspaper in the other.

"Morning," he drawled, one eyebrow raised as he looked between us.

"Good morning," I said, leaning down so I could kiss him on the cheek. Up until last night, I would say I loved and trusted my brother more than anyone else on the planet. We had survived so much together, and trauma like that bonded people on an entirely unknowable level. "Is there coffee?"

"Uh-huh." He nodded to the carafe. "How are you both feeling?"

"Okay," I said, wincing as the wound on my leg twinged. But I'd had worse injuries, so I didn't mind it so much.

"My shoulder aches," Roman said, coming to stand next to me as I made our coffees. "But it'll be okay."

"Hmm," Leo said with a nod. "That's good."

"How are you?" Roman asked. "Have you heard from Davila?"

Leo rubbed at the space between his brows and sighed. "He is still considering our terms."

"Della texted me yesterday," I said. "Gabriella is planning a big arms pickup from the Hell's Knights. That could be why they were on Rose territory." After last night, I didn't know if they'd still have the numbers to back Gabriella. The Roses had taken a lot of them out. "Hannah is missing."

"Missing?" Leo raised his eyebrows. "What do you mean?"

"Della says she was terminated. No one's seen her in weeks." My stomach churned with anxiety for my missing friend. She'd been an informant for years, and to suddenly go missing usually meant terrible things. "Can you ask around about her?"

Leo nodded and grabbed my hand in solidarity after I sat next to him. "I'll see what I can do."

"In the meantime," Roman said, "we can use the Hell's Knights to track Gabriella. I've already got Switch and Castor looking for the rest of them."

"Thank you," Leo said, nodding at Roman, "for protecting Julia... for standing by your promise."

"Hmm." Roman returned the gesture. "I'm a man of my word. I said I'd keep her safe, and I meant it." He lowered his body into the chair next to mine and sipped his coffee. "Where are we with the plans for the wedding?"

"I've secured the caterer and the invitations, and I've planted seeds with the family. They've heard about the big ceremony and Leo's part in it."

"Good," Roman said. "That will draw her to us."

"She will come out swinging," Leo said. "She'll bring the whole army."

"I'm counting on it," Roman said.

"It could be a bloodbath," I murmured, glancing between the two most important people in my life.

Roman cleared his throat and shifted in his seat while Leo rubbed at his lips.

"It will be okay, *mia sorella*." Leo's gentle smile almost calmed my anxiety. "We'll make sure you're safe."

That wasn't what I was worried about. Here I was, giving my heart to the King of Roses, only to chance losing him the same way I'd once lost Hugo and Vittori. I couldn't go through that again. Would I always be cursed because of my Caputi blood? Would they never let me be happy?

For someone in Roman's position, he'd likely find an early grave or a life sentence in jail regardless of what horrible luck I brought to the marriage. I couldn't lose another person so close to me, someone in whom I'd placed my whole heart and soul. I needed to be prepared for this to end in heartbreak all over again.

If I were smart, I wouldn't have those rough nights with him anymore. I wouldn't allow him to use me however he wished or indulge in early-morning fornication. But when it came to love, my silly, stupid heart ignored that type of logic.

Roman and Leo continued to make plans and deliberate the best way to get the other underbosses on their side, but I chewed my lip and stewed in panic.

"We'll need to get most of them in our pockets before the wedding," Leo said.

"Uncle Frankie," I cut in. "You need Uncle Frankie."

Leo sighed. "I've been trying. He won't hear me out."

I knew how to get to him, and it wasn't with threats and underhanded politics, the way my brother had been playing it.

"I'll meet with Chesco," I said. We had been close growing up. He was as good as another brother to me and the eldest son to Frankie. He stood to inherit that piece of territory once Frankie passed, so if there was anyone he would listen to, it would be his son.

"I don't know about that," Roman said, furrowing his brows.

"I agree," Leo said. "I don't trust our cousin, haven't in a long time."

"You can trust him with me," I retorted. Leo had every right to be skeptical. Chesco had always been more of a wild card than him. But where my brother's vices were drugs and beautiful women, Chesco's were violence and unpredictable behavior. He'd once beat a man nearly to death for continuing to pursue Della after she'd told him she already had a boyfriend.

Roman looked at Leo, who pursed his lips and raised an eyebrow.

"Oh, come on," I said, rolling my eyes. "I'm not a prisoner. Della and Chesco were my best friends before all of this. I miss them. I want to see them."

Leo tsked through his teeth and dropped his gaze, but I turned to my husband.

"They're my family. I don't need permission from either of you to see them," I said. "This will be a good thing. Have I not proven to be a dedicated informant? I've faced more dangerous men than Chesco, you included."

Roman ran his hand over my hair and brushed it back from my face. "Okay. But you will take three Roses with you, and if anything happens, I mean *anything,* you'll call me. Understood, *mia cara?*"

"Of course." I smiled and leaned in to kiss him, full and deep, not caring my brother sat on the other side of the table. "It will be fine; I swear it."

Roman glanced at his phone and stood. "I have to head to the clubhouse to clean up before work. You're okay here?"

I nodded. "Yes. I'm okay."

He kissed me one last time before grabbing his coffee, wallet, and keys, and heading toward the door. "Be good."

"I will," I said with a smile, watching his hips sway in his jeans as he left. I took a deep breath to calm the rising emotions in my chest, wondering how this could still be pretend when he set my heart to pitter this ridiculous patter.

When I glanced back at Leo, he still had an eyebrow halfway up his forehead and an indignant smirk on his expression. "What?"

"You are still so very spoiled," he said, laughing as he sipped his coffee.

"You're the one that insisted I marry him," I said. "So what if he spoils me? He understands how to take care of me."

"Uh-huh," Leo said. "And how is the rest of your marriage contract going?"

"You mean the part where you insisted he impregnate me within a year?"

"Oh, I heard how well that's going at two o'clock this morning," Leo teased, and I picked up a napkin to toss across the table at him with a guffaw.

"Don't be disgusting," I said.

"I meant are you happy, dear sister?" he asked. "Is he treating you right? Was this worth it?"

I took a deep breath and remembered our conversation about

kink, about how much I liked when he took control. I thought about how he looked last night when he pointed at me and said I was his in front of his entire club. The look of rage and vengeance in his eyes had been terrifying and emboldening. I shouldn't have liked it as much as I did. I shouldn't like any of this as much as I did, but I couldn't help the smile on my lips.

"Yes," I said. "It was worth it."

"Good." He grinned and ran the back of his index finger down my cheek. "I'm happy to hear it."

"What about you?" I asked. "Are you planning to wed a Rose princess? What will you do when you take over the Caputi empire?"

Leo sipped at his coffee and shook his head. "No Roses in my future, I fear."

"Will you be single for the rest of your life?" I scoffed. "What would our beloved mama think?"

He chuckled. "Now there's a thought."

"Oh, please," I said with a disbelieving sneer. "I'm surprised you've managed this long without some blond gold digger in your bed."

"Well," he said with a playfully innocent shrug, "who's to say I have? But there is no one I'm serious about, and this is a good thing. I've got more important things to worry about than some blond gold digger, as you say."

"Right." I turned my attention to my phone, sending a text to the group chat with Chesco and Della, promising to see them soon.

"Be careful with Della, *mia sorella*," Leo said. "I know you two are close, but she's...ambitious."

"I know." I sighed, a weight settling in my gut. I'd long been ignoring the voice in the back of my head that told me to be suspicious of her for more than one reason. "What are you thinking?"

"It's a gut feeling. Something is off about her and has been for a while."

I scowled but didn't argue. Leo had a sixth sense about these sorts of things. He could get the measure of a person far better than I ever could, and if he told me to be careful, it was in my best interest to listen.

"When you're right, you're right, brother."

Leo smiled and grabbed his newspaper again, flicking it open to the page he'd been on.

16

JULIA

A week went by before I could see my cousins. In that time, I finalized the rest of the arrangements for the wedding and decided on a dress. The girls came with me to try it on, but even as I stared at the beautiful lace fabric in the mirror, I lamented that the rest of my family couldn't be there.

Nothing about it felt right. Della wasn't crooning over how perfect it was, and my aunts weren't gathered around with champagne, barking orders at the attendant. No, it was just me and a few women I'd met only weeks ago.

"It's perfect," Alba said, fluffing out the train behind me.

"How do you feel?" Selene asked, tilting her head from side to side as her bright blue eyes assessed me.

"Fine," I said as I fussed with a piece of the trim on the arm.

"Fine?" V scoffed and came closer, narrowing her gaze at me. "No woman should get married in a dress that makes her feel *fine.*"

"I'm already married," I said. Besides, this ceremony was for show only. It wasn't real, and tears nearly ran down my cheeks at the metaphor. My marriage to Roman wasn't real. My nascent feelings for him weren't real. Even the attention of the women at the bridal shop with me was pretend.

All of this pageantry was just...a farce, a charade, a game meant to put the chess pieces in the right spot before taking down the queen. But if it was only pretend, why did my heart shatter like this at the very notion? I put that in a compartment inside my mind to dissect later.

"You still deserve a beautiful day," Alba said.

Did I? After all my family had done to hers? Roman had told me what happened to Lore on Alba and KC's wedding day, and it had been Leo's fault. Still, I smiled and thanked her and put the deposit down on the gown so I could mark another item off my to-do list. The dress didn't really matter anyway, not if it was likely to be covered in my family's blood by the end of the day.

After that, we went for mimosas and brunch, and I listened to Ru talk about her father's upcoming trial. Aris had been locked up with Crow months ago, and both were having difficulty getting a fair deal. I felt bad for them, truly, and her plight made me even more committed to my nuptials with Roman. It may not be real, but I needed it to end the feud between our families, to finally know lasting peace.

I tried not to let the anxiety affect me, especially when I was around my husband and the rest of the club. I had to play the part of the queen, the steadfast force beside the MC's president, the old lady who set the example for the others. But Roman could tell something was bothering me.

"Are you sure you're all right?" he asked later that night, after he'd spanked me and fucked me and ran me a bath. Now, I sat in the tub with him behind me, massaging my shoulders while I rubbed his tired calves.

"I'm just worried about the wedding," I said. "I don't want anyone else to get hurt."

I don't want you to get hurt.

But I didn't say that. Our whatever-this-was didn't feel solid yet, and until it did, I couldn't admit how much he'd come to mean to me, especially not to him. If I lost him, if he ended up dying in my arms like Hugo, I didn't know if I could handle it. Despite being technically a Montgomery, I hadn't escaped the curse of my Caputi bloodline, not yet. And I may never fully.

He inhaled and let out a deep sigh, wrapping his arms tighter around me. "I won't let anyone touch you, I swear."

I swallowed my angst and changed the subject, confirming he'd set up my babysitters for my cousins' visit the following day. He narrowed his eyes but allowed the conversation to move on, and that was the last we talked about it.

The next morning, Roman and Leo had already left by the time Della and Chesco arrived, which was good because I wanted some alone time with them. As Roman had requested, there were six Roses posted sentry outside, three more than usual given he couldn't be here to guard me when two Caputis he didn't know invaded Rose territory.

"I have to ask you to leave your guns here at the door," Wheels said, raising an eyebrow at Chesco.

My cousin stood six-six with tattoos covering his body and snaking up his neck. He even had one over his eyebrow that said 'Evil Boy' in decorative script. Chesco's dark gaze shifted to me before back to the Rose.

"Are you fucking kidding me?" He crossed his arms and sucked in air through his teeth. "I'm not gonna hurt my little cousin, even if she is a brat who doesn't text her favorite family member for months at a time."

"Chesco, c'mon," Della said, wringing her delicate hands. Despite being cousins, we looked like sisters. She had long dark hair that cascaded down her back and wide cedar eyes that made her seem innocent and docile.

"Don't be a dick. You'd do the same thing if the tables were reversed." I grimaced as Chesco rolled his eyes and unbuckled the harness around his chest, sliding the leather straps down his arms before handing two Glocks to Wheels. He grabbed the pistol from his waistband and shoved it at the Rose before going for the smaller handgun around his ankle. And honestly, I couldn't be sure that was all he'd brought. Chesco was always loaded, no matter the occasion.

Della, likewise, handed over a small nine millimeter from her purse and stepped inside, pulling me into a big hug.

"Gosh, it's so good to see you," she said. "I don't think the three of us have ever gone this long without talking."

"I missed you." I blinked back tears as I looked to Chesco, who pursed his lips and put his hands on his hips.

He'd always been a precious peacock, and standing in his black Versace three-piece on a random Tuesday morning, he looked every bit the arrogant man I had left behind in DC.

"This place is a shit-hole," he said. "What the fuck are you doing here?"

"Shut up," I said, wrapping my arms around him, too. The three of us were born within months of each other, Chesco being the oldest, followed by me and then Della. We were best friends, confidants, and I would not have survived my childhood without them. Having them here after so long nearly broke my heart. "It's temporary."

"Temporary?" Chesco muttered to himself in Italian. "Leo should have moved you to a condo in Miami rather than let you live like this."

"This is actually Leo's house," I said. "My house, Roman's house, recently got shot up by Roses."

Chesco blinked and rubbed a hand over his dark brown hair. "I should have gotten you out before you signed your life away. What the fuck, Julia?"

I laughed and gestured to the living room, letting them walk ahead so I could grab coffee for everyone. I put the mugs on the table between us and sat next to Della, grinning like an idiot from having my two favorite people here in person.

"Tell me," Della said. "Is being married to a Rose absolutely horrible?"

"Not at all," I said. "He's been kind and understanding. We get along surprisingly well."

"Kind?" Chesco whistled in disbelief. "And here I thought I was going to have to cut his balls off for touching you."

I laughed. "No, I'm okay, truly."

"And what about the rest of them?" Della asked. "Are they as vicious and disgusting as I've heard?"

"No, they...they remind me a lot of our family," I said. "If we're like cats, they're like dogs. We've been drawing lines between us for no good reason."

"Christ, she's drinking the poison fruit juice," Chesco whined. "Quick, Dell, get the van. I'll knock her out and throw her in the back."

I laughed despite his playful threats. *Oh, how I had missed them.*

"What about you two?" I looked between them. "Take my mind off wedding planning. Tell me about home. Are you still seeing that guy from the coffee shop?"

"No," Della said. "Chesco scared him away."

"If he can't handle me, he can't handle our family," he said, refusing to feel ashamed of his behavior. Ever the proverbial older brother, he took great pride in swiping his vicious claws at anyone who sniffed too close to his cousins. If they didn't cut back harder, he rushed them off with their tails between their legs.

"And what about you?" I raised an eyebrow at Chesco. "Anyone make it more than one night?"

He laughed and shook his head. "I'm not the warm and fuzzy type."

We caught up on the rest of the family, and I asked about our other cousins, feeling a sentimental weight shift in my heart at how distant I'd become in only a few months. I missed them, and to be so suddenly shut off from the safety of the Caputis made me twinge with sadness. I hoped this plan worked. I hoped I could be back with them as soon as possible.

Eventually, Della excused herself to the bathroom, and I took my opportunity to ask Chesco about his father.

"Have you heard about our plan?" I asked, assuming his father had already spoken to him about it.

Chesco sighed and leaned back in his seat, crossing his ankle over the other knee. "I have. And to be honest, Leo needs to be more careful. He's lucky someone hasn't already leaked it to Gabriella."

I gulped. "Do you think he can do it?"

He licked his lips and ran a finger over his tattooed eyebrow. "I don't know. This alliance with the Roses has garnered mixed reactions."

"Go on." It must have been met with the same combination of agreement and hesitation as the Roses, but I wanted to know more. This war had been going on for so long, everyone in my family had lost someone close because of it. The blood ran thick and heavy in the divide between us; not even marriage could patch that up.

"Uncle Sulli is gunning for a spot at the top," Chesco said. "But he's an old man, and no one wants to see him take over."

"What about your father?" I asked. Of my father's seven siblings, only three were still alive: Gia, Stefano, and Frankie, Chesco's father. Gia had the most sway, but she had always hated Gabriella. She'd side with Leo in a heartbeat, and Stefano would do whatever his older sister decided. Frankie would be the hold-out, but I hoped Chesco could convince him based on our relationship.

My cousin tsked his teeth and shook his head. "Is that what this reunion is about?"

"C'mon, Chesco," I said. "You know me better than that. Of course, that's what this is about."

He laughed and clapped. "You sly little minx. What am I supposed to do with you?"

"Side with me, side with us," I said. "It's time we stop this war, and you know Leo can do that."

"And what happens when he starts snorting pills again?" Chesco asked. "Or fucking his way through the families?"

"Is it enough to say we can cross that bridge when we come to it?" I said. "He's been sober for almost a year, and I think having a purpose will give him direction."

Chesco narrowed his eyes on me. "I agree the war needs to end. We've lost far too many loved ones, and our focus is better spent on expanding our business rather than fighting a gang of disgusting motorcycle enthusiasts."

I bit back a chuckle, remembering how I'd said the same thing when I first met Roman. Now, I didn't think of them like that anymore. My definition of family had shifted. And it wasn't just about blood anymore. It was about life and friendship and happiness, and the Roses had that in spades.

"But I don't see how we can do that without the rest of the families," he explained.

It wasn't just the Caputis that had control in DC, though they were the bosses in charge of all the others. The Morellis, the Romanos, and the Vitales would take more convincing. However, if we placed Leo in charge and poured a more solid foundation, how could they argue this hadn't been the right thing to do? The infighting and the bloodshed would stop, and we'd have a more stable regime. Peace meant prosperity for everyone.

"Your father is influential," I said. "If he were to get on board, the others would surely follow."

Chesco grimaced. "Getting him to do anything new is a testament to patience and manipulation."

"Well, it's a good thing you're the master of that, huh?" I winked as I took another long sip of coffee.

"Oh, dear cousin"—he shook his head—"if I do this, you will owe me. Big time."

"This is the path to end the war. You know that. Frankie knows that. How many more cousins are you prepared to lose because Gabriella can't swallow her pride?"

He hummed.

"Then there's the matter of Gabriella's spy," I continued.

"Yes, I know," he said, leaning forward to rest his elbows on his knees. "I've had my feelers out, but I haven't heard anything."

"Someone snitched to Gabriella," I said. "She set her men to beating me."

He pursed his lips. "Who do you think it was?"

"I don't know," I said, though I had my suspicions, "but whoever it was is still feeding her information. Someone told her thugs to come to Roman's house. They almost killed me, Chesco."

"Tell me about this attack. Were you injured?"

A knock upstairs drew my attention, and I furrowed my brows before standing to investigate. Steps at the back of the house led to the second floor, but Della was only supposed to use the bathroom down the hallway. Chesco walked behind me, probably prepared to fight whoever had broken in, but when we passed the bathroom, it was empty. Which meant that Della must have gone venturing on her own.

Skeptically, I walked up the stairs and down the corridor on the second floor, but she came out of what had become my bedroom before I caught up with her. "Oh, there you are."

"What are you doing?" I asked, peeking inside the room. Nothing was messed up or askew, but I knew Della better than that. "I heard a bang up here."

"Yeah, I was looking for your tampons." She held one up. "Just got my period."

I narrowed my eyes on her and nodded behind me, a sick weight settling deep in my gut. "There were some in the cupboard under the sink."

"Oh," she said with a smile, pointing at her head like she'd become such a ditz. "Stupid me. I didn't even think to check there."

Leo's warning rattled through me, his reminder to watch her because he didn't trust her, and I looked inside my room again.

"Well, come on," Chesco said. "I'll order us lunch, and Jules can tell us about her wedding plans and how we're supposed to accept some Rose gremlin into our family."

"We're already married," I teased. "Technically, he's already a part of the family."

"Ugh, don't remind me," Chesco groaned.

I smirked but followed my cousin back downstairs with Della right behind me. I, of course, knew what this was. She thought she was being smart, but she wasn't nearly as sneaky as she'd need to be to fool me. After all, Della thought we were playing checkers, and I'd been playing chess far longer than she knew.

17

BEAR

"She's the spy," Julia told me later that night, after her cousins had left and she'd frantically searched our room for whatever Della might have seen. "I'm almost sure of it."

"What do you think she found?" Leo ran a hand over his lips and raised his eyebrows. After Julia told us Della had snuck off on her own, we'd had the house swept for bugs or tracking devices, but we turned up nothing. She must have been looking for intel, and seeing as Leo kept his bedroom door locked for this very reason, there wasn't much she could have found.

"I don't know," Julia said. "I was so stupid. I shouldn't have let her go by herself for so long. I got caught up talking to Chesco."

"Hey," I cut in. "Stop talking about yourself like that. He agreed to help us, and that's worth its weight in gold."

"I don't think she saw anything substantial," Julia said. "There's nothing much here. Just wedding plans and seating arrangements. Gabriella already knows about that. We planted that information weeks ago."

"Keep her talking," Leo said. "See if you can find out what she saw."

I could tell Julia didn't like that, but she ultimately agreed. After all, if Della was a spy, she was playing both sides. We got as much from her as she might have been giving to Gabriella. Knowing gave us the advantage, and we could manipulate the situation how we wanted.

That was two weeks ago. Now, we had moved back into my house...*our* house, and I couldn't help staring at the spot in the living room where Stallion had her kneeling and waiting for me to arrive. If we'd been even a minute later, if Leo hadn't answered his phone when he had...I shuddered to think about it.

Despite this, Julia reassured me she didn't think of me any less than she had before. Which was to say she didn't think of me any more than she had when we'd gotten married.

Sure, we fucked most nights, and I loved making her submit to me. But lately, I wanted more. I wanted adoration in her eyes when she looked at me. I wanted her to talk about me the way a wife should about her husband. Fuck me for being a sap, but maybe I wanted my wife to love me.

Do I love her?

It had been almost four months since we signed the marriage contract and three since we'd been living together. Her incredible mind worked faster than mine, and it was her plan that we'd decided to put into motion. She stood by me at every club meeting, holding my hand and reassuring me we were doing the right thing. She matched my sexuality in ways I'd never experienced before. When I woke up before her in the morning, sometimes I watched her sleep just to memorize the way her forehead sloped into her beautiful eyes and pouty lips. She had become a better partner to me than I ever could have asked for.

There was no way Leo could have known this when he proposed we get married, so it must have been fate. And who was I to point a gun at the universe and tell the bitch she was wrong?

"We'll have to pick up our final fittings tomorrow," Julia said, leaning over her vanity to swipe mascara on her lashes. Based on where we were going tonight and what we planned to do, I had every intention of smearing that pretty makeup down her cheeks. I tried to stay focused on the conversation, but daydreaming about the rotten things I would do to my wife had become one of my favorite preoccupations.

"I've already picked up the rings," she said, facing me. "If Titus is right, Gabriella will plan to crash the ceremony as we make our vows."

I fixed the button on my cuff and cracked my neck, ignoring the churning in my gut from the thought of finally facing down that Caputi bitch. This war had been going on my whole life, and to see it end would lift a weight off my shoulders the size of Jupiter.

"Then, there's the matter of my cousins," she said, walking back to her closet and returning with a pair of sparkling strappy heels and a tiny scrap of black fabric. She'd been wearing a robe to get ready, but now shucked it down her arms to reveal lace lingerie under her dress. "Chesco will keep his word, but Della—" She paused to glance at me, and while I was paying attention to what she said (I truly was), I couldn't help running the length of her tanned, satin skin with my gaze. It was as soft as it looked, and even though she had bruises on her thighs from where I'd bitten her two nights ago, I found myself anticipating what other marks I could leave. "Are you listening, husband?"

I quickly shifted my focus to her eyes. "Of course, *mia cara.*"

She raised an eyebrow and stalked closer in her little black dress, turning to sit on my lap as she pulled her hair to the side. "Zip me up, please."

I groaned when her plump, delicious ass rocked up against my cock, nearly half hard from watching her shimmy into her dress. I grabbed the metal and slid it up her body as slowly as I could, delighting in the feminine scent of her hair and the soft feel of her spine on my fingers.

"Della is still playing dummy," Julia said, glancing over her shoulder with furrowed brows. "She thinks she's smart, asking me things in ways that sound innocuous. I've been playing along."

In the weeks since their visit, Chesco had reached out to Leo with hesitant optimism. Frankie and Sulli wanted to meet to discuss next steps, and I tried not to let fear take over. Leo assured me it was a good thing, and Julia seemed accepting of Chesco's help, but the Caputis had tricked us before. I needed to keep my guard up. Della, on the other hand, had always been Julia's best friend, so if she really was betraying her, that had the potential to hurt my wife in more ways than one.

I ran my hands over Julia's hips and down to her ass, giving the flesh a tender squeeze. "I think you're worrying too much for someone who's about to spend all night worshipping my cock."

Her eyes heated, and a blush graced her cheeks before she bit her bottom lip and stood to grab her heels.

"Perhaps you're right," she said, sliding one foot into the shoe before bending over to twist the straps over her lower calf. "Perhaps I can forget about it for one night."

"Come here," I said, waving my fingers at her.

She lifted her leg and dug the heel into my chest, and I bit back a grin while I held her ankle and latched the buckle into place. Meeting her gaze, I leaned down to kiss the top of her foot before letting her go. She gave me that adorable grin before doing the same with the other shoe. I fixed that one into place, kissed it, and stood.

"I think"—I brushed her hair behind her ear and ran my knuckles down the side of her cheek—"you're amazing. You've played this game far longer than almost anyone else. You're smart and capable, and we're going to win. But tonight is about turning off that voice inside your mind that's constantly planning ten steps ahead."

I remembered what she said about wanting to feel calm and peaceful during our scenes. My control over her meant she didn't have to think anymore. It meant she only had to do what I told her and nothing else. It tickled a dark, depraved part of me that she liked it as much as she did, especially considering I was a filthy Rose and she'd been raised to hate everything about me.

"I have a gift for you," I said, reaching into my pocket to retrieve a decadent black silk collar. We'd been invited to the Beacon's first anniversary party weeks ago, but I had no way of knowing the depth of this thing between us at the time. Now, I *owned* this side of her.

Now, she *wanted* me to own it. The collar made it official and signaled to everyone else in attendance she belonged to me. No one was allowed to touch without my permission, and I was a greedy, spoiled shit, so that meant no one touched at all.

She was *my* toy, *my* pet, *my* dirty little Caputi cumslut, and we both liked it that way.

"Do you know what this is?" I asked when her eyes widened and she inhaled a sharp gasp. "Do you know what it means?"

She touched her bare throat and nodded, looking back up at me. "It means I'm yours, that I belong to you. That we're in kink headspace."

"That's right," I said. "Do you want to wear it?"

"Yes, sir. Thank you." She brushed her hair over one shoulder and turned around so I could place it on her delicate throat and latch it into place.

"I know this...relationship...wasn't what either of us wanted." I cleared my throat as she turned back to face me, her delicate fingers tracing over the strap of soft fabric. "But I've grown fond of it. Of you."

Julia smiled and met my gaze with fire in her eyes. "Me too."

"When you wear the collar, it means we're in scene. I have the control, so you don't have to worry. You don't have to wonder what to do or plan your next step. I'll do that for you."

She nodded. "Yes, sir."

"Good." True, I liked it when she fought. The night she held a knife to my throat played in my darkest fantasies on repeat. But I also liked her like this—pliant and willing and *mine*. "Now, take off your panties and put them in my hand."

She snapped her attention up and froze, squaring her jaw like perhaps she meant to argue with me. "What?"

"You heard me," I said, holding my hand out palm up. "Do I need to repeat myself?"

"No, of course not," she said. "It's just...my skirt is short and when I sit—"

"Do you need to use your safeword? We can renegotiate our terms if this is a limit for you."

She considered this for a moment before she shook her head and reached under her dress to shuck the black lace down her legs and step out of it. After bending over to pick it up, she put it in my hand and glanced up at me, expectation in her brown gaze. I thought about making her take her bra off, too. I liked the thought of her being bare and readily available for anything I wanted. But, one step at a time.

"Good girl, my little wife." I stuffed her panties in my pocket and grabbed her chin, holding her still while I planted a kiss on those ruby red lips. I'd have her lipstick smeared on my cock by the end of the night. I'd have her black mascara-laced tears spoiling these expensive pants, too. "Such a good queen."

She smiled and preened, and that, too, delighted me in exquisitely perverted ways. I planned to ruin her, and oh, how much fun it was going to be.

18

BEAR

"Are you sure I'm dressed okay?" Julia asked as we walked inside the Beacon.

"You look beautiful, *mia cara*." I put a hand on her lower back to lead her inside, smiling at her shiver when I touched her. "Who cares what these people think, anyway?"

"Yes, my husband," she said as she glanced around at the surroundings.

I'd been to the dungeon a few times, but never to play. It had once been a strip club, but when Aris signed control over to Ru, she'd turned it into a BDSM playground. Up front, there was a bar and two stages where people like my sister and Hollywood liked to put on shows for the patrons. They could paddle and whip and punish, but because it was the front-facing room, there was a no-penetration policy.

In the back were private rooms for people to do whatever they wanted. The club didn't ask, as long as the patrons cleaned up after themselves and didn't make a mess.

Upstairs was where the real fun happened. There were various viewing rooms to watch whatever the exhibitionists in attendance wanted to show off. It took an extra special VIP membership to be admitted to the second floor, and since the SRMC had a large stake in renovating the club, I could go anywhere I wanted...*within reason*. I already checked with V to see where they planned to be so I didn't accidentally walk in on my baby sister fucking my best friend. She was on general manager duty tonight and Hollywood was playing security, which left the entirety of the club's amenities at my disposal.

I eyed the gorgeous woman tied to a St. Andrew's Cross, her back pinstriped with pink marks while her dominant flogged her. On the other stage, a woman had been suspended from a thick length of bamboo while her rigger poured wax on her legs and stomach.

"Do you want a drink?" I asked, nodding toward the bar.

"Water, please." Julia glanced around and gripped her clutch purse, her shoulders wiggling from her nervousness. I'd have to rectify that. She had nothing to be worried about. She was the most gorgeous person in this place, and I'd think that even if she weren't mine. I got us both water and, when I walked back to her, she was staring at the woman hanging from ropes, rapture and curiosity in her gaze.

"Are you interested in Shibari?" I asked while she took a sip.

"No," she said. "It's just...she looks like she's enjoying herself."

"Hmm." I held my hand out to her, and she placed her palm in mine before we made our rounds. I put on the good show of mingling with the patrons, clapping hands with people I knew, and introducing myself to others. I showed Julia off like the prize she was, territorial pride churning in my gut when everyone stared at her. She was gorgeous, and mine all mine.

Thirty minutes later, after I'd made sure everyone knew we were there, I led her over to the stairs. Hollywood stood to the side of the maroon velvet rope, wearing a black suit and a huge grin.

"There you are," he said, clapping my hand before pulling me into a hug. "I wondered if I'd see you tonight, especially after your APB text to V earlier."

"Forgive me for not wanting to see what the two of you get up to in your spare time."

"You're forgiven, prez," he said with a laugh and opened his arms to Julia, waiting for her consent before leaning in for a hug.

"We're heading upstairs," I said, nodding toward the entry. "I booked room six for the rest of the night." I'd been intentional about telling him that. While the club, its members, and our princesses had always been sex-positive, I had grown into a possessive motherfucker when it came to my wife. I didn't want anyone to see her the way I did. Her moans, her breathy sighs, her beautiful cunt, it was for me and me alone.

"The whole night?" Hollywood blew out a playful whistle and pulled the rope aside. "Pace yourselves. Last call's at three a.m."

I laughed, and Julia smiled as I stood aside to let her go ahead. "Have a nice night, Hollywood."

"Yeah, you too!" he called as we ascended the red-carpeted stairs. The walls had been painted black, adding to the edgy ambiance of the entire place, especially when we got to the second floor and the white, black, and red decor continued. Sconces lined the hallway, giving it a Gothic vibe, and I grabbed Julia's hand to lead her straight ahead. We passed floor-to-ceiling windows with all types of various activities inside. Group sex, needle-play, a wet-works room, all visible from the hallway. But this wasn't what I'd brought her here for.

No, she'd marked voyeurism on her list, among other things, and I planned to make good on that Y column tonight. When we got to room six, I opened the door and nodded inside the dark space, trying to keep my smile genuine and calm despite the anticipation coursing through my veins. Her heels echoed off the walls as she walked, her back straight, her eyes wide with trepidation.

"What is this?" she said, glancing back at me as I entered behind her and closed the door. The room wasn't large, maybe fourteen by twelve, with black walls and various play implements hung around us. Maybe I'd use some of them, but mostly I wanted a safe space to act out a few fantasies without anyone disturbing us. A huge wooden chair sat in the middle of the room, more of a throne than a dining room seat. It faced what I knew to be one-way glass. We could see the other side, but the people in there wouldn't be able to see us.

"A show," I said as I walked toward her.

She bit her bottom lip and glanced at the impact implements on hooks next to the door. "Are we the performers?"

I snorted and shook my head. "No, no one gets to see what I plan to do to you. No one but me."

She seemed to like the sound of that, her cheeks flushing as she preened for me with her arms behind her back. "Where do you want me, sir?"

I tried to ignore the effect that honorific had on me and how powerful it made me feel. She was a Caputi princess, royalty among peasants in her own right. To have her place her trust in me, especially in this den of iniquity, I had transcended the Gods. I could bend her, break her, have her gagging and crying by the end of the night, and then she'd thank me for it. Had two people ever been more perfect for each other?

I grabbed her collar with my index finger and pulled, leading her over to the throne.

"On your knees, pretty wife." I nodded to the ground, and she sank with hardly any complaint. "Fuck, I love how well you listen."

She stared up at me and jutted her chin, thoughts of defiance perhaps echoing behind her gaze. If she wanted to play the brat, I'd tame her, but I sensed that wasn't where the night was going.

"The things I want to do to you, they're downright filthy," I murmured, kneeling in front of her. I traced a finger over the mounds of her breasts, watching as she shivered from the touch. Her skin pebbled, her nipples hardening just under this pathetic excuse for a dress, and that, too, sent another shock of arousal down to my balls. "And you'll let me, won't you?"

The muscles of her throat worked while she swallowed, but she didn't reply, just maintained eye contact as I dragged my hand lower.

"Answer me," I said.

"Yes, sir," she whispered, her voice nearly cracking.

I traced the curves of her body down to her thighs, ducking my fingers under the hemline to ghost them over her soft skin. She trembled harder.

"Are you scared?" I asked, raising an eyebrow. I teased one leg and skipped completely over her cunt to trace down the other.

"No," she said.

"No?" That amused me. "Such fearlessness. If I had brought you here months ago, you would have stabbed me in the throat and run away."

She smirked. "If you had brought me here months ago, you would have been lucky if all I did was stab you in the throat."

I tried not to laugh at her threat, wanting to stay in the right mindset to dominate her. My hand shot around her throat before I could stop it, and I leaned closer, bringing my face inches from hers.

"Careful, *mogliettina*," I said, using the Italian term for little wife. "I can think of a thousand better uses for that tongue."

She grinned as if to suggest I do something about it.

"Open up," I said, and when she did, I shoved my index and middle finger inside. "Suck."

Watching her wrap her pretty lips around my fingers paled in comparison to the euphoria that zapped down my spine and into my cock. She lapped at them, and I pushed them to the back of her throat, preparing her for what I had planned. With the other hand still on her windpipe, I could feel my ministrations through her muscles, and I imagined what it would be like to fuck her like this later. But I was nothing if not a gentleman. When I was satisfied that they were wet enough, I yanked them out and shoved them between her legs, pleased I had made her wear nothing under her skirt. She was already soaked, of course, but I lived to drench this pussy. She moaned when I rubbed at her clit, spearing through her skin with expert precision. I knew how to apply just the right amount of pressure, and when I massaged her while tightening my grip under her chin, she let out the most adorable whine and rocked against my hand.

"That's it," I said. "Get yourself off on my fingers."

"Please, sir." She fell forward into my hold, pressing her forehead against my jaw. "Please."

I knew what she wanted. If there was one thing she liked coming on more than my cock or my tongue, it was my fingers. She wanted me to fuck her hard, to rub at that sweet spot on the inside and break her to pieces. When I pushed inside her, she groaned, and my cock gave another half-hearted jerk, desperate to replace my fingers.

Patience. I'll get mine soon enough.

I fucked her, rubbing into her pussy while she mewled and shivered in my embrace. She gripped my button-down with her delicate fingers, undoubtedly creasing the expensive fabric, but that only spurned me on.

"You're such a dirty girl," I said, spewing the most depraved shit I could think of. "Letting me do this to you. Do you like fucking your king's fingers? Do you like being on your knees while I take you?"

"Yes, yes," she said. "Please. Harder."

"Oh, I don't respond to little sluts that don't respect their lord."

"Please, sir," she said, emphasizing the honorific.

"Do you need to come?"

"Yes, sir. Please, my king. My lord. Please let me come."

C'mon, I couldn't leave her like that. Her thighs quaked around my hand and her cheeks flushed, an enticing pink snaking over her chest and disappearing under her dress. I found that magic spot in her body and played with it while rubbing her clit with my palm until her internal muscles clamped around me.

"Go on," I said. "Come for me, darling. *Mia cara.*" She clenched her fingers harder, digging her nails into my skin as she soaked my hand, but I kept going. I wouldn't stop until she squirmed and begged for release.

Goddamn but she was beautiful like this, even more than normal. It went to my head and made me feel powerful, like I actually was a king and I could command entire legions in her honor.

When she came back to herself, I grinned and kissed her face until she reached down for my wrist to stop my fondling.

"Too sensitive?" I whispered to check in on her.

She nodded.

Humming my approval at her honesty, I stood and ran a hand over her cheek to brush hair away from her face.

"I love this shade of lipstick on you," I said, rubbing a thumb over her bottom lip. "You know where it would look even better?"

"Where, sir?" She looked up at me with that beguiling mix of feistiness and sexiness that had driven me wild all these months.

"My cock." I smirked and sat on the throne, unbuttoning one of my shirt cuffs so I could roll the sleeve up. She watched with rapt attention, gulping and swiping her tongue over her mouth. I did the same to the other sleeve, and once my arms were free to move easier, I nodded down to my lap. "Go on then. I'm going to watch this show and you're going to keep my dick warm." She started to scoot forward on her knees, but I held up a finger and tsked through my teeth. "Crawl."

Julia took a deep breath through her nose and exhaled with a sigh, leaning onto her hands so she could come closer. Fuck, the sight of her literally crawling on my command made me so hard, I had to adjust my hips in my seat. She was beautiful, so regal, in her submission. It electrified my blood, made me burn from the inside out.

When she got to the edge of the throne, she sat back on her haunches and looked up at me while she undid the button on my pants with her dainty hands. I ran the finger that had just been inside her beautiful cunt over my mouth, smelling and tasting *her*, and watched her pull down the zipper to take out my dick with a sly little grin.

"Kiss it," I said, leaning into the lord role-play. She'd marked this as acceptable, so unless she said her safeword, I kept going. "Worship it. Worship me."

She held my dick in one hand and kissed the length of it, pressing her tender lips from root to tip and back down again, leaving red lip marks all over me. When she nuzzled her nose against me to deepen her attention, I couldn't help the groan that barreled out of my chest. The hot, desperate sensation shot down my legs and up the back of my torso, nearly curling my fingertips.

"That's such a good girl," I said, holding the base to angle it inside her mouth. "Now, do what you were made for."

She wrapped her mouth around me and sucked.

I groaned and leaned my head on the back of the throne while she held me there, running her tongue on the underside, over the length of me. When she got to a part that felt amazing, I grabbed her head and held her still, sinking my fingers into her hair. She liked that the most—when I was rough with her, when I manhandled her like the overbearing piece of shit I was.

"There ya go," I murmured, relishing the sight of her lipstick smearing on her chin and leaving red streaks on my dick. "My good little whore wife. You like being nothing more than a cum hole for me, don't you?"

She moaned, the vibrations shooting right through me and into my balls. Fuck, I loved that, and I watched as she worked me. Perhaps getting too excited herself, she put her fingers between her legs and rubbed at her clit, but I couldn't have that. I didn't want her to come again until I told her to, until I gave her permission.

"Uh, uh, uh," I said. "Don't you dare touch my cunt. Only *I* get to play with that tonight. Hands where I can see them, *amore.*"

She froze and glanced up at me, looking too damned cute with that confused expression and my dick in her mouth. But I didn't push the issue. Yeah, I'd called her my love. I'd done it on purpose.

On that night when those fucking traitors broke into my house to defile her, it had taken me five minutes between when she'd called Leo and when I made it to my house. It felt like a damned century because I'd thought I'd lost her. I'd thought Gabriella had gotten to her, that Stallion would kill her, that she'd been abducted and would be gone forever.

The very notion left a hole in my heart. It terrified me more than it should, more than I ever thought it would.

Tonight would be about more than dominance and submission. I wanted to show her how much her affection meant to me. This may have started as pretend, but it had become so much more to me. I suddenly couldn't imagine what my life would be like without her, and waking up with her in my bed these last few weeks had settled in my bones permanently. I wanted her, and I would always want her, and nothing would ever change that. I'd come to accept it in a way I never thought possible.

Of course, I wasn't sure if she felt the same. So I planned to make a show, test the waters, and see how she reacted. We were already married, so what was the worst that could happen?

19

JULIA

more?

I kept his cock in my mouth while I put my hands on his thighs, determined to follow his directions. Sinking into this role-play had always excited me, and a thrill shot into my lower stomach. My thighs clenched, determined to relieve the friction he wouldn't let me handle myself. My clit throbbed, angry and swollen from both his attention and now the lack of it. All the while, that word spun in my head.

Amore. Amore. Amore.

My love.

He'd never used that before. I was his little wife, his darling, his pretty good girl. But his love? Why would he use that word with no one around to pretend for?

This was supposed to be fake. He wasn't supposed to have feelings for me, not real ones. All of this was a game, a play, something we had to do because of our families, nothing more. And in this space, he was my king, and I was his subservient queen. I knew I'd fallen deeper for him, but when had he started to reciprocate?

"There ya go," he said, cupping my jaw before sliding his hand to my throat. The other hand clenched my hair, holding my head in position for him to piston his hips in and out...in and out...so slow, so achingly delicate. Drool pooled over the side of my mouth and my jaw began to ache, but I didn't dare let up. He wanted to smear my lipstick on his dick, and he wouldn't relent until he had done just that. "Such a beautiful little slut, aren't you?"

From anyone else, the degradation would have insulted me. My brother had killed for less. But from him? Shivers erupted over my skin and the sharp burn of humiliation scalded my skin. I was *his* little slut, *his* little whore. And like he said, no one else would ever see me like this.

My heart pounded as he slid farther inside me, hitting the back of my mouth. I yearned to please him. I wanted to be enough for him. I wanted to sink into his control and let him have me because I knew only he could care for me like this.

He went farther in, and I gagged around him. But he hissed in a noise, suggesting he liked that and did it again. My eyes watered, stinging with the copious amounts of makeup I'd put on, but that had been the point. I wanted to be a blurry mess for him by the end of it. He would destroy me, and I liked the look of myself in the mirror after it happened.

"You're so perfect like this. You drive me wild, you know that? I love fucking every part of you." He rambled on, saying the filthiest things I'd ever heard. For a lady of high moral standing, I should have been outraged. But I reveled in it. I wanted more.

My knees began to ache, and I'd have bruises tomorrow, but I wanted that, too. Ages passed with his dick in my mouth. Sometimes, he fucked me. Sometimes, he just pet my hair and my face and let me suckle on him like a pacifier. Shame boiled my blood at how much it calmed me, how much peace I found in between his legs.

Bright lights came on from somewhere behind me, and I wondered what was happening in the center room, but I didn't dare move. If I stopped to look, if I let him fall out of my mouth before he told me to, he'd punish me. And it wouldn't be a spanking or a deep fisting, no. He wouldn't let me come the entire night. He might not let me come for the rest of the week. My poor empty cunt lurched at the very thought, so I held still, gripping his thighs to ground me.

"It's starting," he said, running the backs of his fingers along my jaw. "Would my greedy cumslut queen like to watch?"

I nodded, doing my best to look sultry and adorable despite the thick tears streaming down my cheeks. He pulled himself out of my mouth and grabbed my arm to help me stand. My feet had gone numb and blood rushed through my tingling legs, but he didn't let me go very far. He turned me around and coasted his hands up the sides of my thighs, inching my dress up with him.

"Now, I'm not ready to fuck you yet," he said. "The lovely exhibitionists in there want to give us a good show. But my cock still needs attention."

I gulped and rolled my jaw to stretch it out, trying to hide the trembling in my muscles. My throat was sore, my eyes burned, and my knees were already protesting anything else that might happen tonight. Still, I waited for his command.

"Spread your legs, my lovely queen," he said.

I did.

"Now, come here and sit on my lap. But don't you dare move." He backed me up until I straddled his legs, and he lowered me, lining himself up at my entrance. I moaned when he was fully sheathed inside me, the pressure of the last million years of sucking him finally getting some relief. I arched my back, trying to get him to that special spot inside, but he slapped my ass hard enough to make me hiss and wince. "I told you not to move."

"Please," I said, looking over my shoulder with a pout. My lips were swollen from my ministrations and my voice was hoarse with thirst, but there was nothing in the world I wanted more than to ride him to orgasm.

"I said no." He scoffed and shook his head. "You Caputis, all the same. Pigheaded. Refusing to listen to anyone."

I bit back a laugh and refocused on the center room, finally taking in the scene. A man stood on a platform with two other people kneeling at his feet. He had on a finely tailored suit with a vest, matching slacks, and a black button-down shirt. The two other people wore next to nothing. The woman had been clad in a black lace bra and the tiniest thong I'd ever seen...until I looked at the man and realized his thong might have been the same size. His cock and balls nearly spilled out of it, and it would have been comical if I wasn't so damned turned on and curious to see what would happen next.

"My queen," Roman said, grabbing my shoulders, "lean against me."

I did, holding him inside me while I rested against his chest.

"Drink this." He held a bottle of water up to my mouth and I swallowed a few greedy sips while I focused on the performers. The suited man, clearly the dominant, nodded at his shoes, and each of his submissives kissed one before glancing up at him for further direction. He waved two fingers at the male submissive, who stood and unbuttoned the dominant's vest, shucking it down his arms before walking to hang it up on a nearby chair. The woman stayed on her knees while the dominant ran a hand along her cheek, pausing at her mouth. She opened dutifully for him, and he shoved two fingers inside, reaching to the back of her throat. I marveled at her lack of gag reflex.

How did she do it?

But that thought quickly went away when the dominant unbuttoned his pants and pulled out his beautiful cock, quickly replacing his fingers with it in her mouth. She latched on like it was her lifeline, sucking and pulling from him with amazing eagerness.

A desperate wave of arousal rushed through me, heating my body, making my inner muscles clench around Roman. He felt it, and he groaned behind me.

"Oh, does my little wife like the show?"

"Yes, sir," I said, focusing on not moving, not angling my hips the way I wanted. I was pathetically wet. It puddled out of me, leaving a spot on Roman's pants that I felt anytime I moved my legs.

"Hmm, take this dress off," he said, sliding the zipper down. "I want to play with your nipples."

I yanked it over my head and tossed it to the side, doing the same to the bra when Roman unhooked it. The rush of cool air on my skin made me painfully aware of how clothed he still was, and I gasped when his rough, callused hands ghosted over my ribs and up toward my breasts. Despite the way he talked to me and the way he handled me sometimes, he never treated me with violence. These hands were capable of bloodshed. I'd seen them tear a man's limbs from his body, but like this, they only brought me the pain and pleasure I asked for.

Roman rolled one nipple between his fingers while the other ventured south, toward my aching cunt. I watched the dominant pull the female submissive from him and tell the male submissive to take her to the bed on the other side of the platform. He scooped her into his arms and did as commanded, where she rolled onto all fours, patiently waiting for their next instruction.

I understood then why Roman had wanted us to see this performance. I'd marked voyeurism on my checklist because I liked the thought of getting off while I watched others do the same, but those three were clearly in a similar type of dynamic as Roman and me. That dominant was their lord, and they worshipped him, and he in turn took care of them. Was Roman trying to prove to me what we had was normal? Or did he perhaps choose something he thought I'd be comfortable with for my first time? Had he even known what it was we were going to see?

Roman swept over the lower half of my stomach, toward my hip, and down the inside of my thigh, purposely ignoring my needy clit. It pulsed in time with my rapid heartbeat, and I panted, wanton for friction, needing more than just sitting here with his jerking dick inside me.

"Do you see how powerful he looks?" Roman said, kissing my shoulder, working his way up my neck to my earlobe. "Do you see how it's their submission that gives him that strength?"

"Yes, my king," I said, moaning when he went to the other nipple, pinching and yanking the same way as the first. Sparks went through my nerves, jolting straight down to my cunt. I clenched around him harder, and he twitched inside me, maybe also furious for more.

"That's what you give to me, Julia," he said, biting my earlobe. "When we argue, when we play, when you crawl for me...you give me your strength."

Pressure mounted in my chest, and I didn't know what to do with it. I watched the dominant flip the female submissive over and wrap her legs around his shoulders so he could lick her, swirling his tongue and sucking in the right ways to make her writhe and moan. The other submissive held her down by the wrists, kissing her breasts, biting her windpipe.

"And you see," Roman said. "He cares for her. He cares for both of them. They trust him to do that, to always be there, to catch them when they fall."

I took a deep breath and looked at Roman, his face millimeters from mine. This wasn't supposed to be so intimate. Yes, we were fucking, and yes, we were deep into role-play, but those words changed it from a game to something...more.

Amore.

"I love when you look at me like that," he whispered, touching my face, pressing his forehead to mine. "I love when you bow to me, when you place your trust in me. It makes me feel like I could fly. I've never felt as comfortable doing these things with anyone else, only you."

I swallowed, repressing the tremble that threatened to break through. I sensed where this was heading, and it couldn't... shouldn't...go there.

"Fuck me, please," I said, more to break his concentration than anything else. I was so turned on and amped up, the moans coming from the center room spurred me on. If he didn't take me hard, if he didn't make up for this entirely too sentimental moment, I would burst out of my skin.

His features dropped, his eyes widening as his mouth hung open. I could have slapped him and he might have been more surprised. Just as quickly, he locked it into a scowl and fisted a handful of my hair, yanking my head back so quick, I nearly cried. "Is that all you want from me? A good fuck?"

I reminded myself this was pretend, just role-play, even if the agony in his voice bordered too close to reality. He let me go and sat back, raising an eyebrow.

"Fine. Fuck yourself," he said, resting his arms on the throne. "But turn around so I can watch you."

Finally.

I stood, faced him, and sat again, positioning his cock at my entrance so I could impale myself on him. He slid in easily; I was so ready for this. I'd been ready since we got here. I put my hands on his shoulders and rocked my hips, rolling him inside me, hitting all the spots I wanted. My head fell back, exposing my neck, and I closed my eyes, allowing my anxious thoughts to disappear into this clawing thing between us.

He grabbed my chin and forced my head upright. "Eyes on me, little wife."

I followed his direction, maintaining contact while I worked myself on his lap. The tone was back in his voice, the one he'd used when we first got married. Its sarcastic glimmer should have been the first indication this game had gone awry, but I didn't care. No, I chased the euphoria that usually came when I sank into his dominance, moaning and grinding and...God, I wished he would touch me, grab me, choke me, anything except sit there.

I reached for my clit, but he smacked my hand away.

"Please," I whimpered. "I need to come."

"Oh, now you need something from me?" He ran his tongue over his teeth. "Why should I let you?"

Had I done something wrong?

I'd stopped him from confessing something that would send this precarious house of cards tumbling to the ground, but other than that, I'd followed all of his commands. Emotions weren't welcomed here, not in this space. He wasn't supposed to love me. I wasn't supposed to love him back.

It was only supposed to be pretend between us, and even if I'd started to feel more for him, the thought that he reciprocated terrified me. The wedding was in a few days, and if he went the same way as my other lovers...no, I pushed that thought away. I couldn't face it, not yet, not like this.

"I want to be good," I murmured. "I want to be good for you."

He growled and wrapped his arms around my ass, holding me to him as he stood. He flipped me around so I was kneeling on the throne, my arms along the seat back, my knees on the cushion. With no preamble, he grabbed my hips and shoved inside me. It was hard and deep and I surged forward, almost unable to hold myself still.

"You better hang on, you Caputi slut," he snarled, suddenly right at my ear. "This isn't going to be soft and slow."

The slicing sound of a fleshy slap went through the room before the fiery burn zinged up my right side. He'd spanked me, fucking me rough, digging his fingernails into the injury. He did it to the other side, another vicious smack before repeating the process again and again. I arched into the pain because I deserved it, didn't I? Here I was, married to an MC president, trying to convince myself that loving each other was the worst thing that could happen. This marriage would never be about that, no matter how much we tried to make it otherwise. But how could it be pretend when all I wanted in the world was him?

He grabbed my hair again and tugged, forcing me to arch as he rutted me into the chair.

"That's right, you take that Rose cock like the little whore you are," he said. "My whore. My slut. *My wife.* Mine. All fucking mine." The filth went on until I couldn't stand it.

The dam finally broke inside me, a tumult of ecstasy and nerves sparking into a frenzy. I screamed, my climax yanking me under its tremendous weight. The world stopped spinning. Everything wrong had been set right. My mind went blank and rebooted like a broken computer, and when I finally drew a long, deep inhale, Roman had wrapped his arms around me, holding me up while he jerked and moaned and came deep inside me.

"Can't you see?" he cooed, tenderly kissing the side of my neck and ear. "This is more than pretend now. It has been for a while. I love you, Julia. *I love you.*"

Those three little words dumped ice water on the whole thing. He'd been building up to it through the entire scene.

Oh God. This is real. He thinks this is real.

And so do I.

He grabbed my left hand and held up my third finger, sliding a beautiful ruby ring over the knuckle. It was encased in diamonds, perfectly gaudy and showy and mesmerizing. I wanted to rip it off and throw it at his head. I wanted to wear it forever and be buried with it at the end of my days.

"Roman," I said, my voice breaking as my chest cracked open. I couldn't accept it. I shouldn't *want* to accept it. "I'm sorry."

Whatever response he'd been expecting, that wasn't it. His arms dropped as he stepped away. His cock slid out of me, leaving a cold, wet mess and a trail of cum down the inside of my thigh. When I turned to step off the throne, he blinked and shook his head, his face ashen, his eyebrows halfway up his forehead.

"You're sorry?" he said. "For what?"

"I...um..." I swallowed against a painfully parched throat. "I can't do this."

He seemed not to know how to process that. "Can't do what?"

"This." I gestured to the ring, to him, to the whole thing. "I don't... I'm not capable..."

I don't love you.

I tried to say the words, but they tasted like garbage because they weren't true. I did love him. I knew I did, and I had for a while, and I was a stupid girl who couldn't accept I might be allowed to have something good and true and amazing. If I said it out loud, if I admitted it to him, he would fall at the hands of my family, and it would kill me. I couldn't live through that again.

My eyes burned as tears bubbled at the corners, streaming down my cheeks. This time, it wasn't from gagging on him, but from suffocating under the weight of my own blindness.

"This isn't supposed to be real," I snapped as I gathered my dress from the ground and slipped it over my head.

"Julia, wait," Roman said, trying to stop me. He put his hands on my shoulders, but I shoved him back, swallowing a sob as I grabbed my purse from the floor.

"Julia—" He came toward me again, but I already had my knife in my hand, holding it out to him.

"No," I shouted.

"Is that supposed to scare me?" Roman looked down at the blade before glancing up at me again, holding his hands out to either side. "I'd get stabbed a million times to get to you, little wife. There's no running from me now."

"Is that supposed to scare *me?*" I scoffed. "Mercutio."

With that, I turned toward the door and stomped down the hallway, taking the stairs two at a time until I was on the ground floor.

"Hey, Jules," Hollywood said, pulling the rope aside as I passed. Then, he caught sight of my face and his bright smile dropped. "You all right?"

"Julia, wait!" Roman said, racing after me.

"Leave me alone, Roman." I reached for my phone and called my brother. He picked up after the second ring, and while I was trying to get a ride out of there, I heard Hollywood wrestling Roman behind me.

"You know the rules, brother," Hollywood said. "She said leave her alone. Let her be. Or I'll be forced to get your sister."

With one last look at my husband, I wiped the tears from my cheeks and stumbled out into the humid August night.

20

JULIA

"**D**o I need to kill him?" Leo asked, sitting across from me at the dining room table in his kitchen. He'd come to the Beacon personally to pick me up two nights ago, and I'd refused to talk more about it. Now, he demanded an explanation, and I didn't know how to tell him it was my fault.

"No," I said. "He didn't do anything."

My brother narrowed his eyes and drummed his fingers on the table while he took a sip of coffee. The glint of the silver on his rings reminded me of the monstrosity on my left third finger, the one I secretly loved, the one I hadn't taken off yet.

"Then why are you here?" Leo raised his eyebrows. "Two weeks ago, you were keeping me awake all night. Now you won't take his calls?"

"How do you know I won't take his calls?"

Leo snorted. "He asks about you when I go to the clubhouse."

That made the sinking feeling in my gut turn to lead, and tears built in the corners of my eyes again. I'd been crying for two whole days, and I felt so foolish.

I *did* love him, and being without him, even for only forty-eight hours, had carved out a giant chunk out of my heart. I'd gotten used to sleeping next to him, his massive arms holding me through my darkest dreams. Without him, they came back with a vengeance. I didn't know how much I needed him until he was gone, and it was all my fault. My stomach had soured, and I'd done nothing but cry and vomit since I left.

"*Mia sorella.*" Leo reached across the table and grabbed my hand, squeezing it tenderly. "You look terrible. *He* looks terrible. Tell me what's going on so I know whether to change our plans. If I need to kill all the Roses, that is a different conversation with our uncles."

"No, we don't need to do that," I said. "It's nothing serious, Leo, honestly."

"If it's not that serious, tell me. Let me share this burden with you."

I took a deep breath. "You'll think it's stupid."

"Probably," he said with a laugh. "Tell me anyway."

"He told me he loved me," I said.

Leo raised his eyebrows, waiting for me to go on. When I didn't, he twisted his features in confusion. "Do you think he was lying?"

"No," I said, sniffling while I wiped my face. "He meant it. He gave me this beautiful ring." I showed it to my brother.

"Julia," he said with a small chuckle. "What are you doing?"

"It wasn't supposed to be like this," I said. "Titus says Gabriella is bringing all her allies. We'll be outnumbered. He'll get shot. He'll die."

"You don't know that," Leo said.

"Hugo," I said. "Vittori. They all died because of me."

"Vittori died as a result of our father," he said. "Hugo was because of Gabriella."

"Because I loved them," I said. "I loved them and they died."

Leo took a deep breath and grabbed my hands again, holding them with both of his. "You must stop this madness. You're married to him, and there's no changing that."

"I can live here," I said.

Leo laughed harder, and I had to physically restrain myself from slapping him. "No."

"What? Why?" I couldn't believe this. My brother was my most trusted adviser, my best friend. Would he not have me?

"Because after the wedding, I'm moving back to our home and *you* will go back to your husband. You signed a contract saying you would live with him."

My cheeks burned because he was right. That was something we'd had to agree upon.

"He will keep you safe."

"Leo," I said, shaking my head, blinking against my blurry vision. "I'm in love with him, too."

"That's wonderful," he said, and I sobbed harder. He stood and walked over to me, scooting the chair by my side so he could wrap his arms around me. "Why are you crying?"

"If I love him and he dies, I don't know what I'll do. Any man I love ends up in the ground. Call it fate, call it karma, but our family is cursed. You know this."

"Tsk. Stop being so superstitious." He sucked in air through his teeth and grabbed my face, holding it up so I had to look at him. "I would not have allowed you to marry him if I thought that."

I furrowed my brows, confused. "What?"

"He is the leader of a pack of wolves," he said. "The king of lions. If he's in love with you, he would walk through fire to get to you. I know this because I am the same way. The Caputis and the Roses are two sides of the same coin."

I bit back another sob as my brother wiped the tears off my cheeks.

"They are rough around the edges and ride motorcycles and dress in leather, but they have a code similar to ours. We do not allow disrespect. We do not allow treachery or libel. And we protect our women. They protect us."

"What happens if I lose him?" I said. "I won't survive it."

"Yes, you will," he said. "Because you are Julia Caputi, and you have survived this far."

I hugged my brother so tight I thought I might suffocate him, but he only squeezed me back just as hard.

"Come with me to the clubhouse tonight," he said. "All of the chapters have rallied. They need to see you two together. They need to know your marriage is strong."

I took a deep breath and nodded, my stomach churning at the thought of seeing my husband again after the way I'd left things. But I could pretend. I'd been doing it this long. I could put up my guard and continue to keep him safe.

Tires crunched on the driveway outside, and Leo broke away to check it out. His bodyguards poked their heads inside to alert us that our uncles had arrived. I swiped under my eyes again and took a deep breath to freshen myself before facing these zions of Caputi power.

"And for the love of all my sanity, and yours, stop with this cursed bloodline nonsense. Roman is not Hugo or Vittori. You are allowed to love him," Leo said before turning toward the door and opening his arms. "Sulli! Frankie!"

I glanced up at the men in front of my brother. Uncle Sulli was my father's cousin on his mother's side, practically a brother to Giuseppe Caputi and an uncle to me and Leo. Uncle Frankie was Chesco's father and my father's younger brother. The Caputi resemblance was uncanny. All of us had deep-tanned skin and dark brown hair. We'd all inherited the Caputi nose, even Chesco, who came in behind his father and pulled me into a hug.

"Leo," Sulli said. "It's good to see you sober and healthy."

"Thank you," Leo said, gesturing to the living room. "Please, come in. Get comfortable. Can we get you anything to drink? I don't keep scotch in the house, but I can send—"

"Water would be great," Frankie said.

Chesco helped me get the glasses while Leo, Sulli, and Frankie went into the other room.

"Did you talk to him?" I asked my cousin, keeping my voice low so the other men didn't hear.

"Of course," he said. "Otherwise, we wouldn't be here."

"Was he agreeable?"

"Define agreeable." Chesco winked, grabbed the water bottle with one hand, and three glasses with the other before walking into the living room with our family. I followed behind him with the rest.

"Getting rid of Gabriella will be harder than simply rooting her out," Sulli said.

I bit back my surprise. They'd jumped right into business. Usually, my family liked to beat around the bush until the cigars were lit and the scotch was half gone. Since this was a sober event, perhaps they'd decided to cut right to the chase.

"But you agree she does need to be removed," Leo said. "As Giuseppe's only surviving son, that honor falls to me."

Frankie tsked and leaned back on the sofa, taking a drink of the water after I handed it to him. "That's if Julian were still alive."

I swallowed down the wave of shame and grief that usually accompanied the mention of our elder brother. Alba's husband, KC, had killed him in defense of his sister, and if he hadn't, Julian likely would have killed both of them. We needed to end this once and for all.

"Well, he's not. And I'm all we've got," Leo said.

"Benito and Giuseppe have two remaining brothers," Frankie said. "One of them is sitting in this room."

"And numerous cousins," Sulli added.

"You're both itching for retirement," Leo said with a scowl. "You have been for years. You don't want this action."

I took a hesitant drink of water as another wave of nausea rolled through me. I tried to focus on the conversation, especially when it veered toward the wedding arrangements.

"Everything is set," I said. "My final fitting is tomorrow. The cake, the rings, all of it has been completed. We're just waiting for the guest of honor."

"How many people will be there?" Sulli said.

"How many of Gabriella's associates are planning to come?" Leo cut in, answering for me.

Sulli and Frankie exchanged a look, one that said so much without saying anything at all. They still weren't sure about this alliance. They had spent a lot longer fighting the Roses and had lost more because of it.

"We need to focus on expanding our business," Chesco added. "Letting bygones be bygones. I thirst for Rose blood as much as any respectable Caputi. But we have more important things to worry about."

Sulli sighed and Frankie nodded, seeming to agree with that.

"Sulli, you married a Romano for a family alliance when they came poaching on our territory," I said. "How many of your cousins did Dean Romano kill personally?"

Sulli shook his head. "Too many, but you're right. Now, he's one of my best friends."

That might be hyperbole because I wasn't sure Sulli had *any* friends, but I dropped it.

"And Frankie," I said. "You planned to marry Chesco to a Chekov to keep the Russians from snooping into our business with the cartel."

"God, don't remind me," Chesco said, rolling his eyes.

"Our family has settled disputes far greater than this before," I said. "The Roses are under new leadership. It's time we do the same. We can accomplish so much more if we work together. Leo has the network, the support, and the mindset to do that."

Sulli and Frankie looked at each other once more before settling their combined stares on me.

"We will support him," Frankie said.

Leo smiled and leaned back in his seat.

"As long as you help him," Sulli added.

"What?" I said at the same time Leo added a quick, "Of course."

They wanted *me* to help him? I would admit, of the two of us, I'd always been the brains behind the operation. Even when Julian was alive and we were children, I'd always come up with good ideas and they executed them. What were the Caputi brothers without their brilliant sister?

"Julia is going nowhere," Leo said, winking at me. "She's the queen of the Roses, the link between our new alliance."

I tried not to let my surprise show, but of course. I could no more do this without Leo than he could do it without me. We'd been together all our lives, and now that we had our uncles on our side, we talked about next steps. Despite loving Gabriella as a sister, Frankie and Sulli both agreed her time at the helm was at an end. There was always the possibility they were lying to us, purposely setting us up only to pull the rug out from under us at the wedding. But why would they do that?

They had nothing to gain. They already had Gabriella's loyalty. Even meeting with us would cause her wrath. With them on board, we now had most of the family. The Morellis, the Vitales, and the Romanos would follow suit, as would the underbosses. We had four days to get everything else settled before the wedding, and after that, we would bring in a new world for both the Caputis and the Roses.

Several hours later, after everything had been negotiated and defined, we said goodbye to our uncles and prepared for the next phase. Leo eyed me with that mix of skepticism and judgment, but I ignored him. I could admit I'd been too traumatized by what happened to me before to come to grips with how my new situation might be different. My feelings for Roman were deep and complicated, and even if I'd grown up in a cursed family, perhaps we might make it out of this after all.

I went upstairs to my room and checked my phone, but Roman hadn't contacted me today. I debated biting the bullet and calling him, but what could I say? He deserved an explanation, but that would be better in person. I had sixteen texts from Della, each becoming more frantic.

Della: Gabriella is getting restless. I think she knows something's up.

Della: Did you meet with Sulli and Frankie?

Della: Jules, I need your help.

Leo and Roman had told me not to give up the game, to continue like nothing had happened. But it pained me to do it. She was my best friend, my cousin, and she betrayed me. She was *still* betraying me. It had been a hard lesson to learn that family didn't mean blood, and blood didn't mean family. But learned it, I had.

Blood of the covenant is thicker than water of the womb.

My father used to say that, but only recently had I learned the weight of its true meaning. Sighing, I replied to her, trying to be as nonchalant and as cryptic as I could. Then, I scrolled to Roman's name in my contact list and hovered my finger over the green button to call him. But I hesitated because once I relented to this ache in my heart, there would be no going back.

How was I supposed to keep him safe when I loved him entirely too much for anyone's good?

21

BEAR

The clubhouse was packed tonight, everyone having made the trip for my wedding. We hosted three chapters, damn near two hundred and fifty men, and half of them were here to party. It was the calm before the storm.

I made the rounds like my father usually did. I checked in with the other presidents to ensure they were settled.

"We're ready to tear some Caputi heads apart," Titan said, laughing with a few of his other New England SRMC brothers.

Lizard, the president from North Carolina, clapped me on the shoulder and thanked me for the invitation. "The boys are always thirsty for enemy blood."

I caught up with as many of the visiting brothers as I could before going around to my own chapter, forgoing the tightness in my chest to make sure they all knew I still had their backs.

After killing the traitors so viciously, something had shifted in the atmosphere. The undercurrent of tension that had been there for months had dissipated. But just because it was over didn't mean we were in the clear. Switch was still looking for the ones that had escaped. They could come back any time and hit us harder than before. I wouldn't be able to truly rest until they were all gone.

"We're gonna take her down, brother," I said to Hollister. When Gabriella had attacked us five months ago, she'd tried to shoot Hollister in the head. Her hand jerked at the last second, skimming the top of his skull rather than going through it. He'd been in the ICU for weeks afterward, but now that he was back, he had the taste of Caputi blood on his tongue.

"We better," he said. "This has gone on too long."

"No fucking shit." I joked with him and his brother, Wheels, for a few minutes before moving to KC, Hollywood, Thor, and Saint. They sat on the couches at the back of the room, clearly deep in conversation while they pretended to play poker on the coffee table.

"Hey, there he is," KC said, clapping my hand when I got close enough.

"Heard you already chased your old lady away," Saint said.

"That didn't take long," Thor added with a teasing laugh.

"We're...uh...taking a breather." I cleared my throat and raised an eyebrow.

"It didn't look like a breather," Hollywood said.

I grimaced and took a sip of beer, trying to ignore the ache in the center of my chest at the mention of her. It had been there the entire time she'd avoided me, and the more we were separated, the more my skin shrunk around my bones. Her absence chafed, and that only reconfirmed what I'd told her. I'd never felt this way about anyone before, much less a romantic relationship. I missed her shitty cooking and her biting insults. I missed the way her eyes blinked open in the morning and that adorable pout on her lips. I missed her strong presence and the air of invincibility she carried with her no matter where she went.

"Enough," I snapped. "My relationship with my wife is none of your fucking concern."

Hollywood smirked, and Thor raised his eyebrows, seemingly surprised by the roughness in my tone.

"Is everything in place for the ceremony?" I asked.

"Uh-huh," KC said, inhaling his cigarette. "All the fun and games have been unloaded."

He meant the guns and heavy artillery. Gabriella wouldn't go down without a fight, and if she brought as many of her goons as we thought she would, we needed the extra weapons.

"What about Aris and Crow?" I said, glancing at Thor. He'd been the one in correspondence with their lawyers. As Sarge, it was his duty to get our guys out of the pen, if he could. "How are things going?"

Thor sighed and ran his hands back through his long, dark blond hair, tying it in a thick pink scrunchie. "Not good. The evidence is overwhelming. Jordan says she spoke to you? What'd she say?"

"She wants Crow to snitch on the Caputis in exchange for a deal," I said. "But my old man isn't the type to yap. That's what I told her."

KC nodded. "She's gonna get him killed."

"I told her to look closer to home. Someone in the pigpen is working with them. How did they know we'd be distracted when they came to raid us?" I suspected her partner, Detective Dickface or whatever his name was.

"She might have mentioned that," Thor said. "Said she wanted *you* to spill the beans instead."

I rolled my eyes and scoffed. "Hell would freeze over first."

Thor snorted and KC laughed.

"I told her that, too," I said.

"Hey, shithead!" Verona said from behind the bar. I glanced over at her, surprised when she was looking at me. "Yeah, you!"

Hollywood whistled a low, threatening noise. "You've done it now. Good luck, brother."

Sighing and rubbing at the back of my neck, I headed over to her.

"What the fuck did you do to your wife?" V said, shoving at my shoulder with that stereotypical little sister glare in her violet eyes. "Do I have to cut off your balls?"

Goddamn, would I get my ass chapped by everyone in this fucking club?

Despite my annoyance, my sister demanded an explanation, her hands on her hips, stamping her foot like I was an unruly youth.

"V, lay off him," our brother, Pollux, said, coming up next to me to throw an arm over my shoulders. "He's got enough on his plate without your harassment."

"He sent his submissive *running* from my club," she said. "If it weren't for Hollywood defending you, I would ban you from coming back AND THEN I would cut off your balls."

"I didn't hurt her," I said. "Not like that."

Truthfully, I didn't know what I'd done to upset her. I'd told her I loved her, that I was happy we would have to spend the rest of our lives together. The look of panic in her eyes was definitely *not* the reaction I'd been expecting. Not that I thought she would swoon and confess her undying loyalty, but I didn't mean to terrify the poor woman.

"Then. What. Did. You. Do?" V growled the words through her teeth, maybe preparing to lunge at my throat and tear it from my head.

"I overstepped a boundary I didn't know she had," I said, glancing sidelong at Pollux, and finally Castor, as he came to the other side. "She called her safeword, and she left."

My sister narrowed her eyes and pursed her lips. "I'm going to talk to her, and if she tells me something different, rest assured, you *will* be dealt with."

"Bear," Castor said, flipping open his computer. "We've got a problem."

I took a deep breath and sighed as he explained the situation.

"Even though the Kings of Carnage said they wanted nothing to do with us, they're on Caputi property," he explained. "I can't get a good read on how many people total. But if she called in the cavalry, we could be outnumbered."

I pinched the bridge of my nose and tried not to panic. Letting my fear run wild would help no one, especially not the Roses. We only had four days until the wedding. What the fuck we were going to do?

We had our closest chapters here, but they weren't the only Roses in the country or the only ones that could make it here in time.

"Call Lore," I said. "Find out where he is. If he's still out west, tell him to stop in Indiana. We're gonna call her bluff."

Castor nodded and glanced at Pollux and V before raising an eyebrow back at me. "Are you okay?"

"Besides our sister's perpetual harassment, I'm fine."

"His wife is avoiding him," V said. "He needs to go crawling back with his tail between his legs, but *his pride* won't let him."

I snarled and glared at my sister.

"Is the alliance in jeopardy?" Castor said. "Do you need me to tap her phone or something?"

"No," I roared, slamming my hands down on the bar top, startling the twins but making V double down. She put her hands out on the granite and tilted her head at me. "All of you, drop it. This is hard enough without your fucking pestering."

V sneered and walked away, finding Hollywood on the other side of the clubhouse. Castor grabbed my shoulder and looked at Pollux before heading off himself. It was the younger twin that stuck around.

"Relationships are a pain in the dick, huh?" He laughed and clinked his beer against mine. Earlier this year, he'd been in the hospital after an explosion at the Beacon. He'd become infatuated with one of the nurses, a young redhead named Phoebe. After his relentless flirting, she finally agreed to go out with him, but I wasn't sure how much about our family he'd told her.

"No kidding," I said.

"It's too close to the wedding for things to fall apart now," Pollux said.

"We're already married," I said, resigned. "And part of our contract said we couldn't get divorced. We have to live happily never after, even if she hates me."

Pollux winced. "Listen, it's not my place to say anything, and maybe I should keep my fucking mouth shut, but brother...she's been good for you."

I furrowed my brows, my stomach clenching harder.

"All my life, you've been holding us together," he said. "Especially after Mom died and Dad fell apart. It was *you* signing off on my homework and permission slips. It was *you* giving me lunch money."

I shifted uncomfortably, not sure where this was going.

"I've never seen you happy, truly happy," he said. "I thought it was impossible for someone with the weight of all this on their shoulders." He gestured around to the club and the brothers and all of the bullshit that came with it. "But then she came along."

"Brother," I started, the hole in my chest gaping, splitting open even more.

"Just let me say it," Pollux continued, his bright brown eyes imploring me to shut the fuck up. So I did, deciding to hear him out. Of the twins, Pollux had always been the quieter one, the less ostentatious. I figured if he had something to get off his chest, I might as well hear him out. "At first, I could tell it was awkward between you. She sat out here on her phone and you pretended she didn't exist. But then something changed, and you both decided to be partners."

I gulped and blinked back the burning in my eyes.

It was pretend. All of it—fake, a farce, a charade. Pretend.

It wasn't supposed to be real.

"I'd never seen you look at anyone how you looked at her. Like the world had been in black-and-white until you found her, and now, vivid neon." Pollux whistled and shook his head. "And she looks at you the same way."

"She doesn't look at anyone like that," I said.

"Pfft, of course she doesn't want you to see it," he said. "She seems like the type of person to keep her heart guarded. But she softens around you, like she can trust you, like you are the only one she *can* trust."

Pollux kept talking, but something clicked, some kind of knowing I hadn't put together before. Julia had confessed to losing everybody she'd ever loved, everybody she'd let get close. She'd agreed to all of this in the first place because she wanted peace; she wanted that bloodshed to stop. What was the name of the man Gabriella had taken out? Hugo? And before that, her boyfriend in high school.

Did she think I was just another man she'd ultimately lose? If she let me in, truly allowed herself to open up to me, was she afraid she'd lose me? Christ, I was planning a massacre at our wedding.

I'd been such a fucking idiot.

"You need to fix it with her," Pollux said, drawing me back to the present. "Whatever it is, tell her you're sorry. You'll never get another opportunity like this."

"You know what, brother?" I grabbed his shoulder and pulled him into half a hug. "You're fucking right."

"What? Really?" Pollux blinked.

"Yep." I stood from the barstool and walked over to Alba and Ru, a plan forming. They'd been with Roses for a long time. If anyone could talk sense into her, it would be them. I figured Julia could use the support, and lord knew she didn't have much of that these days.

After that, I texted my brother-in-law.

Me: Is she okay? Is she safe?

Leo: Yes, she's safe. But she is more stubborn than I am.

Me: Is she coming tonight?

Leo: We are almost there.

I cracked my neck and prepared myself to see her. It had only been two days, but that seemed like an eternity compared to how used I'd gotten to having her around.

And when the doors opened to reveal the Caputi alliance, I took a deep inhale and braced myself for her ire.

22

JULIA

When we got to the clubhouse, I felt his hot gaze on me immediately. Like a tractor beam from some alien ship, he reeled me in, coercing me toward him against my will. I held still, choosing instead to walk toward the MC princesses currently at the pool table.

Leo and Chesco greeted the other SRMC members, shaking hands with Roman and KC before laughing at whatever Hollywood said. I sternly avoided my husband, choosing the safer route of Alba and Ru, who looked even more like sisters with their hair bundled on top of their heads.

"Hello, cousin," Alba said, hugging me. "It's good to see you."

"You too," I said. "I apologize for not being around recently."

"I don't blame you," Ru cut in. "Whatever Bear did, he probably deserved your wrath."

I was about to explain how it was my fault, that I'd let the sins from my family's past catch up to me.

"There you are," Verona said, coming up to put an arm over my shoulders. "Now, tell me. Do I need to kill my brother?"

"No," I said, grinning at these amazing women. "It's me. I...I made a stupid mistake."

Alba laughed and Ru shook her head, her ice-blue eyes narrowing at me.

"Listen," Ru said, "we're well versed in these alpha assholes. We know how it goes."

"They're obsessed with you," Alba said. "They'll kill for you. You run and he chases. Trust me, that's the way this story ends. Selene told me that years ago, back when KC and I first started dating. Bear is the same way."

"But sometimes, they can be over the top. That's when you smack them back down to reality," V said. "Or flog them. Whatever you're into."

Ru and Alba laughed while V winked, but I cleared my throat and rubbed at the heat on the back of my neck, knowing he hadn't come after me yet. But the way his eyes tracked me from the other side of the room said he would only tolerate this separation for so long.

"Are you okay?" Ru rubbed my shoulder in a comforting embrace. "Are you ready for the wedding?"

I nodded, even though my anxiety had never been higher. This was madness. This was chaos. We were inviting bloodshed, knowing what would happen. The avalanche was rolling now, picking up steam, and there'd be no stopping it when it descended on our little village.

"Are you still planning to come over the morning of?"

Alba nodded. "Of course. I'm happy to help you get ready."

It sounded normal, as if I really were a blushing bride preparing for my first night as a married woman. Never mind I'd been legally a Montgomery for months now. Never mind the wedding was a ruse.

"It'll be a good distraction from getting my dad out of the pen," Ru said.

"Same," V added.

"How's all that going?"

Ru and V talked about their struggles of trying to find decent legal help, and while the club's lawyer had done well thus far, they'd need a lot more than they could afford.

"We're planning a fundraiser at the Beacon in a few weeks," Ru said. "Make sure you and Bear come, yeah?"

I nodded. "Okay."

"All right, you fucking heathens," KC called from the entrance to the back room. "It's time for church." He winked at Alba, who blushed and brushed a stray piece of hair behind her ear. Hollywood, Saint, Thor, and the others passed us to head inside, but I remained rooted to the spot. I didn't know if I'd be welcomed, not after what had happened. Certainly, I knew the itinerary the best. I'd heard more concrete details from Titus this morning, but would Roman want me? If he did, I certainly didn't deserve it.

Before I could think too much about it, a firm hand grabbed my elbow and nudged me along.

"Let's go, little wife," Roman said, nodding ahead. "We only need to pretend for a few more days." He whispered the last bit in my ear, and the heat of his breath shot down that side of my body. "Then you can go back to hating me as much as you want."

I winced as the lie hit me in the stomach. Of course, that was what he thought. I hadn't given him any reason to think otherwise, but I couldn't deal with that now. We walked into the back room where the leaders and other officers from the visiting Roses stood in their cuts, waiting to hear what we had planned for the wedding. They talked among themselves, the rowdy sounds of mindless chatter drowning out my turbulent thoughts. I steeled my jaw and straightened my shoulders, walking like I had the confidence of every man in this room. Even if there was tension between my husband and me, none of them needed to know it.

No, we were the king and queen of this mess, and we'd have to lead the kingdom through it.

Roman walked to the head of the Steel Roses table, nodding at my brother and Chesco as he went. When we got there, KC banged his rings on the table loud enough to reverberate over the gruff conversation.

"All you motherfuckers, listen up! Church is in session!" KC clapped to punctuate his announcement, and all the talking died down to a rumble and finally to silence.

Roman took a deep breath and glanced around, dropping his hold on my elbow to my fingers, gripping my palm in his.

"Thank you all for coming," he said. "Whether you're a part of the Madison County chapter or from out of town, your support is invaluable to our cause."

Rounds of clapping came from everywhere, hoops of encouragement echoing through me.

"For over four decades, the war has raged on between the Roses and the Caputis," Roman started, glancing at all in attendance. "It started because of love, because of supposed slights one side may have done to the other. A few days from now, it will end the same way."

My husband took my hand and pulled me closer, wrapping an arm around my waist so our bodies were aligned from shoulder to hip. His clean, masculine scent assaulted me, and I tried not to let my memories override the seriousness of the situation. I went back to the first time I met him, how I thought he was evil, but realized I could probably live with that. I thought of when he pulled me into his lap at his dining room table and tilted my face toward his to take my lips with careful deliberation. How I'd shivered in his embrace. I thought of the way he'd made love to me in Leo's guest bed and how he'd worshipped me at the Beacon before demanding the same from me.

I had long ago started to love him, even if I couldn't admit it, even if it terrified me.

"Between Julia, Leo, and their cousin, Chesco, we've managed to secure enough of an alliance within the Caputi family to bring a ceasefire to the violence."

Another round of applause forced pride to swell in my chest, making my heart beat faster.

"I want to thank Copter, Lizard, and Titan." He gestured to the men standing on either side of the table at the other end, all wearing cuts that proclaimed them as presidents of their chapters. "Without your alliance, we wouldn't stand a chance."

After a nod to both of them, Roman went through the logistics of the wedding day. We would meet at the Roses' farmhouse on the fringes of Madison County—close enough to DC to draw out the Caputis, but far enough away to keep the local PD from being too interested. The ceremony would start at noon with the reception right afterward. The food, the flowers, the cake, all of the other pretenses of a real wedding would be brought and set up the day before, making it easy for the rest of the club to show up the day of and complete the setup. The timing would have to be critical because they wanted the women and serving staff on their way to safety before the bullets started raining.

It was lucky we were having the wedding at a farm with wide open spaces and few avenues for collateral damage.

Once Gabriella showed herself, Leo would take her out and position himself as the new head of family. Anyone who didn't side with him would meet the same fate. We used to think that any drop of Caputi blood spilled was a waste, a blight on our honorable name. But now, we had to make a few exceptions for the greater good.

The little girl inside lamented the thought of all my wedding plans gone to waste. How many times had Della and I dressed up in our mothers' oversize gowns and pretended to marry the man of our dreams? How many times had I thought I'd get here with Vittori or Hugo?

I wouldn't even get a real wedding with my real husband.

Once the timetable had been decided and everyone knew what they were going to do, Roman gave the men one last pep talk.

"This could very well be our last few nights alive," he said. "Don't fucking waste it."

The crowd shouted and clapped their enthusiasm, and when KC dismissed them all to party, I stayed by Roman's side as everyone filed out. Leo hugged me before he went with them, and Chesco eyed my husband with a raised eyebrow as he wrapped his arms around me in a fraternal squeeze.

"If you need me to kill him, the safeword is Funky Town." My cousin kissed my cheek as he pulled away.

I laughed and rolled my eyes. "Have a nice night, Chesco."

"Uh-huh." He tsked his teeth at Roman and sauntered back into the front room.

I'd been ready to leave as well, but my husband grabbed my bicep to stop me, and I froze, my pulse racing. I knew what would happen now. He'd given me two days, and in his estimation, that was likely too much.

"You want this door closed, prez?" one of the prospects asked, holding the sliding barn door leading to the rest of the clubhouse.

"Yes, thank you," Roman replied, and the deep tenor of his tone reminded me this wasn't a game, not anymore. Nor was it pretend.

"They'll kill for you," Alba had said. *"You run and he chases. Trust me, that's the way this story ends."*

"Where do you think you're going, little wife?" Roman asked, moving to stand behind me, trapping me between his massive body and the wooden table.

23

JULIA

I gulped and turned to face him, steeling myself for this inevitable face-off. "Roman, I—"

"Shh," he hissed, cutting me off. "I know."

My jaw hung open, and I furrowed my brows. "You know?"

"Of course." He raised an eyebrow and nodded. "You're about to tell me how sorry you are, how much you regret running out on me. You're about to get on your knees and plead for my forgiveness."

Suddenly, the burning shame in my chest gave way to all-out gall. *Get on my knees? Plead for forgiveness?*

Who did he think he was?

I'd been trying to keep him safe. By ensuring we were emotionally detached from each other, he wouldn't become a way for my family to control me, to humiliate me, or cause either of us pain. He didn't know the extent of how terrible the Caputis were.

"I beg your pardon," I said, crossing my arms in clear defiance.

"Good. Go on then. Beg." Roman smirked, his eyes darkening as he dragged a finger up my arm to my shoulder and over the thin strap of my dress. "Beg for my attention. Beg me to forgive you for leaving me at the Beacon, for not answering my calls."

His audacity and arrogance made me equally attracted to him

and frustrated with him. I didn't know whether I wanted to obey or stab him in the face.

"You said you wanted space." His gaze flicked to mine. "You called the safeword and ran away from me."

"After you said you loved me," I snapped. "Don't you remember this isn't about love? This is pretend."

"Hmm." He nodded and crowded me against the table, running his hand over my clavicle to my throat, his cool metal rings biting into my skin as he flattened his palm over the divot at the base of my neck. "Pretend."

"Yes," I reiterated, but even then, my shaking voice betrayed me. It hadn't been pretend in a long time, not for him, and certainly not for me. Still, I couldn't back down. If I admitted it, if I let him in, this would end in heartache. I knew it. I felt it in my gut.

He moved even closer, forcing me to sit on the table to avoid getting caught in his trap. And once my legs were spread, he quickly positioned himself between them.

"When you wear your pretty lingerie and make me dinner wearing nothing else, that's pretend?" Roman's hold on me tightened as he coasted his palm up my windpipe to just under my jaw, holding my head right where he wanted it. I shivered under his control, seeing the speeding train going off the rails but knowing I couldn't stop it. I was addicted to him, and since I'd deprived myself of him for two whole days, I now would do anything for a hit.

"Yes," I murmured, ignoring the drop in my belly and the clench between my legs.

"And when you kneel and crawl to me, that's just pretend?" He tilted his hips toward me, brushing the thick ridge behind his jeans up against my throbbing clit.

I moaned out another, "Yes," tilting my head to the side as he leaned into my ear.

"And when you fall apart under me, gushing on my cock, I'm guessing that's pretend as well?"

"None of it's real." It sounded like a lie, even to my own ears, though I'd been desperate to make it a reality.

"Uh-huh." He shifted his hand around to the back of my neck and fisted my hair in a tight grip, yanking my head so I exposed my throat to him. It hurt, but how I loved it. A groan of pure arousal shot out of me. "Oh, my little wife. I adore how your lips form those pretty lies."

"They're not—" I tried to get out my rebuttal, but he pulled me off the table and flipped me around, slamming me down so hard, I nearly winced. My tender breasts ached on the wood, my cheek pulsing with a sharp smack as he held my face to the side.

"Don't you dare lie to me again," he said, leaning over me. The jeans on his thighs pressed up against the bare skin on mine, my dress having hiked up with the movement. Now, I lay exposed to him, my thin lacy underwear doing nothing to conceal just how much I wanted him—wanted this. "Let's see just how much you're pretending, huh?"

One hand held my head down while the other ducked under my hemline and dragged the satin up...up...up over my hips, completely baring me to him. He straightened and glanced down, letting out a laugh that sent the burn of embarrassment cascading through my body and into my cheeks. He dragged two fingers over my panties, from my ass to my clit and back up again, shaking his head.

"Oh, such a lying little wife," he said, shoving my underwear down to my ankles, exposing me to him. "What am I going to do with you?"

I took a deep breath and sighed, knowing I'd been caught. Yes, I still wanted him. I'd always want him. This game, this magic, between us had enchanted me more than I'd ever thought it would. But still, I wouldn't go down without a fight.

"Such a brute," I snarled, trying to shove my way up. He pushed me back down harder.

"Stay still," he growled. "You've denied me for two days, and now you're lying to my face. I should punish you. I should pull you over my knee and edge you until you can't walk. In fact—" The sound of jingling metal and the soft whoosh of leather made me look over my shoulder. He took off his belt and bent it in half, holding it with one hand while he admired the sight of my wet cunt and exposed skin. "I will give you two chances to tell me the truth. You can call your safe-word and I'll let you up, but if you do that and run away again without an explanation, I can assure you any restitution after that will be much...*much*...worse."

He paused, waiting to see what I would say. *Mercutio* hovered on the tip of my tongue, and perhaps I should have said it. Perhaps I should have slowed this down so we could talk about it like reasonable adults, but I deserved the pain.

I deserved to be belted for having run away. I deserved the hurt for going along with this ridiculous marriage. And worst of all, I deserved the agony because I'd had the idiotic idea to fall in love with him in the first place.

"No? Nothing to say?" Roman tightened his hold on my hair.

"Well, go on then," I snarled. "I don't have all fucking night."

The whip of leather through the air preceded a hard, fleshy smack. I heard it before I felt it, and when the bite sizzled up my back and into my legs, I collapsed against the table, all of the fight draining out of me. The belt came down again, this time on the other cheek, and I arched into it, perking my ass toward him, desperate for more. It hurt. He certainly wasn't being gentle, but the sting on the outside had started to evaporate the fire on the inside.

"Such a fucking stubborn woman," Roman sneered through clenched teeth. "I'm your husband. I'm the one you lean on, the one who shares this with you."

Another hit caused another burn, and a huge chunk of my emotional armor split off, landing somewhere near my heart.

"I love you"—another lash, another sting, another moan—"no matter what you do, no matter what happens. I love you. And you don't have to love me, but goddamn it, I won't tolerate dishonesty."

I dug my nails into the wood under me, struggling for purchase, anything to hold on to to keep me grounded, but my fingertips only grasped the burned outline of the SRMC logo. There was nothing, only him and me and the one thing I didn't want to say.

"Tell me, Julia," Roman growled. This time, the belt hit my cunt and I hissed in a gasp, the torture shooting into my gut and down to my toes. It decimated my defenses, cracking them like shattered glass. Any minute now, I'd lose. I could call the safeword, but deep down inside, perhaps I wanted to lose. Like he said, he was supposed to be the one that helped me share this burden.

Would he still love me if he knew what my returned adoration would mean for him? Would he make fun of me for my fears? Would he accept them, welcome them, soothe them?

Sometime around the tenth or eleventh strike, my gasps finally became sobs. The dam inside me broke, and a flood of torment rose inside me.

"I can't lose you," I finally said through heaving cries. "I love you, and I can't lose you."

"There we go," Roman said, dropping the belt before grabbing my shoulders to ease me up. "There we go."

"Fate abhors me." I sucked in air as tears rolled down my cheeks, blurring my vision. "Anyone I've ever loved has died. I'm not meant to be happy. And if you...if fate takes you from me... I can't do that again, Roman. I can't."

"Shh," he said, scooping an arm under my knees so he could pick me up. When he sat in the president's chair, he put me in his lap and hugged me close while I let it all out—all of the weight I'd been carrying for months. It wasn't just the threat of loving and losing him. It was this whole situation. There was no one else who could go up against Gabriella, no one else who knew the family the way I did. If Leo were going to take over the helm, the burden to keep him in line had always and would always rest on my shoulders.

If he went down, I went down. And now, I shared a similar relationship with Roman. Trapped and surrounded by people that didn't trust me, that barely knew me, I'd been playing a high-stakes game of Jenga, praying I didn't accidentally pull out a piece that would topple the whole thing.

The pressure had become unbearable, and I let that all out on Roman's shoulder while he pet my hair and rubbed circles in my back and dried my tears.

"Oh, my love," he said. "*Mia cara, amore mia.*" He whispered other endearments in Italian, muttering something about never leaving me, no matter what happened. "I'm yours, and you're mine, and I will fucking run to the end of the earth to have you. Do you know that? Nothing will separate us. Not Gabriella, not the Caputi family, nothing."

"Everyone I've ever loved has died, Roman," I said. "And you—" The words came out of me now, the whole truth. "No one has ever meant as much to me as you."

He brushed the hair out of my face and wiped my eyes with his thumbs, leaning in to kiss me so tenderly, it almost broke my heart all over again. "We are meant to be, my wife. My love."

I snorted and shook my head. "We're star-crossed."

"Well, fuck the stars," he said, giving me another tender kiss. "And fuck fate. If it wants to take me from you, it'll have to fight like hell. You understand me?"

I nodded and kissed him, wrapping my arm around his neck, delighting in the safety of his hard body and his strong, capable arms.

"You wear my ring," he said. "You have my last name and my entire family. You have everything I am, and I'll be fucking damned if anything, fate or Caputi, is going to stop that."

"I love you, Roman," I said, leaning back to look him in the eye as I said it.

"I love you, Julia." He kissed me again, this time deeper and slower than before. I pushed my hands up his chest to his neck, intertwining my fingers with the hair on the back of his head. At first, we reconnected with gentle pecks and slow licks, but soon we grew more passionate. He picked me up and twisted me around in his lap so I straddled him, my knees on either side of his hips.

He explored my body, grabbing my hips and sliding his palms up to my breasts to cup and knead like he'd never touched me before. I arched into it, opening my lips when his tongue demanded entrance. I wrestled mine against his, and I loved the spark that went through my center, straight to my nipples and cunt. Rolling my pelvis against him, I ground down to find that perfect cock, which had gotten harder since I'd stopped crying.

Roman kissed down my jaw and lapped at my neck, tugging the strap of my dress and bra down to free my breasts. When his greedy mouth found its way there, I leaned back so he had more room to explore.

"Please," I murmured, gripping at his hair, rocking against him in a humiliating frenzy.

"Please, what, my darling wife?" He grinned while he sucked one nipple into his mouth, and lust shot through my veins, mixing with the heady look in his eyes to amp me up.

"Please, fuck me," I said. "Make me yours again. Show me you love me."

"*Mia cara,* I've been showing you that for months now," he said with that devilish smirk. "I'd do anything for you."

He reached between us to unzip his jeans and free his cock, and when he lined himself up at my entrance, I lowered myself down on him all the way. I clenched against the intrusion, at once painful and euphoric, and I stayed there for a moment to adjust. I met his dark eyes, now almost black with his excitement, and I could swear I saw right down to his soul.

It was bright and powerful, just like him, and more importantly, it matched mine.

We truly were made for each other, and even if our story didn't start the way either of us would have wished, I couldn't imagine anyone else completing me so perfectly.

"Tell me again," he said, rocking into me, gripping my hips to guide me.

"I love you," I whispered.

"Again." He leaned in to kiss me while I fucked myself on top of him.

"I love you." I had to say it through fumbled moans as he hit spots inside of me that set my molecules alight.

"Goddamn right, you do." He broke away to kiss down my neck again, pausing at the spot where my neck met my shoulder while he found my clit, rubbing in that expert way only he knew how to do. "Don't ever forget it."

"I won't." My toes dug into the sides of the chair, my knees aching against the hard wooden seat. I'd surely have bruises later, not to mention the swollen parts on my backside, but who cared about that when my husband's beautiful dick made me feel so amazing and fulfilled?

"Good." He lapped over a particularly sensitive spot, and I melted, my muscles tightening, the euphoria inside escalating, amplifying, nearing a breaking point. "Just to make sure you don't forget it..." He sank his teeth into my skin, sucking and biting the flesh on my trapezius muscle.

The pain combined with the pleasure between my legs and I broke apart, submitting to him and my orgasm and this untenable thing between us. I screamed, my entire body tensing, something pouring out of me that I couldn't control. He covered my mouth with his free hand but kept going, kept fucking me while he claimed me with his teeth. It was so primal and territorial that I almost couldn't stand it.

I loved that about him—how much he owned me, how much he protected me and possessed me. Even though I was fucking him, he had complete control over us both.

When I came back into my body, the explosion having ebbed enough for me to refocus on him, he grinned like a demon and wrapped his arms around me to stand. He carried me to the table and laid me down on top of it, my legs wrapped around his waist, his cock still buried deep inside me.

"Are you okay?" he asked, pressing tender kisses to the ache on my neck.

"That was amazing." I could barely think, let alone operate my mouth.

"I think they heard you in Guam." He laughed and leaned over me, holding my shoulders so he could lazily thrust into me in slow pushes that teased me and eased me down from my climax.

My loudness suddenly made me self-conscious, and I bit my bottom lip. "Is that a problem?"

"Fuck no," he said. "Let them hear how much you love me."

I grinned as my skin burned for him.

"Now, hold on. I'm gonna fuck your brains out." My sexy husband smiled, gripped my hips, and did just that.

It was only afterward, once he'd come deep inside me with his head thrown back on his shoulders and that look of rapture on his gorgeous features, that I realized he'd left a hickey on my neck four days before my wedding. A version of me from six months ago would have been appalled. But now, well, I was grateful for a good concealer.

24

BEAR

Even though it was bad luck to see the bride the day of the wedding, I spent that morning fucking Julia like the world might end. Hell, for all I knew, it would.

She explained her beef with fate, and even though I never believed in any of that shit, I couldn't deny that things between us felt karmic in a way nothing ever had before. She was meant to be with me, and I was meant to be with her.

It was why none of my other relationships had turned into anything serious. In a morose sort of way, perhaps that was why all her previous boyfriends met the business end of her family's high expectations.

It was too late to do anything about it. The wheels were already turning and this fucking train was barreling toward the cliffside. Pumping the brakes would do nothing. When I came deep inside her with whispers of love and adoration on my lips, I memorized everything about the moment—the way her hair smelled like flowers and sunshine, the way her dark eyes got impossibly darker when she climaxed, the way her body gripped me like she was trying to pull my soul into hers.

We lay in that bed worshipping each other until we had to get up or risk being late to our own shindig. Worry lines creased her forehead, and even though she tried to hide it, her swollen, puffy eyes told the tale of how much she'd been crying.

"It'll be okay, my love," I said, brushing the hair behind her ear.

She attempted a smile but didn't commit, and that should have forced me to pull her back into my bed, perhaps keep her there all day. Fuck the wedding.

Then, she got up and ran to the bathroom to vomit, and I tried not to take it personally. She said it was wedding-day jitters, and I took her at her word, even as I held her hair and rubbed her back. When she felt better, I helped her gather her things and loaded them into the truck.

By the time we made it to the farm, all of my groomsmen had already shown up, even Hollywood, and that motherfucker would be late to his funeral.

"Well, look at what the dirty, rotten alley cat dragged in," he said, clapping from his spot at the far end of the groom's dressing room. He wore a white T-shirt, his boxers, and nothing else, clearly in the middle of changing into his suit.

"It's about time," Thor said, already dressed. He'd probably been ready to go since five this morning. "I was about to send the cavalry after you."

"It was difficult to leave her," I said, glancing toward the door leading to the bride's suite on the other side of the hall. It wasn't anything fancy, just an old farmhouse that had been converted into a venue for conferences and weddings. The club had owned it for longer than I'd been alive and paid a company to maintain it. I didn't know how to feel about marrying the princess of the Caputi family when a lot of her family members had disappeared in the back forty.

"No kidding," KC said, buttoning up his black shirt. "They're only two rooms away and I'm twitchy as fuck."

I looked to the other side of the room, finding both Castor and Pollux ready to go.

"What do we know?" I asked the computer genius.

He shook his head. "Hard to say. The ones I've got tabs on are moving this way. But I can't get a read on Gabriella."

"She's coming," said a deep voice from the doorway. Leo rubbed his hands together and walked inside, glancing at me and my brothers in various states of undress. "Trust me. She wouldn't miss this opportunity."

"She must know she's walking into a trap." KC finished with his buttons and moved on to the cuffs. "She can't think this ends well for her."

"After the raid earlier this year, she's unhinged," Leo said. "She wants my head so badly, she'll be too overzealous to resist."

"Not to mention the body count," Hollywood added, finally putting on his pants. "She's got two clubs and most of the Caputi army with her."

Leo smirked. "Only until the bosses turn on her."

I took a deep breath and prayed that plan held firm. I'd imagined this ending a thousand different ways, and in most of them, the bosses turned on us at the last minute and killed everyone I loved.

"It's almost time," Leo said, patting me on the back. "I'm going to go be with my sister. Try to enjoy yourself, huh? It is your wedding. You'll only get one."

I sighed as he walked away because, technically, I was already married to the bride, even if we hadn't proclaimed our vows in front of an audience yet. I changed into my suit while the rest of my brothers made light of the situation, but an undercurrent of tension boiled between us, all nerves and anticipation of the battle to come. Even though we'd planned for it by wearing Kevlar under our shirts, today would be bloody and violent, and at the end, I prayed we got out of it with everyone we had going into it.

Fifteen minutes before the ceremony was supposed to start, my groomsmen and I walked downstairs and through the kitchen to the backyard. Rows of chairs had been lined up on either side with an archway at the head, just in front of a view of the mountains in the distance. It truly was a beautiful spot to get married, and I lamented that today would not be about me proclaiming my undying love for my new wife.

Sure, that was a piece of it, but like so much about my union with Julia, the ceremony would be fake, a ruse meant only to draw the villain out of hiding so we could take her down once and for all.

"How ya feeling?" KC asked, grabbing my shoulder in a fraternal squeeze.

I swallowed my nausea and forced myself to grin. "All right. How about you?"

He laughed. "You've always been a shitty liar."

"Truthfully?" I grimaced and rubbed my fingers over my tired eyes. "I'm pissed my dad can't be here."

KC's features fell, and he nodded, wrapping an arm over my neck to pull me in for a sideways hug. "He would if he could; you know that."

"Of course." But if there ever were a day to regret his being locked up, it would be the day I got married and brought down the bane of our existence. This had been his plan—well, maybe not the whole shooting up my wedding day part, but the rest of it. He'd advocated for peace between our families when Saint spared Leo's life a year ago. He'd fought like hell to keep me from having to marry Julia, but if he could see how strong she was, how happy we were together, I'd bet he'd be proud to call her his daughter-in-law.

"V said she would take lots of pictures to show him," Hollywood added, coming to stand on the other side of me.

I had my real brothers here; no one would ever replace Castor and Pollux in my heart. But these two knuckleheads had been with me through it all. KC and Hollywood were my best friends, my ride or dies, my brothers in spirit if not by blood.

"Thank you both," I said, glancing between them as a wave of sentimentality hit me square in the chest. "Thank you for being here, for always having my back."

"Hey, don't start that shit," KC said, pointing accusingly at me. "Hollywood's gonna start crying and then I'm gonna have to clean him up before V kicks all of our asses."

Hollywood wiped at his eye and sniffed. "I'm not crying, you're crying, you son of a bitch."

KC shook his head and laughed. "You got it, prez. I couldn't have done anything without you, ya know?"

"We're with you till the end." Hollywood clamped my hand and pulled me into a one-armed hug before stepping back and playfully smacking my cheek. "Even if you are a short-dicked, hot-tempered piece of shit."

"Oh, so you want to spend my wedding day on your back staring up at the sky with a bloody nose?" I tapped him back a little harder than he'd hit me.

"You couldn't catch me if you tried." He punched my stomach, and I nearly collapsed. But I wouldn't let him win that easily.

"Hollywood, I've been kicking your ass since—"

"Enough," KC cut in, putting his arms out between us. "If either of you ends up bloody today, Sunshine's gonna kick *my* ass, and I don't make a habit of pissing off my wife. Understand?"

I narrowed my eyes at KC, but ultimately gave Hollywood a nod of agreement. It wasn't the right time to go running off into a wrestle.

"Besides," KC said, "no one's dick is as big as mine, and I could take you both out with one hand."

Hollywood stared gape-jawed at KC, but I burst into hysterics, needing the laugh to soothe my nerves.

My brothers and I took our spots in front of the archway as the rest of the "guests" filled in the chairs on either side. Most of them were members from the other clubs, and when Lore showed up last night with the Indiana crew in tow, I started to feel a little better about all of this. Of course, aside from my family in the club and the MC princesses, neither of us had any real family here. Chesco would arrive when his father did and Julia didn't want to drag Della into this more than she already was. So it was just down to strangers and other Roses to bear witness to the greatest lie I ever told.

Of course, it didn't feel like a lie when the music started playing and my sister appeared at the end of the aisle. She walked between the rows of seats, carrying a bouquet before stopping at the far end of the arch. Ru came next, followed by Selene, and finally Alba. And when I saw Julia standing at the end, wearing a beautiful strapless gown, holding on to Leo for dear life, I almost cried.

My heart pounded and my legs shook, and for a moment, one blissful heartbeat, I pretended this was real. I pretended my father was sitting in the front row and Julia's uncles were on the other side, and she was gleefully walking down the aisle to hand the rest of her life over to me. She looked stunning, her hair falling in beautiful curls down her back, a radiance shining out of her that reminded me of those ancient paintings of Goddesses.

When Leo and Julia stood in front of me, I had to blink myself back to reality.

"Who gives this woman to this man?" Saint said from his spot in front of the arch.

"I do," Leo said, "on behalf of her bloodline, her family, and her friends."

He placed her hand in mine, and the weight of the world suddenly disappeared. I looked into her deep mahogany eyes and saw my entire future play out for me. I saw our kids growing up in a world where they wouldn't have to worry about a war hanging over their heads. I saw her with gray around her temples, looking just as gorgeous for her age, and me with wrinkles at the corners of my eyes. I saw us playing the same games in twenty, thirty, forty years, enjoying it just as much. And I wanted it all.

"Hi, little wife," I whispered, bringing her hand to my lips for a quick kiss.

"Hello, husband." She grinned, and we turned to face Saint as he began reciting the planned ceremony.

"You look amazing," I whispered, trying to keep my voice low.

"So do you," she said. "Such a shame it's going to be ruined."

"Once this is over, I'll take you anywhere you want to go," I murmured. "We'll get married on every island in Greece, if that's what you want."

"Careful," she said. "I may hold you to that."

I prayed she did. I prayed we made it out of this in one piece, that luck really was on our side for once. Saint went on with his speech, praising the merits of union and throwing a little jazz on some of the verbiage we'd selected, but we didn't want the ceremony to last forever. The anticipation of what was to come hung over us like smog, choking everything into a haze.

Gabriella Caputi could come out of the woodwork any second now, and when she did, this idyllic romance would crash down around us.

"And now, the vows," Saint said, gesturing for us to face each other.

"Do you, Julia Gianna Francesca Benita Natali Caputi," Saint said, "take Roman Alexander Montgomery to be your husband, to have and to hold, to honor and protect, to love and defend, for all the days of your life?"

"I do," she said, smiling up at me.

"And do you, Roman Alexander Montgomery, take Julia Gianna Francesca Benita Natali Caputi to be your wife, to have and to hold, to honor and protect, to love and defend, for all the days of your life?"

"I do," I replied, returning her grin.

"Do you have the rings?" Saint turned to KC.

KC reached inside his pocket to pull out the velvet cloth containing the simple white gold bands we'd picked out weeks ago. Even though we were already married, the little circles meant so much for being just chunks of soft metal.

"These are symbols of your vows to one another, signs of your commitment to the promises made here today." Saint went on, but the significance hit me right in the chest. Four months ago, I'd sat in that lawyer's office, going over a contract that stipulated the rest of my life. It mandated we had children, that we share a last name, that we share a house, and I barely knew the person I was supposed to do those things with. I only knew that it could end a war neither of us wanted.

Now, here we were. I grabbed Julia's ring from Saint's palm and held up her left hand, sliding it over the knuckle of the third finger, placing it on top of the ruby one I'd given her a few days ago. She did the same to me.

"And now, in front of your family, the Steel Roses, and all the fucking Gods, I pronounce you man and wife. You may kiss your old lady!"

The crowd erupted into applause and cheers while I stepped closer to connect my mouth with hers. She smiled against me and held my jaw, deepening our connection.

When I stepped back, I knew no matter what happened today, I'd never regret marrying her...*for real.*

25

JULIA

The ceremony and reception went on as if we weren't waiting for the real guest of honor to show up. Della and Chesco had assured us she planned to appear shortly after the vows. But when the dinner had been served, and it was time to cut the cake, we still hadn't seen any sign of her.

"Castor, what the fuck is going on?" Roman asked his brother.

He typed on his laptop and shrugged, glancing at us. "I don't know. The people I'm tracking *should* be here. Like...right here."

"Julia, Bear!" Ru called, waving us over to the cake at the other end of the tent. "C'mon. We're all ready for dessert."

"It doesn't make any sense," Castor said. He glanced at Lizard, whose club was responsible for guarding the perimeter. "Have you heard anything from your guys?"

Lizard shook his head and grabbed his phone, pressing a button before holding it to his ear. One of the servers walked back, his gaze connecting with mine for a moment, barely a heartbeat, but recognition shot through me. I could have sworn I'd seen him before, but I didn't know where. He walked over to one of the tables to refill a water glass while alarms blared in the back of my mind.

"Let's go cut our cake, *mia cara*," Roman said, squeezing my hand and interrupting my train of thought. "Keep working on it, Cas."

We walked to the group waiting by the three-tiered monstrosity, but the pit in my stomach only grew larger. She should have been here by now, and if she wasn't, it could only mean one thing. She had planned something we didn't foresee. Now we waited for the fallout. Today had been wonderful, something from a dream, and that made me more anxious because it was about to be brutally ripped out from under me.

I tried to calm myself.

Roman is wearing Kevlar. Your dress is reinforced with a bulletproof corset. It's going to be okay.

That was, of course, as long as no one aimed at our heads.

"Here we go," Ru said, handing the cake-cutting knife to me with a grin. I tried to reciprocate, but the tightness in my chest grew into a boulder, suffocating me. "Grab it together."

Roman wrapped his hand around mine, and we sliced into the white dessert before plopping a piece down on a plate.

Something's not right.

It rattled around my head like an echo as Roman cut off the tip of the piece and held it out to me to take. We were meant to feed each other a tiny bit, and when he put the portion between my lips, I regretted we had used our pretend wedding for this. I wanted it to be real. We deserved it to be real.

I smiled for the camera and kissed Roman's icing-laced mouth, causing the crowd to applaud again. But after that, I needed a moment to get my head back in the game. Even though this had been my idea, I wanted nothing more than to grab my husband and our family and get the hell out of here.

"I have to use the bathroom," I said to Roman, nodding back toward the house.

"I'll go with you," he said.

"No, I'm fine," I said. "Stay. Take care of our guests."

He narrowed his eyes and glanced around, seemingly uncomfortable with letting me out of his sight, but ultimately nodded. "Be quick. Or I'm coming to find you."

"Always." I kissed him one more time before turning to head back toward the farmhouse. I greeted the two Roses from New England standing guard by the door as I went inside and held my dress up as I climbed the old creaky stairs to the second floor. I went to the restroom in the bridal suite, did my business, and washed my hands. Then, I stared at myself in the mirror and wondered what I was doing—*really* doing.

The people I thought were my enemies had turned out to be the kindest, most loving allies I could ever ask for. And the ones I considered family were more likely to stab me in the back as to help me anymore.

I grabbed my phone when it buzzed, indicating a text message, and I frowned.

Della: *Run!*

Run? What did she mean—

Movement in the mirror caught my attention and I jumped, gasping when a man in a staff uniform stood in the reflection, the same man I thought I'd recognized earlier.

It hit me in a split second. He'd been at Roman's house the night of the attack. He was a Hell's Knight.

Terror launching me into action, I only had a moment to reach for my knife before he wrapped an arm around my neck to put me in a headlock.

But I wasn't the same woman who'd been attacked weeks ago. I stomped on his foot, causing him to let go enough for me to wiggle out of his hold. My blade was still sheathed on my thigh, but I had a million pounds of fabric between me and it. I tried to yank up my dress, but my attacker recovered enough to punch me in the face.

Agonizing pain splintered down my cheek and into my neck, and I stumbled back, unable to defend myself when a different pair of arms wrapped around my chest.

"Good to see you, blood traitor." The voice ricocheted through me, and I froze. Suddenly, I wasn't in the bridal suite bathroom anymore. I was back in that dusty cabin in the woods with those men kicking me and beating me. This wasn't one of my uncles' men or one of Chesco's. No, this was the disgusting, sick bastard that worked for Gabriella, the one that took delight in making me cry.

"No," I tried to say, but blood filled my mouth, tasting like copper, choking me.

"Oh, yes," he said, fisting my hair to yank it back. "You didn't think you'd lay this trap so easily, did you?" He laughed and pointed a gun at my head. "Oh, you stupid bitch. Of course, you did."

"Lenny," came a chilling, familiar tone from the doorway. "Enough." Gabriella stood with her dark hair in a tight bun and her lips painted dark red. She wore her finest clothes, a suit imported from Italy no doubt, and the rarest jewelry. I bet she cost more than my trust in just what she had on. "Let's go say hi, shall we?"

Then she set her gaze on me and shook her head like I was the biggest disgrace our family had ever seen. "Bring her."

I struggled to walk with Lenny holding my hair and my face pounding in time with my racing heart, but we somehow made it down the stairs. When we got outside, I gasped at the two Roses slumped over. They weren't bleeding, so they hadn't been shot, but somehow, my aunt's cronies and the other motorcycle clubs had knocked them out to get inside.

The roar of motorcycles echoed up the road, and a swarm of them appeared on the horizon. Hell's Knights and Kings of Carnage, no doubt. But how did they get past the Roses guarding the perimeter?

We kept going, kept walking, and when we got to the tent, Gabriella strolled inside like she'd been a part of the ceremony since the beginning. The music cut off. The crowd parted as she passed. When the other Roses saw me being manhandled by one of her minions, they reached for their weapons.

But the wait staff reacted by pulling guns seemingly from every-where—under tables, behind the bar, in holsters under their aprons. Castor was right. They'd been here the whole time. They infiltrated our reception staff and now stood with their pistols aimed at the Roses, who pointed their guns back at them. It had gone from a fake wedding to a real standoff in a heartbeat. The horde of Gabriella's MC cronies parked their bikes and stormed toward the tent, and suddenly, both armies were pitted against each other.

This. This explains the knot in my stomach. God, I'd been so blind. I didn't see this coming.

I locked eyes with my husband, who stood at the lover's table with his hand on his nine, pointed straight at Gabriella.

"Easy now," Roman said, shaking his head. "No one make any stupid moves."

Sulli and Frankie walked out of the house to stand along the tent's edge, Chesco at his father's side with a scowl. I tried not to look at him. I didn't want to give the game away, but I didn't see my brother. Where had Leo gone? Did Gabriella snatch him too? Or had she already killed him?

"Well, well, well," Gabriella said, stopping in the center of the crowd. "Is this all for me? I'm touched, truly."

She nodded at Lenny, and he threw me to the ground where I landed in a heap at Gabriella's feet.

"She's got nothing to do with this," Roman said. "Let her go and you and I can—"

"Nothing to do with this?" Gabriella laughed. "My guess is this is *all* her doing." She stared down at me with disdain, her nose scrunched, her eyes evil and menacing. "Oh, my dear." Gabriella tutted and shook her head. "A coward, I'm afraid. Just like your father. It runs in the blood, you see." She looked at Roman. "But what did I expect for someone who would whore herself out to a disgusting piece of Rose garbage?"

"Coming from you, that's a compliment," Roman said.

One of the Caputis stepped aside so another could come through, hauling Della with him by the arm. She'd been beaten and bruised, bloody tears running down her cheeks. She must have just had enough time to text me a warning before they did that to her. I started to stand, to go after her, but Lenny held me down by the shoulder.

"Oh, there she is," Gabriella said, turning to me again. "Your rat."

I swallowed, but kept my composure. I'd already known *who* it was, but I didn't know what information she'd been feeding them. It must have been the plans for the wedding. It must have been the catering crew we'd hired so that they could sneak in like a Trojan Horse.

"Did you know she was the one who sold you out?" Gabriella raised her eyebrows. "Gave you up in a heartbeat. All I had to do was threaten her beloved Matteo, and she sang like Pavarotti."

I sympathized with my dear cousin. Gabriella always knew how to use a person's heart to get them to do whatever she wanted.

Della sobbed and wilted into her captor's hold, murmuring, "I'm sorry," over and over again.

"Well, what should we do now?" Gabriella turned back to Roman and clutched her hands behind her back. "I'll admit, you're not the Montgomery blood I wanted to spill, but a Rose by any other name and all that. I suppose you'll have to do."

"What makes you think you have the upper hand in this?" Roman scoffed.

"Oh, I know all about your trap." Gabriella stepped toward him. "I know my nephew is lurking around here somewhere. I even know this was a charade to lure me out." She turned around, glancing at the tense crowd. When she didn't see him, she looked down at me. "Well, here I am. What do you want?"

I sat back on my haunches and stared up at her, my nose dripping, the space between my eyes pounding. "I wanted you out in the open."

"For what, my darling liar?" Gabriella smiled like a monster. I trembled, my entire body shaking with the weight of what I knew I had to do. Hatred brewed in my gut, spewing through my molecules in a hot, disgusting wave.

The skirt on my dress hid my legs well, and they'd shoved me so haphazardly to the ground, they hadn't thought to bind my hands. They'd been distracted, and I had gone for my knife without them noticing. Now, I had my opportunity.

Memories of me as a child floated to the front of my mind, when my mother was still alive and Gabriella had been someone

I'd looked up to. She always gave the best presents at Christmas and knew how to make anyone laugh. When Alessandra died, a piece of Gabriella went with her, and after Benito, there was nothing human left inside my dear old Zia. Putting her down would be a mercy.

My hand shook. I stared up at her, my jaw clenched, tears in my eyes, knowing I could slash her across the throat and it would all be over. A queen for a queen.

Just as I went to do it, menacing laughter came from my right and I stopped. My brother weaved in between Frankie and Sulli's men, patting Chesco on the shoulder as he passed him. Then, he stopped and clapped in a slow, degrading rhythm.

"Look at you," Leo said, glancing around. "All this posturing. All this scheming. And for what? Why not just ambush the wedding and shoot everyone? Why not kill Julia while no one would see you?"

"There you are," Gabriella said, her features softening. She turned to one of her minions. "Grab him."

No one moved, not even Lenny. The Hell's Knights and the Kings of Carnage seemed unsure about what to do. They looked at each other, confusion etched between their brows. They must be hesitant about who to follow. Their allegiance had been with Gabriella, but if the Caputis weren't behind her anymore, was it still advantageous for them? Everyone else looked to Frankie, who pursed his lips and tilted his head.

"What are you waiting for? Grab him! Bring him to me!" Gabriella turned, aghast at how her orders were being ignored.

And now the time has come.

The walls were closing in on her, and the reign of her mania had finally ended.

"Gabriella," Sulli said, holding his hands out to either side. "I didn't want it to come to this."

Her jaw dropped, her face turning a pale shade of ash as reality caught up to her. No one was on her side anymore. Maybe one or two of her goons would protect her. Maybe she would even have someone willing to go down with her. But the family had rallied behind

Frankie and Sulli, and they'd put their faith in Leo. She'd been outmaneuvered.

"No," she whispered, shifting her wide eyes between my uncles, my brother, and me.

"So you see," Leo said, crossing his hands, "it's over. The war, the bloodshed, all of it is over."

"It's time for a new reign. A time for peace," Chesco added.

"I've got all of the underbosses," Leo said. "The uncles, the Morellis, the Vitales, the Romanos. The only one here who wants the war to continue is you."

Gabriella looked around, waiting to see if someone would stop them, and when no one did, not even Lenny, she let out a loud, mocking laugh. "Him? You're putting your trust in *him?*"

A few things happened after that, and time seemed to slow down and speed up simultaneously. Gabriella lunged for Lenny and grabbed his gun. Roman must have thought she was coming for me, and he fired. I lurched to my feet, my knife in my right hand, ready to pounce. Gabriella started to turn toward my husband, aiming at his head, but Roman's bullet hit her in the shoulder and she stumbled, her finger clenching around the trigger.

I stabbed her in the throat just as her gun went off, a bright white blast blinding me. Suffocating smoke filled my nostrils and coated my tongue as it went down my esophagus. Something hot and fiery burned through my dress, into my gut, and when I glanced down, I saw a bright crimson patch spreading over my beautiful wedding gown. It was completely ruined, of course. I'd never be able to get that stain out.

Then, my brain caught up with the pain. My stomach...Something had happened to my stomach.

Had I stabbed myself?

No, my knife still stuck out of her neck where she collapsed on the floor.

"Julia!" Roman cried, rushing toward me, a look of sheer panic echoing out of his wide eyes.

Oh...

My chest erupted into agony, the burning heat of having been shot cascading down my legs and up my spine. My knees gave out, and I sank to the ground just as Roman's arms wrapped around me, holding me up.

This is it. It was real. The whole time.

But it wasn't Roman that fate wanted. Oh no. This time, it came for me.

As I stared up at his beautifully frightened eyes, I remembered there was something I wanted to tell him, something important.

"It was real," I said, reaching up to touch his face. My fingers were coated red with Caputi blood, both mine and Gabriella's. Despite this, I couldn't feel them, and I couldn't feel his cheek. The world had started to fade away. "I love you, and it was real. The whole time."

Then everything went black.

26

BEAR

The steady beep-beep-beep of Julia's heart rate monitor was the only thing keeping me sane. Watching her go down had pierced through my soul, and for one heart-clenching moment, I thought I'd lost her. I almost did. She bled out in front of me while chaos erupted around us, and I did my best to shield her from the fray.

The bodice of her wedding dress had been reinforced with body armor, but she'd managed to twist in just the right way for Gabriella's bullet to go through a seam and into Julia's chest. It was a one-in-a-million shot, but like Julia feared, fate had it out for her after all.

After Gabriella died, what little remained of those loyal to her either fled or were killed by my brothers. And the fucker that put his hands on Julia, Lenny or whatever the fuck his name was, fell lifeless to my feet when I put a bullet between his eyes.

Then Selene held my wife together until we could get her here. All in all, we'd lost over two dozen men, either killed so Gabriella could sneak onto our property or caught in the fray between the MCs after she went down. We couldn't afford to lose any more, not after Stallion's treachery and the raid earlier this year.

I should have been doing damage control at the clubhouse with KC and Hollywood. But instead, I sat by my wife's side, my hands still stained with her blood.

It had been two days of touch and go, and after surgery removed most of the bullet fragments from her stomach, the doctors told me the rest would be up to Julia. She'd lost so much blood, she'd been sheet-pale by the time they got her on a gurney, and then they'd had to wait until she could even sustain surgery to get the pieces out.

"Have you slept?" came the deep voice from the doorway.

I glanced up to see Leo walking toward me with his hands in his dress pants. Verona had brought me a change of clothes earlier today, but I hadn't been home since before the wedding, choosing instead to sleep on the tiny sofa just in case Julia woke up. I wanted to be the first person she saw. I wanted her to know we'd both made it, that she truly belonged to me now in a way she never could let herself before. We belonged to each other.

"Some," I said, shifting in my seat as he sat in the chair on the other side of the hospital bed. He swept his red-rimmed eyes over his sister before letting out a long, drawn-out sigh. "What about you?"

"Some." He attempted a smile, but it wasn't genuine, not when Julia had paid the price for our high-stakes chess game. "Any change?"

I shook my head. She'd been hooked up to machines since she came out of her operation, and the doctors couldn't say for sure if she would ever come off them. Selene was hopeful, and I'd never known her to mince words. If she thought Julia wouldn't make it, she'd tell me.

"She is strong," Leo said. "Stronger than both of us. She'll come out of this."

I didn't know what I would do if she didn't, and my lungs seized at the notion. It hadn't started as love. Hell, it had barely started as friendship, but we'd built a solid foundation of trust and admiration. Now I loved her more than I'd ever loved anyone who dared stand in her place before.

"How's your rise to the Caputi throne?" I asked, deciding to change the subject before my worries escalated into an anxiety attack.

"Going very well," Leo said. "My uncles have ceded the top seat to me, and the underbosses have already fallen in line."

"Do you expect dissent?" I thought of my brothers who had betrayed me and how hard it was to deal with them. Now, I couldn't be sure if the rest of the club was scared of me or truly supportive of the plan. I guessed it didn't matter either way, as long as they did what they were told and didn't start shit. We would probably be hunting down their allies in the Hell's Knights for years to come.

"Probably," Leo said, picking lint off his shirt. "Some will think it easier to get rid of me than Gabriella. They may have gone along with it if only to topple me once I had the reins."

"Keep me in the loop," I said. "You had our back, we'll have yours."

He nodded. "I asked around about the leak in the PD."

That got my attention. I still owed some pig a visit. Whoever had been responsible for arresting Crow and Aris had done it in conjunction with when the Caputis attacked us. It had been coordinated, entirely too perfect. Months ago, I'd promised Detective Jordan when I found out who it was, I'd be sure to return the favor. I meant it.

"No one knows who Gabriella was working with," he said. "If they do, they're keeping it hidden, maybe in attempts to save their own skin."

I sighed, trying not to let the disappointment overtake the rest of my energy.

"I'll keep my ears open," he concluded.

"Thank you. Truly." I pinched the bridge of my nose and ran my fingers over my burning eyes.

"You should go home for a bit," Leo said. "Take a shower. Get some food. I'll stay with her."

"I appreciate that," I said. "But I'm not going anywhere."

Leo stared at me, raking his gaze over my tired form, like he could see inside my head, perhaps read every thought I'd ever had.

"What?" I raised my eyebrows at his assessment.

"You really love her, don't you?" His tone hinted at amusement, though not too much considering the unconscious person between us.

"More than my life," I said. "If I could, I would trade places with her in a heartbeat."

"I'm pleased to hear it." Leo reached out to grab her hand, tucking his fingers between her thumb and forefinger. "Julia always was a stubborn girl, even as a child. She'd dig her teeth into something and wouldn't let go, no matter what logic or reason you threw at her. Once, she found an injured bird in our backyard and brought it inside to nurse it back to health. 'It's a wild animal,' our mother told her. 'It's going to die, no matter what.'" Leo pulled one side of his mouth into a smile, as if he could see the miniature version of her in front of him. "But Julia wouldn't let the thing go. She tended to its wing and fed it worms until it had the strength to fly on its own again."

She had a big heart. I'd already known that about her.

"Eventually, my father found it and cracked its neck in front of her."

I hated Giuseppe Caputi even more.

"It was the first thing she ever loved, and he took it away from her." Leo clenched his eyes shut, like the memory haunted him. "It wouldn't be the last time he did that. If you ever wondered where her rebellion started, it was with a tiny bird in his big, violent hands."

"That's horrifying," I said.

"She loves you, too," Leo said. "More than I believe she's ever loved anything, including that bird."

Tears burned the corners of my eyes, and I blinked them back and cleared my throat.

"Have you been by the clubhouse?" he asked.

I shook my head. "I haven't left her side."

"KC is taking good care of it," Leo said. "The other Rose chapters are grieving their dead, but everyone who came to help knew the cost."

"He told me we lost three prospects and five brothers of our own," I said. What remained of the Kings of Carnage and the Hell's Knights had tucked tail and ran. We would need to retaliate, but we'd face that day when it came. One step at a time.

Leo nodded. "The funeral is in a few days. You should go."

I knew I should. As the president, it would only be right. But if my old lady was still in this bed, then this was exactly where I would be. I wouldn't leave her to wake up alone and scared.

"Thank you, Leo," I said. "Not just for the information, but for all of it...for agreeing to go along with our plan in the first place."

"Thank you, Roman," he said as he stood and put his hands back in his pockets. "It's a new day for our family. Let's make it a good one, yes?"

I couldn't disagree.

"She'll be okay, brother," Leo said. "I know it."

I watched him walk out of the room as the weight of his words settled in my chest.

Brother.

Two years ago, I would have died rather than consider Leo Caputi my brother, and now he truly was—not just in relationship but by law. The Roses and the Caputis were connected irrevocably by love and marriage, and soon by blood.

The doctor had confirmed Julia had been pregnant and miscarried due to the trauma of being shot. I didn't plan to tell anyone that, not until Julia knew herself. I grieved the young life we'd lost, even if I didn't know about it until two days ago. I wanted children with her. I wanted the family I'd always envisioned.

I stared at the woman on the bed and wiped the water from my cheeks, praying to whatever fate...karma...deities were listening that they heal her and bring her back to me. Hadn't I given enough for this fucking war? My parents, my blood, my fellow Roses, almost my brothers and sister. Hadn't I done enough to end it, to make it right? And now my whole future lay unconscious on a bed, nearly bled to death, and what did I get in return? Nothing but my anger and frustration that I couldn't do anything to stop it.

To distract myself, I answered a few emails from my phone and replied to the sibling group chat including Pollux, Castor, and V.

Verona: Bear, do you need anything? I'm on my way over. I'll bring you something to eat.

Pollux: Get me a chicken sandwich—the one with the cheddar jack cheese.

Verona: I didn't ask you, bonehead. You're not at the hospital with your wife.

Castor: I want extra fries.

Pollux: Get me extra fries, too. We'll meet you there.

Verona: Idiots. BEAR—Do YOU need anything?

Pollux: Yeah, brother. Want me to bring you some clean clothes?

I laughed and tried not to let my emotions overwhelm me. If it was one thing about my siblings and me, we were trauma-bonded down to the marrow. Losing our mother so young, living this life together, it made the foundation of our relationship so fucking solid, nothing would shake it. I could tell them not to come. I could tell them not to waste their time since she probably wouldn't wake up for a while, but they wouldn't listen. When Pollux had been in the hospital, we'd all gone to see him every day, even if there was nothing new to see. They wouldn't let me face this on my own.

A groan from the hospital bed drew my attention before I could reply to my siblings, and when I glanced up, my heart nearly stopped to see her beautiful brown eyes open.

"Julia?" I said.

She moved her lips to try to talk, but there'd be no point with the ventilator down her throat.

"Shh," I said. "Don't move. Don't try to speak." I called over my shoulder for a nurse or a doctor, fucking someone to help her, but when she grabbed my hand and squeezed, I knew she'd be okay. Leo had been right. She was strong, much stronger than me, and she'd pull through.

"You're okay," I told her. "You're in the hospital, but you're okay."

The sound of rushing feet came up behind me and warm hands pulled me away from my wife.

"Let me see her," the nurse said, grabbing the stethoscope from around her neck. A few other people filled in around her, and I reluctantly dropped Julia's hand to let the doctors do their work. But regaining consciousness was a good sign, and I bowed my head to silently give thanks to whatever had heard me and granted my prayers.

27

JULIA

✦

"Why do they call you Bear?" I asked, my throat still scratchy and hoarse from the tube being removed a few days ago. I had never gotten an opportunity to ask, and after almost dying, I wouldn't waste any more time.

Roman smirked and shook his head, holding out a spoonful of cheap pudding. "Because nothing can get through me if I stand my ground. Ever since I was little, I was a juggernaut, too big for my britches." He put the spoon between my lips and I swallowed it down. Even though I wasn't a huge fan of the taste, I needed the calories. "And I protect what's mine."

"Hmm," I said. "Me too."

"Good thing you're married to me, then," he said, scooping up the last bit and offering it out to me. But I shook my head, unable to stomach anymore. He ate it himself and set the plastic cup on the side table. "But don't you ever do anything like that again, little wife."

I scoffed and rolled my eyes. "Your life is good enough to trade for mine, but mine is not good enough to trade for yours?"

"You're goddamned right." He glanced down at my stomach with a knowing look, and I clutched my midsection. After the trauma of being shot and going through surgery, I had miscarried. I'd been crying about it since I woke up and found out. I yearned for the life I'd lost, even though I didn't know I was pregnant in the first place. It wasn't far along, barely six weeks, but it was enough. Up until very recently, I wasn't sure I wanted this with him, and now I mourned the future that had been ripped away from us.

Perhaps that was the sacrifice fate demanded to keep us both alive. Perhaps it wasn't me that had to die, but the baby I carried inside me. I hated Gabriella all over again. But at least it was over now. As much as it hurt, we'd have peace. We could have a new future. We could start again.

"I won't apologize for saving your life," I said.

"Don't worry, *mia cara*," he said, his eyes clouding with that tell-tale sign he had something wicked and debauched brewing in that brilliant mind. "I'll find some way for you to make it up to me." He stood and leaned over me, bringing his lips to mine for a chaste kiss that quickly bordered something much too fiery, considering I'd been in a hospital bed for over a week. But we were both too emotional for anything else, so with one last kiss on my forehead, he sat back down and smiled.

I had a long road to recovery ahead. The bullet had deflated a lung, and pieces would be lodged in my rib cage for the rest of my life. I'd need physical therapy and rehabilitation, but I was already up and walking around for twenty minutes twice a day, which the doctors said was good progress.

Gabriella was dead. Most of her lackeys were dead. The other MCs had gone home empty-handed and missing some of their men. Della had gone missing—either run away with one of the MCs or disappeared on her own. Leo said she hadn't shown back up on Caputi territory and I hadn't heard from her. Not that I'd tried to reach out.

I didn't blame her for what she'd done. She must have felt pressured to give Gabriella information about me once our aunt threatened Della's long-time, on-again-off-again boyfriend, Matteo. But I couldn't see how I'd ever trust her. Perhaps it was best she'd run away. Perhaps she'd taken Matteo with her and they'd ridden off into the sunset together. I'd like to think so rather than brood over what more she might do to ruin my life.

Things had gone the way we wanted, and now we tried to move on with a new goal: peace between our families.

"I love you," I said, blinking back tears. "I'm sorry I ever said I didn't. I'm sorry I even left before the wedding." I knew now it had been hormones and stress and—

"Shh," he said, brushing hair out of my face. "Enough. You're safe. I'm safe."

"We lost good people."

"We did. But everyone who was there was prepared for that. It's not your fault. It's no one's fault," he said, rising to sit on the hospital bed by my legs. "I love you so much. I never thought I'd feel this way about anyone, least of all you."

I smiled as warmth raced through my blood, settling in a warm puddle in my gut. The minute I got out of this hospital, I'd find some way to make it up to him, to prove how much he truly meant to me and always would.

"There she is!" came a deep bellow from the doorway. Hollywood walked in with his arms open wide. Chesco, Ru, V, and Alba walked behind him, followed by KC, Saint, Castor, and Pollux.

"Oh, little coz." Chesco rubbed his tattooed hand over my hair, mussing it up the way an older brother would. "You look like shit."

"Hey!" both Roman and V said at the same time in the same tone.

"You look just fine, all things considered," Saint said with a grin.

"Yeah, when I got blown up, I couldn't eat solid foods for like a month." Pollux picked up the plastic container on the side table and sniffed it. "You're lucky you're getting pudding already."

"How are you feeling?" Alba asked, setting a vase of flowers on the counter behind Chesco.

"Better," I said. "The doctors say I should be able to leave soon."

"Good," V cut in. "Bear needs someone to keep him from barking at everyone."

"I'm not barking," Roman said.

"Castor, find the fuckers that tried to kill my wife," Castor mocked.

"Saint, make sure the Hell's Knights know we're coming," Saint added with a smirk.

"Hollywood, don't fucking touch my wrenches," Hollywood mimicked. "Hollywood, find the Kings of Carnage. Hollywood, go meet with Rico and—"

"I shouldn't have to tell you these things." Roman sighed, clearly exasperated. "You should just do them."

"See what I mean?" Hollywood rolled his eyes. "A fucking grouch since you've been gone."

I laughed as my company carried on around me, teasing each other and fussing over whatever they could do to help me. It felt good to be surrounded by them, to have their love and support in a way I didn't before. The girls had tried to make me feel welcome, I'd known Saint for years, and I'd appreciated Hollywood's antics before I married Roman. But perhaps I'd been keeping a part of myself from them, just in case it didn't work out. They had sensed this barrier and kept themselves from me in return. To see them all here now, despite the history between our families, made me feel accepted in a way nothing ever had before.

I loved Roman, and I loved our family, and I loved these people with everything in me. For the first time since I married him, I was proud to call myself Julia Montgomery, the old lady to the Rose president, the woman meant to carry his children. I was a sister to them, a cousin, a friend, and I'd finally accepted that.

A few days later, once the wound had healed enough and I could stand on my own without toppling over, the hospital released me to go home. I hobbled into Roman's house...*our* house...and relaxed in the living room while he fussed over me. He took off my shoes and rubbed my feet, making sure to massage my calves and thighs, and I ran my good hand through his hair, smiling when he glanced up at me with those piercing dark eyes.

"What do you need?" he murmured.

"You. Just you." He climbed up my body to kiss me. We couldn't have sex how we both wanted, not until I healed completely, but he still rubbed me the way only he could, enough to bring me pleasurable euphoria and calmness.

The next day, Leo came to visit. I'd seen him at the hospital, of course, but now that I was home, we could get down to business. Our uncles had asked me to help him run the family, and even though I didn't think I was qualified for such a thing, Leo had been steadfast in his agreement.

"How are you feeling?" he asked, sitting across the dining room table from me, drumming his fingers on the wood. He'd started wearing the Caputi signet ring, and that made me even more proud of what we'd done. Our father had worn that my entire life, and I was happy it now belonged to a man worthy of it. Leo would never do to me what our parents had, and I had faith he could run the business much better than any of the Caputis before him.

"Okay," I said and sipped at my coffee. "Sore, but that will pass."

He nodded. "And your husband?"

"He's getting ready to take us to the clubhouse. Church is today."

"So much for fate, huh?" He raised his eyebrows and grinned in that cocky way that meant he knew he'd been right.

"It didn't kill my husband, but it almost killed me."

"Hmm. I recall you stepping in front of her gun." Leo tsked and shook his head. "Some fate if you're the one who makes the stupid decisions."

I gave him a nasty look, mumbling Italian expletives under my breath. "I saved my husband, didn't I? What would happen to our alliance if he died?"

My brother shrugged, nonchalant and seemingly too high and mighty to even consider it. "We'll never know now."

He smiled and drummed his fingers again, a nervous tick that clued me into something going on with him that he didn't want to share.

"What is it?" I raised my eyebrows, bracing for the worst.

"I've appointed Chesco as my second," he said.

"Good." I liked that. He would keep him in line when I couldn't.

"There are rumors," he said. "Some of the underbosses are already talking about a coup."

I tsked my teeth. "Benito was almost dethroned several times, even once by our father."

"We must remain strong," he said, reaching across the table to grab my hand. "We must remain united."

"Of course." I sensed something in his stare, an undercurrent of a plot developing, one he wouldn't share unless I pushed. "Leo, what are you thinking?"

He shrugged. "It might be time for me to make my own alliance."

"Oh?" I couldn't imagine him as a married man, but then again, I didn't know this version of him as well as the one before. Getting sober had changed him in a million ways, all for the better. "And who are you thinking?"

He smirked. "You should help me with that."

"Okay." I started to consider the best possible candidates. If one of the other families were talking dissent, perhaps it might be worthwhile to start there. "We need to shore up our trade agreements. The cartel has exclusively been tied to the Roses, but now that we're family, perhaps they would reconsider."

"There are the Canadians and the IRA." Leo continued to talk business as my husband walked into the room and straightened his cut. He wore his jeans and a black T-shirt, but my oh my, how delicious he looked in such a casual outfit. It made me wish I was completely healed. It made me wish I could get rid of my brother and drop to my knees and beg my husband to do despicable things to my mouth. It made me want to start a fight for no other reason than to have him put me in my place.

Roman leaned down behind me and kissed the side of my neck, nuzzling me in a deep show of affection that turned my insides to mush and curled my toes.

"I should head out," Leo said, standing. "It's good to see you, *mia sorella*. Please don't scare me like that again."

"I'll make sure she doesn't," Roman said with a devilish grin.

"I won't," I said. "Trust me. Getting shot once was enough for a lifetime."

28

BEAR

"The war with the Caputis is over," I announced to the club when we'd gathered at the clubhouse for church. "Today marks the beginning of a new reign. A tentative stalemate, but peace nonetheless."

I ran my hand over Julia's spine and curled my palm around the back of her neck, massaging her tense muscles. She'd been nervous to face the brothers after everything that had happened. Understandably so. We'd lost good men because of Gabriella Caputi, but their sacrifice had not been wasted. We were stronger for it, ushering in a new era of trade with people we'd once considered enemies. As our closest neighbors, it made more sense for us to be allies, especially now that I knew how much we had in common.

"What about the Kings of Carnage and the Hell's Knights?" Wheels asked, rubbing his hand over his head.

"They're still a threat," KC said, crossing his arms. "We're monitoring them closely."

"They live far enough away that we'll have ample time to prepare if they decide to come on our territory again," Thor added.

"They sided with Gabriella," one of our brothers said. "They deserve our wrath."

"Definitely," I added. "But we just buried our fallen brothers. We need to let the dust settle and regroup before we do anything reckless."

The mostly positive mumbling echoed through the crowd.

"Anyone have anything to say to that?" I barked. "Speak now or hold your fucking tongue."

No one said anything else.

"Good," I said.

"We've heard from Berkshire," KC added. "The case against Aris and Crow isn't good. The DA is pushing for maximum sentencing, upward of ten years in prison."

More grumbling came from the club, and I heard words like "Get them out," or "We need to rectify that shit." I didn't disagree.

"My family has a few very talented lawyers," Julia added. "I can ask them to take a look, if you'd like."

KC pursed his lips and Hollywood smiled.

"That would be wonderful, wife," I said, kissing her cheek. "The more help we have, the better."

She nodded and retrieved her phone, no doubt sending out commands to the lawyers in question to get involved.

"The IRA is sniffing around," Hollywood said, explaining how our Irish friends had been upset about the supply disruption while we fought off Gabriella. "If we don't straighten it out soon, they'll come do it themselves."

"I'll call their boss and get it sorted," Thor said.

"Perfect," I said. "What about the upcoming run?"

Lore filled us in on what had happened out in Montana. The Royal Bastards were all too willing to keep our business, which was good because we needed to find other customers to buy the arms we got from the cartel.

"They want me to be their exclusive liaison," Lore said. "I'm happy to do it if you think it's a good idea."

I agreed, and the conversation moved on. We had three upcoming runs in the next few weeks, and my time had come up in the rotation. I'd take the ride to New England and back. It wasn't my usual trip, but

I didn't have a problem with that. Maybe I'd even get Julia on a bike by then and take her with me.

After all the business had been sorted, most of the club got up to leave, except for my officers. KC stayed in the spot on my right and Hollywood on my left. Wheels, Doc, and Thor leaned on the table to glance up at the head where I still sat with Julia on my lap.

"How's the alliance coming along?" Thor asked, glancing at Julia. "Is everyone in the Caputi family playing nice?"

She shifted. "We might have a problem, but nothing my brother can't handle."

"Good," Thor said as he crossed his arms. "Because the Hell's Knights aren't gonna stop coming for us. We owe them for what they did to Alba and Julia."

"When we took out their prez earlier this year, it set a precedent," KC added. "They're pissed. It may have started because of some shit Crow did to the prez's brother, but now it's about the whole thing."

"We killed more of them on our turf. It may have created another war." Doc stabbed out his cigarette and looked at me. "The men are right. We should mount an attack now before we find ourselves on the wrong end of a Knights' invasion."

"They'll have to regroup first," I said, clearing my throat to get rid of the lump that had suddenly formed in my gut. I hated the thought of more bloodshed so soon after we'd just ended it on our home turf, but I wouldn't let the Hell's Knights disrespect us any more than they already had. My father wouldn't have stood for it, and nor would I. They were a national club as big, if not bigger, than the Roses. If they wanted to start shit, we could finish it. "Enough. The night is young, and most of you have old ladies to keep happy." I nodded toward the door. "Go."

Everyone stood to leave except for KC and Hollywood, who both looked at me like they had more to say. I sensed this would be better done in private, so I patted Julia's tight little ass and nodded toward the door.

"You too, *mi amore.* I'll be out in a few minutes."

She kissed me before rising to walk out, the click-clack of her heels echoing through the small space. Leave it to her to wear Jimmy Choos two weeks after being released from the hospital, despite her arm still being in a sling.

God, I fucking loved her.

"You two seem great," Hollywood said. "I was worried I was gonna have to kick your ass for whatever you did at the Beacon that made her run away from you."

I raised an eyebrow and smirked. "I told you already. I didn't *do* anything to her that she didn't want." I knew now that she'd been in the very early stages of pregnancy and her emotions had been justifiably all over the place. Telling her I loved her shouldn't have been that big of a surprise, seeing as I killed anyone who touched her. "What's going on? What is this?"

I glanced at KC, who smiled and shrugged. "We just wanted to check in on you. Sunshine tells me Julia was pregnant before she got shot."

"I didn't realize she'd mentioned it to anyone," I said, pleased my wife had confided in her cousin about it. At least she had someone to talk to. "It's sad. We're grieving it, even if we didn't know about it until it was already too late. Don't worry, I'll get her knocked up again soon. The terms of the contract will still be fulfilled."

"That's not what I'm concerned about," KC said. "What will our enemies do when they realize the new president's Caputi wife is carrying his kid?"

"Are you suggesting I *not* fuck my wife?"

KC snorted and shook his head. "No fucking way. I'm saying you need more guards, more protection. You need to take better care of yourself."

Once upon a time, I would have balked and told KC to mind his own business. But now...well...these two boneheads were my second and third for a reason. I trusted them more than anyone else in the club. I shifted at the advice and nodded. "Fine."

"And you need to stop doing runs," Hollywood added. "You're too important, and we're too vulnerable right now."

I snapped my gaze up to him, my jaw clenching. "I'll decide when I stop doing that."

"See?" Hollywood glanced at KC. "Told ya."

"Bear," KC said. "Be reasonable. Your old man—"

"My old man stopped doing runs because we were beefing with the Caputis," I said. "Now that's over, I can—"

"Fine," Hollywood cut me off. "I'm pulling rank. I'm the road captain and I say you need to keep your beautiful, entitled ass at home."

"You can't do that," I said, my tone snappier than I'd meant it to be.

"Watch me." He leaned in, his grin widening into that stupid Hollywood smile that made me want to punch his teeth out.

A tense moment passed between us where I dared him to say more and he dared me to do something about it. I launched out of my seat at the same time he did, and both of our chairs toppled over. He raced out of the back room, and I ran after him, dodging through brothers and sofas as I trailed him. We burst out into the humid night air, his shit-kickers thundering on the grass as we circled the clubhouse to the wooded area in the back. We had a bunch of sheds out here, housing all the shit the club had collected over the decades but didn't fit inside the main building anymore. Hollywood threw his head back and howled as he sprinted, and I growled, knowing he had a point but unable to concede it without a fight.

Truthfully, Hollywood and I had been roughhousing with each other since we met. I couldn't count the number of times I'd had to haul off and tackle him to keep him from doing or saying something stupid. It was part of the reason I loved the guy so damned much. We were brothers by choice, and in a world that kept trying to take my family away from me, I needed that more than ever.

I finally caught up to him toward the tree line a hundred yards away from the clubhouse, and I shoved my shoulder into his gut to take him down. He elbowed me in the chin, and I punched him in the stomach before he threw his weight around and rolled us so he was on top. And just when I would have kneed him in the groin to get the upper hand again, a feminine laugh got my attention, followed shortly by a deeper masculine one.

"Hollywood," Julia said. "I would have shared him if you had only asked. But since you've got him in submission, I suppose I'll let the slight go if I can watch."

"Oh, these two have been inches away from fucking or fighting for years," KC teased.

"Get off me!" I growled.

"You know, I normally like to be the bottom, but I think I can make an exception for you," Hollywood said with a smile. "Maybe just this once."

"You've gotta get him on the side," Julia called. "He's super ticklish."

Hollywood dug his fingers into my ribs and I wilted, trying to scramble away but he had a good hold on me.

"Goddamn it, wife. I thought you had my back."

"Not about this," she called. "I agree with them. You need to leave the runs to the brothers. Now, fuck him up, Hollywood, or let him go. I'm tired and it's too wet out here for my suede heels."

Hollywood rolled off me and I lay in the grass, staring at the fading summer sun and trying to catch my breath.

"Fine," I finally conceded. "I'll stop doing runs."

"Good," Hollywood said, nailing me in the stomach one more time before pushing to his feet and holding a hand out for me to take. "I wouldn't have to kick your ass if you'd just listen to me once in a while."

I sneered at him, but walked to my wife and scooped her in my arms to carry her back inside so she didn't ruin her pretty shoes.

A FEW DAYS LATER, I was at the garage, trying to figure out what was wrong with an old Ford Ranger when the familiar sound of a clearing throat got my attention. I rolled out from under the pickup and sat up, glancing at both KC and Thor before pushing to my feet.

"Mr. Montgomery," Detective Jordan said from her spot at the entrance.

"Detective Jordan." I raised an eyebrow and wiped my oily hands on a rag. "To what do I owe this great honor?"

She nodded back toward her unmarked car. "Can I have a moment?"

Thor shifted onto his other foot and KC shrugged, raising his eyebrows like maybe it wasn't the best idea. I thought back to the last time I'd talked to her, when I told her to find the leak in her department. Someone had been working with the Caputis and the secret of who that was had died with Gabriella and her men.

"You have a warrant?" I glanced around, noticing she'd come by herself. No other police officers trolled the perimeter, nor was her partner Detective Asshat in her car.

"My visit's not exactly...on the record." She stared at me, perhaps willing me to pick up what she was laying down. Her bright hazel eyes sparkled in the sunshine, her body tense with whatever had brought her to Rose territory with no backup.

"All right," I said, shaking my head when Thor picked up a wrench. "I'll be back in a few."

"Uh-huh," he said, watching as I followed the detective back down to her Crown Vic.

"What's going on?" I asked, sudden alarm shooting through my chest and into my gut. "Is it my old man?"

"No," she said. "Randall's fine. Ashley's fine." I hadn't heard Crow and Aris referred to by their legal names in so long, it took me a moment to realize who she was talking about. "It's, um..." Jordan cleared her throat and glanced down to the ground, kicking a rock back and forth with her boot.

"What?" I asked. "I don't have all fucking day—"

"It's about the leak," she said. "You said you thought someone in the Feds had been working with the Caputis."

"I did," I said. "I still do. And?"

She put her hands on her hips, pushing her suit jacket back far enough to reveal her badge and gun. "I believe you."

"Oh." That took me by surprise. I'd been expecting her to tell me the whole thing was ridiculous or perhaps arrest me for my part in any number of the illegal shit my family got up to. I had not expected this. "What changed your mind?"

"I've been a cop for ten years. Not once have my instincts steered me wrong." She shook her head and glanced around. "After the last time we talked, my gut told me you were right, that there was more to what you were saying. I did some digging."

"And?" I crossed my arms, glancing back toward Thor and KC, who stood outside and watched like hawks. If Jordan made one wrong move, they'd descend like a pack of wolves. I tried to reassure them with my expression.

"And...it's not good," she said. "But I need your help. There's no way I can get close enough to do this on my own."

"Help?" I scoffed. "You obviously didn't listen last time. I'm not a snitch, and neither is my old man."

She tucked her lips between her teeth and steeled her gaze, taking a long, slow inhale. "I can make it worth your while."

"How?" I let out a sick laugh. "You gonna let my dad go? You gonna let Aris walk?"

"I can't," she said. "But I can convince the DA to lower the charges. If the evidence was obtained illegally, it's inadmissible in court. And if what I suspect is true, we don't have much."

That lit a small fire of hope in my chest. "What's in it for me?"

"You wanted to see your dad?" she asked. "I can arrange that."

The temptation was too great to resist. For months, I'd been holding the club together by my fingernails, barely sleeping, worrying I wasn't doing the right things. The only person who had visitation rights was my sister, and she'd been tasked with relaying everything he said like some twisted game of telephone. It was one thing for her to say he approved; it was another to hear it from the man himself.

"What do you want from me?" I asked, twisting with guilt at the thoughts spiraling around in my head. If there was one thing we outlaws agreed on, it was that cops were bastards and untrustworthy. All cops. It didn't matter what sweet lies dripped from their slimy lips or how much they promised in return. Making a deal with them was worse than signing your life away to the devil. Snitches routinely got killed in the pen for this very thing. But if I could get my revenge and my father out of jail, what wouldn't I give for that? Was my guilt, my shame, worth it?

"From what I understand, you're married to a Caputi," she said. "Not only that, Gabriella has all but disappeared and her nephew, your brother-in-law, is now the head boss of the Caputi mafia."

I crossed my arms. "It sounds like you have your asset. What do you need me for?"

"Leverage," she said. "I need confirmation that what I suspect is true. Cold, hard evidence. Otherwise, I can't do anything about it."

"And you think *I* can get that for you?"

"I think your wife can," she said. "Your brother-in-law."

"Convincing them to work with the pigs is never going to happen," I said. "No matter what you think you can do."

"C'mon, Montgomery," she said with a smirk. "I heard you were the brains of this whole operation. Surely, you're more resourceful than that."

I raised an eyebrow and pursed my lips.

"Find out who the Caputis were working with in the Feds, and I'll get your dad and Aris Washington a lower sentence."

"And if I can't?" I didn't like being backed into a corner, but perhaps Jordan wasn't as terrible as the rest of the PD. Perhaps she really *could* help my dad.

"No deal," she said. "I believe you when you say someone is doing something shady on the inside, but unless I can prove it, I can't do anything about it."

I took a deep inhale and nodded. "Fine. I'll do my best, but I'm not telling you anything more than that."

"Fine," she said, her eyes lighting up at my very reluctant acceptance.

"Why are you doing all this, anyway?" I said. "You've got no business helping me or Crow. So what if someone in the PD is dirty? It wouldn't be the first time."

She shifted her shoulders uncomfortably and looked down at the ground, crossing her arms in defense.

"I don't like the thought of someone sullying the badge," she said. "Among other things."

The blush on her cheeks gave her away. I'd always been good at reading people, and even if Detective Jordan could maintain that stoic skepticism most detectives had beaten into them, she wasn't perfect. Something more was going on, something she didn't want me to know, something she was perhaps ashamed of.

My father would never admit it, but he'd always had a soft spot for her. I didn't know what it was, but I married the enemy, so who the fuck was I to judge? Did she return the sentiment?

She handed me a business card with a handwritten number on the back.

"This is my burner phone," she said. "I suggest you get one, too. Text me the number when you have it. We'll go from there."

She turned to head back toward her cruiser.

"Jordan," I called out. She stopped and faced me. "Whatever your reasons, if this gets me killed, my wife will come after you."

"Let's hope it doesn't come to that." She nodded, hopped in her Crown Vic, and started the engine.

I tried to swallow down the rising tide of panic in my gut. My father wouldn't like this. My club wouldn't like it. Nor would my wife or new family. But like Jordan said, I'd always been resourceful. I could figure out who ratted us out, slip the info to her, and kill them before anyone knew it was me. And as for the pig who turned traitor, well, I'd let Jordan handle her own.

I put the card back in my pocket and headed toward the garage.

"What'd she want?" KC asked.

A moment passed where I debated not telling Thor and KC. Maybe it might be better to keep it a secret. My club would gut me alive if they found out I was working with the PD. But...I wasn't, was

I? Not really. I was working with Jordan, and I had a gut feeling she wouldn't let her slip show. She'd keep this under wraps until she could take down the dirty fucker herself.

"We've got a problem," I said. Then, I told them everything, trusting they would keep it between us three.

"I don't like it," KC said, scratching the back of his head. He narrowed his bright blue eyes and winced. "This walks a fine line."

"I know," I said. "Which is why we're gonna play our own game."

"Oh?" Thor raised his eyebrows. "What did you have in mind?"

"Vengeance." With a grin, I told them my plan and watched as they pieced it together. For the rest of the afternoon, we schemed and plotted and ultimately decided to keep it between us. The rest of the club didn't have to know, not yet, not until we had more to go on ourselves.

"We'll have to give it to someone else," Thor said. "We just got you off runs. You can't start stuffing your face with pig shit."

"I agree," I said.

"You think she's got it bad for your old man?" KC asked with that charismatic grin.

I laughed. "If she does, I pity both of them. The only thing worse than marrying a Caputi would be falling in love with a cop."

"May the Gods have mercy on them, then," Thor said. "Now, let's get to work."

29

JULIA

SIX WEEKS LATER

It took me longer to heal than I would have liked. Even after I got the all clear from the doctor to resume normal activities, the pain in my ribs still ached, especially if it had been a long day. But I couldn't wait anymore. I had an apology to make, and I'd been dreaming about it for weeks.

I put on my sexiest lingerie, a black lace bra, a matching garter belt and thong, and thigh-high tights before I did my makeup. I attached the silk collar around my neck, a blatant indication of what I wanted, and I braided my hair in two pigtails down either side of my head, knowing Roman would like to use them in delightfully perverted ways. I heard him in the other room, the one we'd converted to his office, rummaging around and adjusting his chair. When I knew I looked too beautiful to resist, I put on his favorite pair of heels and walked down the hallway, stopping just inside his door.

He sat behind his enormous desk, scribbling something on a piece of paper in front of him. He wore a white T-shirt and jeans, nothing else, and as much as I loved to see him in his leather, this, too, sent a yearning spike straight down my spine. His hair had been properly mussed, as if he'd been running his fingers through it all afternoon, and his dark, intelligent eyes sparkled as they scanned over the documents.

I squeezed my thighs together, hoping to alleviate some of the tension building between them. At the sound of me stepping into the room, he glanced up and froze. I could tell I'd interrupted something important, but perhaps he could use the break.

"Husband," I said, sauntering closer.

He ran the length of me with a heated gaze as he leaned back in his seat, resting his elbows on the arms of the chair. He touched his fingertips together, brought them to his lips, and raised an eyebrow. "What's this?"

Donning all the self-confidence I could muster despite the huge pink scar on the left side of my rib cage, I walked to the side of his desk and tilted my chin up, trying not to tremble under his scrutiny.

"I left you in the Beacon with hardly an explanation," I said, turning to lean the back of my thighs against the edge of the mahogany. I put my hands behind me, pushing my breasts out farther before taking a deep breath to slow my racing heart. I didn't know what I was nervous about. My husband had never rejected me, and even if we hadn't been intimate since before our wedding, I had no reason to think he would now. Still, I was very aware of how damaged my body had become since then. I'd lost weight, I had more ugly scars, and I'd never be able to inhale fully without grimacing through it. "You said I owed you an apology. I'm here to pay up."

He twisted his lips into a devastating grin, his eyes lighting up like a little kid who had discovered a bundle of presents under the tree on Christmas morning. I couldn't wait to be unwrapped.

"Hmm." He quickly washed away that excitement, training his features into a stoic mask before turning his chair back to his paperwork. "I'm really busy."

I swallowed against a dry throat, trying not to take it personally. I hadn't told him about this. I had simply shown up at his doorway and expected him to drop everything for me. Still, the heat of doing all this work only to have him so easily dismiss me raged through my blood, burning my cheeks, curling my hands into fists.

"Oh," I said, pushing upright again. "I guess I'll just go fuck myse—"

He shot his hand out to grab my arm. "I didn't tell you to leave, *wife*."

His tone on that one word locked me in place. He only used it when he was ready to play, when he wanted me in the headspace for a scene.

"What can I do to assist you, *husband*?" I bowed my head, pretending to be reverent.

He wrapped a finger inside the metal heart at the center of my collar and pulled, forcing me down to my knees. "Why don't you use that pretty mouth for something other than apologies?" Without taking his attention away from his work, he nodded under the desk, and I got the picture.

After crawling into the space where he'd tucked his long legs, I situated my body between his knees. I grounded myself in his presence by coasting my palms up his thighs to the button at his waist. He canted his hips, allowing me to push the metal through the hole and lower the zipper. Trying not to tremble with anticipation, I reached inside his boxers to release his already erect cock, gently taking hold of his balls, too. His soft groan urged me on, and I leaned in to lick him from the base to the tip. I loved the way his skin felt like velvet over steel, and when I kissed the head, he let out a barely audible whimper that made me smile.

I could turn such a strong man into a pile of mush, and that emboldened me, making me feel powerful and ruthless. Sucking my husband back, I massaged his cock with my tongue, using one hand to grip and guide him while the other held his testicles the way I knew he liked. He hit the back of my throat and I kept going, gagging around him, tears burning my eyes. But I didn't let up. No, this was an apology. This was my way of making up for all the times I'd made him feel like I didn't want him, like he was just a pawn in a much larger game.

Lord only knew how long I was under there. My knees started to hurt, spit ran down my chin, and my mascara had long since dripped down my cheeks. But that was how he wanted me—messy and defiled and soaked in my debauchery. My lips were numb from the friction and my throat ached, but I didn't let up. I kept his cock warm and played with him while he petted the back of my head and clenched his fingers around my braids, using my face like a sex toy.

That shouldn't have turned me on so much, but I couldn't help sliding one hand between my legs when he started gasping and moaning above the desk. I liked being his little wife, his little Caputi whore. It cleared my mind in a way nothing else could and made me feel connected to him.

After centuries under his desk, he finally pulled my head back and slid the chair out from under the desk, staring down at me with his pupils blown so wide, they were nearly black.

"You were enjoying yourself entirely too much for this to be an apology," he said.

I grinned and wiped my chin with the back of my hand.

He crooked a finger, beckoning me upright, and I crawled out, using his knees as leverage to push to my feet. Roman quickly arranged me on the edge of the desk and gently nudged me so I sat on top of his paperwork, the crinkling under my body adding to the ambiance of my sincerest atonement.

"Lie down," he said, his voice gruff and hoarse with his arousal. "Legs up."

I did as he said, eyes widening when he grabbed something shiny from a desk drawer to his right. A knife. Shivers raced over my body when he slid the flat edge up the inside of my leg, teasing the blade along my flesh.

"You know," he said as he ghosted his fingers over the other leg, grabbing my thigh to guide the toes of my heels to the arms of his chair. "You technically owe me *two* apologies."

"I'm not sorry for saving your life," I replied, gasping when he hooked his index finger into the gusset of my underwear and tugged it away from my skin.

"You're not?" He laughed out a dark, sick noise that should have scared me. It didn't. It only made me more excited about what would happen next. "Such a brave little wife."

I opened my mouth to reply, but he slid the knife under the fabric and yanked, slicing my delicate panties in two.

"Hey," I said. "Stop doing that or I won't have any left."

"I'm sure you'll find some way to replace them," he snarled, staring up at me from between my legs. "Now, shut up, and let me enjoy my sweet apology."

I moaned as he dove in, lapping at me like a starved man, like he could make up for all the lost time between us. He devoured me on his desk, on top of all the work he'd been doing for the last several hours. I arched into the contact, euphoria coating my veins as he sucked on my clit and drove his fingers inside me. He rubbed at the pleasure center inside, and I nearly fell apart.

I'd be a quick trigger tonight. It had been far too long since we last fucked, and now that I had him right where I wanted him, I wouldn't be able to hold out. My legs shook, nerves mixing with adrenaline and rattling through me. His dark head bobbed as he licked and fingered me, and when he reached his other hand up to wrap around my throat, the dam inside me shattered.

My orgasm claimed me, hard and intense, and I clenched my eyes shut, my cunt tightening down on his fingers. Something released in my lower half, a great loosening that I'd only ever experienced once or twice. Roman rubbed my clit faster, working me through it, and when I finally came back to my body, he coasted his big palm over me as I panted and sobbed.

"There ya go," he murmured. "Such a good queen, squirting for your king like that."

"Fuck," I said, squinting through the tears currently rolling down my cheeks. All of the pent-up emotions had been unceremoniously flooded out of my body. Grief, gratitude, shame, relief, all of it, all-consuming. When I glanced down at Roman, his shirt and jeans were soaked with my cum, and he grinned up at me, his chin drenched with evidence of how turned on he'd made me.

"That was so fucking hot," he said. "Can you keep going?"

I nodded and reached for him, gripping his shirt to bring him closer. "Yes, sir. Please. I need you."

"Such a greedy girl." He shoved his jeans down to the ground and ripped his shirt over his head, shucking it somewhere to the right before gripping my hips and pulling me to the edge of the desk. "Tell me you love me."

"I love you," I said without hesitation, knowing it to be more true now than it ever had been before. "Please. I love you. I love you. I love you."

"You're goddamned right you do." He lined himself up and surged inside. I melted into the sensation of being full, of being so complete with him like this. We were connected on more than a physical level, and I never could have predicted it would turn out this way. But I was so grateful that it did.

Roman fucked me on his desk until we both were a spoiled, sopping mess, and then he carried me down the hall to our bathroom, where he sat me in the tub and ran me a bath. When the water level got high enough, he climbed in behind me and laid me back across his chest, running his hands over my arms and neck.

"Thank you for that," he murmured, pressing tender kisses to the side of my head. "I needed the break."

"You're welcome, *mi amore*." I hummed in contentment, so appreciative of the tender way he took care of me.

"But as far as apologies go, that barely counted."

When I gasped and shifted to look at him, he sank his teeth into my shoulder, holding me firm. I'd known him less than a year, but I understood the playful look in his eyes. "What do you want instead?"

He grinned, and I knew I was screwed.

30

BEAR

"Roman, please," Julia whined, practically stamping her foot like a toddler. "This is madness."

I grinned and put the helmet on her head, wrapping the buckle under her chin before connecting the two pieces and tightening it.

"You're gonna enjoy it," I said. "Motorcycles are fun."

"Motorcycles are death machines," she said, glancing over my bike with a mix of fear and hesitant excitement in her gaze. "It's a good way to end up as roadkill."

"That's not true," I said with a laugh. "I've been riding one for over a decade, and I'm still walking upright."

She glared at me.

"Besides," I said, "you stabbed Gabriella Caputi in the neck at your own wedding. You're a badass. What do you have to be scared of?"

This did nothing to soften her resolve.

"Okay, okay," she said. "Just...go slow, all right?"

"Oh, *mia cara,*" I said in that teasing tone that let her know exactly how...*slow*...I could go. "I promise to take extra special care of you."

Blushing, she smiled and shoved my shoulder. "Stop it. Don't get me all hot and bothered before getting on that monstrosity."

I licked my lips and smiled harder, remembering Ru joking about what riding on the back of Saint's bike did to her lady parts. "Who knows, little wife. You might like it."

I put my helmet on and straddled my bike, turning the key in the ignition before kicking it to life. It roared between my legs, thunderous and overwhelming, and fucking hell, how I'd missed it. Sure, I'd ridden by myself a bunch of times since marrying Julia, but having her behind me would take it to a whole new level.

There was something to be said for a biker when he had his old lady on the back of his ride. It spoke to the intimacy between them, saying so much without saying anything at all. I had ached to have her legs on either side of mine, her arms wrapped around my torso, her squeal in my ear as I went faster than she'd ever been before.

"C'mon," I shouted over the bike's engine, patting the seat behind me.

She bit her bottom lip in an adorable pout that made me want to take it between my own teeth. Her worried eyes met mine again through the window of the visor. I grabbed the part of the helmet covering her mouth and yanked it close, touching my forehead to hers.

"I would die before I let anything happen to you, *mia cara.* Now get on the fucking bike."

She took a deep breath and swung a leg over the seat, settling in before touching my hips to hold on. I laughed at her naivety and grabbed her hands to wrap them firmly around my stomach. Then, I hiked up the kickstand and took off.

Julia held on for dear life at first, her small body practically trembling behind me. But this was a bandage we had to rip off. She couldn't very well be married to the president of a motorcycle club and not get on a motorcycle.

Besides, she was my new favorite backpack. When I let it loose on the highway, she held on tighter and damned if that didn't make me feel powerful.

After I'd lost my mom, I started to question the existence of God or a divine being altogether. How could such a thing exist and take away a mother from four young kids in such a heinous act? When Leo suggested I marry Julia, I again wondered how a supreme, all-knowing being could put me in a ridiculous situation. For a long time, I waffled back and forth, convinced nothing would ever confirm it one way or the other.

But in that moment, with my wife on the back of my bike and the heavens painting a rosy-tangerine blush across the sunset sky, I knew true heaven. Nothing would ever come close to the calm and serenity of that perfect existence.

Julia eventually loosened up, and I even caught her giggling when I took a hill a little too fast and that flipping feeling bloomed in my gut. After about half an hour, I pulled over on a spot high up in the mountains overlooking Madison County below it. The sun had just dipped under the horizon, and the full moon had risen in all its glory and splendor. It was a beautiful start to an excellent night.

I turned the bike off and kicked the stand out so I could lean it to the side. Julia climbed off behind me, and I swung my leg to stand. When I removed my helmet, she was already smiling with that entrancing mischief emanating from her dark brown eyes.

I didn't even have to ask. "Look at you."

"All right, Montgomery," she said, clasping her hands behind her back, pretending to be coy. "You win. It was a lot of fun."

"See?" I leaned back against the bike and grabbed her hips, pulling her toward me and nestling her in between my legs. "It's almost like I know what I'm talking about."

"I liked when you hit the higher gear and—" She cut herself off, her cheeks turning a gorgeous shade of pink.

"And?" I knew where this was heading. Everyone with a clit liked riding a bike for more than one reason. Sure, it went fast and it was fun, but to have four hundred pounds of vibrating combustion between your legs did things that people with a penis could barely comprehend...or so I'd been told.

She wrapped her arms around my neck and leaned in to kiss me.

"Well, you'll get no argument from me about going out with you again."

"No, go on," I said. "Explain it to me. What *exactly* did you like the most?"

She scoffed and tried to pull away, but I yanked her back and switched our positions so she was the one leaning up against the bike, and I crowded her in.

"It feels...very nice." She licked her lips and glanced away, but oh no, I didn't permit her to be shy in front of me.

If she liked something, she needed to tell me. Those were the rules.

"Use your words, little wife," I nearly growled.

She stayed coy, blushing harder.

"Oh, are you ashamed to admit you liked the way the engine roared against your pretty pussy?"

"Roman!" She shoved my shoulders, but I only laughed and leaned in more.

"If I put my hand down your pants, would I find out how much you liked it?"

She took a deep breath and glared at me, her jaw squaring up for a fight. But I didn't let her. When she opened her mouth to say something undoubtedly mean and infuriating, I cut her off with my lips, snaking my tongue inside to steal whatever it was. She moaned against me, sagging into the contact.

And you know what, when I put my hand down her pants, I learned Julia Gianna Francesca Benita Natali *Montgomery* had liked riding on the back of my bike a whole fucking lot.

EPILOGUE

JULIA
FIVE AND A HALF YEARS LATER

I f I thought I loved my husband wearing oily jeans and a stained white T-shirt, fresh from the garage, it was nothing compared to the way he looked with our children on his chest. Our daughter, Olivia, had just turned four and our son, Noah, would turn two next week. There could be no denying they were his. They'd both inherited his dark hair, the shade of his brown eyes, and the Montgomery face shape. Olivia looked more like V than she did like me, but I didn't mind that so much. They were both Rose and Caputi. They were a symbol of peace and prosperity.

Roman worked tirelessly to be the best president of the SRMC that he could, and I stood by him as his faithful and loyal queen. Together, we maintained the peace we had so desperately fought for. And at the end of every night, after we came home from the clubhouse or he stopped turning wrenches at the garage, he spent his evenings entertaining all three of us. Then he stuffed his massive form into their tiny bed and read to them until they fell asleep. The sounds of his deep baritone had stopped coming a few minutes ago, so I walked down the hallway to check on them and found him with a toddler under each arm, his eyes closed, his chest rising and falling in that steady rhythm that meant he'd also succumb to his subconscious.

I debated leaving him there. It wouldn't be the first time one of us fell asleep in their bed only to wake up in the middle of the night with a stiff neck and shuffle down the hallway to our own room.

But I had other plans for my king. It had been six years of harmony between the Roses and the Caputis, six years of defending our territory as a unit rather than fighting with each other. In that time, we'd seen our fair share of obstacles—other MCs attempting to encroach on our land, dissenters from within struggling for power, and other players wanting a piece of what we'd gained. But with Leo at the helm of DC and the Roses steering the Madison County ship, we were far too powerful for anyone to topple.

"*Amore*," I whispered, giving his leg a tender shake.

He opened his eyes and grinned when he saw it was me. "*Mia cara.*"

"Come," I said, nodding toward the door. "It's my turn to put you to bed."

Roman stretched and smiled like a lazy lion, carefully extracting himself from our children before pushing to his feet. He wrapped an arm around my waist as I turned off the big light and closed the door, heading down the hallway to our bedroom.

Once inside, I checked that the baby monitor was still on before facing my husband. He sat on the edge of the bed, an eyebrow raised, that expectant look on his face.

I knew what he wanted, of course. I wanted the same thing. He'd been edging me for the better part of the day—stealing private moments when he could to shove his fingers between my legs, sending me dirty texts that had me blushing and squirming wherever I was, finding me during his lunch break so he could shove his head under my skirt and suck me nearly to orgasm. Our play certainly wasn't the same as it had been before the kids, but he never let me forget how much he adored me. And I returned the favor.

Six years ago, I'd never dreamed my life could be like this. I'd never thought I'd fall in love with anyone, much less enjoy this type of dynamic. I'd never thought I'd have children, and here I was with two of them that meant everything to me. Enjoying these things with Roman, knowing we would both protect it with our lives, healed the broken pieces inside of me, and I'd never be able to thank him enough for giving that to me. I'd spend the rest of my life trying.

BEAR

MY QUEEN WAS FAR TOO eager to please me that night. After I fucked her damn near into a coma and checked that our children were still asleep, I lay with her tucked into my side, her head resting on my chest as she rubbed circles into my stomach.

"Leo is hosting a Christmas party at the mansion this year," she said. "I've told him we'll go."

I hummed in agreement and lazily ghosted up and down her spine, far too satisfied to argue. Not that I would. In the six years since I'd married Julia, Leo had become a full-fledged member of my family. That was something I'd never thought I'd say, but after everything we'd been through between now and then, I trusted him nearly as much as I trusted my brothers. He had my back, and I had his. Not to mention he was on a very...*very*...short list of people I trusted with my children.

"Your father said he'd take the kids so we could go to Naples for our anniversary," she continued. "I think it's a good idea."

My old man loved his grandchildren with his whole heart, and secretly, I had started to think he cared more about them than he'd ever cared about his own kids. I tried not to let thoughts like that keep me up at night. If it meant he kept them safe, secure, and happy, I'd deal with it.

"Thank you," Julia said, nuzzling closer. "Thank you for building this life with me."

"Of course." I narrowed my eyes and put a finger under her chin to tilt her face to mine. "What's going on? Are you okay?"

"Yeah, just...sentimental." She wiped at an eye and sniffed, making me roll so she was under me, my arms caging her head in, her legs on either side of my hips.

"*Mia cara,* I told you before, and I'll tell you as many times as you need to hear it. I'd do *anything* for you." Yeah, I'd just fucked her within an inch of her life, but my cock didn't pay attention to silly things like that. Rubbing up against her warm, wet cunt got his attention, and all these lovey-dovey things we murmured to each other in the dark only urged him on. "I love you."

"I love you," she returned.

And when I shifted my hips to slip inside her again, I nearly collapsed from the hot, tight warmth of her body. In six years, I must have fucked her a million times, a billion, but it would always be like the first. She engulfed me, mind, body, and soul. I belonged to her in every single way.

Growing up, I never could have imagined I'd end up here one day. I'd never thought I'd ever care about someone as deeply or completely as I did her. She was more than my wife, my queen, my submissive, or the mother of my children. She'd become my partner in every sense of the word, my soulmate.

And heaven help anyone who came for her again. I'd once told her I'd kill for her, and I had. She could merely breathe the word and it would be done.

Together, we owned our ruthless reign, and I pitied anyone who tried to stop us.

The End

WANNA JOIN THE ROSES?

Thank you for reading! If you enjoyed this book, please consider leaving a review. They help other readers find my work, and because of that, they enable me to keep writing.

If you want more **STEEL ROSES** content, check out the prequel novella, **THEY CALLED HIM SAINT.**

I don't have a sneak peek for the next story yet, but a Pollux/Phoebe short is coming later this year. The next SRMC novel will feature **CROW** and **DETECTIVE JORDAN.**

You can stay informed about all things Jena Doyle and SRMC related by signing up for my newsletter.
https://jenadoyle.com/join/

(No spam, only smut. I promise.)

ACKNOWLEDGMENTS

Dear Reader,

When I first set out to write the Steel Roses MC, I had no idea I would see all five books published one day. KC and Alba demanded to be told, and that was all I knew. I plotted out a five book arc, all culminating with the joining of the Caputi and Rose households. To finally have the arc complete fills me with humility, astonishment, and curiosity.

Where do we go from here?

I've got some ideas. Crow and Detective Jordan have been dancing around each other since *Crimson Chaos*, and I desperately want our old man ex-Prez to know true love. He deserves it.

How would you feel about a Caputi spinoff? Chesco is talking pretty loudly, (almost as loud as Hollywood was, but admittedly, no one can top our favorite golden retriever... except for V). And I know Leo will need his full redemption story. There are Caputi cousins upon cousins to spare.

As for the SRMC, the Hell's Knights are still causing chaos, and the Kings of Carnage have it fucking coming. Wheels, Doc, Lore, Hollister, Castor, and Switch all have stories to tell. As long as you want to read them, I'll keep telling them.

To my wonderful partner and husband, I love you. Thank you for continuing to support this little hobby of mine. Onward to the NYT's Bestselling List. *Avante!*

To my beta readers, Maggie Sims, Leslie Grace, KyAnn Waters, and Amethyst Moonchild, thank you for your invaluable feedback. I truly could not do this without the support of my fellow writing/reading community.

To my editors, Misha and Kimberly, you wonderful souls. Thank you for being on my team and providing the best editing skills a girl could ask for.

To my ARC readers, thank you for your early support and your continued willingness to hop on the socials to talk about the Roses. I've had the wonderful privilege to meet some of you in person, and it has truly been an amazing experience.

To my shadow work / old ladies group: Nae, Amethyst, Willow, and Becca — You keep me sane. Old ladies forever. Much love!

And finally, to you, Dear Reader. Thank you for picking this up and giving this indie author a shot. Thank you for journeying this far with me and my motley crew of motherfuckers. I hope you have enjoyed the ride as much as I have.

Cheers!

-Jena

ALSO BY JENA DOYLE

MIDSUMMER

We Wild Things (Prequel Novella)

Midsummer

Samhain

Solstice

Beltane

STEEL ROSES MC

They Called Him Saint (Prequel Novella)

Crimson Chaos

Savage Saint

Oleander Oaths

Mischief Mayhem

Ruthless Reign

ROYAL BASTARDS MC: HELENA, MT

Blood and Whiskey

Blood and Magic